From This Day Forward

Books by Lauraine Snelling

SONG OF BLESSING

To Everything a Season   Streams of Mercy
A Harvest of Hope   From This Day Forward

An Untamed Heart

RED RIVER OF THE NORTH

An Untamed Land   The Reapers' Song
A New Day Rising   Tender Mercies
A Land to Call Home   Blessing in Disguise

RETURN TO RED RIVER

A Dream to Follow   More Than a Dream
Believing the Dream

DAUGHTERS OF BLESSING

A Promise for Ellie   A Touch of Grace
Sophie's Dilemma   Rebecca's Reward

HOME TO BLESSING

A Measure of Mercy   A Heart for Home
No Distance Too Far

WILD WEST WIND

Valley of Dreams   A Place to Belong
Whispers in the Wind

DAKOTAH TREASURES

Ruby   Opal
Pearl   Amethyst

SECRET REFUGE

Daughter of Twin Oaks   The Long Way Home
Sisters of the Confederacy   A Secret Refuge 3-in-1

SONG OF BLESSING • BOOK 4

From This Day Forward

LAURAINE SNELLING

BETHANYHOUSE

a division of Baker Publishing Group

Minneapolis, Minnesota

© 2016 by Lauraine Snelling

Published by Bethany House Publishers
11400 Hampshire Avenue South
Bloomington, Minnesota 55438
www.bethanyhouse.com

Bethany House Publishers is a division of
Baker Publishing Group, Grand Rapids, Michigan

Printed in the United States of America

Library of Congress Cataloging-in-Publication Data
Names: Snelling, Lauraine, author.
Title: From this day forward / Lauraine Snelling.
Description: Minneapolis, Minnesota : Bethany House, [2016] | Series: Song of
    blessing ; 4
Identifiers: LCCN 2016025386| ISBN 9780764218743 (cloth : alk. paper) | ISBN
    9780764211072 (paperback) | ISBN 9780764218750 (large-print paperback)
Subjects: | GSAFD: Christian fiction. | Love stories.
Classification: LCC PS3569.N39 F76 2016 | DDC 813/.54—dc23
LC record available at https://lccn.loc.gov/2016025386

Scripture quotations are from the King James Version of the Bible.

Cover design by Dan Thornberg, Design Source Creative Services

Author is represented by Books & Such Literary Agency

16 17 18 19 20 21 22   7 6 5 4 3 2 1

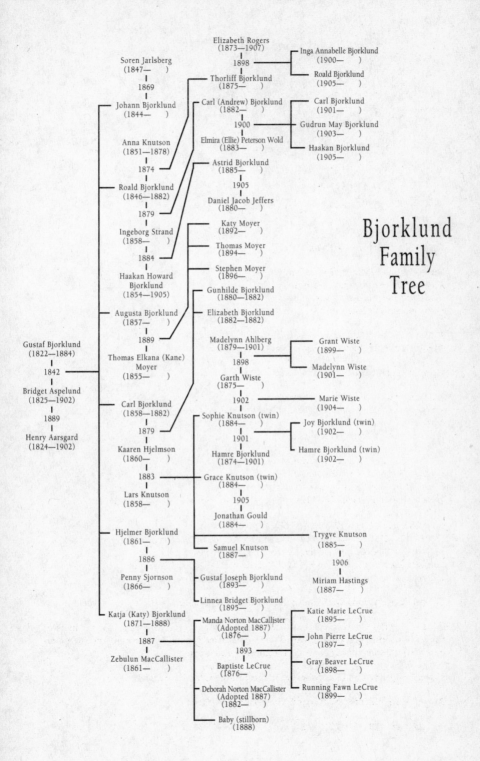

Bjorklund Family Tree

Gustaf Bjorklund (1822—1884)
1842
Bridget Aspelund (1825—1902)
1889
Henry Aarsgard (1824—1902)

Johann Bjorklund (1844—)
— Soren Jarlsberg (1847—)
1869
— Anna Knutson (1851—1878)
1874

Thorliff Bjorklund (1875—)
— Elizabeth Rogers (1873—1907)
1898
— Inga Annabelle Bjorklund (1900—)
— Roald Bjorklund (1905—)

Carl (Andrew) Bjorklund (1882—)
— Elmira (Ellie) Peterson Wold (1883—)
1900
— Carl Bjorklund (1901—)
— Gudrun May Bjorklund (1903—)
— Haakan Bjorklund (1905—)

Roald Bjorklund (1846—1882)
1879
— Ingeborg Strand (1858—)
1884

Astrid Bjorklund (1885—)
— Daniel Jacob Jeffers (1880—)
1905

Haakan Howard Bjorklund (1854—1905)
— Katy Moyer (1892—)
— Thomas Moyer (1894—)
— Stephen Moyer (1896—)

Augusta Bjorklund (1857—)
1889
— Thomas Elkana (Kane) Moyer (1855—)

Gunhilde Bjorklund (1880—1882)
Elizabeth Bjorklund (1882—1882)

Carl Bjorklund (1858—1882)
1879
— Kaaren Hjelmson (1860—)
1883
— Lars Knutson (1858—)

Madelynn Ahlberg (1879—1901)
1898
Garth Wiste (1875—)
1902
— Grant Wiste (1899—)
— Madelynn Wiste (1901—)
— Marie Wiste (1904—)

Sophie Knutson (twin) (1884—)
1901
Hamre Bjorklund (1874—1901)
— Joy Bjorklund (twin) (1902—)
— Hamre Bjorklund (twin) (1902—)

Grace Knutson (twin) (1884—)
1905
Jonathan Gould (1884—)

Hjelmer Bjorklund (1861—)
1886
— Penny Sjornson (1866—)

Samuel Knutson (1887—)
Trygve Knutson (1885—)
1906
Miriam Hastings (1887—)

Gustaf Joseph Bjorklund (1893—)
Linnea Bridget Bjorklund (1895—)

Katja (Katy) Bjorklund (1871—1888)
1887
Zebulun MacCallister (1861—)

Manda Norton MacCallister (Adopted 1887) (1876—)
1893
Baptiste LeCrue (1876—)
— Katie Marie LeCrue (1895—)
— John Pierre LeCrue (1897—)
— Gray Beaver LeCrue (1898—)
— Running Fawn LeCrue (1899—)

Deborah Norton MacCallister (Adopted 1887) (1882—)
Baby (stillborn) (1888)

CHAPTER 1

W hen will it be my turn?" Deborah Mac-Callister paused to sniff a spray of lilac. Heavenly!

Ingeborg Bjorklund looked up from the abundance of lilacs she was arranging in a bucket, her second, to set by the door to the sanctuary of Blessing Lutheran Church. "Ah, Deborah, what makes you say that?"

Deborah reached for another lilac branch to insert into the vases she was filling for the altar. "All the others have married but for me. Some even twice, like Sophie and now Anji. I . . . I always dreamed of being married, and look at me, an old maid."

"And you are how old?"

"Twenty-five."

"Only twenty-five and you are the super-vising nurse at the hospital. That's a lot of responsibility, and certainly more than your fair share of drama and excitement. So many girls dream of that."

Deborah laughed. "True. And you know I love my job." Oops. Here was a ladybug among the leaves. She certainly did not belong in the church. Deborah seized her with two fingers and gently carried her to the door. Ingeborg was right that she led an exciting and useful life. But Ingeborg did not know how Deborah really felt, deep down inside.

The community considered her a member of the Solberg family, and most of the time, she did too. And yet, not really. Not like their natural children.

Ingeborg was right, but in a way she was wrong too. She talked about drama as if it were always a good thing; it was not, not always. Oh my, no. When Deborah's pa and Manda and Baptiste went to Montana all those many years ago, leaving half the family behind, that was dramatic but not good. How many nights did Deborah lie in bed, wishing her pa would come back to take over the ranch again?

Deborah scissored out a dead twig that was spoiling the bouquet. Drama? Dear Zeb Mac-Callister stopping by a soddy dug into a hill near the Missouri River, probably hoping for a meal, only to find two young girls with no parents in sight. That was drama. Zeb did his best for the orphans. When he married Katy

Bjorklund and they adopted Deborah and her sister, it was almost like having a whole family again.

That was it, right there. Whenever she thought of those years, deep in her heart, that was what she wanted. Love and laughter and good hard work to build that ranch.

But then Katy died and the light went out of the world for Zeb. And then the circus brought disease to town and people died. Why did drama and heartbreak so often go hand in hand?

"There now, how is that?" A smile trembled on Deborah's lips as she pointed to the explosion of purple and white that filled the vase to bursting with spring. With a bouquet on either side of the white-painted traditional Norwegian altar, and more on the side railings, spring and joy danced together.

Ingeborg cocked her head, studying it. "So lovely. I always think spring is my favorite season, and then fall slips in with the painting of the leaves and the cooler weather, and I think fall is my favorite. And of course I love summer too, with the garden and the berries."

"And the white and sparkles of winter, until it drags on too long and sends one more blizzard and we all dream of spring." Deborah gathered up the few remaining stems of lilac.

"We humans are so funny, I often think God must just shake His head and chuckle;

but sometimes, especially with the children, I can see Him laughing in love."

Deborah watched Ingeborg. "You really see Him, don't you?"

"In my mind, I guess I do." Ingeborg seemed to smile at an invisible Father. "God has become so real to me through the years."

"Was it always this way?"

"No, I don't think so. I have believed in Him since I was little, but learning to accept His love and guidance, to trust Him with all that I am, has grown through the years. Now I want to walk right beside Him, seeking His face like He tells us. I think of Inga and how when you are walking with her, she is either pulling ahead to see something, or dragging behind to study something else she found. I think we are all like that, and I don't want to do that anymore. I want to walk right beside Him, looking up to see His face and letting Him do the leading."

"Trust is a big word, isn't it?"

"Ja, it is. It is so human to want to go our own way and then say, 'Oh, by the way, God, please bless what I am doing.'" She wagged her head, smiling at the young woman who was watching her so seriously. "Dearest Deborah, you have grown up with a wise man for a substitute father, and he and I have learned to believe this way."

Deborah nodded. "Almost losing Johnny

last summer was terribly hard on him. In fact, I wonder if sometimes his faith wavered. There were many nights he didn't sleep while he and Mary Martha kept vigil at the hospital. We all prayed so hard."

"I know you were a big help with the younger children."

"When I wasn't on night duty. That is one problem with being a nurse."

"Patients need round-the-clock care. And being the supervisor, I know, just adds to it. You have to fill in if someone else can't be there."

"I am grateful that doesn't happen often. But with that diphtheria epidemic, I was so afraid more of our people would come down with it. The wisdom of Astrid and Elizabeth and their contacts with the hospital in Chicago are what saved the rest of us, and getting that antitoxin here so quickly." Deborah heaved a sigh. "I learned so much, but then I am always learning something new."

"So true. We all are." Ingeborg stood up straighter. "But back to your situation. I'm not going to call it a problem, just something for God to work out."

"Seems like a problem to me." Deborah picked up some leaves and blossoms that had fallen to the floor. "But today I will be glad for Anji and Mr. Devlin—er, rather, Reverend Devlin." She frowned. "That seems stiff. Does that church call their pastors *Reverend* or *Mister* or what?"

"I heard John say that some are called *Rector*."

"Rector?" Deborah's eyebrows disappeared into the fringe that curved over her forehead. "I heard some ministers are called *Father*."

"That is the Catholic faith. The Jews are called *Rabbi*."

"This can get confusing." Deborah looked around the sanctuary. "I think we are all done here. At least the blossoms will stay nice for church tomorrow." She inhaled. "And the whole sanctuary smells heavenly." She looked at the lilacs in her hand. "I'm going to put these as a bouquet on Ma's table."

"Good idea! Mary Martha does love flowers. We'd better hurry." Ingeborg looked around the big room one more time, and then gently closed the doors.

Three hours until the wedding started.

"Now remember, you children will be sitting right in the front row of the sanctuary, so *no fidgeting* during the ceremony. Understand?" Anji Moen stared right at Annika, her youngest.

Melissa, her eldest, who had just turned eleven, said, "Don't worry, we'll all be right there too, and Annika will sit by me, right?"

Annika nodded. "I'll be good." She twirled

to enjoy her new dress. "How come my dress is pink and Melissa's dress is yellow?"

"Because this is spring and these are spring colors. And yours is really peach."

"I like mine better."

Melissa rolled her eyes, just barely putting up with her five-year-old sister. "Let me tie your bow again. Twirling like that made it get tangled." She grasped Annika's shoulder.

"Ouch! Ma, Lissa is being mean."

At Anji's feet, her younger sister, Rebecca Valders, tugged at Anji's skirt. "There. I sure don't know how that hem got so crooked." Rebecca stood and set the pincushion on the table by the window.

"Ma is like me, she can't stand still either." Annika giggled with her hands over her mouth.

Gilbert, Anji's son, who would turn ten next month, wandered into the bedroom. "Do we have to call Mr. Devlin *Pa*?"

"That would be proper."

"But we already have a pa, or rather we had one. Do you think he's watching us from heaven? What if he doesn't want you to get married again and us to leave Blessing? He liked being in Blessing better than Norway."

"Why do you say that?"

"Because I heard him say that one day. He and some lady had an argument."

"Gilbert, the things you come up with."

"Where is Joseph?" Rebecca asked. Joseph had been born between Gilbert and Annika.

"Out playing with Benny."

"Out playing where? I told you all to stay in the house so you could keep clean." Anji turned to her sister. "Can you go call him?"

"Them, you mean." Rebecca looked up at the clock. "I'll send Joseph back in and then get dressed. Lissa, can you read to the younger ones, please? You all want to look nice for the wedding, don't you?"

Melissa nodded and took Annika's hand. "Come on, we'll go sit in the parlor. Gilbert, are you coming?"

"I guess. I'll be glad when this is all over," he muttered just loud enough for his mother to hear. He stopped at the door. "When we move away, we won't see Benny anymore. Why can't I stay here with Tante Rebecca?"

Anji started to scold him, but instead sat down in a chair and beckoned him over. "Gilbert, I know you don't want to leave Blessing and all your cousins, but you will make friends in Michigan. Our house will be right near Lake Michigan, and there are lots of trees and hills, more like we had in Norway. You'll be able to go fishing and even hunting, maybe. Thomas said there are boys there just your age, and the people are very friendly."

"But here we have our family." His blue

eyes shimmered with tears. "We might as well go back to Norway."

Ah, my son, one day you'll have to, but not now. She smoothed his hair back with both hands. "You look very handsome. Can you keep a secret, if I tell you?"

He glared at her from under his brows. "I guess."

"Thomas said there's a dog living at the house and he needs a boy to love him. And there are two cats."

"Will we have a horse too?"

"Ja, Thomas has a horse that can be ridden or hitched to a buggy. It sounds like a fine place to live. You and Joseph will share a room that looks out to the lake, and the girls' room will look over the garden. And we will have an extra room for company. Maybe one day your cousins can come there to visit."

"How could Benny go on a train?"

"Knowing Benny, he could do anything he sets his mind to." Anji paused to listen. "I think it's time to go to the church. After the service we will have cake and ice cream."

"Can we go fishing after?"

"Probably not today. We have to finish packing so we can catch the train on Monday."

"I packed all my stuff in that box you gave me."

"I know, you have been very helpful." She stood up.

"What about our garden? We got some of the seeds planted and the lettuce and peas are up. The onions too."

"Onkel Toby will have a fine garden. Now, go wash your hands." She looked up to see Joseph stop in the doorway. *Oh, please Lord, get me through this day.* "Joseph, come with me." The tone of her voice brooked no argument.

By the time she'd scrubbed the dirt off the knees of his pants, tucked his shirt back in, scrubbed a dirty spot off his shirt, and washed his hands and face, he was squirming.

"I told you to stay in the house to stay clean and you did not mind me." She hung up the washcloth, grabbed a comb, wetted his hair, and combed it—again. "Now it's almost time to leave for the church, so go listen to the story Lissa is reading aloud."

"Is Benny going to the church too?"

"Ja, we are all going." She pointed to the stairs. "Go! Sit!"

"How can a grown Irishman be feeling almost terrified?" Thomas Devlin stared at his friend and officiating pastor.

John Solberg fought to keep a straight face. "I think marriage sounds wonderful in the courting phase—you're in love and all is well. Or at least in your case, it finally became well. Thoughts and dreams are great, but when it comes down to the actual ceremony, your life flashes before your eyes."

Devlin stopped his pacing and asked, "How be ye so wise?"

"I've not only been there myself, you know, but I have performed the weddings for many, and I can't think of a man—or woman—who hasn't had a panicky feeling when that music starts to play. Some manage to go through with it stoic as can be, and others nearly pass out." He thought for a moment. "In fact one did."

"Man or woman?"

"The man, actually. I think his collar was too tight."

Devlin barked a laugh. "Well, me collar is not too tight, but I do want to get this shindig on the road. I'm sure I'll feel better after we get started."

"Breathe deep and think about something else while I go check on Anji. I'll come back for you, and we'll go wait at the front just like we practiced. You performed weddings in the old country, didn't you?"

"Aye, but being the clergy be far easier than being the groom."

"Breathe!"

"The veil feels lopsided." Anji wished there were a mirror in the room.

Rebecca tweaked the veil and reset the hairpin keeping it in place. "Now remember, you cannot talk to Thomas before the ceremony. They say it is bad luck for the groom to see his bride before the wedding." She stepped back to make sure her sister was ready. "You look lovely. That ice blue makes you look like an angel."

Some angel who nearly scrubbed her young son's face off. Anji kept her thoughts to herself. "Gerald has all the children?"

"No, Clara is taking care of my two little ones. I decided they did not need to be at the wedding, so I asked her to help. Being a bride's matron of honor is about all I can manage at the moment. And I want to enjoy myself too."

Once they were at the church, Anji clamped a hand over her middle. The butterflies now felt more like a swarm of bees inside. Was she doing the best thing for her children? She knew she was doing the best thing for herself. Once she realized that her commitment to take care of Thorliff was finished, she'd been so afraid that Thomas Devlin might have changed his mind. But he hadn't. He said real love was not turned on and off like a faucet, and the thought of facing life without her had made him miserable. But he figured God had other plans for him, for a priest can remain single and still be a good priest.

"Getting on that train and leaving you was the most difficult thing I ever did," he'd said.

"Even worse than my discussion with the archbishop that sealed me fate and forced me to leave the auld sod."

Then he had cupped his hands around her face and stared into her eyes, mesmerizing her. And then he kissed her and her world had exploded.

She jerked herself back to the present. She could hear the piano playing. People coming in. "Rebecca, I have a bad case of the jitters." She held out her trembling hand. "What if . . ."

A knock at the door spun her around. "Ja?"

"Reverend Solberg here. May I come in?"

"Of course." But when Anji started for the door, Rebecca laid a hand on her arm and shook her head. She opened the door and welcomed John Solberg inside.

"Ah, Anji, you look so lovely. When I conducted the wedding for you and Ivar, you were like a shy maiden, and now you are a lovely grown woman with four children. You have been through many hard things and now you are about to start on a new adventure. I want to pray for you, and then we'll meet again at the altar. All right?"

"Ja, I am shaking."

"Brides are nearly always shaking, and usually their grooms are too." He took her hands. "Lord God, today we celebrate the marriage of two of your finest children. You have brought this union about and helped them work out the wrinkles. Bless them, Father, as they join together in holy matrimony, as they become one flesh. Calm Anji and fill her with joy. Remove from her mind the concerns about the children being just so. We love her, her soon-to-be husband and her children. Help them all become a family in their new home, in their new parish. We thank you and praise your name, that this union will bring glory to you. Amen."

He stepped back. "Now I have one very important piece of advice."

Anji waited.

"Breathe. Take several deep breaths to calm yourself. Right. Breathe again." He nodded, his smile bringing even more calm. He turned to Rebecca. "Are you ready?"

"Ja, we are all ready."

Anji licked her lips and reached for the glass of water Rebecca had brought her. She took a drink, then another deep breath and blew it out. "I'm ready."

I hope.

CHAPTER 2

The piano prelude changed from something gentle and melodic to something stately. Anji had trouble listening to the music; her mind and heart fluttered too much.

Rebecca kissed her on the cheek. "I know Mor and Far are smiling down on us and are so glad you will have a husband in your life again. I am sure they have been worrying that you needed help."

"You think people worry over what is going on down here when they are in heaven?"

"The Bible has places that talk about people looking down but not able to change anything." She opened the door. "Here we go, just like we practiced."

Anji watched her sister step into the sanctuary and start down the aisle. Anji moved to the wide doorway. The glorious flowers drew her gaze to the altar, where it fell upon the three men waiting. But really Thomas Devlin—tall, handsome, his deep red hair combed back—was the only one she saw. *Thank you, Lord, for this man,* she whispered to herself and stepped forward as everyone stood.

Her eyes locked on his, and it was as if a glimmering line drew her forward. She clutched her bouquet of purple lilacs with white spirea and paced the length of the aisle. As she drew closer, he shimmered through the tears she ignored. Could one drown in another's eyes? When she reached him, he took her hand and drew it through his arm, she handed her bouquet to Rebecca, who was unashamedly sniffing, and they turned to face Pastor Solberg, who nodded with a smile. He then looked to the congregation.

"We are gathered today in this house of God to unite these two people in holy matrimony. Let us pray. Lord God, who instituted marriage as a union, we thank you for the blessings of love and marriage. We thank you that if we keep you as the center of our lives, we become stronger because of your strength. Bless Anji and Thomas as they repeat their vows and begin their life together. Amen."

He nodded to Jonathan Gould on the piano, and as his fingers danced on the keys, Linnea Bjorklund and Truth Hastings, Miriam

Knutson's little sister, came to stand beside him. The girls' voices blended in a lovely old Norwegian wedding song and then floated into an amen together.

Anji looked up at Devlin, her eyes wide in delight. He smiled and patted her hand. *I didn't know they could sing like that. How long have they been practicing?* The questions floated away as Reverend Solberg raised an eyebrow before the next part of the service.

"Let us hear what our Father has said about holy matrimony." After reading the passage about leaving father and mother and cleaving to one another, he nodded toward Sophie. "And remember what I have told you so often; the word *charity* here means 'complete and utter love.' *Agape.*"

Sophie Wiste stood and took a deep breath. "First Corinthians 13, verses four through eight and thirteen. 'Charity suffereth long, and is kind; charity envieth not; charity vaunteth not itself, is not puffed up, doth not behave itself unseemly, seeketh not her own, is not easily provoked, thinketh no evil. . . . And now abideth faith, hope, and charity, these three; but the greatest of these is charity.'" She smiled at Anji and Thomas and sat down.

"Anji, Thomas, as your pastor here, I have some words of advice for you." Reverend Solberg raised his eyes to the congregation. "And to all those for whom this applies now—and if not now, ponder it for the future. Some of the wise words in the Scriptures apply not only to married couples but all of us." He paused. "Do not let the sun go down on your anger. We all get hurt and angry at times, that is part of life, but if we can say we are sorry and ask for forgiveness before that night falls, we will have fewer fights, deeper friendships, and we'll all sleep better.

"In that Corinthians passage, we are told what real love is. We can't manage all of that all the time, but that is the way that God loves us. Be the first to say, 'I'm sorry, please forgive me.' Don't cross your arms and blame the other person. We are called to live together in love, as He loves us. And when we do love like this, our families will be closer, our marriages stronger, and our hearts lighter. We are all His children, brothers and sisters in the family of Christ. How blessed we are. Amen."

He turned back to Anji and Thomas, bade them face each other and read the vows, waiting for them to repeat after him.

"Aye, I do," Thomas said, never taking his eyes off the woman before him.

"And do you, Anji Moen, take this man to be your wedded husband?"

Anji made her pledges to Thomas firmly, looking into his eyes, her voice only wobbling once or twice, especially on the "till death do we part" portion. She'd been through that once, with Ivar, and knew the pain.

"I now pronounce you, Anji, and you, Thomas, man and wife. You may kiss your bride."

As they kissed, a boy's voice came from somewhere in room. "Oh ick."

As the congregation chuckled, Thomas whispered, "I used to think that too."

Anji rolled her eyes, trying to stifle a giggle.

Reverend Solberg laid a hand on each of their shoulders. "The Lord bless thee and keep thee . . ." When he finished the blessing, he looked to the congregation. "Meet Rector and Mrs. Thomas Devlin." He beckoned to the four children in the front row. When they came forward, he added, "And their family."

With the four children in front and their arms locked together, the family made their way down the aisle, stopping to greet their friends and families as they went.

"Join us under the trees for cake, coffee, and whatever else the women have put together," Thomas invited in full voice.

The piano played them out the door and down the stairs.

"I'm so glad we set this outside. So many were praying for no rain." Anji couldn't stop smiling at the man beside her as she held tight to his arm.

"Ye make a muckle fine bride, Anji Devlin."

Anji Devlin! Oh my!

The party lasted through the meal, and

then everyone gathered close to watch the couple open their gifts. One was a sheet with a strip of bright fabric wrapped around it and tied in a bow. Anji let Melissa untie the bow to find a wedding ring quilt folded carefully. Anji held it up and read the embroidered tag: *To Anji and Thomas Devlin with love, the women of Blessing Lutheran Church.*

Anji stared around at all the women who usually quilted. "When did you have time to do this? I mean, I often attended and . . ."

"We've been busy," Penny said, grinning at the others. "It was hard to keep the secret, especially when you were part of the group." The other women nodded and smiled.

After opening packets of flower starts, household items, linens, canned goods, dried beans, and an embroidered picture of snow-capped Norwegian mountains, one more box appeared.

"This one is for the children," Daniel Jeffers announced, beckoning the four forward. "Come on, you can open it together." He held the big box carefully.

When the box whimpered, Joseph's eyes grew wide. He unfolded the flaps and all four of them peered down at a fluffy red-and-white puppy. Anji gasped and looked at Thomas.

Gilbert looked up at his mother. "Is it really ours?"

Thomas nodded. "Yer mum didn't know

about this gift, but they asked me first. We have an old dog at the rectory that needs a friend something fierce, like this little fellow and you children. But you have to come up with a name. Oh, and 'tis a male puppy."

Melissa reached inside the box and lifted out the bundle of fur, which tried to lick her face and her hands, then gave Gilbert a swipe, nibbled on Annika's fingers, and wriggled all over as Melissa handed it to Joseph, who got piddled on.

"I think Piddler would be good," someone called out.

"Nah, name it Fluffy," a child called out.

The other children gathered around, and as the puppy made the rounds, more ideas were volunteered among giggles and glee.

"I want to name him Benny," Joseph announced.

"My name!" Benny grinned from his wagon. "That's a good name."

Melissa nodded. Gilbert shrugged, and Annika giggled as the puppy licked her chin again.

"I guess Benny it is," Devlin agreed. "The old dog's name is Frank, so we'll have Benny and Frank. Sounds fine to me." He shook the human Benny's hand. "If that pup has half the guts ye have, lad, 'twill become a right wondrous dog."

He stood and raised his hands. "Thankee

all for the lovely gifts and for joining us here to celebrate. Ye have all made this day even more beautiful than ever I dreamed."

Andrew Bjorklund stood up. "I have another gift for you, but Mor said I should ask first. So do you have a place for a pig to live? If you do, I'll build a crate and load it on the train with you Monday."

"We would have sent chickens, but you already have those. So we boxed up some rhubarb roots instead," Ingeborg announced. "And strawberry plants, because I know how much Melissa loves strawberries. These will all be at the train, ready to go."

"I'm surprised you didn't crate up a heifer calf," Anji said, shaking her head.

Ingeborg laughed. "We thought about it, but Andrew figured a pig would be easier. And there will be baskets for the train ride. Thomas, I know how you love my cheese; there will be plenty."

"And I thought we didn't have much more than clothes to ship." Anji looked up at her new husband.

"You should have known better," Kaaren told them. "As if we would send six of our own off without provisions."

❧

On Monday afternoon, Sophie watched from the end of the platform as the eastbound train spent extra time at the Blessing stop. The men loaded the pig crate and various other boxes and crates. The canine Benny was to ride with his new family. Sophie joined the happy crowd as all the people exchanged hugs and many wiped away tears. The impatient conductor kept trying to hurry things along, but some things cannot be hurried, like all the good-byes and advice. He did keep his smile in place as he finally got the Devlin family ushered up the steps, waving as they went. Once inside, they plastered themselves to the windows, as everyone at the station waved good-bye until only the trail of smoke was visible.

The school-aged children returned to school from their all-too-brief holiday. Sophie pondered the school situation. Thorliff was assisting Pastor Solberg by substituting at the high school, and Isabelle Rumly had all the grade school children. But it was obviously more than any of them could handle; seven new pupils had entered the system since last year.

"I sure hope we can fill those teacher positions before school starts again," Sophie said as she and her aunt Penny walked back to their places of business.

"Who would have thought last summer that we would need two more new teachers this year?" Penny said.

"Life has changed in Blessing, that's for

sure. But that should be no surprise. We've been through a lot the last couple of years." Sophie looked toward the grain elevator that had been rebuilt after it exploded and nearly took half of Blessing with it, all due to a man smoking against orders. An apartment house and various other homes had grown up to add to the town. An expansion of the deaf school, to the north of town, would be starting as soon as possible. They hoped to have it weather-proofed before winter.

"We have to make plans on how to get our new schoolhouse built too." Sophie leaned closer to Penny. "The way the men are drag-ging their feet on this, it looks to be up to us women to get it rolling. I'm going to have a women's gathering at my house next week. I'll make it sound like a party, but we can begin the plans. What do you think?"

"We need to start with ideas to make money. You know that is what is holding the men back."

"I know. I'll ask everyone to come pre-pared."

"And let the men think we are sneaking behind their backs?"

Sophie shrugged. "We just have to get it started. We need two new teachers—actually three: another for the high school unless Thor-liff wants to stay on. He's doing a good job, but teaching isn't his dream."

"Neither is being a wounded widower." Penny sniffed. "Life sure is hard at times."

"Having lost a husband, I know how he feels. When that boat went down and took Hamre with it, I thought I would die too. I was living all alone out there in Seattle and wanted to come home to Blessing so bad, but I was terrified of what people would think of me after the sneaky way I left."

Penny patted her shoulder. "Like Ingeborg says, God often works in spite of us. When we lived in Bismarck for that year, I kept dreaming of coming home too. I could not make myself see Bismarck as home. I missed my family here, and my store, so when Hjelmer decided to not run for office again, I was overjoyed."

The two parted, Sophie to go to the boardinghouse and Penny to return to her store.

"chool's out for the summer, Grandma!
What are we gonna do today?" Inga asked.
"Can we go fishing?" Emmy and Inga danced
around Ingeborg, clapping and giggling. Emmy
was ten, almost eleven, and Inga had just turned
eight. Inga had run, not walked, to the farm as
soon as school was dismissed the day before,
and stayed.

Ingeborg drew in her chin in mock dismay.
"Fishing? Why would we ever want to go fishing when there are weeds to pull and . . . and
besides, no one has dug worms yet."

"I'll call Carl." Emmy ran to the telephone
and climbed up on the low bench Haakan had
made for the grandchildren to reach the sink,
cupboards, and telephone.

Inga clapped her hands over her mouth to

try to stifle a giggle when Clara motioned to the baby boy sleeping in the sling she wore on her back.

"Sorry, I forgot about him." She grabbed Ingeborg's hands and they spun in a circle. "Can Clara go too?" She stopped and looked at Clara. "Do you know how to catch fish?"

Clara signed back "No, never went fishing."

Inga stared at her, mouth in an *O* of horror. "You never went fishing? Not ever?"

When Clara shook her head, Inga turned to Ingeborg. "Grandma, she has to learn how to catch fish. Can't Clara come too?"

Clara shook her head and motioned to the baby on her back again. Then signed "No, no."

"Carl will be here as fast as he can run," Emmy announced. "I'll go start digging worms. Inga, you get the fishing poles."

Ingeborg grinned at Clara. "Since we went fishing the last two years on their first day after school was out for the summer, this is no surprise. We should be able to have a fish fry for supper, but go ahead and start the stew anyway. We can always have that tomorrow."

When the sling moved and whimpered, Clara smiled.

Never had Ingeborg seen a young mother more entranced with her baby than Clara. Every day he seemed to do something new, bringing love-light to his mother's eyes. She had blossomed like the sunflowers that lined the garden fence last fall, their heads so heavy with seeds they had needed to be tied to the fence to keep from toppling over.

How did a mute name her newborn son? Ingeborg had long puzzled over the problem as Clara's delivery approached. But when the baby was born, Clara solved the problem herself. For hours she went page by page through every book she could find. Freda was the only one in the house the day Manny came in from school, plunked his books on the table, and headed out to the barn to do his chores. Clara, Freda said, stared open-mouthed at the book on top of the pile for the longest time. Then she ran to her room, where the baby was sleeping. She snatched the infant up and brought him to the kitchen. She thumped the book with her index finger, pointed to her baby, and then thumped the book again.

Freda had no idea what the girl was saying; then she caught on. The book was called *Martin Van Buren, a Life.* "Martin. Is that what you've named your baby? Martin?"

Clara had beamed, her head bobbing up and down.

While she had never mentioned the baby's father, sometimes in the long evenings of the winter, Clara mentioned her life in Norway before she came to America four years earlier at the age of fourteen to work for a family. From the sounds of things, life in Norway had not been any easier than life here, or vice versa. One time she had made a reference to life before she went mute. Ingeborg and Kaaren were always puzzling on ways to help her regain the use of her vocal cords.

"Something terrible must have happened to her to make her go mute," Kaaren said once. She had read all she could find on *aphasia voluntaria*, the scientific term, but no one held out much hope. But Clara learned to sign in English and finally to write in English, proving that she was intelligent and should not always have to rely on doing heavy manual work.

"You go nurse him now before we leave," Ingeborg urged the young woman, "although Freda won't be out in the cheese house all day."

"You will take food?" Clara signed. When Ingeborg nodded, Clara signed "I will make sandwiches."

Ingeborg had given up trying to argue with Clara. Instead, she lifted Martin from the sling and went to change his diaper. She never tired of seeing him laugh, wave his arms, and try to imitate the sounds she made to him while she cleaned him up. As miserably as Clara had been treated, such a happy and healthy baby was near miraculous.

Sandwiches were wrapped in a towel, cookies in a napkin, and a jug of pink water joined the food in the basket. Ingeborg thanked Clara.

Inga had found the fishing gear and made

sure each pole had a line with a cork bobber with an embedded hook. "I couldn't find the lead sinkers," she muttered. "And a couple of the hooks are rusty, but we can rub it off with sand. Didn't Grandpa have extra hooks and lines?"

"I thought so." Ingeborg kissed Martin's cheek and handed him back to his mother. "Did you check in the cellar?"

"No." Inga shook her head, setting her braids to swinging. "Where's the tackle box?" Her eyes narrowed as she puzzled. "Manny's room." She pelted up the stairs. Manny had kept as many of Haakan's things as he could find, as if the treasures might keep him closer to the man who had taught him so much in the brief time they'd had together. A couple minutes later, she came down the stairs triumphantly. "Under the bed."

"Surely they have enough worms by now." The two gathered the gear, and after waving at Clara, who sat in the rocker with a dish towel covering the loudly nursing baby, headed for the barn—and the worm diggers.

"We have enough," Carl announced and jammed his pitchfork back in the aging edge of the manure pile. "Some are really big, they'll catch a big fish."

As they followed the path to the river, Ingeborg listened to the cousins chatter, the meadowlarks heralding their way. What better

way to spend an early June day than going fishing with these little—well, no longer quite so
little—ones of hers?

Inga dropped back to walk beside her.
"Grandma, will Pa ever get over his sad eyes?"

"Ja, I think he will."

"You did."

"Takk, I'm glad to hear you say that."

"Sometimes he smiles now, but not often.
Not even when Roald is so funny. Me and
Astrid, we—" She shook her head. "Whoops,
Astrid and I can get him giggling so hard, and
then we are laughing too and even Thelma, but
sometimes I think Pa isn't even there. I mean
he is sitting right there but . . ." She shook her
head again. "I want him to be like he used to
be. Before Mor went to be with Jesus." She
heaved a sigh. "I sure miss her. Do you think
she is happy in heaven?"

"Ja, I do. God promises us that heaven
is beautiful beyond what we know here and
there are no tears or pain in heaven." As they
followed the path into the shade of the trees
and down the riverbank, they all sighed in
pleasure.

Carl put his finger to his lips to shush them.
"Don't scare the fish," he whispered.

"Pa said," Inga added in a whisper. Carl
was certain his pa knew everything and was
always right. The girls giggled very quietly and
Carl frowned at them anyway, which made

them giggle all the more, which made Ingeborg nearly choke, suppressing her own laughter.

To Carl, fishing was serious business. But then, he was a serious little boy. Had Andrew been like that? Ingeborg pondered her son's boyhood and couldn't come up with an answer. Andrew was the son of Roald and Ingeborg. Then along came Astrid, Ingeborg's only child with Haakan. There had been no more children, something Ingeborg had at times lamented but finally accepted as God's will for them. Since then, she'd learned that often when men have mumps as adults, as Haakan did, they could no longer father children. Sad, but she'd finally come to acceptance and was grateful instead for all the other children God brought to her, often the needy and the broken, for her to love.

"Grandma, aren't you going to throw your line out?" Carl whispered to her. He handed her a pole with a wriggling worm already on the hook. The others had already cast theirs out and were sitting on a log, waiting.

"Thank you for taking care of your grandma." She reached to hug him and then took her pole. "Where do you think I should cast?"

Carl studied the river. "Try near that snag over there." He pointed across the river.

"Okay, I will." Ingeborg cast her line and watched the bobber eddy along. Before she even had time to sit down, she had a strike.

"Set the hook!" Carl cried.

Ingeborg jerked her pole, and a fish came flying through the air to land behind them. Patches barked, dancing around the flopping fish.

"Grandma got the first fish!" Inga danced in place, making sure she kept one eye on her own bobber.

"Shush!" Carl scowled at her.

Ingeborg settled down on the bank in the shade of a gnarled old willow. How many fishermen had this willow seen and shaded? At least the elephants had not reached it. When the circus was in town last summer, the elephant keepers had brought the huge animals down to the river shore to browse. What a mess the poor starving animals had made. The bank where they had been was not yet beginning to return to its old self.

Inga caught a fish and so did Carl, so apparently everyone had been quiet enough that the fish were not frightened away. Ingeborg's bobber disappeared, but she did not try to set the hook. Let the children catch fish. In a few moments it came to the surface, so she drew her line in and replaced the worm that had been stolen.

Haakan used to love to take the children fishing. Back when his son and daughter were this age, there had not been enough help in the fields for him to take time off, but in his later years, he had whopper fishing and hunting stories to tell.

Ah, Lord, how he would have treasured a day like this. Is there fishing in heaven?

No, of course not. If you were happily swimming around in a heavenly river and someone caught you, cleaned you, and had you for dinner, that was not heaven, at least from the fish's point of view. Fishing must be done here in this life.

Ingeborg smiled and let the glory of the day and muted chatter of precious children surround her with joy. For a moment, this moment, nothing in the world could possibly go wrong. Right?

Her mind and memories drifted. She had to be careful not to fall asleep. Sometimes it was hard to believe this placid river could break over the banks and threaten the lives of both animals and humans along the entire Red River Valley. Her mind drifted back to the last of the great floods in the '90s. Every year she prayed against such devastation. They had moved the cows to higher ground a few times, and the muddy water made it up to the porch, but pumping out the cellar was nothing compared to rebuilding houses and burying the dead.

A fish whizzed by her head as Emma giggled and Carl hushed them all. Within moments another flopped on the bank. They might have a fish fry after all. When Ingeborg reached to help Inga, her own cork bobbed and her pole snaked down the bank toward the water. She grabbed for her pole, slipped in the muck, and plunked down on her rear—with no pole.

"Grandma, you got a fish!"

"I know. Grab my pole!"

Patches barked at the rapidly fleeing fishing pole, and Inga got the giggles. But Carl was the hero. He ran over and stomped on the end of her pole just as it was about to slide into the water. He handed his pole to Emma, grabbed hers, and another fish flip-flopped beside her.

"That's a big one." She looked from her fish to her eldest grandson. "Takk. Carl, you saved my pole."

"And the fish. Grandma, you gotta pay better attention."

That did it! Ingeborg tried to keep a straight face, but Inga and Emma's giggles did her in. "Ja, Carl, I will try but . . ."

"Carl, you better land your own fish." Inga clutched her pole and tried to pull his in with her other hand.

Emmy whooped. "I got one too!" Biting fish and laughing grandchildren left Ingeborg no more time for thinking of past floods.

Inga jerked her pole, and a large fish whistled by Ingeborg's head.

"We have a new rule here. No hitting your grandmother with a fish."

"Sorry." Inga picked up her flopping fish,

removed the hook from its mouth, and instead of handing it to Ingeborg, added it to the stringer herself.

"You did well."

"I watched you." Inga grinned and dug another worm out of the bucket. "Rolly ate a worm yesterday. Thelma was not happy. She said he might get sick and it served him right. She said *ishta*. Ma once told me not to say that. What's wrong with saying *ishta*?"

Ingeborg wanted to hug her little grand-daughter to her side and keep her there. "It's just not a word that proper ladies use."

"Isn't Thelma a proper lady?"

"Well, that's not what I meant. Of course she is, but . . ." How to explain the difference between common language and polite language? "Uh, some things just are not as polite as others." She could feel all their eyes on her. She glanced out at the water. "Your bobbers."

Even as they returned to fishing, Ingeborg knew Inga would not let go of this. She landed another fish of her own and started a new stringer. If they wanted a proper fish fry, she should contribute her share. Good thing they were all getting stronger to help carry their fish home.

Perhaps she should suggest to Thorliff that he bring the children fishing instead of burying himself in work so that he didn't have to think. She remembered doing that herself after

Roald died. Kaaren had accused her of trying to kill herself with work. All she knew was
that when she was idle, the pit came closer to
sucking her in. She tipped her head back and
stared up through the tree branches, which
were mostly leafed out. Back then she didn't
understand that God really meant it when He
said He would keep her from the miry pit and
put her feet on solid rock. The pit had tried
to come for her after Haakan died but with
nowhere near the strength, as she had learned
to stand on God's promises—at least most of
the time.

Her pole twitched, she jerked, and another
fish landed on the bank. After accompany-
ing her to the stringer, Patches lay back down
beside her, nose on his paws, watching the children. He took his job of protecting them very
seriously.

"I need to go," Inga whispered to her
grandma.

'Okay, but be careful of poison ivy."

"I will." She headed for the big tree the
girls often hid behind for this purpose. Patches
sighed as he rose to go with her.

Ingeborg puzzled on remembering how old
Patches was getting to be. He was their third
dog since coming to North Dakota, and this
was 1908, so he must be six or seven. She'd
need to ask Thorliff.

She heard Patches growling before she saw

him, ruff raised, tail not wagging, staring up river.

"Patches, what is it?"

As if the dog could say.

"You all stay right here," she said softly as she flipped her line out of the water, rose, and staring at the brush beyond the big tree, made her way toward Inga. She picked up a big knobby stick lying where the high water had left it.

"Inga, are you finished?" She kept her voice soft.

"Ja." Her skirt settled back in place as she came around the tree.

"Come stand behind me."

"What is it, Grandma?"

"I don't know, but Patches does, and he's not happy." She stopped beside the quivering dog and tried to see what he saw.

Emmy appeared and pressed hard against her. "Grandma, we're in trouble. I know, because wild dogs were a real problem in our village."

"So it *is* wild dogs."

Emmy nodded, still pressed against her. "They hunt like coyotes hunt, but they're meaner and stronger. See that dog halfway up the bank? Over there! See?" She pointed, but though Ingeborg followed her pointing finger, she saw nothing.

Until it moved.

It was huge, gray, and shaggy.

Inga asked, "Could it be a wolf, Grandma?"

Ingeborg's mind flashed back to the time she had seen a wolf here, but that had been Metiz' wolf. Not that she'd known it at the time. But Metiz' wolf had not returned after it brought its family back to introduce them—and later, Metiz died.

Inga whispered, "Grandma, I'm scared. Could this be the dog pack the men were talking about?"

Ingeborg heard a snarling growl. "Inga, go tell the others to wrap their poles up and pull the stringers. Quickly! I'll try to chase it off."

"No!" Emmy wailed. "Don't! That's the decoy. It wants us to chase it. Then the rest of the pack closes in behind us and traps us in the middle!"

Patches slunk forward. Emmy grabbed his collar and held him back.

Inga didn't have to tell Carl what to do. He had already gathered the poles and stringers together. He had a big knobby club too. They clustered in close to Ingeborg.

Inga's voice trembled. "Are they gonna eat us?"

"They'll take Patches for sure, and maybe a little child. Not Grandma or Carl or . . ." Emmy shuddered.

"Emmy, hang on to Patches if you can so

he can't chase them. Carl, give me three or four of those fish. Hurry!"

Carl unthreaded three flopping fish from his stringer.

"Let's get home." Ingeborg gripped the fish behind the gills and started up the bank.

The children moved quickly, scrambling up the bank and out into the meadow. Emmy hauled Patches along with her.

"Don't run!" Emmy ordered. "Don't anybody run. If you run, the dogs will chase you and they're faster. They can pull you down easier if you're running. Walk in a straight line."

Fear grabbed Ingeborg's breastbone. *They can pull you down easier if you're running.* Emmy's warning almost turned her knees into melted butter. But Emmy obviously knew a lot about wild dogs, a lot more than Ingeborg or these children knew.

Lord, our lives are in your hands. Please, Lord God! Please!

Ingeborg stopped, wheeled, and threw a fish toward the big gray dog. The dog lunged forward and grabbed the fish as two other dogs appeared out of nowhere. Emmy was right; they had been hiding, waiting to ambush their prey from behind. The dogs fought viciously for the fish. Ingeborg threw the other two fish as far as she could.

There were two more dogs, and another,

and another. They fell upon the fish, snarling and snapping at each other.

"They can't see us anymore," Emmy cried. "Run!"

Once up on the open fields, they headed straight for home, saving their breath for running.

As they drew closer to the buildings, Ingeborg slowed to a fast walk, fighting to catch her breath. Her lungs ached. She glanced back; the dogs had not followed.

When they passed the back of the barn, Carl dumped the worms back on the manure pile.

"You even brought the worms back?" Ingeborg tried to laugh but coughed instead.

"We will need worms again, and besides, we didn't leave the fish either. Just the ones you threw at them, and they were the smallest we caught." Carl held up his string and each of the others did too.

Ingeborg's cough turned to laughter, and one by one they joined in. Patches danced around them, yipping and whimpering. The danger was over, for now.

Finally, Ingeborg tipped her head back to stare at the sky. Leave it to her brave children. She was concerned about a pack of wild dogs, and they were more concerned about getting their fish home—and the worms.

Back at the house, Freda brought two knives

out to the bench where they cleaned fish and often scrubbed vegetables. "I just sharpened these. How many you got there?"

"Not enough for all three families. Freda, that pack of wild dogs showed up."

"And Grandma threw them some of our fish, and we had to leave real fast." Carl's tone was slightly accusing.

"You better take the rifle next time," Freda said.

"There will be no next time until the men destroy that pack. They must live along the riverbank. It provides the only cover within miles. As soon as we scale and clean these, I'm getting on the telephone and making it clear that this has to be done now before more than a lamb or chickens are snatched." She paused. "And if the men are reluctant, I'll go track them myself."

Freda made one of her noncommittal sounds, like a cross between clearing her throat and snorting. "I'll take care of these and you go make that telephone call." She frowned. "Who will you call?"

"My two sons to start with." Ingeborg smiled slightly and shrugged at the same time. Her nerves were still tingling, agitated, unsettled. *What if the children . . . What if Patches had not been there to alert them?* "When I tell them the story, they'll probably be out the door before I finish. After all, we are protecting their children."

"Let alone their mother."

When Ingeborg had finished telling Thorliff what had happened, he assured her the men would take care of it. Did they have any dead lambs or chickens he could use as bait?

"Andrew just had a litter of pigs, so he might. Do you want me to ask Lars?"

"No, I'll take it from here. You better tie Patches up or put him in one of the box stalls in the barn. How far upriver from the path were they?"

"Maybe a hundred yards. Not far. But surely Patches would have smelled them earlier if they lived there. I think they live somewhere farther up the river and were hunting, and we just happened to be there."

"I'm calling Andrew now, Mor. We'll get them."

They said good-bye, and after hanging the earpiece back on the prongs, Ingeborg joined Freda at the cleaning bench. "Where are the children?"

"Down at the barn. I told them to start sweeping out the haymow."

"Do we have any swizzle made?"

"No, but there are still canned raspberries in the cellar."

Ingeborg nodded absently. That would do. "Where's Manny?"

"Lars has him helping repair machinery."

Ingeborg smiled to herself. Lars had slowly

stepped into Haakan's place in teaching fifteen-year-old Manny all the skills needed to be a farmer. Just the way he had trained his own sons and some of the boys in the deaf school. Thomas Devlin had been teaching woodworking and carpentry to some of the deaf boys. Who would step into his place? Part of the training was homemaking for the girls and skills to prepare the boys to make a living. Surely with all the new folks in town, someone had those skills and would be willing to teach. Perhaps she'd put the word out. *Ingeborg, it's not your problem to solve.*

Her jangled nerves brought her mind right back to the dogs. Emmy knew what to do, but most of the children, especially the small children, did not know. They would run away, and the dogs . . . *Lord God, protect us all!*

Emmy said that wild dogs hunted the way coyotes did. Coyotes hunted at night, or at least dusk. But those dogs were out hunting in the afternoon. Dogs with rabies hunted at midday. If rabies was in the area, no one's dog was safe, not even Patches. What if a pack of feral dogs was not the worst of it?

On the outside, Ingeborg tried to appear calm for Freda's sake.

On the inside, she was trembling.

CHAPTER 4

I think we need a girl party," Deborah surprised herself by saying to Sophie one Sunday after church.

"I think you are very right. What shift are
you working?" Sophie half closed her eyes to
think better. "Like next Saturday?"

"I have the weekend off."

"Then I'll set it in motion. We are long
overdue for a meeting." She studied Deborah.
"Any special reason?"

Deborah half shrugged, then rolled her lips
together. "Can we talk then?"

"Of course. Just us oldies, or should we
include some newbies like Miriam? Astrid, of
course, will be on call . . ."

"But we don't call her anymore unless we

can't handle the case. I would like to include Miriam."

"Good. And remember, at our girl party, confession is not only good for the soul but mandatory." Sophie chuckled. "Besides, I think we're no longer girls. Our children are girls. I'll tell the others, and as always, bring whatever you want for food. I'll banish my tribe to their aunt's house for the night. Remember when we all used to spend the whole night together?"

They shared a smile.

"We have so many good memories." Deborah waved good-bye to Sophie and walked out of the church.

Where was Toby? By habit she looked around for him, the way she always did after church. He was over there among a knot of young men, talking. Gerald said something and they all laughed. Just like always.

She was about to head home when she stopped. Offering. Did she drop it in the plate? Or . . . she was helping little Swen find the penny he had dropped, and the offering plate had gone right on by. She groped around in her reticule. Yes, there it was. *What an oaf, Deborah. Why can't you remember?* She carried her tithe back inside.

She didn't think she was mooning about husbands, but Toby had passed through her mind. He had sat practically right across the aisle from her, yet he had not spoken. He had smiled and waved, but that was all. Surely if he were even halfway interested in her the way she was interested in him, he would have stopped and talked to her after the service.

The collection bag had not been taken to the back room yet. She tucked her offering inside it and went back outside.

"Deborah? Deborah! There you are." Toby! He came running over to her, and her heart soared. There was hope!

"Good morning, Toby!" Oh my, he looked handsome today.

"May I walk you home?"

"Please do." Her heart was now soaring somewhere beyond the clouds.

"I have a favor to ask of you."

Her heart thudded to earth. Oh. Here she thought he was interested in her, and all he wanted was some favor. "What do you need?"

"Well, you know the guys who are planning the Fourth—we were thinking we should invite the well drillers to come in for it—all of them, not just the ones who live here—and the fire brigades from up north who helped us last year. They probably won't come, of course; they have their own Fourth of July celebrations. But it would be a nice gesture, and we'll have plenty of food."

"I heard. Beef *and* pork."

"Right. So we were thinking, maybe you could help us out by writing all the invitations."

"Writing the . . . wait. You guys, as you say, came up with the idea. Why don't you write them?"

"Well, we all have jobs that take a lot of time. But the hospital isn't very busy right now, so we thought that since you're just sitting there . . ." He paused because she had stopped walking and had turned to stare at him. Probably she was glaring at him, but she didn't care.

Just sitting there? She hardly had a spare moment at work, and they thought she just sat there? Besides, this wasn't a favor to Toby after all, it was a favor to all the men. He was just the one who'd asked her.

"Why are *you* asking me? Why not Pa, I mean Pastor Solberg, since we live in the same house?"

"Well, uh, the pastor thought I might be a good one to do it, since you seem to . . . uh . . ." He licked his lips, opened his mouth, and closed it again.

Her thoughts and feelings all churned up together, and she couldn't sort any of them. She kept her voice flat and modulated. "Thank you very much for walking me this far. I can find my way home the rest of the way." She turned on her heel and started walking. Of all the emotions fighting in her head, fury burned brightest.

Just sitting there indeed!

But then he called to her departing back, "Besides, I kind of like you!"

The days crawled by, and that was not like Deborah's usual week at all. What had Toby meant? How did he feel, really? She couldn't tell. Just when she thought he cared nothing for her, something suggested otherwise. She needed the advice and support of her girlfriends more than ever.

When Ingeborg had once asked her what she wanted most in life, Deborah's first thought had been, *to be married to Toby Valders*. Now here it was, so many years later, and Toby was still the only man she thought of.

In a way, she sleepwalked through her duties at the hospital and at home, keeping one part of her mind on the task of the moment and the other part in that now-familiar churning mix of emotions. But confusion plagued her the worst, especially now, as she walked home from her day shift at the hospital. What would her wisest form of action be? The girls had always depended on one another for counsel. She, Rebecca, Sophie, Grace, and Astrid, along with Anji, before she moved away to start her new life with Thomas. All of them born and raised in Blessing, except for her and Manda. And yet they were included as if they had always lived there too. In fact, most people had probably forgotten that she and Manda weren't born there.

She mounted the steps to the ranch house that long ago became home to the Solbergs and herself.

"I'm home," she called, walking through the front door.

"Back here," Mary Martha called from the back porch. "Iced tea is in the icebox. Come join us."

"I'll change first." She always left her nurse's apron at the hospital, and now she changed out of her skirt and waist into a loose summer dress and left her nursing shoes in the closet, instead choosing to go barefoot. Nothing felt better than bare feet in the summer, especially in the morning with the dew on the grass. In the kitchen she poured herself a glass of tea and, taking a sip, wandered out to the back porch that extended about halfway down the north side of the house. The front porch extended the full length, and both had shingled roofs like the rest of the house.

"Welcome home," Mary Martha said with a smile. "We're playing hooky."

"Hooky from what?"

"From work. I decided to have cold things for supper, all of which are made. The garden is sort of weeded. We should be planting the pumpkins and other late crops, but we needed a breather." She motioned to the four children, two sitting on the back step, playing cat's cradle with red yarn, two leaning over the low table between two chairs.

Johnny and Thomas looked up from the checkerboard. "I'm checker king today," Thomas said, grinning, and held up three fingers.

"He cheats," seven-year-old Emily announced from the step. She passed the yarn to her older brother, Mark.

"Do not. I don't have to cheat."

Mary Martha rolled her eyes. "I don't suggest you challenge him. I haven't won a game with him since he was six." He was fourteen now, which she could hardly believe. She motioned to the settee. "We saved that for you."

"Where's Pa?" Deborah had taken to calling the Solbergs *Ma* and *Pa* not long after Manda and the others left.

"Meeting with Thorliff and the others. Planning the Fourth of July celebration. Every year they make plans, and every year we do the same wonderful things. Other than that year we women tried to have the fireworks. As you know, the men have not forgotten the near miss and decided not to let us do the planning anymore."

"And that's why it is already June and they are just starting?" Deborah asked with all innocence.

Mary Martha laughed. "We'll never tell.

But we'll take care of the food as always. I think they've agreed on half a steer barbecue again. I know someone mentioned that a hog would be good that way too."

"If I remember right, we didn't have a lot of leftover beef last year. Do we have more people here now than last year?"

"I'm not sure, but the children are growing and will eat more." Mary Martha glanced across at her brood. "If these are any indication."

"Word has gotten out about how our celebration has such great food, so others might come too." Deborah sipped from her glass and held the chilly surface to her cheek. It wasn't unseasonably warm yet, but when the perpetual breeze died, like now, one felt the heat more. "I need to make something for the party at Sophie's on Saturday. Any suggestions?"

"We have lots of eggs; what about deviled eggs?"

"Good, I'll put them on to boil. Do we have any popcorn left?" Last summer they had grown a patch of the special kind of corn for popping, and after drying it, they had treats all winter.

"We planted the last of it."

Johnny studied the checkerboard. "We planted twice as much this year."

"Good thing. We had such a fun time making popcorn balls last winter." Emily grinned, then glanced down at her hand. "But that syrup burned some."

"They didn't last long, that's for sure." Mary Martha smiled at her daughter. "Makes me hungry for one right now."

"So deviled eggs and . . . ?"

"How about those crispy crackers you make? We can make a big bunch so we can have some too." Mark abandoned the cat's cradle game. "I'll help roll and cut 'em."

Emily clapped her hands. "I'll help eat 'em. Better make lots."

"You know those biscuit rolls you made with cinnamon and sugar, like cinnamon rolls? Those went over really well." Mary Martha thought for a moment. "What if we put butter and grated cheese and some herbs on the flattened dough and rolled them up? That sounds really good."

"What if we made those for supper?" Deborah pushed herself to her feet. "I'll get the stove going. Come on, Mark, you can measure out the flour and other ingredients."

"But . . ." Mary Martha shook her head. "Oh well. If the stove is hot, I'll put coffee on too. John will appreciate a cup when he comes home." She poked Thomas's arm. "Come on, you can bring in a brick of cheese and grate it."

By the time the stove was hot enough, the cheese roll-ups were ready to bake, and they were rolling out cornmeal and flour dough thin enough for the crackers. Deborah had chopped parsley and chives very fine and added them to both kinds of dough. "Okay now, sprinkle on salt, lightly, and we'll slide this pan in on the top rack."

"We have to taste them first, right?" The three younger children circled around the table while Deborah rolled out more. Johnny had picked up his guitar and was playing it in the next room.

Mark frowned at the bowl. "We made lots of dough."

"I know, we might be baking them forever." Thomas didn't look a bit sad. "This is fun."

Just as Deborah was taking the eggs off the stove the barking dog announced that Pa was home. She would finish making them tomorrow.

Emily ran to meet him at the door. "We're baking crackers for Deborah to take to her party and we get to keep some too." She grabbed his hand. "Come on."

"Crackers? What about cookies or pie or a cake?"

"Sorry, Ma said cold supper, but then Deborah came home and we're baking cheese roll-ups and crackers. And now the kitchen is hot, but . . ." Emily paused and stared up at his face. "I'm glad you're home."

John Solberg smiled down at her. "Me too. Is the coffee pot on?"

"It is." Emily leaned her cheek against his arm. "Ma said we could eat outside tonight."

Mary Martha met them at the doorway into the kitchen and kissed Pa on the cheek. "Welcome home. I tried for peaceful, but . . ." She motioned to the mess in the kitchen. "We are trying two new things."

Deborah pulled the first pan of cheese roll-ups out of the oven and set them on the cooling rack. "Just in time to try our new recipe." She bent back down and pulled the first pan of crackers out too. "Recipes."

Emily pointed. "Look at the way the crackers curled up on the corners, like they are flying." She danced around Deborah. "Try them, try them."

"You're going to burn your fingers. Wait at least a couple of minutes." Deborah slid the crackers onto a towel spread on the counter. "Mark, load this pan up again."

"You have a full bakery going here." Pa accepted the coffee cup from his wife.

"So, anything new for the Fourth of July?"

He smiled. "A pie social to earn money for the new school building, the governor agreed to be our speaker, and we added wheelbarrow races to the games. We vetoed the fireworks again, but Sophie keeps trying."

"Beef or pork?"

Pa chuckled. "Toby talked us into both this

year. Says there are enough people around, we won't have much left over."

Silently, Deborah mused, *And Toby Valders is a pillar of the community, another characteristic in his favor.*

"Sounds like a good day," Mary Martha said. "And did you put in the order for good weather?"

"That we did."

"Ma, Mark snitched a cracker." Emily glared at him.

"Did not, it fell on the floor so I ate it."

"You knocked it on the floor."

"Did not." Mark looked up at Deborah. "I didn't. . . . Okay, I did, but not intentionally."

Deborah smiled at him.

"An accident." Emily shrugged and then nodded sagely. "But they are good. Can we have some now?"

Mark jostled her. "You had yours."

"Did not. It was a broken one."

Deborah tipped the roll-up pan over to release the rolls. "These smell heavenly. We have to eat them warm, while the cheese is still melted." She broke the rolls apart, and everyone helped themselves.

Johnny took the first bite and shook his head. "They're no good. You better not eat them."

"Why, so you can have them all?" Thomas asked.

Johnny shrugged and grinned at Deborah.

"Okay, only one." Mary Martha set down her roll and reached for a cracker. "Good crunch. These are really good. You'll need to put them in a tin with a tight lid to keep them crisp."

Deborah checked the two pans in the oven. "I think we need to poke them with a fork to help them lie flatter. Mark, do you have the other pan about ready? It's a good thing we have so much help or these would take forever."

John snatched another roll. "Those crackers are good but these are superb. What do you call them?"

"Cheesy roll-ups," Deborah replied.

"John, you and the little ones go out on the porch, and we'll bring supper out. Although how anyone can have room for supper after all these treats is beyond me."

He frowned at the children. "Did you kids do your chores yet?"

"I took care of the chickens." Emily watched a tray of crackers come out of the oven.

Johnny glanced up at the clock on the wall. "Not time to milk yet."

"Let's eat right now, and then we'll finish the chores." Mary Martha headed for the icebox and began handing out things to be carried to the table. "Everyone dish up in here and take your plate outside."

That evening, after Deborah was all washed

and sitting on her bed, propped against pillows with a breeze coming in the window, she added a few more lines to the journal she had kept ever since high school. Once she had gone back and read the whole thing. So many dreams and prayers about life with Toby Valders. Sometimes she had been so sure that would happen, and other times she wrote that she hated him because he'd gone off to work with the windmill crew and it didn't look like he'd ever come back, or he had been interested in someone else. Sometimes she declared she was done dreaming over him and would just concentrate on being the best nurse possible. Once she'd written that perhaps she should go off and be a missionary in some far-off place where she would be too busy to dream of him.

She shut her journal and tucked it under her Bible on her nightstand. She'd taken to writing in pencil so she could carry it with her more easily. Pens and inkpots were a real encumbrance if one were not seated at a desk or table.

Dusk had not yet turned to full dark, but she needed to get to sleep. She had so many things to get done before going to the girls' get-together. Did she really have the courage to confess this quandary of hers?

CHAPTER 5

Ingeborg held the phone's black earpiece to her ear. "I'll go along with you if you want."

"Mor, we have plenty of men to take care of this. Maybe I should ask Manny if he wants to join us." Andrew sounded excited. "Now, you say this was your usual fishing spot?"

"Ja, and the dogs came from upriver."

"Clever idea, throwing them the fish, but Carl is still grumbling that you threw good fish away."

Ingeborg chuckled. "He even held onto the can of worms. What a bunch of troopers we have."

"We have a couple of dead piglets we can use for bait. Tell Manny that if he wants to come, Lars and Samuel will meet the rest of us in the big barn at nine or so. No point in staking it out before dark."

Ingeborg remembered tales of hunters tying out a live sheep or calf to draw the predators that needed to be disposed of. "Takk for taking care of this."

"Stealing a lamb or calf is one thing, but challenging people, especially our children, means war. I need to get the chores done. I'm glad you and the little ones had so much fun fishing—before the dogs, of course. 'Bye, Mor."

She hung the earpiece back on the prongs. Here she was, recently turned fifty years old, and she wanted to go hunting the pack of wild dogs. What was the matter with her?

She heard little Martin cry and hurried to the crib. Clara was out in the garden with Inga and Emmy.

As she leaned over to pick him up, she crooned, "Surely you are not hungry again already, baby boy. Oh, you are soaked. No wonder you woke up." She held him away from her apron and laid him on the changing table they had set up in her bedroom. "Look at you, smiling and even trying to talk." He gurgled and cooed at her, waving fists and feet. "O Lord, how I love having a baby in this house again. Thank you for this little fellow and his mor. We sure need your wisdom to discover how we can help her the best."

She kissed one of the waving fists and, dry

diaper and soaker in place, tucked him into his sling and returned to the porch, where she had been writing a long overdue letter to Manda and Baptiste. Talking with Deborah at the wedding had reminded her that she owed them a letter. Not that they had written for a long, long time either, but oh well.

She caught them up on the local news and then added one more paragraph:

> *Deborah really misses you. Is there any possibility that you could return for a visit? I know that is asking a lot, but she is not the only one to ask about you. You will be surprised at how much Blessing has grown, with new people and new buildings. Please write soon and tell us how you are.*
>
> *With love,*
> *Ingeborg*

The baby stretched and gurgled. Patches, at her side, lifted his head and scrambled to his feet, his toenails clicking as he yipped and tore out to greet Manny, who was returning from working with Lars. Even with the special shoe Lars had made for him, he limped, but nothing like before.When Ingeborg thought of the sullen boy who had come to live with her after breaking his leg during an attempted bank robbery, she was overwhelmed with wonder at the bighearted young man Manny had grown into.

"You look a bit weary."

He waved and nodded. "Fixing machinery takes lots of thinking, like when Haakan taught me farming things. Farming machinery is complicated." He patted Patches, who was jumping at his side, and waved at Emmy and Inga, who hollered to him from the garden. He sank down on the steps and grinned at Ingeborg while fluffing Patches' ears. "I see you've got Martin."

Ingeborg patted the baby's bottom. "He's such a good baby. So, are you planning on going with them tonight?"

"I want to." His jaw tightened. "If we don't get 'em, they might get a child. Grandma, they coulda hurt all of you real bad or even killed somebody. If wild dogs pull you down, you're in trouble, and they could pull down a child real easy."

"Ja, but God kept us safe—with three fishes. Just like the story where Jesus fed the people with five loaves and three fishes. Only here He protected us with three fishes."

Manny shook his head. "Too close."

"Do you want something to drink?" She started to rise, but he waved her back.

"I'll get it." He stood and yelled. "You hardworking gardeners want lemonade and cookies?" At their chorus of yeses, he grinned at Ingeborg. "It is lemonade, isn't it?"

"Made this morning." Ever since Penny

started carrying lemons at the store, she made lemonade, often mixing it with their own canned fruit or juices.

He stopped at the door. "Where's Freda?"

"Up at the cheese house. She'll be here soon. She mentioned she's about out of shipping crates again." The first shipment of the summer was nearly ready to send out, along with sharper cheddar that they had aged through the winter. Their customers were already clamoring for cheese, but they didn't set much cheese until the cows could graze in the pastures. This year spring had come a bit early and without flooding the Red River, which meant the pastures greened up sooner. They already had ten calves out in the barn and calf pasture, to the delight of Emmy and Inga, who fed and played with them.

In the past, Inga had spent as much of the summer at the farm as her mother would allow. But since her mother, Elizabeth, had died of typhoid, Grandma's farm became Inga's summer home. Ingeborg let it go since Thorliff did not seem to mind.

Manny returned in a few minutes with full glasses for all and a large plate of molasses cookies. "Come and get it!" His shout brought on giggles and running girls.

As they all took their treats and found a place to sit, Ingeborg laughed along with them, loving every minute of their teasing. While

Manny was growing into a fine young man, taller than Ingeborg now, he was still one of the kids when they got together.

"Come on, Freda, before the cookies are all gone," he shouted at the woman who had just closed the door to the cheese house and was returning to the main house.

"You better save me one."

Sober Freda could now take part in some of their antics. Another of the miracles Ingeborg recognized around her all the time. Would wonders never cease?

"Do you want me to take him?" Clara signed after swigging half a glass. She wiped the perspiration from her forehead with her apron.

"Clara, now you have dirt on your face," Inga whispered loudly enough to be heard across the river.

She shrugged and waved her hand, turning back to Ingeborg.

"He's going to be asking for you pretty soon, but right now you just sit there and catch your breath." For a change Clara did as Ingeborg said and collapsed back against the cushion on the settee.

The sling Ingeborg wore started to wiggle and emit little squeaky noises.

Clara leaned forward to reach for her baby, but Ingeborg waved her back again. "You sit a couple more minutes; he won't get wound up that quick." She gently jiggled the sling and pushed to start the chair rocking. "Sweet, sweet baby, you could let your ma rest a few minutes at least."

"May I have some bread and cheese or something before I go help with the milking? I'm really hungry." Manny looked to Ingeborg, who half shrugged.

Freda stood up from the other cushioned chair. "I'll get it for you."

"I can do that." Manny rose to his feet, but even so, Freda beat him to the door.

"I wouldn't argue with her; even I never win." Ingeborg sat back, rocking. There was nothing, absolutely nothing, as satisfying as rocking a little baby.

Inga frowned at Manny. "You ate five cookies."

"How d'you know?"

"I counted them." Inga stared at the empty plate. "I only got two and Emmy the same. Not fair, huh, Grandma?"

"If you are hinting for more cookies, it won't work. Those were the last of them." The bundle squeaks were growing more demanding.

Clara stood and reached for her baby, alternately shaking her head and grinning at Ingeborg. Ingeborg lifted the sling from around her neck and one arm and handed him to Clara.

"Since supper won't be for an hour or more, I suggest we each have a piece of cheese, and the three of us can mix up a batch of cookies and get the stove heating. We're having pork chops and rice with gravy, so Freda won't need the oven."

"Grandma, are they really going to shoot those wild dogs?"

"Ja, they are."

"But why are they wild? Coyotes and wolves are wild, but dogs are tame and live with people." Inga propped her elbows on her knees, sitting cross-legged on the porch floor.

"Who knows? People must have left them or they got lost. Then the females have puppies, and before long there is a whole pack, a dangerous pack, because they hunt together like wolves do."

"They sure sounded mean."

"Maybe because they're so hungry," Emmy added softly.

Later, after supper, with the sour cream cookies cooling on the table, they watched the men gather down at the barn. Everyone carried a shotgun, Manny using one of Haakan's. They headed out across the field, following the trail that had been worn through the years. They left Patches in a stall in the barn.

Fairly soon the mosquitoes drove the women and girls back indoors. After cookies and milk, Ingeborg read the next chapter in *Little Women* until the clatter of June bugs slamming against the screens reminded them it was getting late.

"Grandma, I don't want the dogs to die." Inga leaned against Ingeborg in her rocking chair.

"I know, but we have no choice. The men tried to find them several weeks ago and they had disappeared."

"Well, they sure came back."

At midnight, when Ingeborg got up to use the necessary, Manny's boots were not back by the door. "Lord, please keep our men safe and do away with the danger." Back in bed, she listened to the night sounds, the singing crickets, an owl hooting, the breeze lifting the lace curtains. One by one, she went down her family. *Heal Thorliff's heart from Elizabeth's death.* Then she thought of Deborah and her dreams, and prayed that Anji and her family were settling in well in Michigan.

A volley of shots woke her some time later, a howl cut off with another shot. *Lord God, keep them safe.* She knew too well how a load of buckshot could go astray. When the normal night sounds took over, she drifted back to sleep.

"So how did the hunt go?" she asked when everyone was gathered at the table for breakfast the next morning.

Manny reached for a second helping of eggs. "We were startin' to think the dogs wouldn't show up. We waited and waited, and even though we smeared comfrey all over us, them wretched mosquitoes wouldn't leave us alone. So we finally put mud on too. Right about when we were starting to talk about giving up, here they come. Seven of them. They were right suspicious, but then the big gray one grabbed a dead pig, and we opened fire. One almost got away, but Andrew saw it and shot real fast. We made sure they were all dead and left the pig and the carcasses for the coyotes. It was already getting light in the east by the time I washed up and went up to bed." He stretched his eyes wide open. "Not that that little bitty sleep helped a whole lot."

"What if there are some dogs that didn't come along?" Inga asked.

"One of the females was nursing pups," Manny said around a huge yawn. "But far as we know, we got them all."

"What about the puppies?" Inga asked.

"Depends on how big they are," Ingeborg said, "but most likely they'll starve to death. Or the coyotes will get them."

Inga and Emmy stared at each other, eyes and mouths wide. Clara looked alarmed too.

"And don't you go getting any ideas of finding 'em either," Manny said, wagging his finger at them. "We'd just have to shoot them too. They're wild." He shoved the last of his biscuit in his mouth. "I'll build more crates later today,

Freda. Lars said we're about done over there. You girls wanna go ride Joker? He needs some attention, like a good curry to get the last of his winter coat off. He needs to be ridden, you know. He's getting fat and lazy out in that pasture."

The girls grinned at each other. "That means we can both ride." They looked to Ingeborg. "Grandma, you used to ride. You could ride too."

Ingeborg stared at the girls. All of a sudden she thought riding sounded like the best idea in the world. How she used to ride the plains, hunting for herbs and other wild plants she could use for medicines.

"Please, Grandma, please come." Emmy moved to one side of her and Inga to the other. "We've never gone on a real ride."

Why not? She could saddle Jack the mule. He was retired from heavy farmwork a few years ago, and he'd been ridden since then, just not often. He'd always been a gentle animal, unless something attacked the sheep, and then he went into fiery attack mode. He was better than a guard dog for some things. Funny, but she'd not remembered those things for years. *Lord, you have given me so many memories of both good and bad things. I don't mind forgetting the bad, but I do so want to remember the good.* Was it wise to even consider saddling Jack? He and Joker would both come up to the fence for grain or other treats. The girls snuck them cookies, thinking she didn't know it.

"All right. This is the situation. We have chores that need to be done first." She emphasized the *first*. "While you are doing your chores, I am going to get the bread dough going, and Clara can knead it when it is time."

"Bake it too" Clara signed.

"I don't plan on being gone all day, you know."

"So what do we have to do?" Ever-practical Emmy started gathering up the breakfast things.

"Wash the dishes, sweep the porch, make sure all the beds are made, fill the woodbox and . . . oh yes, did you already feed the chickens?" They both nodded. "Then let's get moving."

"I will wash the lamps" Clara signed, "after the dishes are done."

"Takk. We need to be thinking about Sunday dinner too. Ellie said she wanted to have it at her house for a change. So tomorrow we'd better bake pies."

Later, Ingeborg was kneading bread dough when Patches announced that someone was coming. He had a special bark for family, and this wasn't it.

"Yoohoo, anyone home?"

Ingeborg headed for the door with a welcoming smile. "Sophie, what are you doing clear out here?"

"I'm on my way to see Mor. Do you want to come with and we can have coffee together?"

Ingeborg could feel two pairs of eyes drilling into her back. She heaved a sigh. "I would love to, but I promised the girls we would go riding."

"As on horseback?"

"They'll ride Joker and I'll saddle up Jack the mule."

"Well, my lands, but that sounds like fun."

"You can come sit a minute or so while I finish kneading the bread dough, can't you?"

"Tell you what. You go riding; I'll go visit with Mor and stop here on my way back to town. As warm as it is getting, I should have brought the buggy."

"I can hitch Jack up to the buggy when we get back."

"We shall see."

Inga joined them. "Garth and the others could come out and play with the calves in the barn. We're supposed to sweep the haymow before haying starts."

"Yes, they could," Sophie said, "but not until later this week. Garth went with Benny out to the Baard farm to stay a couple of days. See you later." With a wave, Sophie walked back to the gate and waved again.

Ingeborg watched her go, mulling over this surprise. Sophie out walking to her mor's instead of taking the buggy. She always said she was too busy for coffee during the day. Something was up, but what?

CHAPTER 6

W e'll get the horses ready," Inga yelled back as she and Emmy leaped off the porch and headed for the barn.

"They can lift the saddles that high?" Freda asked.

"Good point." Ingeborg set the bread dough in the sunshine to rise. She put a few cookies in a tin for the ride and another cookie in her pocket. "Where's Clara?"

"Out on the porch, nursing himself."

Ingeborg chuckled. "He is getting rather demanding, isn't he?" At nine months old, Martin was a wonderfully happy baby, except when he got hungry. And he went from being sound asleep to starving in about three wiggles and a whimper. "What are we having for supper?" she asked as she clapped the lid onto the cookie jar.

"You know that crabby hen that thinks she should set all the time without laying her own eggs?"

"Ja, she pecked Inga a good one the other day."

"Let's just say she won't be pecking anyone else."

Ingeborg smiled. "When did you have time to butcher her?"

"I woke up early, so I got that out of the way first thing. She's cooling out in the well house. That batch of chicks looks about old enough to let loose with the rest of the flock, and the barred Rock is acting broody."

"Let her set. We need some fryers."

"Have you heard anything from Anji?" Freda asked as she helped herself to a cookie.

"Other than the card that said they got to Michigan, no." Ingeborg glanced out the front window to see how the girls were doing with the horses. "I'd best go help them saddle up."

"You might take the rifle along."

"Really? Why? They got the dogs."

Freda shrugged. "Just a hunch. You know, better safe than sorry."

"You know something we've not had for a long time?"

Freda almost smiled. "Rabbit. I'll ask Manny to go set some snares. Right around the garden would be a good idea."

With the cookies and a jug of water in a

cloth bag, along with a small basket for berries if they found any ripe ones, Ingeborg clapped a straw hat onto her head and strolled down to the corral fence. "'Bout ready to saddle up?"

"Almost." Inga tossed her brush and curry comb in the bucket. "Talk about dirty."

"They look good now." Ingeborg took the cookie from her pocket and broke it in half for each of the animals. Jack nodded as he munched, big ears flopping, then nosed her pocket for more. She set her supplies down on the ground and slid through the barred gate to lift the saddles in place and let the girls tighten the cinches. "Watch out for Jack, he likes to suck in a belly full."

She pulled the fence bars back and the girls walked the horses through.

"Britches would make this easier," Inga muttered as she fought to get her foot high enough for the stirrup. Ingeborg gave her a boost, and when she was settled on Joker, did the same for Emmy.

She handed up the bag and the basket and mounted Jack, letting out an *oof* as she settled into the saddle. Maybe a mounting block should be on the list of things needing doing. "Good thing you stood still, old boy," she said, patting his neck. "I thought we'd head west and then angle up to the Little Salt. There used to be plenty of strawberries out that way. We can see if any of them are ripe yet."

Inga nudged Joker into a walk, then looked over her shoulder. "Aren't you coming?"

"Just a minute, I'm going to get the rifle."

"Why?"

"Freda suggested it, and her hunches are often right." She rode to the house, and Freda met her at the gate with scabbard and rifle—and a decidedly un-Freda-like grin.

They followed the trails caused by moving machinery from place to place to the end of the Bjorklund land, edged on both sides by fields of waving wheat. To the north, cottonwood trees lined the Little Salt River as they did the Red, along with oak and brushy thickets. Ingeborg pointed to the west, where the river bent to the south.

"Over there in that dip. You can hardly see it from here, but there used to be wild strawberries, which are far sweeter than ours in the garden."

"I don't see how they can be sweeter." Inga shook her head. "The ones in Thelma's garden are blooming, even."

"Ours too. But what if these are already ripe?"

They topped the bit of a rise and stared down into the miniature valley, lined with tiny white blossoms in the midst of deep green leaves. The growing grass shaded the plants. Ingeborg dismounted and led Jack over to a low branch, where she tied him. The girls did the same, and the three of them stepped carefully among the low-growing plants.

"They're so tiny."

Ingeborg knelt down and moved the leaves, searching for ripe berries. "Here's one." She picked it and held it out on her palm so they could see. "If there is one, there have to be more. As soon as we find two more, we can eat them together."

Emmy found the next two and handed one to Inga.

"On three." They counted to three together and popped them into their mouths at the same instant. Ingeborg closed her eyes, the better to savor the flavor. "I don't think there are enough ripe ones to take back, so I suggest we just pick what we find and eat them."

And so they did. When the sun got hotter, they left the berry search and went to join the horses in the shade. Sharing drinks of water and cookies, they looked out over the prairie, now dotted by houses and barns, trees and windmills.

"Whose land is this?" Emmy asked.

"I'm not sure any longer." Ingeborg lay back, propping herself on her elbows. "Look up. What do you see?"

"Clouds," Emmy, ever practical, answered.

"But don't you see the dog's head over there?" Ingeborg pointed to the west.

Inga squinted. "It makes me think of those puppies."

Uh-oh, Ingeborg thought. "You already have a dog. Scooter wouldn't like any wild puppies coming to his yard."

"Scooter is getting old and fat. And grumpy. Roald was pulling his ears and he snapped at him."

"Did he bite?"

"Nope, but Roald cried anyway. Thelma picked him up and kissed his fingers." She was quiet for a moment. "I sure miss Ma. And Pa is never home, so I'm glad I can come to your house, Grandma. Our house has sad eyes."

"Grandma, look," Emmy whispered, staring off to the west.

Ingeborg caught her breath. A deer came up from drinking at the river, the antlers on his head announcing his sex. A doe followed him, along with a small deer.

Emmy whispered, "A fawn."

"How come they don't know we're here?"

"The wind is from the west, so we are downwind of them. See him sniffing the air?" Ingeborg stared at the rifle in the scabbard. They could use the meat. The buck looked to be in good shape, not skinny from lack of forage in the winter. If she waited any longer, it might be out of range. She laid her finger on her lips and eased over toward Jack. Carefully she stood and slid the rifle free. Taking the safety off, she stayed in the dappling shade of the trees, looking for a good shot.

The buck froze, and the fawn disappeared. Ingeborg zeroed in with the sights and squeezed the trigger. The buck dropped to the ground and the doe disappeared into the thicket. Inga groaned.

Emmy seemed happy. "Good shot, Grandma. Maybe we can dry some of the meat. Do you think I could have the hide?"

"Of course, if you want. You two stay here with the horses and I'll go take care of him."

She'd done it! Dropped him with one shot. Rifle in hand, she pulled the knife out of the pocket on the scabbard and walked carefully toward the deer. She nudged him with her shoe, but when he didn't move, she bent over and slit his throat to bleed him out.

"Emmy, Inga, would you two ride home and find Andrew, ask him to come help me dress this carcass out?"

"Can't I stay with you?" Inga asked.

"No, not this time. You tell him to bring a wagon."

"We could dress it," Emmy said.

"I know we could, but this will be faster."

She watched as the girls climbed aboard Joker and loped off toward home. Jack opened his mouth and nearly split her eardrums with his honking bray.

"I know, you'd much rather go home with them."

Wishing she had sharpened the knife, she went ahead and gutted the beast, laying the heart and liver on the bag that had carried their cookies. Her stomach rumbled. Cookies and strawberries didn't do a lot to fill one up. The sun was flaming toward the horizon when Jack brayed again, this time welcoming the coming team.

She could see two men up on the wagon seat and the girls in the bed behind.

"Land sakes, Mor. Let you go looking for strawberries and you bag a deer." Andrew halted the team, and he and Manny climbed down. Andrew stared down at the bled and gutted deer. "He's a big one."

"One shot. Grandma only fired one shot." Inga grabbed one of the antlers and grinned at Ingeborg. "See, Onkel Andrew, I told you so."

"That you did." Andrew looked around. "What did you do with the guts?"

"Threw them over the bank for the scavengers. I think he bled out pretty well, even if I couldn't hang him." Ingeborg looked over at Manny, who was shaking his head. "What?"

"Are we gonna have fried liver for supper?"

"Freda was going to stew that chicken."

"She didn't know we'd have liver."

"Get that pole from the wagon, Manny,"

Andrew said. "We'll tie his feet round that and hoist him up in the wagon."

Ingeborg chose to ride Jack on home, loath to leave the joys of the day behind. Riding, time with the girls, eating strawberries, and bringing home fresh meat. What a day! They'd share some of the meat, smoke the haunches, and let Emmy tan the hide. What a thank-you-Lord day.

While Manny and Andrew hung the carcass in the barn to skin it out, Ingeborg helped the girls unsaddle and left them brushing the horses down while she took the liver and heart up to the kitchen. "I brought something different for supper."

"You really did shoot a deer?" Freda glanced at her with slightly raised eyebrows.

"Yes, and thank you for reminding me to take the rifle. I have a feeling you meant it more for protection, but when that buck strutted out from the river, I couldn't resist trying."

"You haven't lost your shooting skills."

"He wasn't that far away, but we were downwind and shaded by branches. Even the horses were quiet until Jack announced his displeasure at being left behind. I'm surprised you didn't hear him." While they talked, Ingeborg rinsed the liver and heart in cold salt water. "We can have the liver tonight and stuff and bake the heart tomorrow."

"Oh, I almost forgot. Jonathan rang and wants you to call him back."

"He didn't say what he wanted?"

"No, but it sounded like something was wrong."

Ingeborg frowned. "Where's Clara and the baby?"

"Out in the garden. She hung the sling in the shade so she could use the hoe while Martin naps."

"Between her and the girls, we'll have the best tilled garden anywhere."

Ingeborg went to the oak box on the wall and asked the operator for the Gould residence. Jonathan had set up an office in his and Grace's house so he could spearhead building the addition to the deaf school. All the plans were drawn, but he was hoping his father could come and be there for the ground-breaking ceremony.

When he answered, Ingeborg apologized for not calling sooner.

"Is it all right if I come over to talk with you?" he asked.

"Of course. Any time."

"I'll be right there."

Ingeborg stared at the telephone for a bit after setting the earpiece back in the prongs. Something was wrong, she could tell by his voice. "We'll be out on the porch," she told Freda.

She poured two glasses of raspberry swizzle, made from canned raspberries from last summer, and set a plate of the sour cream cookies on the tray. She'd just set the tray on the low table on the porch when Patches announced that company had arrived. She watched the tall young man bend over and ruffle the dog's ears, then stand again as if carrying a heavy load.

"Welcome, Jonathan. What's wrong?" She handed him a glass and pointed to the chair next to her rocker.

"You are too perceptive." He closed his eyes for a moment, then released a breath that spoke of heaviness. Iced glass between his hands, he looked at her. "My mother died last night."

"What? I mean, oh Jonathan, I am so sorry." She reached for his hand. *Oh, my dear friend David, to lose another wife. And so surprising as this.*

"I think I am in a state of shock. According to my father she wasn't sick and it wasn't an accident. She died in her sleep. Father said he went in to see why she was still in bed and she was lying there, peaceful as could be. I'll catch the morning train; they'll hold the funeral until I can get there."

"How is your father?"

"He sounded businesslike, but the catches in his voice told me he was trying to keep things together and to deal with all the things that need to be done. I know he would prefer that only family and close friends attend the funeral, but she . . . she did a lot of philanthropic things for the city and was active in society. I am sure it will be a big affair." He rolled his eyes. "That's one reason I live here, to be away from all those expectations. I'm like my father in that way."

"Except you left that life entirely."

"Except when we needed money for the school. Mother worked to get donations for us." He leaned back in his chair. "She was very good at raising money for good causes. As long as she didn't have to get her hands dirty." He swallowed. "Sorry, that was uncalled for."

Ingeborg could hear behind his words. His mother had not been as gracious as she could have been to Grace, especially before their wedding, but afterward too. While she did come to Blessing for the wedding, she left immediately afterward, and then threw a huge reception for them in New York. Grace and Jonathan had suffered through it with all the grace and patience they could muster. Grace had told her about it after they returned home. They made biannual visits out east to visit the Goulds, but Grace was always so relieved to return to Blessing.

Jonathan shook his head slowly. "I really don't want to go."

"I can tell. But you and Grace will go and do all the proper things to honor her memory, and then you can come home again."

"Mother wanted grandchildren, and here she died before we could tell her our news."

"Grace is with child."

"You say that like you know. Did Astrid tell you?"

"No, Freda did. After the last Sunday dinner here. She and Thelma both have this sense that recognizes the signs often before the woman herself knows for sure. I don't have that sense so acutely, but I trust them when they say so."

"And here we were waiting until Sunday dinner again. And now we won't be here for it. Grace is sad to miss the girl party too. She's been looking forward to the get-together."

"I love that they still call it a *girl party*. It's so many years since they were young girls. They're the daughters of Blessing in my mind." They sat in silence for a while.

"How come your house always feels so peaceful?"

"I imagine because the Lord of peace lives here. And He fills our house and hearts with His love."

"I imagine so." He took her hand in his. "Thank you for helping me think straight."

"You've forgiven her then?"

"A long time ago, between you and John Solberg, I learned I had to. But this brought up a lot of feelings again. I was pretty angry with her for a long time. But now I'm sad that she won't get her wish to see this baby and for my father. I know he loved her, and they had a good marriage. I guess. I'm hoping he will come out here and spend some time. He has trained my brother to take over all his business affairs, and besides, with telephones and telegraphs, it's easy to stay in contact. So many modern inventions." He drained his glass and stood up. "Again, thank you."

"Go in peace, Jonathan. Home will be waiting for your return."

"I have a lot to do here."

"You do. You have a foot in both worlds. Farming and construction and then who knows?" She wrapped her arms around him. "Tell Grace we will all be praying for you both."

"Her mother said the same thing earlier today. She says becoming a grandmother is such good news." He hugged her back and headed for home, walking straighter, as if he'd left the load behind.

"Thank you, Lord," she whispered. That was rather a shock. *But you ordain the times. Help me not to take the days you have given me for granted.*

She looked out to see Clara pick up her baby. More babies coming. Would that her daughter, Astrid, would become one of the new mothers.

CHAPTER 7

W ill you come with us to see them off?"
Kaaren asked on the phone the next
morning.

"Of course I will."

Ingeborg was ready and waiting when the
buggy stopped at the gate. Jonathan helped her
up and then climbed up with Lars, who was
driving.

"Are you as all right as you can be?" Ingeborg signed to Grace.

"We will get through this. You and Mor
have taught us well."

"And Jonathan?"

"I think he always hoped things could be
made right with her, for my sake. But I did the
best I could. I manage to carry on conversations with those who can hear . . ."

"You do very well." Kaaren signed also. Grace made herself speak to keep in practice, but signing was much more comfortable for her, and when she was in an emotional situation like a funeral, her speech was a bit more difficult to understand.

Lars stopped the buggy right beside the platform between the station and the tracks. A water tower with a long swinging arm filled the boilers with water going both east and west. They could hear the train whistle coming from the west.

"I already have our tickets," Jonathan said after he assisted Grace down from the buggy.

"And here is a basket of cheese, bread, and cookies to tide you over, in case you don't feel like going to the dining car."

"Takk, Tante Ingeborg," Grace said when she kissed Ingeborg. "I know you both will be praying for us."

"I'm sorry you will have to miss the girl party."

"Me too. We'll just have to have another one when I get back home. And yes, I will visit the deaf schools there, and no, I will not agree to teach either students or teachers. If they want to know how we do things here, they'll just have to come see."

As the train screeched to a stop and the steam billowed out around the wheels, Lars and Kaaren hugged the young couple. "Now you take care of yourself," Kaaren admonished her daughter. "Some things might not set too well, you know."

Grace smiled her gracious smile and hugged Ingeborg. "Take care of Mor, will you please? Get her away from the house and school. Ilse can manage just fine."

Ingeborg nodded. "I will try, but you know your mor."

The three of them waved after Jonathan and Grace climbed onto the train and found a window on the car to wave to them. When the train picked up speed beyond the edge of town, they turned away.

"I think a soda would be a good thing right about now," Ingeborg said, "and then I have some things to pick up at Penny's. So I will walk home later."

"So do I. So Lars, do you need to get right home or . . ."

"I heard the word *soda*. After that I can go talk with Thorliff while I wait for you both."

They ordered their sodas and took them outside of the Blessing Soda Shoppe to drink in the shade of the oak tree Penny had planted years before. Rebecca had moved a couple of the tables along with chairs out for the summer.

"Ah, what a treat," Kaaren said with a smile after the first sip. She looked to Lars. "How come we don't do this more often?"

"Tell me how often I come to town."

"You'd think we lived five miles away instead of less than one."

Ingeborg swirled her glass. "Strange, isn't it? You know, the young chicks are having a girl party; I think we need an old hen party— other than Sunday dinners when everything is just too crazy for much real visiting. Let's see, you and me and Amelia, Mary Martha, and Penny."

"What about Mrs. Odell and Mrs. Magron? They've been around forever too."

"Of course. I hate to leave out the newer ladies but . . ." Ingeborg shook her head. "And you know how quickly everyone hears the news. No matter what we do, there are bound to be hard feelings. I know, let's just tell everyone we're having a lunch for all the ladies at my house, and whoever comes, comes. Young ones, older ones . . . Everyone can bring whatever they want to share for the meal."

"Fine with me. When?"

"A week from Tuesday. Noon. There's no canning to do yet, and no haying. We can set up the tables outside or even along the porch. I just ask that . . . no, they just come."

"Maybe this would be a good time to start brainstorming about how to raise funds for the addition to the primary school," Kaaren said.

"And for building a new high school," Ingeborg added.

"Good. We'll have some fun just being

together, but we'll come up with some good ideas too. We can start by telling Penny. She'll spread the word."

Lars finished his soda and stood. "I'll leave the horse and buggy here. You two come find me when you are ready to go home."

He headed toward the newspaper office, and the women strolled over to Penny's store, the Blessing Mercantile.

"Well, I'll be blown over by a small breeze, look who is here, and both of you at the same time." Garbed in a new print apron, Penny came around from behind the battle-scarred counter to meet them halfway. "To what do I owe this honor?"

"We saw Jonathan and Grace off on the train, then we stopped for a soda, and here we are. You probably haven't heard yet that Jonathan's mother died suddenly."

"Oh, how awful. So they're going out east for the funeral?"

"Yes. It's a sad situation for so many reasons."

"That it is. I recall that Jonathan's mother had a hard time accepting Grace as her daughter-in-law."

"I can't begin to understand it, but it's true."

Penny nodded. "But I'm happy to see you here in town. Do you have time for some coffee?"

"We just had a soda." Kaaren looked to

Ingeborg, then back to Penny. "Of course we do. Lars and Thorliff have plenty to talk about."

Penny called behind the curtain to her daughter, Linnea, "Come watch the counter for me; we'll be out in back." She wagged a hand at Ingeborg and Kaaren. "You go out and sit down while I bring a tray. Would you rather have something hot or cold?"

"Whatever is easiest. We could leave our lists here for Linnea to fill."

Penny handed the lists to her daughter. "Any questions, come get us."

Out at the table, Ingeborg tipped her head back, feeling the cooling breeze on her neck. "Ah, such a delight." With quick fingers, she unpinned her straw hat and laid it on the table. "There, now that's even better."

Birds gossiped in the branches above them, and the laughter of playing children came from other yards. Hammering and sawing, men working on another house, came from the west.

"Soon we'll hear more construction at the school too." Kaaren shook her head. "And to think Blessing used to be a quiet little town."

"Like all of us, it's growing up," Penny said as she went back into the store for the drinks.

"Or older."

"Whoever would have dreamed all this?" Ingeborg waved her hand to include the whole town. "All we wanted was the free land to farm."

Their shared gaze spoke plenty of their knowledge of the word *free*.

Kaaren asked, "Do you ever think of our families still in Norway?"

"Some, but not as much as I used to. I dreamed about Gunlaug one night. Makes me wonder how she and her family are. You'd think as close as we were, we'd have managed to keep in touch."

Kaaren nodded. "Especially after her far passed away."

"He was cruel to keep our families apart like that. All because he could not forgive the way his brother divided his inheritance. No wonder the Bible talks about the importance of forgiveness so often."

"Looks like you two are in a deep discussion," Penny said as she set a tray on the table. Taking a chair with a sigh, she passed out the glasses of lemonade. "I mixed canned strawberries with the lemon juice. Tell me what you think." They raised their glasses to each other and first sipped, then savored.

"Very good. Better than swizzle even." Kaaren set her glass back down.

Ingeborg picked up a sour cream cookie and passed the plate. "What did you put in different?" she asked after her first bite.

"Lemon juice and grated the peel in too. Whatever did we do without lemons? Mrs. Garrison said that lemons are now out of season, so we better buy what we can. She's getting a big order in on tomorrow's train. They keep a long time, though."

"What if we canned some, including the peeling?"

"Or dried the skins."

"To think we get fruit all the way from Florida."

"And my cheese goes all over the country."

Ingeborg and Kaaren told Penny of their idea for a ladies lunch. "We decided to just announce it and see who comes. So tell everyone you see. Or we could put up a sign."

"And I can bring anything I want?"

Ingeborg could see the wheels turning. Penny had an idea, and like most of her surprises, they would all benefit.

"We'd better be going," Kaaren said after a bit. "Lars is probably anxious to get home. Taking time off in the middle of the week is unheard of."

"He should do so more often."

"Maybe we should all do so more often," Penny said. "Look at us sitting here, and no one is even knitting or piecing. My mor would be horrified. Idle hands . . . you know the rest."

"Tsk, tsk." Kaaren pinned her hat back on her head. "Back into the fray. Come along, lazybones."

Ingeborg and Penny swapped eye rolls. "Takk for the new drink. You might have started a craze." Ingeborg pinned on her hat and the two started for the boardwalk along Main Street.

"You better stop in at Garrisons' and place your order for lemons," Penny called after them.

"Takk." Ingeborg turned to Kaaren. "What if we split a box?"

"How big is a box?"

"I don't know. Let's just do it. While you do that, I'm going to go by the hospital and see if Astrid has a moment. I'll meet you at Thorliff's."

"Fine by me."

Ingeborg waved at Amelia Jeffers out working in her garden and admired the hospital as she strode up to it. The trees were growing well, the two spirea shrubs looked to be blooming soon, and someone had planted rosebushes under the windows. When she pushed open the door, the scent of lilacs greeted her. The big vase on the entry desk held a wealth of drooping lavender lilacs. Her own were almost done blooming, but Mrs. Geddick had planted some on the north side of her house to bloom later than the others. Resolving to do the same, Ingeborg greeted Deborah, who was behind the desk.

"Is Astrid around?"

Deborah pointed to the closed office door. "She's trying to catch up on her paper work. Go on in, she'll be delighted to see you."

Nurse Miriam Knutson waved while helping a patient down in the ward. Ingeborg waved back and tapped on the office door, then opened it enough to put her head in. "Do you have time for a quick visit?"

"Oh, Mor, of course I do. Come in." Astrid pointed to a chair. "Have a seat and I'll order us up some coffee."

Ingeborg sat down, shaking her head. "I just had something over at Penny's. I should have brought you one of her cookies. Sour cream, but she added lemon juice and grated lemon peel. They were so good."

"I'll have to suggest that to Amelia. I haven't had time to bake cookies since who knows when."

"You're looking tired."

"Takk for nothing. We need an administrator to run this hospital so I can do the doctor things." Astrid glared at the stack of papers in front of her. "Deborah takes a lot of the load, but . . ." She straightened her shoulders. "You didn't come to hear me grumble."

"If you need to grumble, who better to listen than your mother?"

"All grumbling does is make me feel lower than a beetle's foot."

Ingeborg raised her eyebrows. "How did you think up that one?"

"All the June bugs that are sacrificing themselves at the doors and windows to get to the light. We've taken to sweeping them up every morning. I wonder if the fish might like them if we threw them in the river."

"I'm sure the chickens would delight in them. If you have them in a bucket or something, I'll take them home and try them." Ingeborg studied her daughter. Astrid needed to get out in the sun; she was as pale as a fashion model out of some old *Godey's Lady's Book*. "Are you sure you're feeling all right?"

"Why do you ask?"

"Are you not sleeping?"

Astrid shook her head. "Funny you should stop by today. I was planning on coming to see you tomorrow before the girl party. I have a good reason for feeling so tired. I have a hard time keeping food down too . . . mostly in the morning." Her twinkling eyes gave her away.

"Well, I've missed two cycles and Thelma told me I am, so I guess that makes it all definite."

The two met in a hug and shared several tears before going back to their chairs.

"Oh, what splendid news. I will be a grandma again." Ingeborg's medical side kicked in. "So you are getting extra rest and eating properly?"

"As much as I can. I do know a bit about the process, you know."

"And get your feet up when you can." Ingeborg clasped her hands under her chin. "Amelia knows?" she asked, referring to Astrid's mother-in-law.

"Of course, and it has been killing her not to tell you. She said if I didn't tell you at dinner on Sunday, she would. She is so excited. This baby will be in our house, and she can love it all she wants."

"Have you told anyone else?" When Astrid shook her head, Ingeborg asked, "Can I tell Kaaren?"

"Yes, you may. I will tell the girls tomorrow night, and by Sunday everyone in town will know."

Ingeborg grinned. Another grandchild! "Will Kenneth Johnson be returning as soon as he finishes his year in Chicago?"

"I'm counting on him. He said he would, otherwise I would advertise for a new doctor to come to Blessing."

"Another resident won't be coming?"

Astrid wagged her head. "I'm hoping Red Hawk will send more nurses for training. He is in desperate need on the reservation. I suggested that Chicago send someone down there for a resident year. Mor, they need so much. Do you think our church could send some help again?"

"I will talk with Lars about it. It's always better if it comes from one of the men, like Haakan led the drive before. You find out what they need the most."

"I mentioned a trip down there, and Daniel about banged his head on the ceiling."

"I'm sure." Ingeborg couldn't quit grinning. "I need to go. Lars is talking with Thorliff and then we'll head on home."

"See if you can get Thorliff talking. I am having a hard time keeping my mouth shut."

"More than his driving himself so hard?"

A tap at the door. "Dr. Astrid, your next appointment is here."

"Thanks, Miriam. Examining room one." Astrid stood and smiled at her mother again. "Your timing was perfect. Thank you for showing up right when I was thinking about you."

"God did it; I wasn't planning on coming." Ingeborg stood too and hugged her daughter one more time. "See you Sunday. Dinner is at Andrew and Ellie's."

As Ingeborg headed to the newspaper office, she pondered and prayed, *Lord, is it time for me to have a real heart-to-heart with my son?*

CHAPTER 8

I think I'll stay home," Deborah whispered to Mary Martha.

"Why? Are you sick?" Mary Martha automatically felt Deborah's forehead.

"No."

"Do you want to tell me why?"

"Um, well, I told Sophie I'm about to give up on Toby and she said they'd fix a plan." Her words came out in a rush, and she was grateful no one else was around to hear.

"You've loved Toby for a long time."

"How did you know?" Deborah searched her mind to remember if she had ever mentioned her feelings.

"Ah, dear Deborah, I've been your mother for all these years, and you think I haven't paid attention?"

"But . . . but I never said anything."

"No, you didn't, but your eyes and face told me." Mary Martha reached for Deborah and hugged her close. "You've never even gone walking with anyone else. And when he pays attention to you, well, let's say you glow."

"Do you think other people notice?"

"John has. That's a father's job, you know."

"How embarrassing."

"You needn't be embarrassed. We've been praying for the right man for you for years. Like we do for all of our children, and I hope you will do the same when you have a family."

"At the rate I'm going, that might be never."

"You go to the party and just have a good time. You girls haven't done this for so long." She tipped Deborah's face up with a finger under her chin. "Is there anything else?"

"Sometimes it's hard not to be jealous of the others. I'm the only one not married."

"True, but remember, God's timing is perfect. And maybe Toby is not the man He has in mind for you."

"I think I'll just leave Blessing and go for more training so I can become the hospital administrator that we need so much. Astrid needs help and—"

"And you will take one day at a time, and we will all pray that God makes your path clear. Now, do you have your crackers and biscuit rolls?"

"I do and I *will* have a good time." Deborah reached for her basket, paused, gave Mary Martha another hug and a thank-you, took up her basket again, and marched out the door.

As she started up the steps to Sophie's front porch, she could hear laughter through the screen door.

"Come on in, you don't need to knock," Sophie called from the parlor. She took Deborah's basket and set it on the dining room table with the other offerings.

Deborah smiled at Rebecca and Astrid, who were already sipping from their glasses. "Where's Ellie?"

"She should be here any minute. And of course Grace is nearly to New York City. I know she'd rather be here." Sophie handed Deborah a glass with ice and some kind of drink.

"Did you invite Miriam?"

"We did, but she is on duty so that the rest of us can be here."

"I told her to come anyway. We're not far if there is an emergency, but she's just like you." Astrid propped her feet up on a hassock.

"I'm here," Ellie called from the front porch.

"Come in, come in. I'll get your drink."

Ellie set her basket on the table with the others and sank into a chair. "I didn't think I would ever be able to get away. Andrew has a sow farrowing, so he is back and forth to the barn, and Carl did not want to go to bed yet because it isn't dark."

"All right, now everyone has something to drink. We'll put out the goodies after a bit, but first let's just get caught up." As always, Sophie took over running their girl parties, but since she did a fine job, no one objected. "Astrid, what's happening at the hospital?"

"We have a new doctor coming in August, but right now that seems mighty far away. Two more student nurses too—in August. I could manage better if we had an administrator for the business end. Deborah does as much as she can, but we need more help, that's all. Just pray no major crisis happens this summer."

"I thought last year's intern was going to come back," Ellie said.

"He is."

"Don't tell me. In August?"

"Yes, he wants to join our staff, and I'll be so happy to have him here. He's another one of those who thought they were being sent to the outer regions and fell in love with our town."

"Like Miriam and Vera?"

"Right, and as Dr. Deming gets better known, his dental practice is expanding too." Astrid paused. "Red Hawk needs help too, far more than we do."

"But what can we do there?" Rebecca asked.

"Send a railcar full of supplies, like we did

before. Mor said she'd get the quilting ladies to working on it."

"Another one of the times when we miss Haakan."

Astrid blinked. "I know. Some days all I want is to hear his voice again." She sniffed and blinked again.

"Ingeborg has accepted his passing better than about any of us." Sophie dabbed at her eyes. "Let's talk about something else or we'll all be in tears."

"I have one other thing." They all looked to Astrid. "Daniel and I figured we'd better tell our friends before they find out another way." She paused and grinned at all of them. "We will be having a baby in late December or January, if I have counted right."

Squeals and laughter, even clapping hands, greeted her announcement.

"Really? For sure?" Ellie asked.

"I've missed two cycles, and I'm not at my best in the morning, which is the polite way of putting it. I have all the symptoms. I don't know how Amelia kept from telling Mor and Thelma either. She was the first to ask me about it, before I even realized it. And I'm a doctor, for pity's sake."

"She has a sixth sense, is what Ma says," Deborah added. "No wonder those two haven't been out socializing much. Of course Thelma wouldn't say anything. She can keep a secret better than a sphinx." She refused to start to feel sorry for herself. This was wonderful news for Astrid. But how would she work so hard and stay healthy?

Sophie looked around. "Who else has news?"

"It's hard to top that," Rebecca said.

"Right now, I'm glad I am not pregnant." Sophie flipped open the fan she kept handy. "Maybe we should go outside, where it might be cooler. Anyone want more to drink?"

"I want some of those crackers Deborah brought," Astrid said.

"All right. We'll lay the food out, refill our drinks, and stay in here. I'll just open all the windows."

When they settled back with small plates of refreshments, Sophie looked to Deborah. "Are you going to tell, or do you want me to?"

Deborah heaved a sigh. "I need help. Sophie suggested we get together and hatch a plan."

"A plan to what?"

Sophie broke in. "To make Toby Valders realize he loves Deborah and it is time to make up his mind. No more running hot and cold."

Deborah stared at her hands. "I don't want to be an old maid, but I'm sure getting there fast."

"So, my dear friends, what shall we do?" Sophie looked to each woman.

"First," Astrid said, "do you love Toby Valders?"

Sophie snickered. "She's been in love with him since the sixth grade."

"No, we were just good friends for all those years, but one day I caught myself saying 'Mrs. Toby Valders.' And when he was off building windmills, I missed him a whole lot."

"He was seeing someone at some point, wasn't he?" Ellie asked.

"Yes, but it didn't work out, apparently."

Sophie bobbed her head. "I think he's afraid to commit to marriage. I mean, he loves Benny and all his little nieces and nephews. He's great with kids, and they all think he can walk on water."

"You mean he can't?" Deborah asked, raising her eyebrows innocently.

"Good grief."

When they all quit laughing, Astrid said, "I think we should sic our husbands on him."

"Well, Pa tried that, in a way." Deborah told them about Toby asking her to help with invitations and saying he kind of liked her. "But then most of the time he ignores me. But Pa put him up to that, and it didn't go well."

"Men are useless at that," Sophie sniffed. "But what else can we do? Let's make a list." She picked up a pencil and school tablet and licked the pencil tip.

"Well, start with Gerald," Ellie said.

"Rebecca, you have a talk with him. Maybe he knows or would be willing to ask about—I mean, couldn't he ask him straight out? Do you love Deborah?"

Deborah hid her face in her hands. "I'd be mortified."

Ellie grimaced. "Well, you might find out more than you know now."

"Another good ploy is to use jealousy," Rebecca added. "It's a shame there isn't some other man in town who might show some interest in you that would make Toby wake up. I mean . . . the staff coming in from Chicago, for instance."

Deborah watched Sophie write *Jealousy* on her pad. "It won't work. When the new nurses and intern come, I'm going to register for school in Grand Forks."

Astrid snorted. "If you go anywhere, you're going to Chicago. No one knows more what we need than they do. Mrs. Korsheski would love to give you training in administration. I just can't bear to have you gone. I depend on you."

"Let's talk about something else, okay?" Deborah pleaded.

"But we don't have a plan yet," Sophie reminded her.

Rebecca raised a finger. "We need to have a barn dance before haying season starts. We need to raise money for the new schoolhouse, so we can have a box social. Get him to buy your box."

Suddenly all the voices came in a rush; Deborah couldn't keep up, and Sophie was jotting things down wildly.

Do silly things where he can see you.
Do favors for him without being asked.
Act like you're not interested; let him come to you.

Rebecca added, "And if he doesn't come around or ignores you, why, just quit mooning and wishing, and instead do something nice for him."

Sophie added that and held her list at arm's length. "Good. That will get us started. Thank you. What other problems should we solve?"

"We need a teacher more than a new schoolhouse."

"We need both. I don't know if Thorliff is going to continue teaching, but now that Anji and Thomas moved away, we need two more teachers."

"Jonathan could teach music and probably other classes too."

"He's got his hands full with farming and the deaf school."

"Devlin." Ellie sighed. "We are really going to miss that man come fall."

"My children miss them all so much,

especially Benny. He lost his best friend, Gilbert. But they are having a good time out at the farm."

Deborah nodded. "Pa doesn't say much, but I know he misses Devlin too."

"Just think, Anji would be here tonight had they not moved." Sophie waved her hands. "All right, no sad thoughts. We need to find out if an ad for a new teacher has gone out. And we need to come up with some more fundraisers to build the school. Any more suggestions for this list to solve Deborah's problem?"

Ellie asked, "Is there a plan in place to do a fundraiser like we did before, where people agree to donate a certain amount?"

Sophie shook her head. "We'll have to ask the men about that. I know they have a lot on their minds, what with planning to start construction on the deaf school addition."

"That is a big project." Astrid leaned her head back. "Oh, how easy it would be to drift off for a bit of a nap."

"Surely we have enough men in town to build more than one building at a time," Rebecca said.

"But are they convinced that a new school is necessary? I'm sure Thorliff is, since he was teaching there, but . . ." Sophie glanced from Astrid, who looked perfectly relaxed, her eyes closed and her head slightly leaning to one side, to Deborah, who rolled her lips to keep from smiling. Someone else chuckled.

As one, they all stood, tiptoed over to the table and out to the back porch, Sophie making sure the door didn't slam.

Giggles drifted on the evening breeze, a rooster bade the sun good-night, and birds twittered their final messages of the day.

"This is my favorite time of the day." Deborah leaned back with a sigh of contentment.

"I'm like Ingeborg, dawn is my favorite."

"Any time of day is Ingeborg's favorite. Someday I want to be like her. And my mor." Sophie sipped from her glass. "Deborah, these crackers are the best."

"The cheese roll-ups need to show up at every event." Ellie reached for another of each. "Rebecca, now that summer is here, is your business picking up?"

"Especially when the train arrives, I have people standing in line. Even though Benny's only ten, he's the biggest help, when he's there. I scoop the ice cream, hand it to him to put in the syrup, and ring it up. He sits on a high stool and does great. Lissa was hoping to work for me this summer, until she found out they were moving. Linnea is busy helping Penny at the store."

Deborah asked, "What about Emily? She's young but so capable. And Goodie loves to help.

We made the crackers together. Well, all of us did. They take a lot of rolling and cutting."

"Wouldn't it be nice if we had a bakery in town?" Sophie said. "Baking has never been my favorite part of cooking."

"You have Mrs. Sam at the boardinghouse and Helga helps you out at home. When do you cook anyway?"

Sophie shrugged. "Well, I think about it at times. Speaking of Mrs. Sam, if you think about it, pray for her. Her heart is not good, and even though we have more help now, she likes to do things herself and not just supervise."

"She and Mr. Sam are getting up there in years, aren't they?" Ellie asked.

"They must be. I'll ask Mor or Tante Ingeborg. They'd have a better idea than anyone."

Ellie caught back a yawn. "I need to be thinking of getting home. Dawn comes too soon."

"We need to do this more often if for no other reason than it makes us feel good," Sophie said. "The men get together and talk all the time."

"They call it business," Rebecca said. A chuckle skipped from one to the next.

"Strange how half the businesses in town are owned by women and we never get invited to the *business* meetings," Sophie replied. The squeak of the door caught their attention. "Well, sleepyhead, welcome back."

Astrid blinked and stretched. "Sorry. I didn't mean to fall asleep." She leaned against the wall and drank from her glass. "You know, I tell women they will be tired and need extra sleep when they're with child, but I had no idea it was like this."

"As long as you don't fall asleep in surgery." Deborah picked up the dwindling cracker plate. "Everyone says you are hungry all the time too, so here, help yourself."

Astrid laid a hand on her rumbling stomach. And did as she was told.

"That's what you told me with every baby," Ellie scolded. "Get lots of rest and be prepared to be hungry. After all, you are eating for two."

"And if you heard it once, you heard it a hundred times." Sophie paused, her eyebrows arching. "Get your feet up."

"Do you have any honey, Sophie?" Astrid asked.

"Of course, do you want me to get it?"

"Just thought I might not dislike eating my own words as much if they were drenched in honey." Astrid sat down.

Deborah smiled sadly. "Doctor Elizabeth used to say that."

"I know. I find lots of words coming from my mouth that she put into my mind. I need to head home. Ellie, did you walk to town?" At her nod, Astrid continued, "I could ask Daniel to hitch up the buggy and take you home. He said he would."

Ellie smiled. "No, I'll walk with Deborah and cut across the fields."

"You track through the wheat and your name will be double mud," Rebecca said as she gathered the used dishes.

Sophie raised her hand. "Just leave everything. Helga will clean it up in the morning, bless her."

"It was good of her to take your brood home to her house tonight."

Sophie snickered. "I know, I'm spoiled. But at least I'm not pregnant this summer. All babies should be born in the spring, like the animals bear their young in the spring."

Rebecca set her glass on the low table. "I'm thinking that bakery idea is a really good one."

The others paused in their packing up and stared at her.

"I wonder if someone else might like to go in on this with me. We have a ready market with the train customers. I remember someone coming on the train with a tray of sandwiches and baked goods to sell when it stopped. We'd have to winter-proof the Soda Shoppe and probably add to it."

Sophie nodded. "You know, I think the boardinghouse did just that back in the early days. We need to start asking around. See who is known for their baking, besides Ingeborg's bread. I think I remember someone trying to talk her into it years ago. Penny, I think, wanted to sell it in her store. You might talk with her. Perhaps the two of you could—"

"Mrs. Geddick is a marvelous baker, but we sure can't lose her cooking at the hospital." Astrid looked weary despite her catnap. "Deborah, do not even mention such a thing to her. Please." She caught another yawn.

"I know, I'm just trying to think of all the bakers. She used to do all the cooking for the traveling harvest crew for Lars and Haakan."

"Last year her daughter did it—in fact, the last couple of years, since before the hospital opened," Astrid said.

"What if baking was a skill taught at the deaf school?" Sophie asked. "They teach farming, woodworking, and carpentry for the boys."

"And household skills for the girls. Amelia is talking about teaching sewing out there this fall." Astrid nodded. "We need to talk with the other women. We've got some good ideas here. I know Mor says Clara is taking over some of the baking there and really enjoys it."

"Yes, but can she make bread just like Ingeborg's?" Ellie asked.

"I have no idea. But I heard there is going to be a hen party since we had this girl party. Let's face it, you get the women of Blessing started on an idea, and who knows what will happen." Astrid grinned at Deborah. "Including educating a certain young man into the path he belongs on. With Deborah. I think a December wedding would be nice."

Sophie cackled. "Watch out, Toby Valders! The girls of Blessing are on the march."

CHAPTER 9

Nothing so fair as a day in June." Astrid stopped in her walk to the hospital to feel the sun on her face. First the girl party Saturday night, then yesterday had been such a fine day, the ball game played with only their own families. The men coaching Manny to be a catcher, teaching the younger ones to bat, including the girls. Not surprisingly, both Emmy and Inga caught on quickly. Even though Carl was a bit young, he managed to hit the ball that Thorliff pitched nice and slow. Samuel surprised them all by hitting one pitch almost to the river.

Astrid pushed open the door to the hospital. Three roses, the first from Amelia's garden, graced the counter, the buds still tight but already fragrant.

Her nurses were already hard at work,

serving breakfasts and getting their patients up and ready for the day. "I'll be ready for rounds in ten minutes," she said to Deborah.

"We have so few patients. Everyone around Blessing must be healthy."

"Now, that is good news. Maybe we can get caught up on ordering and restocking." The paper work was always an unending burden. "Is Dr. Deming in today?" The dentist's office was in the north wing of the hospital.

"Not so far, but he didn't say he wouldn't be here."

"I'm thinking of asking him to take a trip down to the reservation to help Dr. Red Hawk for a week or however long he wants to stay."

"What a great idea."

Deborah responded to one of the nurses, and Astrid went into her office. While she always tried to leave it neat, the stack of paper work seemed to multiply when she was gone. She flipped through a couple of telephone messages, surprised to find one from Mrs. Korsheski at the Chicago hospital. She'd call after rounds and before office hours. Since Astrid was the only doctor in town now, she no longer saw patients at Thorliff's house. After Elizabeth died, they'd removed all the medical equipment to the hospital, and everyone came directly here.

On rounds she checked on a seven-year-old child with a broken leg and told his mother, "We can take the traction off soon, but I want to keep him here mostly to keep him quiet. If he forgets and tries to run on that leg now, you would end up back here with a lot more problems. Do you understand?"

She nodded. The boy stared at the far wall, sullen.

"Good." Astrid patted the boy's shoulder. "We'll get you healthy again."

No response. Did he understand what she'd said? No matter; his mother did.

On her way back to her office, Astrid swung by the kitchen for a cup of coffee. "Sure smells good in here."

Mrs. Geddick waved a hand toward the table. "The bread just came out of the oven. Do you want a slice?"

"Being as I am always hungry, I won't turn it down."

"Do you feel better today?"

"I do, thank you. Mrs. Geddick, I wonder if your daughter is interested in helping start a bakery business here in Blessing."

"Adelaide wants to be a nurse here."

"Really? I didn't know that. Have her come talk to me." Addy had been an aide for the last few months and sometimes helped her mother in the hospital kitchen.

Mrs. Geddick handed Astrid a plate with the heel of the loaf slathered in butter and strawberry jam. "The last of the jam. It's a good thing the berries will be ripe soon."

"Danke." Astrid bit into the warm bread, and for a change it did not send her stomach into revenge.

"Put more cream in your coffee. It'll be easier on your stomach."

Astrid nodded and, cup and plate in hand, headed for her office. What a gift Mrs. Geddick was to the hospital; she not only cooked and baked but put up jams and pickles and did some canning too. And one of her sons, Elmer, was an orderly.

She'd just settled back in her desk chair when she heard Deborah say, "Examining room one, right here." Astrid was already on her feet when Deborah stuck her head in the door.

"Thelma is here with Roald, a head wound. It's bleeding bad."

Astrid hit the examining room in full stride. "What happened, Thelma?"

"He was running in the house. I keep telling him not to run, but . . . and he tripped and fell and hit his head on the settee. He was screaming, and by the time I got to him, there was blood everywhere."

"Keep the pressure on it," Astrid instructed as she scrubbed her hands in the basin of water by the door. "Did you tell Thorliff?"

"I'm not sure where he is."

"I see." She smiled at her nephew, who lay on the examining table. Thelma looked like she'd been wounded, blood soaking into her apron and dress. "How's my boy?"

"Owie." He started to put his hand up to his head.

"I see. Bad owie. Let Tante Astrid look at it and make it better. Now this might hurt, so you must be a big boy."

When she started to peel back the blood-soaked towel, he screamed and tried to roll away. "No! Owie!"

"Deborah, we need some help. Send Elmer for Thorliff."

"Roald," Thelma soothed, "Rolly, listen to me. Shhhh."

He reached for Thelma. "Ma. Ma."

Thelma leaned over him. "I am here." She looked to Astrid with apology. "He started that. I tell him no, but . . ."

"Don't worry about that right now. See if you can hold him still enough for me to look at the wound."

In his writhing, the blood flow had kicked back up. She palpated the area through the towel. It was already swelling, but the bone seemed firm. His pupils reacted equally to light, so he probably didn't have a concussion.

"We'll need to clean it and stitch it up. Probably shave the area first."

"Do you want to sedate him?"

"I need to ask Thorliff first."

Thelma murmured to Roald, and he quieted down.

"How did he manage to hit the back of his head? It seems more like he was pushed."

The older woman shook her head. "Unless Scooter knocked him over or something. I don't know. They were running up and down the hall."

"I'm going to try to remove the dish towel. See if you can hold him still."

But Roald arched his back and screamed again and again.

"How can one little guy be so strong?" Astrid took a wet cloth and stroked the blood off his face. "See now, that didn't hurt, did it, Rolly? You can let me look at the owie and make it all better, so you can go home to play."

He turned his face from her, hiding in Thelma's bosom. "No."

Astrid heard Thorliff ask, "Where is he?" He pushed open the door to the examining room. His face turned white when he took in the blood and his son whimpering against Thelma's chest. "What happened? How bad is it? What do you want me to do?" He threw the questions like darts at a board.

"He fell when he was playing," Astrid told him. "I don't know how bad for sure, but the skull palpates solid, so it is a flesh wound. Head wounds bleed a great deal. I need you to help hold him down. He is mighty strong and not cooperating. I need to clean the site, shave it, and stitch it closed. We might have to sedate him. I wanted you to know all this before we start the treatment."

Thorliff stopped by Thelma's side. "Here, let me hold him."

He started to take his son, but Roald shrieked, "No, Pa! Want Ma."

"Roald, I will hold you so Tante Astrid can make you better."

Roald arched his back and reached for Thelma, screaming, "Ma!"

Thorliff clamped his jaw.

"Let him be for the moment," Astrid said in a calming voice. "We're going to lay him back down on the table, and Thorliff, if we need to, you lie across him to hold him down. Thelma will hold his head. Or we can sedate him."

Thorliff shook his head. "Let's try this."

"I need you to scrub and put on one of the aprons to cover your clothes so we can keep this clean." She glanced at his shirt speckled with sawdust. "I'm going to give him a bit of laudanum to help him relax, but it won't put him under." She turned to Deborah. "Bring us some juice please. Just a bit."

While waiting for the juice, Astrid handed Thorliff an apron and indicated the basin.

"You need to scrub your arms too." Astrid looked at his hair now that his felt hat was hanging on a peg by the door. "How about just wiping that wet cloth over your head and face? The apron will cover the rest."

Thelma got Roald to drink the juice, and within a couple of minutes, the little boy's eyes drifted closed.

"Here we go. Lay him down, Thelma, and hold his head to the side so I can work on the wound. Thorliff, be ready to lie across him. But first hold his hands with one hand and his feet with the other. We're going to work as fast as we can."

She removed the dish towel and dropped it in the basin on the floor just for that purpose. Using a sterile cloth, she washed the blood out of Roald's hair. Blood welled up out of the wound, so she pressed a sterile pad against it. "Scissors, please, so we can cut the hair away. I'm afraid he might jerk when I am shaving and . . ." She started trimming. Roald convulsed and whimpered again. Thelma started singing to him, a little song she had taught Inga first and now Roald.

Once the hair was clipped, Astrid studied the laceration. "We need some ice in here. I am going to sponge it with cocaine, and that can hurt, but then it will go numb. Be prepared."

Roald arched his back and ripped his arms and feet out of his father's hands. Thorliff muttered something and threw himself over his son's small body, effectively pinning both arms and legs.

Astrid let the blood flow a bit, giving the cocaine time to work. "They developed a new topical that is less toxic, procaine, but I haven't been able to afford it." She picked up her threaded needle. "This shouldn't hurt, but he may think it does." She put in six small, neat stitches, with both she and Thelma crooning to the blubbering child. When she had them in place and the bleeding stopped, she covered it with another sterile cloth and rested the ice pack against it.

"All right, we can relax for a bit now. I just have to bandage him, and that won't hurt." She patted his little chest. "Good boy, Rolly. I'm going to give you a big bandage all around your head."

"No!" He reached for Thelma again, never even looking at his pa.

Astrid looked at Thorliff, however, to read anger in his eyes, even though he schooled his face to a bland expression. *So who is he angry at? His son? Thelma? Me? Or does he realize he brought this upon himself?* She doubted the latter.

With Roald sitting up, groggy but easier to bandage, Astrid did exactly that. Once the pad was wrapped in place, she looked at Roald. "Now, you have to leave that in place until I take it off. You hear me?"

He nodded.

She tipped up his chin to check his eyes again. No sign of concussion. "He's probably going to have a headache, so if you can keep him quiet this afternoon, he should be fine. But you'll hear plenty if he bangs it again. Bring him back immediately if he starts to act strangely or doesn't wake up from his nap. He might be mopey from the medication, but he might not be. Bring him back to see me in a week, and we'll decide then when to remove the stitches. Any questions?" She looked to Thorliff first, then Thelma. They both shook their heads.

Thorliff stepped forward to pick up his son, but Roald reached for Thelma. "Ma." He raised his arms to be picked up. When his pa picked him up instead, he started crying again, small fists rubbing his eyes. "Ma, Ma," he called between sobs. Without a word, Thorliff stomped from the room with his son, Thelma following after one last look at Astrid.

Do I talk to him now or later? If he lays into Thelma because this little guy is calling her Ma, *I swear I will take a two-by-four to him.*

How to approach this? The puzzle consumed her all day.

Finally Miriam came in to take over the night's duties. Astrid briefed her on the day's activities—patient needs were so light, it did not take long—and left.

But she did not go home. She did not go to Thorliff's house. She went to his office, and there he was, hunched over his desk, with a pencil and paper in his hands. She entered without knocking.

He snapped his head around to stare at her. "Is Roald . . . ?"

"I presume he's all right; haven't heard. I'll stop by there on my way home."

He grunted and turned back to the figures on the paper. "Good."

"Obviously, you have not been home since he hurt himself."

"I'm very busy."

"So I see." She took a deep breath. "Thorliff, I could tell you were really angry today, but I wasn't sure if it was directed toward Roald or Thelma."

"Look, Astrid, this is none of your business." Thorliff pretended to be working. He wasn't, and that was obvious. He wrote something unintelligible on the paper.

"That's my nephew I treated today, not just your son. Yes, it is my business. I'm sorry you feel that way, but you are my brother, and that makes us family, and our family takes care of each other. But Roald calling Thelma *Ma* was not her fault. I have heard her saying her name to him and making him say *Thelma*, but she is the one raising him. You are never there."

"I never said it was her fault."

"Well, you sure acted that way in the surgery. The looks you gave her could have sizzled her hair."

"No. You're imagining things. I was . . . Look, I'm very busy. Please leave."

"Not until you leave also and go home to your children. They need you."

He turned slowly and his eyes frightened her. They were dark and sunken, and they crackled with anger. He looked like he hadn't slept in a week.

"And sleep," she added. "You haven't been getting enough sleep."

He straightened his arms on his desk and leaned forward. "You are not my supervisor; you are not my conscience or my guide." His voice was rising. "You do not belong here at all. Leave."

Her voice was rising too. "I don't think you realize what you are doing to your children. You are so tied up in your own grief, you can't see that you're neglecting them, and they're grieving too, especially Inga. Thorliff, those two children need their father. They need you right now!"

"You have no idea what you're talking about, so take your advice and go home."

"Oh, I think I do. I have eyes to see with. Roald calls Thelma *Ma*, because that's who he sees all the time. He's too little to remember Elizabeth clearly, but he's big enough to know he needs a mor. Inga needs you too. She knows she lost her mother, and she might just as well not have a father either. It makes her grief all the worse."

"Well, her father has two businesses to run and—"

"And he works until he collapses. How many nights have you spent out here because you fell asleep on your desk?" She knew she'd hit home with that one.

His eyes flared and then narrowed. "Astrid, leave now!"

"Thorliff, being pigheaded isn't going to help!" She was shouting now, and she knew shouting wouldn't work, but she couldn't help it.

He stood up so suddenly she took a quick step back. He extended his arm, pointing at the door, his whole hand trembling. *"Out! Now!"*

"Thorliff, think! You can't—"

"Now!" His teeth were clamped so hard the word hissed between them. The red in his face flamed even more.

Astrid was shaking now herself. She walked to the door and turned to look over her shoulder. Sorrow invited anger in. "Of all the stubborn, asinine—Thorliff Bjorklund, you don't deserve the two precious children you have! Take your eyes off yourself and think of them!"

Glaring venomously at her, he snatched up a paperweight.

Without waiting to see if her brother really would have thrown it at her, she left, slamming the door behind her. She was sobbing, and that never won arguments either. She stood for a moment, sucking in barrels of soft evening air.

It did not cool her rage. How could he abandon his own children like that? She thought again of Rolly turning away from him, screaming.

And Thorliff himself was suddenly acting like a stranger. Never had she seen such fury.

She walked to the end of the block, trying to pull herself together, then started home. She was still trembling a little and so angry she could not think. She stomped up the steps and into her own house.

Daniel was sitting in one of the cushioned chairs on the back porch. He twisted to look at her. His mouth dropped open and he leaped to his feet. "Astrid, what's wrong? Why are you crying?"

"Because as far as I'm concerned, Thorliff is no longer a brother of mine!"

CHAPTER 10

We'll have rounds in about ten minutes," Deborah whispered to Miriam. While the two of them weren't usually on duty at the same time, today Miriam had waited to see what would be needed.

Astrid entered the building and headed down the hall. Deborah followed her into the office and closed the door behind her. "What's wrong?"

Astrid hung her hat on the wall peg and reached for an apron. "You aren't supposed to be so perceptive. I thought I was dealing with this off duty."

"No one else would know."

"No? Both my husband and my mother-in-law saw it immediately too." As Astrid sank into her chair, she rubbed her forehead.

"Headache too. Just tell me so we can pray about it and go out on the floor ready to treat our patients with all your usual calm."

"I attacked Thorliff about his children after I left here yesterday."

"Attacked? That's rather a strong word."

"That's the way he saw it. And he's probably right." Astrid raised her eyes. "You saw it yesterday. He's destroying his son."

Please, Lord, help us and bring Ingeborg or Pastor Solberg here. Deborah blew out the breath she'd been holding without being aware. "I saw that he was terribly hurt yesterday when Rolly turned to Thelma."

"And called her *Ma*. But what does he expect? He's not done a thing to help that baby, let alone Inga. She gets all her help at Mor's, or what she can."

"I agree. But right now we need to pray about all this and know that our Father is handling this." *Like He does everything.*

Astrid stared at her friend, head nurse, administrator—all the roles that Deborah felt herself stepping into. "When did you get so wise?" The slight stutter on the words revealed more than what she said.

"I have several good teachers. I asked for Him to send one or the other of them here."

Astrid's eyes widened just slightly. She sniffed and dug a square of muslin out of the drawer to blow her nose. "Let's pray." She closed her eyes, sniffed again, and heaved a leaden breath. "Dear God, Father, Jesus, Holy Spirit. Oh, please help me."

Deborah reached across the desk and clutched Astrid's hands. "Lord God, you know our hearts, our breaking hearts. Only you can love Thorliff and those children more than we do. How to help Thorliff is so far beyond our capabilities. All we can do is leave it with you, and that is so terribly hard." She mopped her own eyes.

"Help, Lord. Oh, help. Mor would say, '*Trust Him*,' and I know that, but . . . I . . . I don't think I really know how."

"Repeat with me: 'Lord, I trust you.' Now, Astrid, say it. 'Lord, I trust you.'" Deborah squeezed her hands. "Now!"

"Lord, I . . . trust . . . you."

"Louder! 'Lord, I trust you.'"

Astrid glared at her. Deborah felt it as well as saw it. "Lord, I trust you!"

Deborah fought to hide the grin tickling her mouth. "All right. Now we dry our faces and go out there on His strength, because He sure is with us." She blew out a breath as she stared around the room, fully expecting to see Jesus standing right beside Astrid's shoulder. *Lord God, I've never experienced anything quite like this before.* She blew her nose, wiped it, and stood, watching Astrid do the same.

Astrid took a deep breath and pulled herself straighter. "Ready?"

"Yes, the clipboard is out on the desk. Miriam is still here, so we are all set."

"Are my eyes red?"

"A bit, but we will do this." *Thank you, Lord.* Deborah took the few steps needed to open the door and ushered Dr. Astrid ahead of her, both of them with not quite smiles but no more tears.

"Good morning," Astrid said to Miriam. "Thank you for waiting."

Deborah joined in the greeting and picked up the clipboard. "Our boy with the broken leg is asking when he can go home. Or at least his mother is."

"Let's go."

Dr. Astrid greeted the boy's mother and smiled down at the sober child. "I heard you walked with crutches yesterday."

He nodded.

Deborah wondered if the boy would ever talk to them. She knew he could, because she'd seen him talking with his family. *Inga and Emmy,* she thought. That was what this boy needed. Her mind flashed back to Inga and Benny at the window when Manny wanted nothing to do with anyone in Blessing. He had been one hard shell to crack, but those kids did it. She jerked herself back to the bedside, scribbled a note on the paper clipped to the chart, and watched Astrid gently feeling the leg as they kept a close eye on the child's face for any pain reaction.

"Did it hurt yesterday when you walked?"

"He not put the foot on floor."

The nurses and Astrid all smiled at the boy's mother. She was taking the English class with Amelia Jeffers, and it was obvious. All the immigrants were taking the language classes, and this family had only arrived in Blessing last year. "Today we will remove the traction," Astrid explained slowly, so Mrs. Chikachev could understand her, "and your Sergei can rest his foot on the floor—not stand on it yet, but balance. Keep using the crutches."

"I think we need to bring Emmy and Inga in to read to Sergei this afternoon. They can play down at the end of the hall." Deborah motioned to the opposite end, beyond the private rooms.

"Good idea. Any questions?" Astrid looked to the mother, who flashed her a smile, shaking her head.

By the time they finished the rounds of their six patients, the first appointment was waiting to see Dr. Astrid. Many of their patients were from the countryside surrounding Blessing, some like this one five miles away or more.

Deborah sent Miriam and the other night nurse home to sleep and gave the orderly instructions to bring the breakfast trays out. Despite the hard beginning for the morning, the day swung into normal hospital motion.

She glanced up from writing on the charts at the front desk when she heard the door open and Reverend Solberg's cheery greeting.

Thank you, Lord, she whispered inside around the grin that leaped to her face. "Good morning, sir, so good to see you." When he stopped at her desk, she slipped out of her professional nurse persona for just a moment, leaned across, and whispered, "How did you know to come now? You usually come in the afternoon. Thank you, Pa."

He patted her hand. "Private messenger." He glanced around. "Looks pretty normal to me. What was the emergency?"

"Not a physical one, more emotional." She nodded toward the exam room.

"Astrid?"

"And me. Please talk with her when you can."

"Can you give me a clue?" He leaned over to sniff the opening roses on the counter. "Bless Amelia."

She gave him a three-sentence description of the day before.

"It's been coming and was much needed," he said.

"I'm calling the young troops in to help our boy over there."

"Ah, Inga and Emmy to the rescue." He grinned. "Wise." He left her and moved off to greet the patients and family members.

Deborah cranked the telephone and

answered the cheery good-morning of phone company manager Gerald Valders with a request for Ingeborg's.

After the greeting, Ingeborg asked, "How soon do you want them?"

"You read my mind. How about after dinner?"

"We'll be there."

"Reverend Solberg is here now, but perhaps you could kidnap your daughter for a while."

"Of course. What a joy."

Deborah put the earpiece back in the prong and closed her eyes for a moment. When thoughts of Toby shoehorned themselves into her head and took over, she ordered, *I will trust you, Lord. I know even you need time to work. Trust. I think I need a visit with Ingeborg too.*

"Whew, it's getting wet out there." Ingeborg closed her umbrella as she came through the door, which Inga and Emma were holding open, one on each side.

Deborah came around the counter for a hug. "I didn't think you would come after the rain started."

"It feels so good. There was a tiny cool breeze and not much more than sprinkles until we were almost here." Ingeborg smiled down at her girls. "If they look a bit damp, it's because they ran ahead of the umbrella."

"We didn't see a rainbow yet." Inga grinned up at Deborah.

"We brought two schoolbooks to read from," Emma said, waving them. "One is about raccoons."

"And checkers. Do you think he knows how to play checkers?" Inga and Emmy finished each other's sentences as if they shared one mind.

"I have no idea. You'll have to ask Sergei. We just finished dinner. He and his ma ate in the dining room for the first time. You could probably read and play in there."

"Okay." The two shared a smile and headed for the dining room.

Ingeborg wagged her head. "I should have thought to bring them before. Ah well. We'll make amends now."

"He was just released from the traction today, so this is perfect. I was hoping you and Astrid could go take a walk but . . ." She glanced out the window, where raindrops were running down the glass pane.

Ingeborg asked, "Does she have any more appointments this afternoon?"

"No, so perhaps you could talk her into going home and possibly taking a bit of a rest." Deborah rolled her eyes, making Ingeborg's face warm in a smile.

"I will try." She hurried off to Astrid's office.

Moments later, the two of them came out. Astrid crossed to Deborah's counter. "Call me if you need me. I should stay here and work on that horrid self-breeding paper stack, but"—she motioned to her mother—"she is dragging me away."

"Good!" Deborah grinned at Ingeborg, and the mother and daughter walked out the doors.

Deborah stood at the counter for a few minutes, rather mindlessly catching up charts from the morning rounds. Some patients were sleeping, and several were visiting with a family member. She enjoyed the job most when it was quiet and orderly like this.

Over by the window, sweet Mrs. Ohnstetter sat rocking slowly and knitting away, her hands flittering. She was too frail to live alone any longer, so since she had no family, she lived at the hospital. She spent her days sitting in the rocker they had brought in for her, knitting. Ingeborg kept her in yarn to create hats and mittens, which Penny sold at her store. Mrs. Ohnstetter claimed that she much preferred living in the ward, where she could watch people, rather than in a separate room.

She wondered where Toby was working today. Out on the new house going up for Dr. Deming? The young dentist said he was tired of living at the apartment building, where he'd been since not long after he and Vera were married. Or perhaps Toby was running that barn building for the farmer southwest of town. She knew the men were excited about starting the addition to the deaf school, and if they were going to have it roughed in before winter, they needed to get at it.

There Toby was in her thoughts again! This intruding-thoughts disease seemed to be getting worse. She was just sitting around, huh? The thought irritated her all over again, and it wasn't just Toby, it seemed, but all of them. Even on a quiet day like today, she had so many chores and jobs.

Wouldn't it be lovely if Toby came at the shift change to walk her home? In her fantasy, Toby would smile at her and take off his hat when he walked through the door and—

And suddenly a vivid, wild thought grabbed her head. She had been urging Astrid to trust God, and she had been trusting God herself— to do what she had wanted her whole life. But most of all, to know His plan for her. What if God's plan was not hers? What if God did not intend that Toby be her husband? What if God had someone else in mind altogether, and Deborah was, as it were, barking up the wrong tree? And here she was sitting at the base of that tree, barking and barking and barking, when really, God's will was some other tree?

No, that couldn't be! Look how Deborah had carried a torch for Toby all these years.

Surely that was from God, right? But what if . . . ?

She was so confused. *God, if Toby is not intended for me, please show me the man you want for me. Please send the man, whether it is Toby or someone else.*

"Nurse Deborah?" The voice came again, jerking her back to the here and now. She felt her face flame. How long had Mrs. Chikachev been trying to get her attention? Wishing for a fan, she smiled. "I'm sorry, guess my mind. . . ."

"I go home now. Class with Mrs. Amelia, then I come later?"

"Of course. Sergei will be fine. When the girls leave, we'll find something for him to do." Now Mrs. Chikachev could start taking some time off. Good. Sergei was no longer trapped in the traction splint, and their lives could return to normal—well, soon anyway.

Deborah shook her head. To think she'd let Toby dreams take over her mind like that.

Sharing the umbrella, Astrid and Ingeborg mounted the steps to the front porch of the Jeffers' house. "Amelia is over at the school, teaching her English-speaking class, and I'm sure Daniel is at one of the offices or the other. Since it will be chilly out on the porch, how about tea in the kitchen or the parlor?"

Ingeborg waved a hand. "The kitchen is

always cozier. I'll stir up the fire while you set out the cups. I brought cookies."

"You and Amelia. You must think it's a sin to have an empty cookie jar. Have you had her new lemon drops?"

"Her what?"

"She rolled out the cookie dough and sprinkled crushed lemon drops on top. Better than raisins any day." Astrid hooked her straw hat on the hall tree and waited for her mother to unpin hers.

"I guess you assume we will be here a while?"

Astrid caught a yawn. "I just hope I can stay awake. I seem to drop off to sleep any time my body finds a chair."

Since her mother-in-law had supper cooking in the oven, the coals in the stove flared immediately with some kindling. Ingeborg added more wood, then pulled the still-warm tea kettle over the hottest part of the stove. Taking the tea tin from the cupboard, she measured several teaspoons of tea into the china pot and set it up on the warming shelf. "Isn't it interesting that the day barely has a chance to turn chilly, and I go for hot tea instead of coffee or the cold drinks in the ice-box?"

"I'll drink tea or coffee anytime." Astrid settled at the counter.

Lifting a plate from the basket always on

her arm, Ingeborg set the molasses cookies on the table. Astrid grew quieter as they finished up the preparations and sat at the table, where a low bowl of roses perfumed the room.

Ingeborg pulled the bowl closer and inhaled. "Oh, how I love the smell of roses."

Astrid poured the tea, and the clinking of teaspoons on china was the only sound in the room.

O Lord, please help this daughter of mine. She is carrying such a heavy load. Waiting could only be tolerated by praying at the same time. "So what happened?"

All the while studying the table, Astrid described the scene at the hospital when Thorliff's screaming son turned away from his pa, seeking Thelma and calling her *Ma*.

Finally, with tear-filled eyes, Astrid looked to her mother. "I yelled at Thorliff after I left the hospital later yesterday, screamed at him. Mor, that was not the way to handle this and I know it. I knew it at the time too, but the words just spewed out like a runaway prairie fire. I was so furious that he's neglecting his children so. Before I could apologize, he ordered me out of his office. I think he would have thrown me out bodily had I not left. By the time I got home, I was sobbing so I could scarcely walk. I thought Daniel was going to go over there and . . . Oh, Mor, it was awful. We've never had a fight like this." She laid her head on her crossed arms on the table, the sobs rocking her body and even the chair.

Ingeborg left her chair to wrap her arms around her daughter, letting her cry it out. Her prayers were woven amongst her own tears. She was beginning to wonder if Astrid's well of tears would ever run dry, but finally they slowed to hiccups and shoulder-wracking sobs. Ingeborg handed her a dish towel and continued to smooth the soaked tendrils of golden hair back from her wet face. All her mother murmurings slowed as needed.

From the sink she brought a cloth and wiped Astrid's swollen face. "All will be well, my dear daughter, all will be well. I know it doesn't seem that way right now, but somehow, our Father will work this out. We have to trust Him for that."

O Lord, break through Thorliff's sorrow and anger. How do we help him? Please, work your miracles. Protect his children. Bring him home from that far land where he is suffering so. What can I say? What can I do?

CHAPTER 11

Do I ever think of anything besides the job?
Toby leaned himself and his hoe
against the garden fence. The garden Anji and
her brood had so lovingly planted and kept
weeded no longer wore the look of diligent care.
So far this evening, he had liberated the carrots and lettuce. Whoever decreed that weeds
would grow faster than cultivated plants had a
sadistic nature. He well knew who was behind
weed growth.

Here it was late June, the garden had gotten
ahead of him, and he wasn't even really working full summer hours yet. Once they started
the deaf school addition, everyone would be
working from dawn to dusk. A robin heralding
the sinking sun caught his attention. When did

he take time to appreciate the birds and the bursting forth of summer?

Face it, he missed Anji and the kids. With Benny still out at the farm, and Rebecca's other kids busy with various activities, it was too quiet around here. And he rattled around that big house since they had left.

He grabbed his hoe again and bent to the destruction of weeds. Pigweed and grass. Maybe he should hire Manny or one of the other boys to come work in his garden. Benny could pull weeds. That was who he'd talk to. But then, Benny had been helping Rebecca at the soda fountain whenever Ingeborg didn't need him for something.

"Hey there, looks like you could use a hand."

His brother! "I could, especially one with a hoe attached." Tipping his flat-brimmed hat back, Toby dried his forehead with an arm partially encased in a rolled-up sleeve. "Good to see you, Gerald. When is Benny coming home?"

"You'll have to ask Rebecca. Do you have another hoe, or do I need to go get one?"

"You're really going to help me?"

"I am. The hoe?"

"In the shed, right where Ma always kept everything, sharpened, cleaned, and hung on the wall."

Gerald fetched the hoe. "Where do you want me to start?"

"Wherever. I'm thinking to ask Benny to come weed."

"He'll be a couple of days catching up in our garden." They both chopped weeds out of the dirt and threw them in a pile.

Toby paused. "Then why are you here?"

"I figured since the only time we get to talk is at church . . ."

"I know." Toby threw some more weeds on the pile. He knew his brother well enough to know there was a reason they needed to talk today.

"Have you given any thought to sharing your house?"

"*Our* house, you mean?"

"No, yours. I have one, and one is enough. But I was thinking, if we hire a male teacher, you could possibly rent a room to him."

"Not a woman, eh?" Toby loved to tweak his brother's not-so-evident sense of humor.

"Well, of course, if you married one." Gerald grinned.

"Whew, I thought there for a moment you were serious." Toby slammed the hoe into the soil.

Gerald stopped and leaned on the handle of the hoe. "I always thought you'd be married before I was. You've always been the ladies' man, after all."

"Life just doesn't go the way we think it might, does it?" One of the bean plants met its demise. He muttered a gentle expletive. "Keep hoeing, might keep you from thinking." Although it didn't seem to help him. "It was great having Anji and the kids here. Every once in a while, I find something they left behind. I've been putting them in a box to ship." He stopped hoeing at the end of the row and surveyed his efforts. "That sure looks better."

Gerald hacked away. "Benny really misses Gilbert and Melissa. And Rebecca mentions Anji at least once a day. Their leaving again left a hole in Blessing. She was a good schoolteacher too."

"The Fourth of July won't be the same without Thomas and his Irish brogue and humor."

Gerald finished his row. "An hour with a hoe can make a big difference. What are you going to do with all that you reap here later this summer?"

Toby shrugged. "Find someone to give it to. Probably some of the folks in the apartment house. That garden they have isn't enough for all of them and canning too." The thought made him smile inside. He'd wondered the same thing. "Ma sure put up a lot. There are still plenty of full jars down in the cellar. Tell Rebecca to come help herself."

"You tell her. She told me to ask you to come to supper on Friday and to bring a friend."

"A friend? Just my company isn't enough?"

He attacked the next row, being more careful with where he slammed the hoe. "Does she have someone specific in mind?" *As in female?*

"Who would you like to bring?"

"How about me, myself, and I?"

"You going to put a dress on one of them?"

Toby gaped at his brother. "Gerald Valders, you made a joke."

"That's what living with prankster children can bring out. As Mor used to say, 'If you don't laugh, you might cry.'"

"Did our mor actually say that?"

"More than once. I sure wish we would hear from her, from them. One letter since they took off. I have a hard time forgiving Pa for dragging her away like that." Gerald mopped his forehead.

"He sure messed up their lives. He was insufferable that last year or so." Toby wagged his head.

"Two years. She's a tough old bird with a heart afraid to show itself."

Toby stared at Gerald. "Really? You think so?"

"Well, they took us in, didn't they? And she was busy in everything, including running the post office."

"I know. She always needed to be in charge. Bossy fits." Toby leaned his hoe against the fence and started tossing the piles of weeds into the wooden wheelbarrow he had made under Lars' tutelage while in high school. Mr. Sam had taught them how to make the iron wheels.

With the weeds dumped onto the compost pile, the brothers put the hoes away.

"Come on, I have some iced tea in the icebox and cookies from Ingeborg."

Gerald frowned. "Did you have supper?"

"Ja, I can cook, you know." They took their drinks out to the back porch and sat at the table he'd made another year.

"So you're going to ask Deborah to come for supper with you on Friday?"

Toby studied his brother. He was beginning to smell a plot. "Why?"

"Actually, that's who Rebecca suggested."

"Figures." Toby ran his tongue over his back teeth. "I could ask Mercy. You know, Miriam's sister."

"You could. I thought you might be getting serious about Deborah. You gave up gallivanting with that girl from Grafton."

"Too far away. Besides, Deborah is fun to tease."

Gerald snorted. "You've been teasing her since grade school."

"I have, haven't I? All right, I'll ask her. And if she says no, I'll ask Mercy."

"She's kind of young for you." Gerald set his empty glass on the table and stood. "You can come help me hoe next week."

"I'm not done here." They both looked out at the garden. A swallow dipped and dove after some bugs. Toby slapped a mosquito on his arm. "Nasty things." A cottontail rabbit slid under the fence. "Maybe I'll ask Manny to set some traps. Fried rabbit would be good."

Gerald lifted a hand in a casual wave as he ambled back over to his house. Toby watched him go. Deborah, huh? So that was why Gerald had come by.

Actually, asking Deborah to dinner wasn't such a bad idea. Better than asking her to write invitations. Come to think of it, she never did say she'd do it or she wouldn't do it, but he remembered how he could feel her turn from warm to icy cold the minute he'd suggested it. Obviously, the answer was no. He would have to be more careful now. They were both grown up, after all, and the teasing days were over—or should be.

Should he telephone Deborah or stop and see her after work tomorrow? But then, she might not be on the day shift. He shrugged. All he could do was ask.

Back in the kitchen, he washed the glasses and put them back in the cupboard. One thing his ma had done well—not that she ever did anything not well—was teach her sons to be neat, to put things away. He draped the dish towel over the wall rack and took the kerosene lamp into the parlor. He'd rather stay outside, but if he took the lamp outside to read, the mosquitoes would have a feast.

Taking a seat in his pa's leather chair with its well-worn footstool, he picked up his book. Anji had started him reading *Ben Hur*. He was enjoying it, which was surprising even to him.

He glanced around the room. Maybe he should get a cat or a dog. Something to bring some life to this house now.

He'd invite Deborah tomorrow at the early shift change. Maybe he'd ask if she wanted a soda too.

The phone rang while he was eating breakfast the next morning. Toby grabbed the receiver off the hook as he was finishing his oatmeal.

"Thorliff for you." Gerald clicked the call through.

"Yes?"

"Jonathan got back yesterday afternoon, so we're meeting here at the office at seven. How far did you get on that barn?"

"The crew can continue without me. I'll let Trygve know to get started and I'll be late."

"How far are you?"

"We should be ready to roof tomorrow. They delivered most of the shingles yesterday. We need to get it done in time for haying, you know." Toby sipped his coffee.

"Ja. We'll get more labor out there for the roofing as soon as you say the word."

"We'll know by the end of the day."

"Good, see you in a bit."

Toby finished his oatmeal, put the pot for the next day in the icebox, and rinsed out his dishes. Anytime he thought to leave some dishes in the sink, he heard Hildegunn's chiding voice.

As he shut the door behind him, he thought, *Ma and Pa could simply telephone, or how long does it take to send a note?* If only he had an address, he'd write to them.

He stopped at the Knutson house to put Trygve in charge of the barn construction, then headed for the office. It felt and smelled like the rain would return. It had watered the gardens well during the night. That should set another burst of weed growth.

Someone else was already there; he could hear voices from the construction office that had taken over the back of the newspaper building. From the fragrance of cinnamon, he knew Thelma had been up early baking. He pulled open the screen door and stepped into the construction world.

Coffee cup in hand, Jonathan Gould stood to greet him. "Good to see you."

"Good to have you home again. I, uh, I hope all went well."

"Thank you. As well as could be expected. You know me and high society. I did my one appearance at the official memorial service; we had a private family one as well, for which I was very grateful."

"How is your father?"

"Better than I feared he might be. He'll be out here in about two weeks, I think."

"Really?"

"He wants to be part of the deaf school addition, not just financing from a distance." Jonathan shook his head. "To say I was surprised . . ." He shrugged. "But then I well know the draw that Blessing is."

Daniel Jeffers had arrived while they were talking. "That does change things, doesn't it? Welcome home." He glanced around. "Where's Hjelmer?"

"Should be here any minute. Kaaren and Lars might be a bit late." Thorliff had the school plans weighted down on the table. "Get your coffee and rolls, and let's begin with you, Jonathan."

Jonathan pulled some papers from a leather case, glancing up when Hjelmer let the door slam behind him.

"I'll need to go open the bank, but I'll come right back if we have more to do." Hjelmer set his briefcase on the table. "Thank God for Thelma." He took a bite of a cinnamon roll and filled his coffee cup. Sitting down, he stared at Thorliff. "You couldn't look any worse if you tried. Ever thought of sleeping?"

Toby watched the exchange. He saw Thorliff's jaw tighten as he straightened his shoulders, almost said something, and took a swig of coffee instead. He heard a *Whoa* from outside. "Lars and Kaaren are here."

After the greetings and with everyone finally seated around the table, Thorliff said, "Jonathan."

After standing and smiling at each of them, Jonathan began. "I brought back several things. The financial papers from my father, including a surprise." He picked up another paper. "This is an added bequest from my mother's estate. She wanted to make sure there would be operating money for the deaf school, so this will be a yearly sum for at least the next five years. I brought you a copy, Kaaren. I had no idea she had done this."

"Your mother had a big heart for the causes she undertook. I understand from Grace that she helped the deaf school in New York where Grace used to work."

"In spite of her love of society events, my mother took her philanthropy very seriously."

Kaaren read the paper and her mouth fell open. "Are you sure, Jonathan?"

"I am. I know you will use it wisely, and my father reiterated the same thing." He turned back to his case and passed copies of the proposed budget to each of them. "If you have any questions, these are the numbers we had agreed on and how the funding will be managed. Hjelmer, the funds will be flowing through the Blessing Bank, so that should assist your liquidity too."

When Jonathan sat down, Thorliff took over. "Let's move on to construction, then. Toby, you will be in charge of the actual construction, under me, with Joshua Landsverk and Trygve reporting to you. Deming's house should be ready for the final interior. Mr. Belin is running the finishing crew of three. Once the barn is roofed and finished, all crews will move to the deaf school construction site. Since the grading is done, we'll lay out today and tomorrow and start on forms next week." He looked around the table. "Questions, comments?"

While Toby had known he'd be in charge of crews, the added responsibility made him swallow. He watched Thorliff's face for any trace of doubt. "When will the lumber for the forms get here?"

"On the train today. It was supposed to have been here yesterday. I checked this morning. We're getting a full flat car load. It was coupled onto the train last night."

Sometime later, after more discussions and Hjelmer returning from opening the bank, Thorliff looked around the table. "Anything else?" By now the coffee pot was empty and the rolls eaten.

"Sorry—I have an application for a schoolteacher." Jonathan handed Hjelmer the paper. "My father thought this might be a good fit. My cousin, Anton, after his fiancée died of tuberculosis, decided he needed a change from where he was, and my father told him to apply here. He has taught mathematics, sciences, and both Latin and Greek, not that Greek was listed. My father said he is an excellent teacher."

"And he wants to come west why?" Hjelmer asked with one raised eyebrow. "And does he understand how little we pay?"

"I might have an idea." Toby surprised himself by not giving this more thought before mentioning it. "I have a big house."

"We can work on the teacher topic later." Thorliff stood up. "Let's get the construction rolling."

Lars and Kaaren stood too. Kaaren smiled at them all. "Whoever dreamed when I learned sign language to help Grace communicate that we would come to this? Thank you all for taking what I was fearful of dreaming and growing this school into not only what it is today but what it will become. God is most certainly using you to take care of the 'least of these,' as the Bible says. I know you are looking at this as a business, but we go so much farther than that. 'Thank you' seems so insignificant, but I have nothing else to give you. Except changed lives."

Thorliff nodded. "You're welcome."

Toby left with the others. His latest task was to drive the wagonload of new shingles just unloaded from the train out to the barn. Grateful for no rain, he picked up the wagon at the station and stopped at the hospital. When he pushed open the door, Deborah was standing behind the front desk.

"Toby, is someone hurt?"

"Good morning to you too." He stopped in front of her, cleared his throat, and dropped his voice. "Ah, if you have nothing else tomorrow night, Rebecca has invited us for supper." His words came out in a hurry.

"Really?" She shrugged. "Well I . . . I guess I could. I'm on day shift all week. If there are no emergencies." She shrugged. "Fine. I . . . Yes."

"Good." He turned and headed for the door.

There, he'd done what Rebecca had said he should do, and it wasn't as painful as he'd thought it would be. He smiled at the memory of Deborah's face. She'd looked a bit surprised, hadn't she? Or was it a whole lot surprised?

CHAPTER 12

Is something wrong?" Astrid asked.

"Uh, no, I . . ." Deborah shook her head. "I . . . I think I'm in a state of shock."

"Wasn't someone just here?" Astrid glanced around the hospital entry.

"Toby." Deborah's voice squeaked. She cleared her throat and drew in some air, trying to regain her normal adult voice. "He asked me to, um, he said . . . Toby Valders just asked me to go to Rebecca and Gerald's house for supper tomorrow." She turned to Astrid. "He really did . . . I mean . . ." She paused. "Astrid, he's never asked me to anything before. Rebecca is matchmaking, right? You know, the girl party?"

"Of course." Astrid leaned in. "She might have suggested it, but she didn't drag him in here to ask."

Deborah exhaled in a sigh. "You're right." She nodded as she spoke, trying to convince herself as much as Astrid. "He asked. He came here to where I work to ask me to supper." She blew out another breath. "I will just accept this and not look a gift horse in the mouth." She peeped at Astrid from under her eyelids. "Right?"

"That's right. And you will not work late tomorrow. Good heavens, it just occurred to me that the Fourth is already this Saturday. I sure hope the rains blow on past by then."

They both turned at the sound of giggles coming from the dining room. "They came again today, bless those two little girls." Deborah shared a smile with Astrid. "Mrs. Chikachev got a break again, and her Sergei can talk. The girls even taught him some English words. Inga says he wins almost every game of checkers." Her eyebrows wiggled and her voice dropped to a whisper. "Do you think they let him win?"

"I wouldn't put it past them." Astrid headed for her office. "If anyone calls, I am neck-deep in paper work."

"Right." *And if you think I'm going to call you for anything other than someone broken or bleeding* . . . She knew Astrid, loved her more like a sister than a friend, and no matter how hard Astrid tried to cover it up, she could tell their doctor was carrying a heavy load again. And her falling-out with Thorliff had to be the cause. Deborah shook her head. Who would he listen to? How could they help him if he didn't want to be helped? Stubborn didn't begin to describe that Bjorklund specialty, even though it was a major family trait.

The question for her was, how could *she* help?

⁓

That night after supper at home, Deborah made a decision. Who better to talk to than her pa?

John Solberg smiled at his eldest daughter. "Of course, come on, let's go in my office." When they were seated in the sewing room that was jokingly called the office, used thusly as needed, he leaned toward her, elbows on his knees. "I heard you have been invited to Rebecca's house for supper Friday night."

"That is rather big news, I know." She could feel her smile trembling. "I'm not sure how you heard, but that actually isn't what I wanted to talk to you about. I don't know how to help Astrid and Thorliff. Their big blow-up is breaking her heart. I can see it in her eyes no matter how she tries to hide it. Apparently they've never had a falling-out like this before."

John nodded and sighed at the same time. "I know this sounds trite, but it isn't. Only Jesus and the Holy Spirit can handle this. Until Thorliff is willing to let go of his anger and

grief, praying is what we do. He has to be willing, even a crack."

"Sometimes I wish God wasn't so polite. I
mean, I'm not blaming Him, or . . ." She shook
her head in frustration. "I mean, I wish He'd
yell at Thorliff."

John covered her hands with his own,
almost stifling a chuckle. "I know you're not
being facetious, and I so often have asked our
Father to hit me with His two-by-four when I
am being stubborn or not getting it. We will all
pray that He speaks in a way that gets through
to our beloved, stubborn Thorliff. We plead
God's protection over that house for both the
children and Thelma. Little Roald is acting
the only way he knows how. Thelma is ma to
him."

"You think Thorliff will take this out on
Thelma?"

"Not intentionally. He is wiser than that. He
knows he could not get along without Thelma,
but this will only make her work harder with
that little one." He paused, obviously contem-
plating the situation. "We will pray now and we
will all join in these specific prayers, mostly that
God will indeed have His way." He patted her
hand. "Polite not withstanding. He will find a
way or many ways to get around our stubborn
friend. Do you believe He can do that?"

Deborah stared into her pa's eyes. "I know
He can. I believe, like you have taught me, that

God has a plan and will do what is necessary, but . . ." She stared at her lap.

With a loving hand, he tipped up her chin. "*But* . . . We all get hung up on that little word. *But* when will He? Right?"

"I . . . I don't want anyone else to get hurt." The picture in her mind was of Astrid, then Thelma and the children.

"That's why we pray protection for them all. God has given us all a chance to grow in our trust of Him." He shook his head, a barely perceptible movement. "We have our work cut out for us. But we *will* trust Him, our loving Father. Lord God, we trust you."

Deborah let the tears flow. "I want to."

John gathered her into his arms. "Holy Father, we serve you and you only, but right now . . ." He heaved a sigh. "This hurts. Thank you, that you are here with your mighty arms around all of us. You are the only way we can turn. You bring us comfort and you have promised us peace. That we can rest in your assurances, your promises to never leave nor forsake us." His voice gained that peace. "And you love your daughter Deborah and have given her a tender heart for loving her friends and family. You know far better than we what this will take. Lord, you love Thorliff beyond what we can imagine, as you do all of us. We rest in that assurance, in your peace. Please remind us to be constant in prayer and to keep our mouths shut unless you give us the words to say. In your holy and mighty name, we offer praise and thanks. You, O Lord. Mighty God and healer of all broken hearts that turn to you. Thy will be done." He hugged Deborah. And they said together, "Amen."

He hugged her again, blew out a breath, and sat back. "This is in His hands. Our job is to trust."

Deborah melted against the chair back. "I am a boiled noodle."

"Me too."

Deborah watched him flex his shoulders and hands. "You'll talk with Astrid and Ingeborg?"

"When the time is right."

Her nod scarcely moved her head. "I think I'm going to go to bed, if I can walk that far."

"Getting prone is a good idea." He stood carefully and held out his hand. "Thank you."

She let him pull her up, confusion making her ask, "For what?"

He put his arm around her shoulders. "For caring enough to ask me. Which is what precipitated this incredible . . ." He snorted. "I can't come up with the right word even." He hugged her. "Just thank you." He opened the door and motioned her ahead of him. "'Night."

Deborah reached up and kissed his cheek. "'Night."

In her room, she started undressing for

bed and instead collapsed on top of the summer bedspread. And didn't wake up until she heard the birds heralding the morning. Looking around, she realized that at some point she had changed into her nightdress and crawled under the blanket. She could feel the smile lifting her face and see the morning breeze setting the lace curtain to dancing. Stretching her arms above her head and gripping the white iron bedstead, she exhaled and touched the foot rail with her toes.

Work! I'll be late for work! She leaped from the bed to the window without touching the floor. Or so it seemed. While the sun had gilded the sky and burnished the land, it was still lifting from the horizon. "Thank you." She dressed in record speed, grateful for indoor plumbing, and still wrapping her hair in a knot, headed down the hall to the kitchen, where she could already hear laughter.

Her ma's smile greeted her. "I feared I might need to come wake you."

"Thanks. I need to run."

"I know, but you will eat first." Mary Martha handed her a slice of bread with cheese. "Praying you a blessed day." She kissed Deborah's cheek and pointed out the door. "Grab the umbrella, just in case."

Deborah did as she was told and took bites from her bread as she headed for the hospital, dodging the puddles as she hurried.

❧

"If this rain keeps up, we'll have to move the whole shindig over here to your warehouse." Hjelmer and Daniel stood in the front window of the machinery building, watching the rain pelt down again. It was late Friday morning, and the storm seemed to have stalled right over Blessing—again.

Daniel nodded. "I know. That's why I had the men clean it all up, get it fit for company. We could always cancel the whole thing, you know."

"We could, but you know it could blow off and the sun could be shining again within the space of minutes." Hjelmer shook his head. "We don't cancel parties for rain here in Blessing. Fewer people might come, but you never know. I told Toby that since he is in charge of roasting the meat and the trench they dug is now full of water, to get a tent up, trench around it, and we'll pump out the fire pit. The load of firewood was already under cover, so we'll be safe."

Daniel shrugged. "You can count on the governor not making it."

"He, or rather his aide, already called with his regrets. Made me laugh. Now if there's a blizzard whiteout or we get flooded out, then we'll reconsider canceling." Hjelmer reached for his still-dripping umbrella. "I gave you that packet, right?"

"You did. Thanks. Toby was disgusted that they couldn't finish that barn roof. I think everyone is beginning to be concerned. The Red River rose, but not even a foot. See if you can get back to the bank without swimming."

Daniel headed for his office with a quick trip by the warehouse. "It's a good thing we're low on stock right now," he muttered to himself. He could hear the racket from the metal stamps cranking out parts for seeders and another section refitting the milling machines that made the new part for threshing machines. He'd be on the road next week taking orders. Should have been there several weeks ago. He waved to the young men on the ends of brooms, finishing the cleaning. They needed to bring the tables over from the school and the church, or rather the sawhorses with plank tops.

While this rain was certainly needed, this wasn't exactly a convenient time. And not all at once like this.

Promptly at three o'clock, Astrid announced, "You get out of here now." She almost pushed Deborah out the door.

"Thank you. Good thing, thanks to Ma, I brought an umbrella." She turned and grinned at Astrid. "Can you believe we're going to do the celebration tomorrow, rain or not?"

"I know. Crazy, but we of Blessing are determined." Astrid held the door open. "Go!"

Deborah opened her umbrella and stepped out from under the portico. While the wind tried to snatch away her umbrella, she hung on and hurried up the street. Her shoes and skirt were soaking up water like a dishrag in the sink. She hadn't worn boots; what an oversight. Closing the umbrella and leaving it to drain in the umbrella stand on the front porch, she stepped inside and untied her shoes on the rug.

Ma called from the kitchen, "Sorry I didn't mention boots this morning."

"I saw enough blue for Dutchmen's britches in the western sky. Glad we weren't needing to take the wagon anywhere." Deborah shivered in spite of her shawl. "I'm going to change clothes right now."

"Good idea. Oh, Rebecca called to say that Benny is home and he can't wait to see you and Toby."

"To gloat, you mean?" Deborah stopped in the archway to the kitchen.

"Ah, never doubt the power of we Blessing women when we start on a mission." Mary Martha handed her a biscuit left over from dinner. "Here, to hold you over."

"Where is everybody? The house is never this quiet."

"John put them to work out in the barn to

get the haymow swept and manure cleaned out. I'm sure that rooster is giving them a beakful."

"Thank you." Nibbling the biscuit and honey, Deborah meandered down the hall to her bedroom.

After hanging her skirt to drip in the bathroom, she pulled her blue dimity dress from the chifforobe and held it in front of her to stare in the long mirror on the bedroom door. Shaking her head, she hung it up and pulled out the navy-and-white-gingham one. *What to wear? Silly, you never have this problem. It's not like you're going to a dance or something.* She shivered in spite of wearing her wrap and glanced at the closed window. Leave it to Ma to remember these things. But she still felt a draft around her shoulders.

"Oh, for—" She jerked a yellow one-piece print dress out from the others and pulled it over her head without holding it up for the mirror. After twisting and turning to fasten the buttons, she smoothed the more fitted bodice and shook the skirt straight. Nodding at the reflection, she sat down at her dressing table and pulled the pins out of the knot of hair that was already sagging. She stared at her face in the mirror.

What if Toby was only doing this because he felt forced into it? "Ha!" Nobody had ever forced Toby into anything.

Brushing out her waves of brown hair, she

gathered it back with a green-and-yellow-plaid ribbon and tied a small bow on top. After putting the brush in the drawer, she leaned in to pinch her cheeks, hoping to bring out some more color. "Deborah MacCallister, what is the matter with you? Stop this nonsense immediately." The smile on the face in the mirror refused to dim.

"Don't you look lovely," Mary Martha said with a wide smile when Deborah joined her in the kitchen.

"Thank you. How can I help?"

"Here, an apron. That bowl of peas needs shelling first. We're having creamed peas and ham over biscuits. I didn't find any potatoes large enough to use, but maybe next week. Go easy on eating them raw, we barely have enough." A grin accompanied the admonishment.

When the clock hands showed five o'clock, Deborah hung up her apron, washed her hands, and retrieved her shawl from the bedroom. Good thing she was wearing her boots and carrying her black leather slippers. Again Ma's suggestion.

"You look lovely, my dear," her mother said again in reassurance.

The dog's barking announced a visitor. Deborah blew out a breath and went to answer the knock on the door. *Lord, please.* But please what, she had no idea.

When she opened the door, Toby looked the same as always—too handsome for his own good.

"Are you ready?"

"Come in." She stepped back and motioned him inside, then reached for her shawl.

He smiled and nodded. "Better bring the umbrella. Dark clouds in the west again."

Mary Martha joined them. "Was the fire pit full of water?"

"We drained it and added more rocks to the bottom. Getting that fire going in a couple hours will be a challenge, but if you pour enough kerosene on it, you can start anything. Never fear, we'll have plenty of meat for the party." He tipped his hat. "See you tomorrow at the machinery warehouse."

Mary Martha smiled. "We'll be there bright and early. I sure hope God answers our prayers to move the rain on."

"Me too."

Deborah flipped her shawl around her shoulders and joined him on the porch. He grabbed the umbrella out of the stand and glanced down at her feet. He grinned at her. "Smart."

He didn't make some funny comment about my boots. She smiled back at him. "Thank you." Was that all she could say?

As they walked, he even guided her around the puddles.

They kicked mud off and mounted the steps to Rebecca's house. "And we didn't even need the umbrella." He stuck it in the stand and knocked on the door.

They heard Benny yell, "They're here!"

"You'd think I never came for supper." Toby grinned at the boy on his crutches and wearing the prosthetics Lars and Mr. Sam had made for him. "Hey, what is this, company manners?"

Benny's grin lit up the doorway. "Ma said." He stepped back very carefully and motioned them in.

Toby handed Benny his hat. "I'm sure glad you finally came back to town. I was beginning to think you'd moved to the farm."

"I like it out there a whole lot." He stopped and took a breath. "I'm glad to see you too, Miss Deborah."

Deborah caught back her giggle. "Thank you, Mr. Benny."

Puzzlement twisted his face, and then his laugh broke through. He reached for her hand and whispered loud enough to be heard in the kitchen. "Ma said."

She leaned closer. "You did a fine job as a greeter. I'm glad you're back home too. We have a little boy at the hospital with a broken leg learning to use crutches who needs a Benny visit."

"Oh good. Tomorrow?"

"I'm hoping they can come to the celebration. If they do, could you make sure he has a good time?"

"Sure. I could go to the hospital too."

"I know. Inga and Emmy taught him how to play checkers."

"Maybe we could have a checkers tournament."

"Leave it to you, Benny," Toby said. "You should have been on the planning committee."

Gerald stopped behind his son. "Come on in. Rebecca has something special to serve before supper." He rolled his eyes and looked at his brother. "I know, don't say anything."

"You go ahead. I need to change my shoes." Deborah sat on the chair by the door for that very purpose.

"I'll wait." Benny stood beside her and sniffed. "You smell good."

Toby gave Deborah a surprised look, as if he hadn't thought about how she might smell.

"Why, thank you, Benny." She slid her feet into her good leather shoes.

"Gerald, will you put Agnes up in the high chair?" Rebecca called.

In the kitchen, the table was all set, and Rebecca greeted Deborah and Toby like company. "Here, try these. Since we got rained out at the Soda Shoppe, I tried something new."

"I helped," Benny informed them.

"He sure did. And best of all, he kept the

little ones out from under my feet." The plate she passed around held sour cream and chocolate sandwich-style cookies with almond frosting in the middle, artfully placed in circles. "It's a bit muggy in here, but now that the rain has stopped, we can open the windows and the doors."

Toby took three of the cookies and popped them into his mouth, one after the other. "These are good. What are they?"

"Chocolate sandwiches. Glad you enjoy them."

"You sit by me," Benny said, motioning to Deborah's chair as Rebecca settled Mark and Swen into their chairs. Agnes banged her spoon on the high-chair tray. "Onkel Toby, you sit on Deborah's other side." He looked to Rebecca, who nodded. "I sure am hungry."

"Didn't they feed you out at the farm?" Toby asked.

"Ja, but that was yesterday, and we had to walk to town because the wagon would get stuck and I didn't have a soda forever."

"Can I help?" Deborah asked.

"We have it all under control." Rebecca and Gerald set the platter and bowls on the table.

Deborah paused in surprise when Toby pulled out her chair for her. What in the world?

Gerald did the same for Rebecca, and after sitting down, bowed his head. Benny helped two-year-old Mark fold his hands and nodded when Gerald asked him to say the blessing.

"Thank you for Onkel Toby and Deborah coming, thank you I am home, and thank you for the food." He paused and everyone joined in the amen, including one-year-old Agnes, who dropped her spoon and banged the tray with her hands.

"Will you be ready to start the fire tonight?" Gerald asked as he put a small portion of meat on three-year-old Swen's plate and then cut it.

"Oh, ja. Trygve and Samuel will pour the kerosene on the wood any time now so we get coals built up. We'll put the beef on at about four a.m. We took it out of Garrisons' cooler and set the spit, so we just have to set it in place on the frame. Mrs. Sam took over getting the pork ready. Her ovens are about the only ones big enough." Toby turned to Deborah. "You're not on duty tomorrow, are you?"

"No, but I start on nights next week."

"You need more help over there." Rebecca cut some potato and carrots into small pieces for Agnes and put the spoon back in her hand.

"She likes to use her fingers best," Benny said to Deborah.

"Babies do that."

When they finished the meal, including cake and ice cream, Toby patted his stomach. "I sure like your cooking better than mine."

Rebecca grinned at him. "You know you're welcome any time."

"'Cause you're our onkel." Benny turned to Deborah. "And when you and Onkel Toby . . ."

"Benny!" Rebecca slapped her hand on the table. "Pass your plate, now!"

Toby snorted. Deborah felt flames attack her cheeks. Would that she could clap her hand over Benny's mouth. What had Rebecca and Gerald said? Had Benny heard?

Deborah pushed back her chair. "I'll help you with the dishes." She picked up her plate and nudged Toby to hand her his. Would that she could cool off with a wet cloth to her face.

Toby failed to completely hide the laughter dancing in his eyes. "Thank you."

Gerald rose. "Come on, Toby, we men will adjourn to the parlor."

The younger kids were already chasing each other out of the room.

"We could play checkers." Benny slid off his chair and reached for his crutches, leaning against the back of his chair.

Toby ruffled his hair. "Good idea. You sure have gotten stronger on your new legs. The way you're growing, we might have to make new ones soon."

"Really?" Benny grinned at his pa, who shrugged and led the way to the parlor.

"Sorry about that." Rebecca shook her head as she and Deborah set the dirty dishes in the sudsy dishwater. "I think Benny talks more than ever, and we never know what will come out of his mouth."

"Thanks for your efforts."

"Gerald had a talk with him recently and said he would again. I know Toby likes you."

Like is not enough. I want . . .

CHAPTER 13

Johnny Solberg rang the church bells at noon.
Penny smiled at Ingeborg. "Now, that's
a fine way to get people to gather together."

"I agree." As one, they stepped back and
studied the tables already loaded with pans and
cast-iron pots of the food people had brought,
with more still arriving. "Funny how we always
fret a bit about what people will bring, and there
is always more than enough."

"That's because we all prayed too." Mary
Martha set two custard pies on the table. "I was
hoping there would be enough strawberries,
but this rain sure drove them into the dirt."

"Rebecca didn't have any fresh ones for
the ice cream. I gave her what I had left of the
canned." Ingeborg set her basket up on the
table, and Clara, baby sleeping in his sling, set

to slicing bread while Freda unwrapped the platter of sliced cheese.

The couple coming through the door caught Ingeborg's attention and she set out to meet them. "Dr. Deming, Vera, so good to see you. Welcome."

"Hello, Ingeborg. I told the men I'd help with the meat cutting, but I apologize for being late."

"I don't know why it is when you are ready to go out the door. . . ." Vera shook her head at her son.

"At our place it might be the cows got out or some crazy thing, so we all understand. He is growing so fast that I can see it from one week to the next." Ingeborg reached a finger toward Phillip, who grabbed it and pulled it toward his mouth. "Uh oh, teething time."

"See, he has two on top and four on the bottom, but this one is being stubborn." Vera rubbed her finger over one of the nubs in Phillip's gum.

Dr. Deming smiled at Ingeborg. "I'll leave you ladies and go do my duty." He headed for the rest of the menfolk.

"Set the basket on the dessert table," Vera called after her husband. She turned to Ingeborg. "This one can get in more trouble when I'm baking pies."

When Ingeborg reached for him, the baby leaned into her arms.

"He's heavy," Vera warned.

"Oh, but full of sweetness." Ingeborg kissed the little fist that reached for her face. "Little Phillip, you are a charmer. Come, let's join the others." She settled the baby on her hip and slipped her arm through Vera's. "We never see enough of you."

"Good to see you, Vera." Mary Martha set the Demings' pies out on the table. "These look so good. What kind are they?"

"One's buttermilk and the other rhubarb custard. Sophie gave me some rhubarb, and Dr. Deming loves rhubarb, so I kept one of those at home."

"I canned some of the rhubarb this year and made strawberry rhubarb jam," Mary Martha said. "How would you like to start cutting pies? And Ingeborg, I get Phillip next. You have to share."

Ingeborg handed him over. "He's sure strong. He'll be running before you know it."

"He can pull himself up on the crib rails now, and when I put him down, he crawls off to inspect everything around him. I have to keep the doors shut to whatever room I'm in, or he'd be up helping the carpenters." Vera picked up a knife. "Six pieces to a pie or eight?"

"Let's do six, and they can go back for seconds if there is enough."

Emmy and Inga were gathering the children to play a game away from the tables of food.

They had been cautioned that even though the sun was out, no one was to play outside and get muddy, at least not before dinner.

"I'm going to see how the men are coming with the meat." Ingeborg greeted new arrivals as she made her way to the tables outside, where four men were wielding knives at the side of beef.

Hjelmer stepped back to stretch his shoulders. "It's a shame we can't serve by the pit like we did last year."

Mr. Garrison handed him a newly sharpened knife. "I had my doubts we'd get this done at all." He waved Garth Wiste over. "You take over for Hjelmer for a minute, please; our banker isn't as strong as he thinks he is."

"Be right there." Garth tied one of the butcher aprons around his waist. "Hey, Mr. Belin, bring that over here, please."

"Da, coming."

"I can see you all have this under control." Ingeborg stepped closer to Hjelmer. "Have you seen Thorliff?"

"No." His tightened jaw said more than his mouth. "He'll show up, but I know he said the special edition would be here."

"I hope so. Thelma and Rolly came a bit ago."

Andrew joined them. "Do you want me to go get him?"

"No, I think not but takk."

Lord, please bring him here. Surely he wouldn't miss this. Concern heaped on concern, in spite of Ingeborg's efforts to leave it all in God's hands.

Answering greetings as she made her way back into the hubbub of the warehouse, she especially welcomed the newer folks in town, absolutely refusing to even think of them as the immigrants any longer. After all, when you counted time, they were no longer new. She admired a babe in arms, thanked others for coming, and oohed and aahed over the dishes many brought of specialties from their homeland. That was getting to be one of the best parts of community happenings: the variety of food.

"Please save me one of your marvelous blintzes," Ingeborg said to Marina Rasinov, who had become one of the quilters.

"I brought lots." She leaned closer. "You no worry. I bring some to quilting next time. I miss no quilting in summer."

"Me too."

They discussed what they were working on, and several others joined them. One woman smiled when they heard the musicians tuning up. "Dancing later?"

"Ja, for sure."

"How long until the beef is ready?" John Solberg asked Ingeborg.

"They will start bringing it in any time."

"Good. I'll tell Daniel. I'm glad he volunteered to be our announcer." They both knew that Thorliff, the usual announcer, had refused the position this year.

Ingeborg joined the women as they gathered the children together and pointed to the raised platform where Reverend Solberg and Daniel Jeffers were talking. Jonathan was sitting at the piano, with Joshua Landsverk and Johnny Solberg ready on guitars. The man who played the concertina joined them, as did a fiddler. The orchestra was growing. John clanged the iron triangle to announce the start of the celebration.

Daniel lifted the megaphone to his mouth and shouted for their attention. "Welcome, folks, to our Fourth of July celebration. We aren't outside like usual, but you all know why." Chuckles and bits of applause skittered over the crowd as they quieted. "Thank you. Thank you for coming." He waited again. "We'll start with the march of our flag." He motioned to the musicians gathered just behind him on the platform.

Jonathan hit the opening chords. As the oldest male of the original settlers, Lars carried the red, white, and blue flag, accompanied by the two oldest immigrant men. He joined in singing. "'My country, 'tis of thee . . .'"

Ingeborg blinked and sniffed as she sang, knowing others were doing the same. She and

Kaaren always had a hard time singing the powerful song.

"'. . . let freedom ring!'" The flag parade reached the front and turned to face the audience. When the final chords died away, applause rocked the room.

"Join me, please," Daniel called. "'Our Father which art in heaven . . .'"

They finished the prayer, and from the back of the room, a trumpet sounded with the call to assembly. People turned to stare, and applause broke out again when the man lowered the horn.

"Reverend Solberg will now lead us in our blessing." Daniel handed off the megaphone.

John shook his head with a smile as he refused the megaphone. He raised his hands and voice. "Ministers are taught to speak to crowds. Let us bow our heads in homage to our God." After a settling pause, he began. "Our Lord God, heavenly Father, maker and keeper of us all. We praise your mighty name as we gather here to celebrate the birth of our great nation. You have brought us from many corners of the earth to build our homes and lives together here in Blessing, North Dakota, a state in this union of states. We cannot say thank you enough for all you do for us and through us. Thank you today for this privilege of gathering together to celebrate this land, this day, these people. Bless this food and those who prepared such a feast. In your holy name, we all say . . ." He paused a heartbeat before they all said amen.

He looked out over the gathering. "You know how to do this. We'll form two lines at each of the two tables. Hopefully this will speed up the serving. Thank you for bringing your chairs and blankets for our indoor picnic. Ladies, guide us please." He motioned for the serving to begin and stepped down.

Penny's crew took over getting the lines started with the huge baking sheets of beef and pork set at the ends of the tables.

"Grandma, come with us." Emmy and Inga grabbed Ingeborg's hands and dragged her to one of the tables. "You're supposed to go first, with Onkel Lars and Tante Kaaren."

"No one told me."

"Sorry. Get in front of us." Lars motioned her to the front. "You're the oldest settler."

"We're the same age, so we'll go together, but I don't have my plate. Oh my word."

"Fret not." Kaaren raised her eyebrows. "I think they are trying to start some new traditions. Since Thorliff came over with you, he should be here, but I'll tell him about that later."

Inga held out a plate. "Here, Grandma. I'll get in line with Thelma and Rolly."

Mary Martha took it from her. "Good thing we have children and grandchildren to help us. Which do you want? Some of each?"

"Some of each, of course. But I was going to wait to see if we had enough."

"I know. But today you three are our honored dignitaries."

"Uff da." Ingeborg rolled her eyes and made her way down one side of the tables with Kaaren and Lars on the other. They took their full plates and followed Emmy to a table set up for them.

"You sit here, Grandma. I'll go get in line with Freda and Clara."

"Takk."

Kaaren sat next to her. "Next year we make sure our children join us, especially Thorliff." She shook her head and muttered, "The newspaper could have waited a few more hours. We have to find someone to help him now that Thomas Devlin and Anji are gone."

Ingeborg cut into her slab of beef. "Tender."

"Good thing, since you donated the steer." Lars looked content as he chewed. "Very good—maybe better than last year."

Kaaren leaned closer to be heard. "I'm thinking you and I need to corral Thorliff and remind him about how you were working yourself to death after Roald died. I'm sure he doesn't remember that year very well, since he was only seven."

Ingeborg chewed and nodded at the same time. "You know, that's not a bad idea. I was thinking John should talk to him."

"Ja, Thorliff needs his counsel too." Kaaren cocked her head. "Like mother, like son?"

Ingeborg smiled. "The only difference is I did not fly into a rage when someone suggested something to me. Poor Astrid is still heartsick over that fight. And he shows no sign of wanting to make amends."

"That's why my heart aches so for him. Maybe tomorrow afternoon after family dinner." Kaaren paused then mused, "Let's let the Holy Spirit tell us when."

"Ja, that's wise."

After everyone was served, Daniel picked up the megaphone again and the triangle clanged. "I know you are enjoying your meal, and from the looks of those meat trays, there is plenty for seconds. No one better go home hungry." The sound of people enjoying themselves picked up again.

Ingeborg turned her head at the tap on her shoulder. Marina Rasinov handed her a beautiful little painted plate with three blintzes on it. "For you."

"Oh, oh, you are so kind. You know, next December we should have a baking day where we all share our family recipes and make them. Wouldn't that be a wonderful day?"

Kaaren nodded. "We need to write that down so we don't forget, busy as we get."

"Not just for Christmas," Mrs. Rasinov said.

"But we all do the special things then." Ingeborg bit into the tender pastry. "Oh, these are so good."

Smiling, Mrs. Rasinov patted her shoulder and returned to her children.

"She took me seriously when I asked her to save me some." Ingeborg held out her treats. "Here, you and Lars can each have one too."

"You eat those. I'm going for pie." Lars pushed his chair back and headed for the dessert tables.

"You know Lars and pie." Kaaren wagged her head.

When the people were finished eating and cleaning up their utensils, Daniel took over the platform again. "Since our governor didn't brave our weather"—he paused for the snickers to pass—"we have a special treat for you. Mr. Andrei Belin has asked if he could say a few words." He motioned Mr. Belin forward and held the megaphone out to him.

"No, I can talk loud." Sweat running down his face, Mr. Belin looked over the crowd. "When we come to Blessing to work, we come to new home too. Here we have plenty of work, good place to live, food. We bring our families, school for our children, we learn to speak English. Thank you to Mrs. Jeffers." He motioned for her to stand up. "She make all our lives better." He bowed to her as the crowd applauded.

"We grow up in Novgorod, in Dalneye,

near the Volga River. Lots of swampy land, wet,
lots of mosquitoes." He grinned, "Like here,
eh? Mosquitoes. But in Dalneye, the tsar say
'sing,' we sing. He say 'join the army,' we join
the army. Here we get better jobs as we learn,
not like life before.

"I come a carpenter, now I am foreman.
My son, he will be what he wants to be. That
would never happen in Dalneye. That time,
that world, no longer home to us." He touched
his chest. "Here is my home now, and I thank
our God."

Mr. Belin mopped his forehead with a
handkerchief. Applause broke out in various
parts of the crowd and grew. Folks stood up and
continued clapping, cheers and whistles added
to it. He nodded and smiled, then motioned
them to be seated again. He said something
in his native Russian, then grinned and said,
"That means my heart is full. Thank you all."
He turned to Daniel, who grabbed his hand
and pumped it.

"You were better than the governor any
day, and more sincere, that's for sure." Daniel
clapped a hand on Mr. Belin's shoulder and
turned to the crowd. "Thank you, Andrei
Belin. You spoke so well. No wonder you make
such a good foreman for our company."

As the man stepped down, Daniel continued. "Because of the mud and because it looks
like it might start raining again, we are going

to clear space down the center of this room for the races, and then our musicians will return for some dancing."

He motioned for the people to begin clearing the center of the warehouse. Tables were hauled out and chairs pushed back to the walls. All the doors were opened to let a breeze blow through, and Reverend Solberg announced the first race, wheelbarrows in three age groups—children, big kids, and men.

Some of the women with babies and young children left, Thelma and Clara included. Ingeborg kept an eye out for Thorliff, thinking perhaps she should go look for him in case he had fallen asleep on the job again, but when Astrid came to sit beside her, she smiled at her daughter instead.

"I asked about Thorliff," Astrid said, "and he is adamant about bringing today's special edition of the paper over before the party is over. He was planning on having it here first thing, but . . ."

"I guess that is a plausible excuse." Ingeborg patted her daughter's hand. "Takk. Of course, someone might have told me, had I asked. Who's helping him?"

"I think Lemuel helps him with the printing and folding now and probably still the delivery too. At least that's what Daniel told me." Astrid patted back a yawn. "I hate to miss anything, but I think I'll be like Rolly and go home for a nap."

"Wise move. One thing we've always told young mothers, sleep when you can."

"Do you enjoy making me eat my own words?" The two shared a smile. "Mr. Belin sure did a fine job, didn't he? I think Amelia has been coaching him extra. He is working to overcome that Russian accent so everyone can understand him. I would love to hear some of his stories of the old country." Another yawn caught Astrid by surprise.

"Go home."

"Yes, Mor."

Applause broke out when Reverend Solberg announced the winners of another event and handed out the ribbons. Sometime later, the final event of the day was announced. Lars agreed to be a pole to be run around, as did Dr. Deming. The route for the three-legged race would be up, around the pole, and back, three times. The contestants had to be one school-age child with either an adult or an older youth. Some fathers paired up with one of their children, Samuel Knutson grabbed Emmy's hand, and Andrew snagged Inga, since his brother wasn't there to take his place.

"Come on, Hjelmer! Get your daughter," Daniel hollered. "Solberg, you and Johnny will make a great pair." When the group swelled to more than ten, Daniel announced, "We are going to run this in two groups, and the winners of each will run again. Now, don't knock the poles over, no intentional tripping, and all four feet have to be on the floor, meaning men, you cannot carry your partner. Now count off by two, and the ones will run first. Everyone give them lots of room. If you fall down you are out of the race."

Ingeborg, Kaaren, and Ellie looked at each other. "We'd better pray everyone runs safe," Kaaren said. "This is craziness."

"They're having a great time," Ellie assured the other two. "Although the ground would be softer to fall on if they didn't mind mud baths."

Eight pairs lined up, using a variety of straps, ropes, and scarves to tie their inside legs together. When everyone was ready, the triangle clanged and the three-leggers staggered, getting their balance. Samuel and Emmy wrapped their arms around each other's waists and counted as they ran. Andrew and Inga looked at each other and tore after the other two. Until Andrew slipped on the final lap and he and Inga dissolved into giggles.

"And the winners of group one are Samuel and Emmy, who understand what teamwork is. Now, group two, line up here. Is everybody tied together? Alright then, ready, set . . . go!"

And they were off. The winners of the second group were a father and son from Haarlem in Holland, although he called it Nederland. What an odd and wonderful mix of people Blessing was becoming.

"These two pairs will race for the win now. I have to tell you we have one delicious prize. The Soda Shoppe will give each of the winners free sodas or ice cream once a week for the summer. After this race, please line up for the ice cream part of our celebration." He pointed to the rear of the room, where the tables were now set with tubs of ice cream and someone waiting at each one with a dipper in hand.

The triangle rang and the race began. The two teams were even on lap one, then Samuel and Emmy led on lap two until two steps from the finish line, when the other team pulled ahead.

"And our winners are Pieter and Willem Noort. Pick up your certificates from Benny at the table, please. Thank you to all who were game to play today. We are grateful no one was hurt. While we are eating ice cream, the musicians will get ready for the dancing."

Laughter and folks yelling to each other to be heard above the others made the walls of the warehouse nearly bulge out. The ice cream lines went quickly, with everyone thanking Rebecca and Gerald and the other servers.

"Whew, what a day." Ingeborg fanned herself as she sat down. "It might be muddy and wet outside, but it doesn't hold a candle to this."

"This is one celebration that will be talked about for years to come. The folks of Blessing know how to celebrate the Fourth of July." John

Solberg stuffed the handkerchief he'd mopped his head with back in his pocket. "I'm getting too old for this."

"You gave it a valiant attempt." Mary Martha handed him a dish of vanilla ice cream. "Here, just the way you like it. They ran out of strawberry almost right away."

The musicians took their places and tuned their instruments while people of all ages slowly moved out to the cleared dancing area.

Daniel Jeffers stopped in front of Ingeborg. "Since my wife, your daughter, is home sleeping, may I have the honor of this first dance?"

"What about your mother?"

"She is dancing with Mr. Sam, and that is perfect."

"Then I am honored. I hope they do a slow one."

"They are."

As they waltzed around the room, Ingeborg noticed that Toby and Deborah were standing off to the side, talking. Deborah laughed. Toby laughed. Good! If only Thorliff were here. She caught her breath on a pang of memory. *Ah, dear Haakan, I'm sure you are dancing in heaven, but right now I wish you were back here with me.* She sniffed, and Daniel drew back to see her face.

"Are you all right?"

She nodded. "Ja, thank you. Haakan used to love to dance, especially a waltz."

"Ma said the grief never goes away entirely."

"Not entirely. And sometimes it grabs you, but the memories grow more gentle. I'm so grateful God seems to hide the bad ones and make the good ones stay."

As the dance ended, they applauded along with all the others, not just the dancers. Daniel leaned closer. "By the way, Thorliff is here now with the newspapers. They'll be given out at every door as people leave."

"Good. Thank you." *What a lovely way to end such an amazing day. Lord, about Thorliff . . .*

CHAPTER 14

Toby was glad the games were over. Gerald had casually suggested that maybe Toby and Deborah should enter the three-legged race. Gerald was becoming something of a pain. But dancing, now that was different, and there she was over there, talking to Sophie. A square dance was next. Perfect—lively but not too terribly intimate, like a waltz would be.

He walked across the room to Deborah. "May I have this dance?"

She nodded and took his hand. As they joined three other couples in a square, they waited for the caller to begin. At his nod, the musicians behind him swung into the introduction, starting everybody's feet to tapping.

"Bow to your corners, bow to your own . . .

allemande right . . . first couple balance, first couple swing . . ."

Deborah did look lovely today. Not that she didn't always, but he never bothered to tell her. Following the caller took concentration, especially since he'd not square danced since who knew when. They did a do-si-do and handed their partners off to the next dancer. He winked at Deborah when they met in the middle in a grand right and left. They were back together again, all the dancers with their starting partners, when the music hit the final bars and everyone clapped.

"Well, I see you've not forgotten how, either," he said.

Deborah smiled at him. "I've heard dancing is like horseback riding. You never forget."

"Good thing." Toby led her off the dance floor. "Thank you."

Samuel reached for Deborah's hand. "Come on, let's get in this next one."

"You didn't give me time to catch my breath," she protested.

"Well, breathe quick, because here we go."

They stood shoulder to shoulder and clasped hands in the proper way for a schottische, and after counting the beats to catch up, moved off around the circle with all the others.

Ah, there was Mercy, just standing, watching the dancers closely. Toby stepped in beside her. "Shall we?" He took her hands in his.

"I've never . . . I mean, I didn't . . . I've never done this. I'm just watching."

"Don't worry. Just listen to the music." The gentleman led, so Toby would lead. He more or less shoved her around, and she was obviously trying to do what the other women were doing. It wasn't perfect, but it worked, kind of.

At that tempo of music there was no time to do any polite conversing. He caught a glimpse of Deborah laughing at something with Samuel. Now twenty-one years old, the boy he had known for so long was fast becoming a real ladies' man.

Toby didn't have to work so hard now as he led Mercy in the final movement and walked her back to the side, where one of the construction crew claimed her next. There was certainly no lack of eligible men in Blessing. For some reason, that thought was a bit disturbing. Toby looked around to find Deborah. One of those single men was leading her back out onto the floor.

Folks came and went as chores needed doing and the food ran low. It seemed everyone was loath to let the day come to an end.

Toby and a face-mopping Hjelmer paused for a moment.

"I've not even had a chance to sit down." Hjelmer turned to his daughter, Linnea, who had grabbed his hand.

"Come on, Pa, before I have to spell Jonathan

at the piano. He wants to dance with his wife. Can you beat that?"

Toby saw that Deborah was free for a moment. He grabbed a glass of punch and made a beeline for her, handing her the glass just before someone else asked her. "Dance?"

She drained the glass, set it down on a table, and smiled at him. "Thank goodness, a slow one."

This one was a slow-paced four-beat, slower than a polka, and since the dancers held each other in a close embrace, the kind of intimate dance Toby had been avoiding. Except now he wouldn't avoid it for the world. He was really enjoying having her close.

"Before someone cuts in, may I walk you home afterward?" he asked.

She looked up at him from the corner of her eye. "I s'pose."

"Good. Remember that." True to his prediction, the dance wasn't even half over when someone tapped him on the shoulder and he released her to whirl away with someone else. Staring after her, Toby rubbed his chin.

When Jonathan announced the last dance and then nodded at Linnea at the piano, Toby reached for Deborah's hand before someone else did and settled into the final waltz. He sniffed her hair as he held her in his arms. "You smell good, like a spring day in May."

Her cheeks reddened. "Thank you." Then

she tipped her head to smile up at him. "I think this has been one of our best celebrations ever."

"I have to agree." As if they danced together all the time, the two turned and swayed with the music.

After the last chord, Jonathan announced from the dance floor, "That's all, folks. Thank you for coming and helping make this such a grand celebration. Oh, and the special edition of the paper is waiting for you at all the exits."

The room broke out in applause as folks chatted with those around them.

Toby had not let go of Deborah's hand. "Come on, let's get a glass of punch before they put everything away."

"Good idea."

"Deborah?"

She turned at the call. "I'll be there in a moment."

Shaking his head, he went to get punch for both of them just as Thorliff was thanking Penny for his drink.

Toby lifted a glass toward him. "Glad you got to come for at least part of this. You really missed a fine party."

"That special should have been out last night, but the press conked out on me. Again." Thorliff swigged his drink and shook his head. "I'm either going to have to order better equipment or just give it up." He rubbed his right arm, which was still weak from his scare with diphtheria last summer. "I must be getting old."

"You can't give it up. That newspaper has always been your life." Toby held out his cup to Penny for a refill. "And it's one of the good and forward-looking things about Blessing. I mean, you've gotten awards for your articles, and you'd be lost without it. And so would we."

"I suppose you're right, but since this construction company took over . . ."

"Once we get the deaf school addition done . . ."

Thorliff grimaced. "Then we need to build a high school and remodel the primary school. Sophie's been after us on the school, and I have a feeling the women are going to up the pressure."

"They have to find the money first."

"Oh, they will. You get that band of women working on something and they are indomitable, like being flattened by a runaway steam tractor."

Hjelmer joined them. "I'll be, you decided to grace us with your presence." He shrugged off Thorliff's glare and took the glass offered him. "That edition looks really good. You wrote that story on the second page?"

"One night when I couldn't sleep. Writing usually helps me relax." Thorliff rubbed his forehead. "Isn't it awfully muggy in here?"

"You ought to try dancing." Hjelmer

mopped his forehead. "What a day this has been."

"A grand day. I wouldn't have thought we could pull this off yesterday when it was still pouring." Toby checked to see where Deborah was. She *had* agreed to his walking her home, hadn't she?

"You and Trygve and crew were a hit with the pork and beef." Hjelmer clapped Toby on the shoulder. "If you didn't already have a job, you could hire out to do real Texas bar-bee-cues."

"Don't give him any ideas," Thorliff muttered. "He's got a two-story school addition to build."

Toby shrugged off a grin. "I'll man the crews, you do the paper work. Say, we wanted to paint that barn tomorrow, but I doubt it will be dry enough."

Hjelmer raised his hands, palms out. "Hold it, no business talk today, even this late. If we get caught, my wife will nail my hide to the back of the store. I promised her the men would not get together and talk either business or politics."

"Well, since you need your hide, I'll help with cleanup." Toby started for the tables but Daniel interrupted.

"You've been up all night cooking, or at least most of it, and completed your mission. Let some of the others do this."

Toby raised his hand. "I'm not arguing. Thanks." He stopped behind Deborah, who was looking around, hopefully for him. "May I carry your basket, miss?"

She gave him a side glance. "Do I know you? I mean, you look like Toby, but . . ."

He took her basket. "That's my kind of line. Maybe we can get home without wading in mud up to our knees." They both picked up their copies of the paper from the dwindling stack by the door and stepped outside.

An evening breeze blew from the west, heralding the sinking of the sun. They stopped and lifted their chins to enjoy the cooling gift. "That sure feels better than in that building," he said. "I thought the walls were going to melt."

"But what a grand time everyone had in spite of the humidity and being packed in that warehouse."

"Can you believe two hours ago it was raining again? Not sprinkling—raining. See, the mud puddles are running into ponds." They looked up Main Street. "Boardwalk or no, let's go the other way."

With him swinging her basket, they dodged the puddles as much as possible until they were beyond the houses, where they could cross to the verge of the road to Ingeborg's. The lots there were empty and the grass squished more than slopped. Instead of the fairly recent crossroad, they stayed to the grass.

"At least it's mud free."

"Barefoot would be better." Deborah grinned at him from under raised eyebrows.

Toby stopped. "Are you suggesting what I think you're suggesting?"

"Well, how long has it been since you've gone barefoot?"

"I have no idea. You can't work on a construction site in bare feet."

She leaned over, untied her soaking shoes, and kicked them off. "There, now I feel better." She lifted her skirt a little and they both stared at her feet, toes digging into the wet grass. "Oh my, but that feels good." She looked up at him and heaved a sigh. "It's probably not proper, but oh, dancing creates hot feet. I just couldn't bear to put my boots on again."

Toby rolled his lips together but in spite of himself, laughter burst through. He held out his arm for her to take, but she planted her hands on her hips and stared at his boots.

He looked down, then up at her. "No." It wasn't a convincing no; it wasn't an adamant refusal.

Deborah wrinkled her nose and tipped her head, then put a forefinger on her chin. "I'm surprised. I didn't know the great Toby Valders was such a chicken."

His eyes slitted. "Are you daring me?"

"If the shoe fits . . ."

He stared at her. Who was this woman? A

grin fought to break out. He shoved the basket into her hands. "Hold this!"

Getting out of men's shoes was not as easy as women's. He unlaced both boots, used his toes to force them off, and stood straight.

"Your stockings are soaked now."

"I know. Thank you for reminding me."

"You can hang on to me so you can take them off."

"I don't need to hang on to you." He pushed and pulled his socks off, almost landed on his rear, and stood up with a huff. "Happy now?"

"I wasn't unhappy." She pointed. "You might want to roll up your pant legs."

I can't believe this. Toby rolled his eyes, shook his head—and bent to the task. When he stood again, he noticed her nibbling her bottom lip. He'd not seen that in a long time.

"We could go splash in the mud puddles. I distinctly remember a rainy day when a certain boy deliberately splashed mud over some unsuspecting girls. And Pastor Solberg—"

"Set him to splitting wood." Toby shook his head. "I split a lot more wood in my school years than I want to remember." He turned to face her and sighed. "We did have fun, though, didn't we?"

"You did. Astrid reminded me that you teased me unmercifully and left me trying to hide my tears more than once." She turned and started west, her toes swishing through the wet grass.

He watched for a moment and then joined her, both of them swinging their shoes. *Should I apologize? Did I really hurt her feelings that much?* "Is it too late to say I'm sorry?"

"For the teasing, or. . . ?"

He almost couldn't hear her. Maybe he didn't want to hear her.

Grateful for a sudden noise behind them, he turned to see who was driving a wagon in this mire. The Knutsons waved to him and he waved back. Deborah turned and waved too.

Before she could face back toward home, Toby stopped her. "Deborah, look at that rainbow."

She turned back and her mouth dropped open. "A double one. I've never seen a double rainbow before, have you?"

"Once, when I was out drilling wells. It rained so hard we had to stop even though the sun was out. And there one was, but not as vivid as this."

"I wish I could paint it, but the paintings I've seen never can match the colors of real life. Not when it is like this." She shrugged. "Not that I've seen all that many paintings."

"I read somewhere that some people believe that someday they will be able to take photographs in color, and much faster than they do today. In Grand Forks one time, I saw a display of photographs by a man who travels all over the west, taking pictures of ranches and the people, cattle and horses and all kinds of wild animals too. The pictures were big, like this"— he spread his hands—"and you could see all the details."

She sighed. "All I've seen are ones in books and magazines. You can't tell much, they're so little."

"Haven't you been to Grand Forks?"

"Nope. When Pa found Manda and me, he brought us to Blessing and I've never left. I've thought of going to nursing school. Astrid said she'll pay for me to get training in administration."

By now they were nearly to the Solbergs' ranch house. Toby could hear laughing from out back.

She asked, "Do you want something cold to drink?"

The sun had started its speedy downhill slide, painting the sky and flat strokes of clouds many more shades than the rainbow possessed.

"Thanks, but I've got plenty of paper work to do before Monday. Do you have tomorrow off?"

"I go to work at three, so it sort of seems like it." She reached for the basket and set it on the house-length porch. "Thank you for walking me home and carrying this." Her grin didn't quite meet her eyes until she snorted. "And for not splashing me—this time."

"So, I'll see you in church then?"

He wasn't sure how to interpret the look she gave him. True, he didn't always make it to services, but right now he figured it might be a good idea. Should he kiss her good-bye? On the other hand . . .

She made the decision for him by saying "Good-bye, Toby," scooping up her basket, and going inside.

Swinging boots and socks, he headed for home. The pull to turn around and see if she might be watching him tickled. Instead, he whistled the tune of one of the dances.

His house seemed mighty empty when he stepped through the door. It was a good thing he had so much to do. It might keep him from thinking of how he'd felt around Deborah today.

CHAPTER 15

Ingeborg again thanked God that this church had good cross-ventilation. It was warm but not stuffy. The warehouse yesterday had been hot and stuffy and humid, but the people of Blessing sure didn't let that slow them down.

Reverend Solberg closed the worship service with the blessing, and conversations picked up instantly. Friendly. That's what this congregation was, just plain friendly.

As worshipers poured out the door, she and Kaaren swapped pleased smiles at what a great day the celebration had been.

"We'll see you all at the house," Ingeborg reminded the members of her family. She looked for Thorliff and saw him already halfway home, carrying his son. She'd call him as soon as she got home. Surely he wouldn't deprive Rolly of time with all the family.

Inga squeezed her hand. "Pa . . ." She stopped and sighed. "I . . . I wish . . ."

Ingeborg watched her granddaughter take a deep breath, wipe her nose with the back of her hand, and swipe it on the back of her dress. Ingeborg hadn't the heart to correct her, so she dug a hankie out of her pocket and placed it in Inga's hand with a smile.

"Other pas danced with their girls," Inga said.

It was all Ingeborg could do to keep from taking her hankie back and using it herself. *Lord, help us. Please help us.* She felt a hand on her shoulder and turned to see John Solberg nodding at her.

"He will come around. I don't know when, but he will."

"Sometimes I wonder."

"I know, but . . ." He turned to Inga. "For both of you, for all of us. Your daddy will come back—the real one, I mean." He nodded and they both followed his example. "We keep praying and thanking God for the wisdom He is giving us too."

"But Pa . . ." Inga sniffed again and wagged her head. "But . . . but . . ."

"We don't see the answers yet, but we asked, and we know God heard us, right?"

Emmy joined them, taking Inga's other

hand. All three of them nodded, the girls albeit a trifle hesitantly.

"Then now, we thank our Father for the answers He has sent on the way. Remember the verse we read this morning, Isaiah 65:24: 'Before they call, I will answer; and while they are yet speaking, I will hear'?"

"We will read that one again tonight, John, thank you." Ingeborg could see the questions building up in Inga's mind.

"I know this is a real stretch for us humans, but—" He smiled at Ingeborg. "I think I feel a sermon coming on, maybe several." He nodded as he spoke. "I better get this written down so I don't forget it. Thank you, girls, for helping me."

Inga stared at him. "But we didn't do nothing."

"You might think so, but this is one of those things we might not see, but they are there anyway," the pastor said. "Just try to believe it, all right?"

Ingeborg nodded. "We will. You know, John, you and your family are all welcome for dinner."

"Takk. I know. But first I've got some notes to write."

She swung the girls' hands, one on each side. "Have you seen Manny?"

Emmy tugged at her hand. "He went home with Clara and Freda. They need us."

"Let's walk fast, then." And so they did.

By the time everyone except Thorliff had arrived, the tables were groaning with food. At least Thelma had brought Rolly. Andrew raised his voice to be heard above the others—hopefully. He grinned at his mor and nodded to Manny, whose piercing *listen up* whistle was becoming legendary. "Let's have grace before the food is all cold."

"Or the flies get it," Freda muttered after throwing dishtowels over the meat.

"I Jesu navn, går vi til bords . . ." They all joined in the Norwegian grace, as the younger generation had taught their children too, including Rolly, who finished with his loud "'men." He also clapped as soon as Thelma released his hands, making the other kids giggle.

"Ah, the joys of toddlers." Kaaren's smile was as wide as Ingeborg's. "At the rate he's going, he'll be leading Thelma on a merry chase—and his father, when he wakes up."

Ingeborg grinned as she looked around. "I never get enough of seeing us all together like this."

"It's good to have Sophie and hers here for a change too. Come on, we'd better get ourselves some food before it's all gone. That baked rabbit that Freda put out is sure popular." Kaaren tugged on her arm. "Come on."

Ingeborg followed. "Did you know Benny

is trapping rabbits at Toby's and their own garden? Maybe with the ones Manny is getting here, we'll run out of rabbits."

"Ha." Kaaren handed Ingeborg a plate. "As if that could ever happen. The cat brought in a baby bunny this morning."

"Still alive?"

"No, she had killed it, at least."

After everyone had had dessert, the women set about clearing away the dishes, and the guys formed up teams for baseball.

"We didn't announce the women's party at church!" Sophie grumbled.

Kaaren scooped the few leftover turnips into a smaller bowl. "That's okay, we did last week. We probably should have set it at the church rather than at a house, but no matter. Several of the quilters have already asked if we will be sewing."

"Not this time. We'll be planning."

"Uh-oh, we're in for it this time. I see a wicked gleam in your eye." Kaaren and Ingeborg both gave mock shudders.

Sophie added, "Besides, you know everyone will bring handwork, no matter what we say."

Ingeborg picked up the platter that had held the rabbit. "Times like this—well, other times too, but . . ." She gave a slight shake of her head as she continued, "I know you might not believe it, but I really miss Hildegunn." She reached for Rolly, who was rubbing his eyes, and smiled at Thelma. "You sit down for a change. In fact, let's all sit down."

She led the way to the chairs. With Rolly settled in her lap and sucking his finger, Ingeborg kissed the top of his head.

"Ja, I sure wonder where she and Anner are and why we've never heard from them." Kaaren sipped from her glass of swizzle.

Thelma stared at her glass. "Me too."

Out in the field, Lars called, "Play ball." The smaller children played around the women's feet. The middle children were down at the barn, where Manny had saddled Joker before heading for the ball game.

Only Thorliff's presence was missing from this perfect July day.

Fifteen guests and more are still arriving! Sophie marveled. This was turning into some party. After discussing the plan after church on Sunday, the women had decided to have the party at Sophie's house instead of Ingeborg's. It was more convenient for the ladies who worked or lived in town. Penny had even closed her store, and Mrs. Garrison had left her husband alone at the grocery store.

Women were setting their food offerings on the table in the house, where Penny had said the food would be served to circumvent the flies, and then they picked up either a cool glass or a cup of coffee before joining the others outside. Those with toddlers or babies gave them to the young girls, who were helping mind the little ones next door.

"Isn't this fun?" Sophie squealed as her sister came up the walk. She gave Grace a hug. She was in her element, playing hostess to all these women.

She patted Grace on her well-disguised mound. "So glad you are having an easy time. You are blooming."

Grace smiled. "Thank you. Me too."

Ingeborg and Kaaren had walked there together and were now sharing hosting duties with Sophie, making sure they welcomed some of the more recent arrivals.

When it appeared everyone had arrived, Ingeborg stood on the back porch and clapped her hands. "Welcome, ladies, to our first ever Women of Blessing Party. After Mary Martha says grace, each of you will serve yourself in the dining room and bring your plate back out here. I have a request: Would all of you please sit with someone you don't know well when you have your food? More chairs are on the way." She nodded to Mary Martha, who stood beside her with a smile as big as Ingeborg's.

"Thank you all for coming today. Let's bow our heads, please." After a moment's pause, Mary Martha began. "Heavenly Father, thank you for arranging for us all to be together. Thank you for the food we have, for the friendships always growing deeper, and for the ideas you will give us today. We praise you and thank you. Amen." She spread her arms wide. "Please, come and help yourselves."

Reverend Solberg and Johnny brought in more chairs from the church, then left with waves to Sophie.

Up on the porch, Sophie whispered to Ingeborg, "I can't believe how much food the ladies brought. I had Mrs. Sam and Lily Mae fix some extra food too, just to make sure we had enough." She shrugged and grinned. "Oh well. I guess we'll have plenty for everyone to take home for supper."

"Takk and thank you and danke and any other way you can say it."

Daniel's mother, Amelia, joined them. "Isn't this absolutely delightful?" She leaned closer to Ingeborg. "Several of these women have been learning English from me."

They joined the line of laughing and chattering women.

When everyone was seated, Ingeborg whispered to Sophie, "Eighteen ladies are here, and several have apologized for someone else who wanted to come but couldn't. This is so absolutely incredible."

"Remember to speak slowly so the newer immigrants can follow you," Amelia cautioned.

"I will, but if I get carried away, you flag me."

When all the plates were back in the house, and the glasses and cups refilled, Ingeborg stood on the porch so everyone could see her. "May I have your attention, ladies?" Slowly the conversations ebbed and all of them looked at her. "Thank you. Thank you so much. I am absolutely delighted so many could come. I know it wasn't easy for some of you, but one thing I think we agree on, we are grateful to be living in Blessing and"—she grinned at Amelia, who'd made a slow-down motion with her hands—"want to help make it better."

Amelia nodded.

"While we all know of things that need to be done, our main focus today is to talk about our school. We all know the building we have is getting too crowded for our children to all attend and have a place to sit, books to study, and teachers to teach them. We need to build an addition for the primary school, and we need to build a high school as well. As always, when we want something like this, we have to figure out a way to pay for it."

Nods and smiles and a smattering of replies swept the group.

"We women know that when you add up a lot of little things, you can have something big, right?" Again nods and titters. Someone was explaining to her neighbor what was said. "So we are going to decide on lots of little things and maybe some bigger ones too."

Sophie smiled and nodded. Ingeborg was choosing her words carefully and she had indeed slowed down so the newer immigrants could understand. Ingeborg smiled at Amelia, who was grinning like a little girl with a new hair bow and a red lollipop.

"We need to start with ideas, so raise your hand when you want to offer one. Amelia will write them all down so we don't forget."

Amelia held up one of the school tablets and a pencil.

"Anyone?"

"Well, one thing we talked about was a box social," Kaaren said.

"I have a feeling not everyone knows what that is," Sophie said. "Amelia, do you want to explain?"

She stood up. "A box social is a party where the women and girls"—she swept her hand to include them all—"make a box or basket pretty, if they can, and make their best foods to put in the box and bring it to the party. But they don't ever say which is theirs. The men bid on them, like an auction, and they are surprised to see who they are sharing supper with." She paused and glanced around. "Any questions?"

One woman raised her hand. "No understand."

"Mrs. Dalnoski, will you please explain to her what I said?" While that happened, Amelia looked to Ingeborg. "We should have brought a sample."

"Don't worry, we'll all get it straight."

Amelia waited a bit longer and then raised her hands. "Let's continue. The party is for the grown-ups only, not small children. Then all the money that is bid for the boxes goes into our Blessing schools fund. After everyone finishes eating, we have a dance."

"Thank you, Amelia," Ingeborg said. "Now we need some more ideas."

Heads nodded while the women waited for someone else to speak. One woman raised her hand. "We bring good foods, uh"—she wrinkled her forehead to get the right word—"cookies and special things to buy, like pie and—"

Someone added, "Blini! Must have blini."

"Thank you. A fine idea," Ingeborg said. "A bake sale."

"Sell a quilt."

"Auction it? Bid like for a box social?"

Nods and *ja*s and other words of agreement came from the group.

"Take collection at meeting?"

"I work for someone and give money."

"Me too."

The ladies were really into it now. More suggestions poured forth.

Finally, when the ideas seemed to be exhausted, Ingeborg looked down at Amelia. "Please read the list again for us."

Amelia read off the list. "If you have more ideas later, please bring them to me. Thank you."

"Great ideas. Now we have a couple of announcements."

Rebecca raised her hand and stood. "We are thinking about opening a bakery. Mrs. Garrison would sell the baked goods at her store, and if this works well, we will open a special shop, maybe add floor space to my ice cream shop. So we are looking for someone who loves to bake." She sat down.

Sophie added, "We will also need someone to take trays of these baked foods to the train when it stops in Blessing. And perhaps we would open a place at the train station, so the people riding the train can buy them. If this sounds like a good idea to one of you, let me or Rebecca know. We will talk about this a lot more, but we know it will not happen right away." She looked to Ingeborg.

"I know of people who want someone to work for them," Ingeborg told the group. "Both men and women are needed. For housework, farm and field work, and cooking."

Kaaren stood up beside her. "When we open the new part of the deaf school, we will need more help too. A lot of help. So if you have friends or relatives who want to come to America, please talk with me."

Ingeborg stared at Kaaren. "What a grand idea. We need to bring this up with the men."

Sophie bobbed her head. "We'd need more housing . . . more of everything. How come we never thought of asking everyone before? But then, perhaps they've already been doing so and just never mentioned it to us." She raised her voice. "Anyone else?" She paused. "Thank you all for coming."

"We meet again, ja?" one woman asked eagerly.

"Uh . . ." Sophie shrugged. "I . . . uh, guess we could do that. When summer is over, we will be making quilts and sewing for others like we did before summer. Thank you for asking. Please pick up the dishes you brought, and I thank you again for coming."

One woman clapped and the others joined her. Pretty soon every one of them was standing and clapping.

Sophie made sure she said good-bye to everyone as they left. When it was only she and Grace, her mother, Tante Ingeborg, and Amelia remaining, they stared at each other. "I think they talked and gave their ideas so well today because no men were here."

"That's why I have separate classes for men and women," Amelia said. "So many of them are used to never saying anything when their husband is with them. They usually let him do all the talking. That's the tradition where they come from, and old traditions die hard."

"Or live forever," Sophie muttered, making the others laugh.

"Do you know what we need here the most?" Ingeborg asked.

"What, besides buildings and teachers and—"

"We need to find someone who can help Thorliff with the newspaper."

"Of course!" Sophie wasn't too sure, though. "Will he accept anyone's help?"

"I have no idea, but we will pray that he will."

CHAPTER 16

Toby, Manny, Samuel, and Lars paused to look out over the fields on the edge of town. The sun was just starting to peek above the horizon.

Lars grimaced. "Thanks to the rain and wind flattening the hay, we're going to have to postpone haying. It's too wet yet. Besides, some of it might perk up and stand upright again; easier mowing."

"We'll just have to lower the cutting bar to pick it up." Samuel glanced at his pa.

Lars was staring off across the fields. "At least the wind blew it down in one direction."

"So we get less hay?" Manny asked.

"Most likely. Even lowered, the cutting bar will miss some," Toby explained. He had to admire Manny, who was always asking questions, always eager to learn. "But we have to get it off the fields for the second crop to grow."

"If we get a second cutting." Samuel kicked a clod of dirt. "It all depends on the weather."

"In farming everything depends on the weather," Manny muttered.

"Well, let's go check over the machinery," Lars said.

"How come you don't use the steam tractor for haying?" Manny asked.

"Knocks down too much hay, but we'll use all three mowers with teams of three."

"Are you gonna shoe the horses first?"

"Usually not until time for harvest, when it's drier. Unless we see they need it." Lars nodded. "Good thinking. Get this done and you boys might want to go fishing."

"The little kids too?" Manny asked.

"Of course."

"Fish fry tonight!" Manny's grin near to split his face. "C'mon, Sam, let's get the machinery cleaned up quick." And off they went.

Sure, Toby was still young, but he envied the way those boys slammed into everything. He wasn't slowing up yet, but he didn't slam into work as much.

The men gathered in Thorliff's office at six o'clock.

Thorliff motioned them all to the coffee

pot. "Coffee's hot. Thelma said she'll bring breakfast out soon."

Daniel turned and clapped Trygve on the shoulder. "Glad you joined us." Since this was the first real meeting since Trygve and Joshua were promoted from foremen to supervisors, the group had grown.

Toby laid the plans he'd been studying on the table and poured his coffee. "Thanks."

"Morning sure came fast." Joshua Landsverk joined Toby at the coffee pot. "I swung by the Hegdahl farm. That barn is dry enough to paint today if we start on the south side, but that wind knocked down some of the scaffolding."

"You'll have five men. Is that enough?" Toby asked.

Joshua nodded. "Should be. Guess we could use one or two more, one for each crew. Got that kid of Hegdahl's too. He might be young, but he's sure a good worker. Maybe his younger brother can be the helper. He's a good worker too. They probably won't be haying like they figured."

"Probably not." Toby turned to Mr. Belin. "How's the finish work coming on Deming's house?"

"Slow. Cabinets not arrive yet in kitchen. Hope for today but . . ." He shook his head. "Said same last week. Doors all hung."

"Bathroom done?"

"Da, cabinet and mirror. Plumbing. Upstairs done, mostly. Finish needed on stairs."

"Takk." Thorliff joined them around the coffee pot. "So we need more finish men, don't we?"

"It would help."

Thorliff shook his head. "It's a shame Devlin left."

"Don't I know it. His work was perfection. I'll put out the word." Toby looked at Mr. Belin. "Can you think of any men on the other crews who could do finishing work?"

"Hm. Da, maybe." Mr. Belin grinned. "See? This I try to say on four of July. Got some boys, beautiful work. They do good work, go up in the world. I see."

Toby bobbed his head as he refilled his coffee mug. "We don't have to work on housing so much if we make better use of the people we have. Thank you, Mr. Belin."

Lars asked, "What about that Tony kid? Tonio Hastings."

"He has one more year of school, but he likes working with wood and makes sure the cuts are perfect. He was in Devlin's class last year."

"Is his wood better than his steel?" Daniel asked. "He did well in machining class too. Hate to lose him." He swirled his coffee. "He's a good boy."

"At least for the summer. Good thing we have some young fellas coming up."

"That Manny . . . Haakan started him on carving, and he's been going at it ever since. He has a real love of wood. He can work with us until the hay is dried and ready to haul."

Hjelmer finally joined them, apologizing for being late when he came through the door.

Daniel poured a cup for Hjelmer. "I've got a shipment to have ready for today's eastbound."

Thelma entered the open door carrying a tray piled high with big, puffy rolls.

"Let's get seated." Thorliff tapped the table. "Bring that tray over here and we can pass it around."

From the big patch pockets in her apron she pulled spoons and jars of jam and honey and set them on the table.

"Takk, Thelma." Thorliff stuck a spoon in the honey and spread it across a roll.

Toby reached for a roll. "By the way, your special edition looked real good."

"Takk. Now that you've divided up the young blood . . ."

"Just we need more."

After everyone gave their reports, Thorliff pointed to the school schematics nailed to the wall. "We lay it out today and tomorrow, and we'll be ready to dig out the basement. That building has to be weathered in before winter gets here. To make that deadline, we need to pour walls by the end of the week." He pointed to the calendar with numbers circled. "Those *are* the deadlines. I will do my best to make sure all the materials are here when we need them." He shook his head. "Now if only our suppliers were as committed to this as we are."

"I can give you a hand with that," Hjelmer suggested. "Thanks to Mr. Gould, all our funds are in place. That's good leverage. Tell 'em we'll pay cash the moment the order arrives and take off a percentage for every day it's late."

"Good idea! I'll give you the contracts. Next item." Thorliff wagged his head and snorted. "Talk about a first. Jonathan said that since haying is postponed, he'd like to be on a crew."

"We'll get him a shovel."

Thorliff slapped his palms on the table. "Anything else?"

"My painters should be available to dig in two days, weather permitting," Toby said.

"Good. Hjelmer, come back, please, after you open the bank."

As the men were leaving the room, Daniel stopped beside Thorliff. "Things are slow right now at the flour mill. Did you mention this to Garth?"

Thorliff stared at him. "Thanks. Didn't think of that." He scrubbed his forehead and smoothed his hair back. "Do you want to talk with him?"

"Of course. You know, something tells me you can't work all day and all night too."

"I know, but there's so much to do."

"Maybe you need to delegate more."

"Easy to say. Like I just did? And to whom?" He swigged his coffee. "Cold. Blech!"

"Perhaps Jonathan would be better helping you. This is as much a part of the building as being out there digging and hammering."

"Better here than out on a mowing machine, but Lars needs him too. They've got both places to cut. Face it, Jonathan wants to farm—that's what he went to college for. He's in that barn milking both morning and evening. "

As Toby left, he almost added to what Daniel had said. Thorliff seemed almost too tired to think anymore. Would there be a good time to just suggest he stick to the printing and let Jonathan or someone else help with the construction? Sure, Jonathan loved to farm, but the construction work was necessary immediately.

He hitched up his wagon, picked up more painting supplies, and met his crew of painters at the boardinghouse. Driving this rickety old wagon was a war, fighting mud all the way to the barn job. Hegdahl and his two boys met them as Toby finally halted the steaming team.

"We got the scaffolding back up," Hegdahl told him. "My son will paint too."

"Good. Anybody big enough to wield a brush."

The farmer whistled, and a younger boy

came running from weeding the garden, his face beaming. Obviously, painting was more fun than weeding. Toby would agree.

"Paint fast, but do a good job," Toby told him as he climbed down from the wagon. "We don't have time to redo anything." While the others unloaded the supplies, he walked around the building, checking the roof and all the siding. Back where they were stirring paint cans, he spoke to his lead man. "That corner trim isn't finished. Get the others painting and you take care of that, please."

The man nodded. "I do."

"And remember, we have to get it right the first time because we don't have time to do it twice. Understand?"

"Ja!"

Toby climbed back in the wagon. Now to Deming's house. He clucked the team to a jog, doing his best to avoid the ruts and mud puddles. All that rain had left them the gift of Red River mud that stuck to everything. Not like walking in the grass, and barefoot no less. He smiled at the memory.

He swung the team around an especially large puddle. The wheels bogged down, and the horses leaned into their collars. But when one of them slipped and went down on his knees, Toby blew out his frustration and climbed down from the wagon. He'd need more horses and men to dig it out. He got a stick from under the seat and moved to the team, both of whom were blowing.

"I should have known better than drive out here today." He patted the horse's near shoulder and leaned over to scrape mud from its leg, then scraped out the hoof. He felt the horse blow on his back. "Yeah, I know, you did your best." He unhooked the team, mud crusted to his knees by the time he was done. Leading them to the grassy verge, he cleaned them up a little more and then swung aboard one and led the other. Maybe Hegdahl could pull out the wagon, or maybe they'd just leave it there. No, bad idea. Once the mud dried, it would be even harder to dig it out. "Come on, boys, let's go."

Lord, I hope the rest of the day goes better than this.

Riding sure beat walking. He stopped at the door to the stables and swung off. "You'd better wash them down—legs anyway," he told the man at the stable.

"Where's the wagon?"

"South of town on the road to Hegdahl's place. Maybe a four-up could pull it out. I had to get that paint out there."

He ignored the grumbling groom and strode out to Deming's house. Another two-story, but at least the dentist had not wanted as much gingerbread trim on it as some of the others. Toby stepped past the piles of milled walnut they'd had shipped in specifically and stored covered by tarps on the porch.

Dr. Deming met him at the door. He glanced down at Toby's muddy legs. "Uh-oh. Another slowdown?"

"You could call it that. What can I do for you today?"

"Any idea when we can move in? We're so tired of that apartment and someone else needs it. I just checked here, and the upstairs is pretty much ready. We could bring our belongings here. We'd stay out of the men's way. After all, we're at the office much of the time."

"You can't cook here, and the bathroom's not all done."

"I know, but the toilet works, and we'll eat at the boardinghouse." He paused. "We were supposed to be able to move in two weeks ago. We have crates of furniture stacked up at the train station. Come on, Toby, I hate to beg."

"Let me talk to Mr. Belin and see what he says; he's in charge here."

Dr. Deming frowned. "I thought you were running this."

Toby brushed him off and made his way to the kitchen, where he could hear men talking.

"Nyet!" Mr. Belin was gesticulating, arms waving wildly.

The man he was talking to—or yelling at—nodded. "Ja, we fix that." His accent made him hard to understand too. The man picked up his plane and went back to a plank of walnut mounted on the sawhorses.

Somewhere in Mr. Belin's tirade, Toby thought he heard something close to *Get it right the first time*. When Mr. Belin got angry, his English went out the window. Obviously they were all harping on that. When it came down to it, there was no way to rush finish carpentry like this. One of the other men was finishing with a fine sanding block.

Toby motioned Mr. Belin into the other room and lowered his voice. "The Demings want to move into the upstairs. What do you think?"

"Dust all over, in air. Not good."

"I know. But they could use the big bedroom. Store some crates in the others."

"Wallpaper not up." Mr. Belin shook his head. "Not good."

"Do you have the wallpaper?"

"Nyet."

Toby bit back an expletive. He had resolved to no longer say even the mildest of swear words, but this morning was certainly testing that. "Do you have paper hangers?"

"Da. Women can do that. My wife, two others. They do that as soon as paper get here."

"All right. I'll look into that and tell Dr. Deming. Hopefully they can move into that room by the end of the week."

Shoulders slumping, Mr. Belin nodded. "Not good, but da."

Toby made his way back to the empty construction office and looked around for Thorliff. They needed someone in the office all the time now. Surely one of the women or older girls could do that. After all, this wasn't writing or layout for the newspaper. He scribbled a note for Thorliff about the wallpaper.

Thelma met him at the door. "Dinner is ready. You need to eat."

"Thank you. Thelma, did anyone ever tell you you're a lifesaver?"

"Pshaw." She grinned. "Oh, Thorliff is on the porch." She was headed back to the kitchen before he could answer.

"Ah, she snagged you too?" Thorliff greeted him as he mounted the steps to the back porch that stretched the length of the house. Looking down at Toby's legs, Thorliff almost kept a straight face. "I see you had some other jobs this morning?"

Toby took one of the chairs at the round table. "The wagon is half buried back from Hegdahl's. I don't know how I made it out there loaded. There's no wallpaper at Chet's and—"

"Just eat before Thelma comes to check on us." Thorliff passed a bowl of potato soup and reached for the platter of sandwiches. "Coffee or . . ." He motioned to the pitcher.

"I thought I'd get something at the board-inghouse later, but this helps a lot." Toby could hear Rolly and Thelma in the house as he ate half a sandwich in one bite. Now that he thought about it, he'd only had bread and cheese for breakfast at home and the rolls Thelma had brought to the meeting. He swallowed. "So we're ready to lay out the new school this after-noon?" At Thorliff's nod, he continued. "Me and who else?"

"You and me with the transit, Trygve and Samuel pounding stakes and stringing. Trygve has men ready to start digging in the morning, so we have to get this right the first time."

Toby nodded and chewed. *If I hear that one more time today I might have to . . .* "Where is all the gear?"

"Behind the office. Wheelbarrows included. Decided not to use the wagon today."

After they ate, Trygve and Samuel met them halfway to the deaf school site. "We need a construction shack out here so we don't have to haul everything around like this."

"I know, one more thing."

"How about borrowing the cook wagon we use at harvesting?" Samuel suggested.

"Now, why didn't I think of that?" Thor-liff snorted. "Good idea. See if you can have it here tomorrow."

"Or tonight. It's at Ingeborg's, but I'm sure Pa will bring it over."

"Tell him if any of the deaf boys want work, they can help with the digging tomorrow."

They stopped at the site for the new school, already graded and free of sod.

"It looks mighty big, doesn't it?"

"Ja." Toby shook his head. "And this needs to be weathered in before winter. Pastor Solberg would say we need a miracle. Or ten. How will we ever get this done in time?"

"We'll pray for a late fall, for starters." Trygve handed the transit to Toby. "Let's go."

CHAPTER 17

Grandma, we can go fishing!"
She heard Manny yelling before his boots hit the steps. She met him at the door. "What on earth—"

"We can't start mowing the hay 'cause it's too wet and laying flat and Lars said we could go fishing." His words ran together in his excitement. "And I ain't gone fishing in forever." He almost paused. "Haven't. Can we go? I'll telephone Carl, 'cause I know he'll want to go. Where's Emmy and Inga?"

"Down at the barn with the new calf."

"Can we go, huh, please?"

She raised her hands, palms out. "Give me a minute to think."

She looked to Freda, who only shrugged. "A fish fry sounds awful good."

"See?" The look on his face made Ingeborg chuckle.

"I have a lot to do, you know."

"That's all right. I'll help when we get back. We have to hurry, it's almost noon." Manny shifted from one foot to the other.

"You telephone and see if Carl can come. It's a shame Benny isn't out here; well, next time we'll plan ahead so he can go too. Freda, please pack our dinner in a basket, and why don't you and Clara come too? We can have a party."

"Uff da, I never have liked fishing much." Freda reached up on the shelf for the big basket. "Clara, you can go, and I'll take care of Martin here."

Clara shook her head no.

Ingeborg stopped and looked at her. "Martin will be fine here, you know. You can leave him for a while."

Clara signed "Do I have to?"

"Well, of course you don't have to. You just don't like catching fish?" Ingeborg heard Manny babbling excitedly on the phone.

Clara made a face.

Freda and Ingeborg exchanged looks but went about packing the food and filling the jug they used for picnics and anywhere they needed cold drinks.

"He's coming. I think he's running. I'll go down and get some worms." Out the door Manny charged.

Ingeborg followed him, catching the screen door before it slammed. "Tell the girls to come up." They probably heard her clear to the barn.

"How come?" Inga asked when they hit the porch only seconds later, it seemed.

"Lars said so." Ingeborg made a funny face. "I guess they can't mow and he figured Manny . . . Just get the fishing poles. The basket is almost ready."

Within minutes, they were heading for the barn, where they saw six-year-old Carl running on the path from his house, shrieking, "Going fishing!"

Inga took her grandma's hand. "It's a good thing they got those wild dogs." She looked up. "They sure scared us. We never ran so fast."

Carl slid to a stop and checked the worm bucket. "Do we need a few more?" Manny turned over another forkful of aged manure, and Carl dug out the worms. "Good. There's plenty."

Emmy and Inga swung the basket between them and they headed down the path, fishing poles in their free hands, and Ingeborg carrying the jug by its handle and marveling at the change in her day. This most certainly had not been on her list of things to do this glorious day.

As if to make up for the time before when she had to throw part of their catch at the attacking dogs, today the fish seemed to bite practically before the worms hit the water. The fisherfolk ate their dinner while snagging fish. Sometime later, after the catch had swelled to three stakes in the shady water, Manny snagged one that had him digging in his heels to keep from being dragged down the bank.

"Hang on, Manny." Ingeborg handed Carl her pole and grabbed the back of Manny's shirt. "Do you think you have a dead tree?"

"Huh-uh. Whatever it is, it's alive."

Up to his knees in the water, he fought with the fish on the end of his line, Ingeborg right behind him, hanging on.

Carl looked up at Ingeborg. "Maybe he caught a big turtle."

"Carl, your bobber!" Inga yelled, earning a scolding look from her cousin. Fishing was supposed to be a quiet event.

Today was anything but quiet. The girls shrieked when a black head with barbels broke the surface.

"It's a big ol' catfish," Manny breathed. "Biggest one I ever saw, and we had big catfish in Kentucky."

"Ew, ugly." Inga made a face. "Did you ever see anything like that, Grandma?"

"Not that big. They usually head for the deepest water and hide in the mud."

Bit by bit, Manny eased back, keeping the line taut. "Carl, find something to club this thing."

Back on the bank, her skirt weighted with muddy water, Ingeborg wagged her head. "Son, you are some fisherman." Oh, if Haakan were here, he would be so proud of Manny. Haakan had caught plenty of catfish through the years, but none this big.

Manny dragged the thrashing, slimy black fish up on the bank. It flopped around clumsily.

"Don't touch him, Carl. That monster is dangerous. My grandpappy warned us." Manny took the knotted stick Carl handed him and whacked the fish's head, once, twice, three times before he pulled it farther up the bank. When the fish finally lay still, he sucked in a huge breath. "Did it. Thought for sure I'd lose it."

"How are we getting it home?" Inga asked, looking up at Ingeborg. "Drag it?"

Manny used his knife to cut the fishing line a ways back from the monster's mouth. "I'm not puttin' my fingers near it. Might not be all dead yet. We shoulda brought a chain or something."

Ingeborg looked over at the four stakes that held the other fish in the water to keep them cool and alive. "We can fish a little longer or head home."

Carl checked the worm bucket. "We still got some more. Can we stay a while?"

Ingeborg looked down at Patches, who sniffed the fish and looked up at her. "I know, fella. It's a shame you can't go home and get us some help." She passed the jug around; she was thirsty, so she figured the others were too. What to do?

"I know." Emmy jerked on her line and another fish whizzed by their heads. "When we're done fishing, I'll run home and get help." She looked at Manny. "Are the chains in the machine shed?"

"Oh!" Inga pulled in her line. "Lost one." She headed for the worm pail and dug out a wriggler to rebait her hook. "Grandma, you got one!"

Ingeborg's line went slack.

"Grandma, you keep forgetting to pay attention." Carl made it sound like a cardinal sin.

Ingeborg rolled her eyes at her eldest grandson. "Ja, Carl. Takk." She rebaited her hook, still trying to keep from laughing. Carl took his fishing so seriously. Had Andrew been like that?

Sometime later, when the fish had slowed their biting and the mosquitoes had increased their buzzing and biting, Emmy ran home for a chain and returned with it looped over one arm and a bigger knife in a sheath.

Manny took the knife, nodding. "Good." After chopping a bigger branch, he chained the catfish to it and looked to Emmy. "Can you help me carry this thing? You're the tallest."

They made two trips up the bank and

staggered across the field toward home. The cows had started bellowing that it was time to milk them.

Andrew broke into a run when he saw them. "What in the world?" His mouth dropped open and he skidded to a stop. He stared at the monster fish, then at his mother and the others, all the while shaking his head. "You've got more fishing stories than anyone I know." He walked around them. "That has to be the biggest cat ever dragged from the Red." He stared at the rest of their catch, the muddy clothes that had dried, and at his son, trying not to snicker like the others.

"Manny caught it."

"And you, Mor?"

"I had to keep him from being dragged down the river. You ought to come fishing with us sometime. I think next time we'll take the wagon or a wheelbarrow."

Carl held up the worm bucket. "Empty."

Ingeborg said, "I'd say we're having fish tonight."

"Ja, I'll tell Ellie to bring the other kids. Do you want some help cutting that thing up?"

"No thanks, Freda and Clara can handle it." Ingeborg pointed to her skirt. "I think I might change clothes." The look on Andrew's face was about all she could handle. She and the children hauled their bounty to the cleaning bench.

"I wish Haakan could see our cat." Manny looked to Ingeborg, who rolled her lips and sniffed.

"Ja, me too. But I think he has."

"I hope you're right. You want me to stay and help clean the fish?"

Freda joined them and could hardly stop shaking her head. "Clara is sharpening some knives. Let's lift it up on the bench." Even with four of them scaling and gutting the fish, and Carl and Inga hauling fresh water, no matter how good they were, supper would be late.

When Ellie arrived, she set her baby basket on the porch and started the fish frying. "I could have come sooner, you know."

"Can I ask Pa to come?" Inga asked.

"Of course, but don't be surprised if he says they are still working." Ingeborg nodded toward the deaf school. "They started digging."

Inga nodded. "How about Thelma and Rolly? Pa can come later."

"Ja, go ahead." Ingeborg paused to heave a sigh. *Please, Lord, make him come.*

Clara went in to help Ellie, and finally Freda threw the last scaled and gutted sunfish in the tub of cold water.

She and Ingeborg stared at the fish. "We have enough here to feed half of Blessing."

"If I don't clean fish again for a month or more . . ." Ingeborg kneaded her lower back with her fists. "What else are we having for supper?"

"Do we need anything else?" Freda sluiced a bucket of water over the cleaning bench. "Maybe we'll send fish home with everybody and some over to Kaaren's."

"Ja." Ingeborg picked up the scrub brush. "We have enough guts here to bury beside all our corn and—"

"Ja." Freda took the brush. "You go get a clean skirt and apron. I'll finish this. Maybe we should do as Emmy wants and dry some. Her folks dry all their fish."

Ingeborg grabbed the stair rail to the porch and almost hauled herself up. She couldn't remember being this tired for a long, long time. But she stopped to smile at Martin and his newest best friend playing, if you could call a baby and Patches facing each other on a quilt on the porch floor "playing." When Ingeborg saw her bed, the urge to flop down on it made her snort. Bedtime would come soon enough.

By the time everyone had gathered for dinner, including Thelma, who had brought Roald out, Freda had potatoes and carrots prepared. What a feast this would be. They all settled themselves at the table, and Andrew looked at Carl. "Will you say grace, please?"

Carl dipped his head. "God, thank you for all our fish and that Manny didn't lose the cat and not even his fishing pole. Oh, and thank you for all our other food too. Amen." Carl looked to his pa. Andrew smiled and nodded.

Twelve people at the table, pulled out as far as it could go, attacked the fish, the fresh lettuce salad, potatoes and carrots, and the peas Freda and Clara had spent the afternoon shelling. Creamed with the last of the canned small potatoes from last year, they disappeared nearly as fast as the fish.

"We have lots more. We don't want the fish to spoil," Freda admonished more than once until everyone was groaning.

"Give 'em away," Andrew muttered, then rolled his eyes at the glare Carl sent him. He looked to Freda. "You didn't fry them all?"

"No. We had plenty, so Emmy wants to strip some of the catfish to dry. You and Ellie are taking plenty home, Thelma is taking fish home, and that should do it." Ingeborg and Freda exchanged nods. "And we will eat more tomorrow."

"Ja, for breakfast, dinner, and supper?"

Ingeborg snorted at her son's answer. "We can never get too much fried fish. Besides, you know Carl would go again tomorrow if we let him."

"Not me." Manny groaned from his chair. Then he grinned at Freda. "What's for dessert?"

"Gingerbread." Emmy started gathering

up the plates and thumped Manny on the head. "Ha."

"Out on the porch," Freda said from her post at the dishpan on the stove. "If the mosquitoes don't drive us in."

Andrew and his family left for home before dark, and before they left Ellie had salted a tub of fillets.

Manny brought the buggy up for Thelma and the sleeping Rolly. When he saw a man walking up to the gate, he called, "Hey, Thorliff, there's lots more fish."

"Takk. I'm hungry as a bear." He lifted his hat to wipe his forehead. He looked to Thelma, who was about to climb up in the buggy. "Do you want to wait a few minutes?"

"I have your supper all here." She pointed to the basket at her feet.

"Pa, you came!" Inga raced down the steps and threw herself into his arms. "We caught so many fish. Manny got a monster catfish and—" She stared up at him, the deepening shadows nearly hiding her face. "You could write about him for the paper. Make Manny famous."

"Ah, ja." He stared down at his daughter, then looked to his mor, who had joined them. "I think we have a fledgling newspaper writer here." He motioned to the buggy. "You get up there, and you can tell me about it on the way home."

Inga looked to her grandma, obviously torn

between staying and going. Ingeborg nodded. "We'll see you early tomorrow, because Emmy needs you to help dry the fish." She handed the sleeping Rolly up to Thelma.

"I will come fast."

Thorliff nodded to his mor. "Takk."

Ingeborg stared after the buggy. Perhaps there was hope for her son after all.

CHAPTER 18

Two days passed, then three days, and now four and not one single word from Toby. Deborah kept reminding herself the construction crews were working from dawn to dusk, but still.

"What is the sigh for?" Astrid asked. "By the way, weren't you supposed to leave by now? As in go home and sleep so you can come back tonight."

"I will. Is there anything more you need here? I mean, I could help with the ordering or . . ."

Astrid stared at her. "What is going on?"

"It's not what is *going* on but what is *not* going on."

It was Astrid's turn to heave a sigh, along with a slight head shake. "Toby."

"I know they are so busy and all, but I thought . . . I mean . . ."

"He walked you home from the celebration, and you had such a wonderful time, and now, typically Toby, you've not heard a peep from him?"

"How did you know? I've not said anything."

"You were walking on air and now you're back in the, uh . . ."

"Mud?"

"Your face says it all." Astrid nodded toward her office. "You need to go home, but we can talk for a couple of minutes. Miriam is here, you know, and she will do her job."

They both turned to see Miriam smile and wave from the nurses' station. She mouthed, "Go home," and pantomimed sleeping.

Astrid pointed to her office, then to the chair when they closed the door. Astrid propped herself on the front of her desk. "On again, off again?"

"Ja, but this time I think he almost kissed me." *What am I doing? I know better—don't I?* "Stupid me, getting my hopes up." She started to stand, but Astrid pointed to the seat. Deborah sat.

"Back to the girl party. Remember the list we made?"

Deborah nodded.

"So what was the suggestion if this on-again, off-again stuff happened?" Astrid waited.

Sucking in a deep breath, ignoring the burning behind her eyes which surely must be the need for sleep, Deborah swallowed and clamped her jaw. "I will quit mooning and do something nice and friendly, like . . . I know. I will leave a plate of . . . of something good on his kitchen table. And if I still don't hear anything from him, I'll get on the train and head for . . ."

Astrid rolled her eyes. "You know you have a standing invitation to go to Chicago for more training." It was *not* a question.

"I know, and more and more I'm thinking that when the doctor gets here in August and the student nurses are in place, I will do that. Go there, I mean."

"And August is how far away?"

"Thank you." Deborah stood, unpinned her nurse's hat, set the starched-to-stiffness badge of the hospital on the proper shelf, removed her apron, and rolled it up to stuff in the hamper. "Thank you. See you next shift."

"If I am still on duty." Astrid's voice softened. "You will get through this, Deborah. I still pray Toby will wake up, but I'm beginning to wonder about some men."

"Pa is so sure Thorliff will see the light."

"He's more sure than I am. He inherited a double dose of the Bjorklund stubbornness. It hurts to see him like this."

"Have you two spoken to each other since the fight?"

Astrid sighed. "Like I say, stubborn." She made shooing motions. "Greet Mary Martha for me."

Deborah marched out the office door and then out the front door to meet a warm breeze, birds singing, hammers pounding, and children laughing, all the sounds of a July morning in Blessing. Words floated into her mind from her father's Sunday sermon. "Trust Him. Above all else, make your requests known to our Father and then trust Him for the answers." *You said you trusted Him, but do you?* Sometimes that inner voice could be a nag. She headed for home at a brisk walk.

Exhaustion caught up with her as she stepped onto the front porch. She greeted Mary Martha in the kitchen.

"Good morning to you too. Your breakfast is in the warming oven. We're picking strawberries today and making jam." Mary Martha paused. "You look ready for bed."

"I am." Deborah took her plate out. "Ah, French toast."

"I'll make you eggs if you want."

"No, thanks, this is plenty." She smiled as her mother spooned fresh crushed strawberries on the egged and fried bread. "Oh, wonderful. You are so good."

She fell to eating, turned down the offer of coffee, and when finished, washed her plate in the dishpan, rinsed it, and set it in the drainer.

A quick kiss on her ma's cheek, and Deborah headed down the hall. Since her room was on the north side of the house, a pleasant breeze set the lace curtains to dancing. Her brother and sisters were out in the garden, laughing, picking away, and if she knew them, eating about every third one. Perhaps she could leave something with strawberries on Toby's table.

Smiling, she hung her things on the wall peg, donned a soft cotton nightdress, and crawled under the sheet and light blanket. Ah, bed felt so good. She said her prayers and was almost asleep when she remembered her Bible reading. Like so many other times, she promised herself she'd read it when she woke. But she did stay awake long enough to mentally make a list.

When she woke up later in the day, she had to form the to-do list all over again because she could not remember what she had planned.

Day 1: Cut and sweetened strawberries on his kitchen table

Day 2: Bowl of strawberry jam and half a loaf of fresh bread

Day 3: Meatloaf, cooked peas, and broken lettuce in his icebox (leave note on table to tell him it's there)

Day 4: Shortcake on table, strawberries and cream for shortcake in the icebox

With the plan in place and ready to start the next day, she had supper with her family and later went back to work. The following day she executed her plan for day one. The next day she left the bread and jam. Then the meatloaf, and then shortcake on the fourth day. And the result?

Nothing. Nil. No comment, no thanks, no acknowledgment. So much for that brilliant idea. Should she keep up the treats or forsake this whole idea, perhaps even forsake hope? Now she did not know what to do.

Wait. She did know what she should do. Toby lived alone. To fix a meal, he would have to get a fire going in the stove, prepare ingredients, then cook them, and after he had been working hard all day. Or she could leave a supper for him and he could rest. Whether he ever spoke to her or not, she could do that much for him. So many people were working long days to finish the summer's building projects. She could contribute to that effort by feeding their bachelor foreman.

She was off the next night and after two days would be back on days for five. When she woke, she lay in bed for a few minutes and stood to stretch. It was a good thing she could go to sleep like everyone else tonight. After dressing in a loose shift, she picked up her Bible and diary and, barefoot, ambled out to the empty kitchen. Cutting a slice of bread and chunk of cheese, she dished up a bowl of strawberries and took her meal out to the round table on the back porch. There was no one out in the garden either. Curious, but not enough to go looking, she sat to eat and catch up on her reading and writing.

The last three days in her diary were brief. "No word from Toby." Alternately chewing and reading, she reread Psalm 91 and contemplated the words while staring out over the lush garden and brilliant flower beds, her mother's delight. They looked to need weeding. Back in her diary, she thanked God for His word, made note of her prayers for her family, and yes, Toby. *Lord, I don't know what to do. Is there something I should be doing? Or not doing?*

As she reached for a strawberry, her elbow knocked her Bible off the table. Angry at her own clumsiness, she reached down and brought it back up. It had fallen open to . . . she gasped. Psalm 40, verse one: *I waited patiently for the Lord; and he inclined unto me, and heard my cry.*

But God, I am so tired of waiting!

Patiently.

Very well, if she must exercise patience, she would do so. But it was so difficult, this being patient.

She heard noises of someone back in the house.

Mary Martha set a plate of cookies on the table, along with a pitcher of water with chips of ice. "I'm glad you are up. I volunteered us to bring supper to the construction crew over at the school. Or rather, John asked me to and I agreed."

"Is this a new thing?"

"No, some of the others have been doing it, but John finished his sermon and went to digging. I have rabbit stew in the oven, thanks to Johnny—who, by the way, is also over there digging, along with Thomas and Mark. The others are playing at Sophie's. Since we ran out of strawberries for a couple of days, they earned a treat too."

"Speaking of treats, all of a sudden I would love a soda or at least ice cream." *No, you will not think of Toby,* she ordered her wayward mind. "What do you want me to do?"

"Since we had sourdough pancakes for breakfast, I set the rest of the dough to rise for buns. I put the dough in the sun, so it should be ready soon." Mary Martha patted her daughter's hand. "You make the best buns and biscuits."

"What else?"

"I thought we'd make a cake and frost it."

"Chocolate?"

"How about that chocolate spice recipe we have?"

"What time do we take supper over?"

"They take a break at six. I hoped you'd help me."

Deborah groaned inside but nodded. How could she refuse?

In the kitchen, she crossed to the area of the table devoted to the rolls as she measured out the dry ingredients for the cake.

Her mother commented, "I take it you've heard nothing from Toby?"

"How did you know?"

"Your eyes don't sparkle. You know, if you'd rather not help . . ."

I'm a big girl. "Of course I will help." She flipped the dough over and punched it down, probably harder than necessary. She'd always heard kneading bread was good for—

Mary Martha completed the thought for her. "I once heard a friend say that there was nothing better for getting rid of anger than kneading bread. And besides the anger abating, the bread was always lighter that way."

Deborah snorted. And kneaded the dough some more.

With the sun starting to angle toward the west, they loaded their baskets into the wagon and pulled it out to the construction site, where they set out the dishes and food on a table set up for that purpose.

"Sure looks good," Pa said after wiping his brow. "What a job." They paused for him to say grace, and the two women dished up plates and handed them out. There wasn't much laughing and joking; in fact, the men were mostly silent other than thank-yous and appreciative mutterings as they shoveled in the food. Toby wasn't there.

Am I relieved or disappointed—or both? Deborah breathed easier and smiled at her pa and Johnny, both of whom looked ready to drag home. As they finished, the guys all muttered thanks and climbed back down into a hole that looked over half done, if one counted the stakes. Deborah and Mary Martha packed up the empty food containers and headed home with a much lighter wagon and plenty of dishes to wash.

"You can sure tell who works in construction regularly and who doesn't." Mary Martha shook her head. "I hope the kids did not devour everything in sight. I left more stew in the oven and we can have bread and butter in place of the buns."

"I kept out some." Pulling the wagon behind her with both hands, Deborah managed to stay out of the ruts. While the ground was drying fast, the ruts cried out for the men to use the grader to smooth the roads again. One more thing that needed doing—preferably before haying.

They heard the telephone ringing when they pulled the wagon up to the porch. Emily met them. "Mr. Valders said for you to call Ingeborg. I just took the supper out of the oven when I saw you coming."

"Good girl." Mary Martha handed her one of the baskets. "Is the dishpan on the stove?"

"No, but I'll put it there," Emily called back.

While their ma went to talk with Ingeborg, the kids set the outside table and brought out the cast-iron stew pot to sit in the middle, along with a serving spoon. All the while they chattered about their day of fun and how Mrs. Wiste had treated them all to ice cream and somebody fell off the swing but only bled a little.

Deborah made sure she answered the kids' questions, teased them about ice cream, and kept so busy she had no time to think of Toby.

After they ate, Mary Martha announced that several of the women were gathering to pray for the building projects and getting sufficient help, funding, teachers for the school, and whatever else anyone brought up. She looked to Deborah. "Would you like to go with me?"

Deborah stared at her mother. *Dare I ask for help?*

"You don't have to, but really you *are* one of the women now, you know." Mary Martha tipped her head slightly to the side and waited.

Her ma was good at waiting. Deborah stared up at a corner of the room, loath to look at her. *Why not? What could it hurt?* There was that voice again. She gave an emphatic nod. "Yes." Then sucked in a deep breath. *Just . . . I've not done something like this before.*

Usually I'm working. She picked up her plate and put it in the dishpan along with the rest.

"My turn for dishes tonight." Mark stopped beside her. "You go on with Ma."

"There's plenty of food for the men when they get home—if they want it."

Mark grinned. "Johnny will eat. Johnny will always eat."

Deborah asked Mary Martha, "Do I have to pray out loud?"

"Not if you don't want to. Just pray along with us for whatever the topic is. We usually do this during the day but not regularly. Perhaps I shall suggest we make this a standard practice. Like John says, 'Blessing exists on prayer.'"

She was relieved to see Sophie was sitting with the group that was gathering in front of the altar at the church. The others were all older: Ingeborg, Kaaren, Penny, and Mrs. Jeffers.

"Mrs. Odell wanted to come, but her man needed help fixing a broken wheel," Mrs. Jeffers said, her smile including Deborah. "I'm glad you are here. We pray for the hospital all the time."

"Thank you." *Do you pray for husbands for the staff?*

Mrs. Geddick hurried down the aisle and blew out a breath as she slid into one of the seats. "Sorry, late."

"We are just beginning," Mary Martha assured her. "Let's have a time of silence to confess our sins and clear our minds, and then I will begin. As usual, speak what comes to your mind." She clasped her hands and bowed her head.

Deborah did the same and felt a peace flow over her that caught her by surprise. Her tight shoulders relaxed and she breathed slowly in and out, hearing the others do the same. *Thank you, Lord, for bringing me here. I had no idea.*

Mary Martha began. "Lord God, thank you for sending Jesus to bring forgiveness and restore us to you. You know the desires of our hearts and you, dear Lord Christ, are right here with us as you said you would be. We thank you and praise you and bring to you now the needs of our town that you have blessed so mightily."

Even the silence felt alive and waiting.

Prayers of gratitude started to flow, then moved into praying for the men building the addition.

"Lord, they are working so long and hard, please keep them safe from accidents."

"And make sure the materials get here when they are needed."

"Father, you brought the deaf school into existence and we have always trusted you for all those who come, and that all of our needs would be met. And now, thanks to all your blessing and guidance, we are building more. You provided the funding, you know all our needs, even before we do."

"Please put a hedge of protection around it all."

Deborah listened and added her unspoken requests for the school. The silence between the gentle requests seemed alive. Could she pray aloud too, like the others?

"And Father, that brings us to the public school. The too-small school buildings, since you bring more families here to live and work."

"And the need for good teachers who care about their students like all those we have now. You have blessed us over and over, and sometimes you move some on to other places. Lord, we miss Anji and Thomas Devlin and others who have left in the past."

"Thank you that you know who you are calling here and you will bring them so we don't have to worry about that." A pause. "You know I try not to worry."

Deborah fought a chuckle. Was this really the way these women had been doing it all these years? She'd seen Ingeborg and her father joining to pray for healing for patients, and God making it happen. She'd seen some die or be crippled anyway, but they kept on praying.

Was this what the Bible talked about when it said to pray for others? She jerked her mind back to the group.

Could she pray for Toby—here—before the final amen? She felt Ingeborg's hand on her knee. Permission? A benediction. That word too had new meaning. Benediction, blessing—peace.

"Father, you care about every little bit of our lives. You know our daughter Deborah desires to be loved and married." Ingeborg paused and patted Deborah's knee. "If Toby is the man you desire for her, help him grow into the man you want him to be, that she needs as a husband. If he is not, please bring the one you want for her."

Someone else added, "Fill his heart with love for Deborah, take away any fears, and Lord, as in all else, we will give you all the praise and all the glory."

"Thank you," Deborah said softly as she sniffed back tears. Somehow a handkerchief found its way into her hand.

"Ja, Lord, we know you can do even this, but if this man is not who you intend for our Deborah, you will bring someone else here for her."

Deborah found herself nodding and agreeing. *Thorliff and Astrid.* The names floated through her mind. "Can we pray for Astrid and Thorliff?"

"Takk," Ingeborg said. "Lord God, the terrible breach between my two children. I know you love them more than I do, but this mor's heart is breaking for them."

"Heal him, Lord, of his grief so he can trust you again. Only you are wise enough to straighten out such as Elizabeth dying. He doesn't understand because his mind is blind with grief and he cannot—"

"Or will not let it go."

"Lord God, we trust you in this as in all things, that you are working as you have promised. You see inside them and us and know the desires of our hearts."

This is for me too. You see the desires of my heart. You are not ignoring me. Deborah had to catch her breath. Another voice floated into her inner ear. *You are mine and I love you.*

Tears bathed her face, soaked her handkerchief. She knew the arms that wrapped around her were her mother's, so she leaned back into the embrace and used the next cloth pressed into her hand. They were all gathered around her, patting her knee, her shoulders, her head. When she could breathe without crying, one by one, they returned to their chairs.

Thank you and *praise you, Lord* lifted from around the circle. "Thank you." Deborah hoped they all knew she meant them as well as God.

After a long silence that vibrated with peace, Mary Martha whispered, "And we all say . . ."

They joined her as one. "Amen. And amen."

One by one they dragged their chairs to the back of the room and silently left for home. Outside, Deborah paused on the steps to stare up at the stars, the band of golds slowly joining the sun below the horizon and allowing the brightest stars their reign in the cobalt night sky.

She took her mother's hand and the two walked home. The light Mary Martha always set in the window greeted them.

"Thank you for praying for Blessing and us all." John's voice came from the shadows, as did the fragrance of smoke from his pipe. "Only God knows how much we need Him."

Deborah bent and kissed his cheek, hugged her ma, and headed for her room. Did her dear pa know something he wasn't telling—yet?

CHAPTER 19

B ut do we dare hire him, what's his name?"
Toby sprawled in his chair at the early-
morning meeting of the school board.

Jonathan said, "Gendarme, Anton Gendarme. He's my cousin on my mother's side.
We spent time together when we were young,
but I've hardly kept in touch with him since I
moved out here. He's taught a number of sub-
jects, and he can pick up foreign languages like
chickens pecking grain. He graduated from
college with honors."

Daniel frowned. "Is there such a thing as
a teacher being too well educated for a small
town like Blessing?"

"Good point," Toby said. "And since he's
not married, if he's expecting to find a nice little
country girl in Blessing, he's going to have to get

in line behind a whole herd of other bachelors."
A sweet girl like Deborah. Suddenly Toby didn't
think this Anton fellow was such a hot prospect.
The thought surprised him. He knew perfectly
well he wasn't jealous at all. But then he thought
of the odd feeling he'd had when Samuel and
Deborah were dancing and laughing.

Jonathan shrugged. "My father says my
mother was unhappy that Anton took a job
teaching at a public school. She felt he was
working beneath his station and should be
teaching at an exclusive boarding school or
college prep somewhere."

"But what if—" Daniel paused. "I don't
want to sound skeptical, but . . ."

Hjelmer completed the thought. "But what
if he's going to feel he's superior to country
people? First of all, what is bringing him to
Blessing? Why is he leaving his present position?" He leaned back, a frown giving his opinion.

"And will he fit in here? That's what I've
been wondering too," Garth mused.

Jonathan referred to his father's letter. "He
says Anton wants something new and different
since his fiancée died. He loves teaching and
making a difference. That's why he went into
the public school system."

"You have to admit Blessing is a good place
for new people. Look how Thomas Devlin fit
in here."

"And you've got to admit, he was different."

Jonathan laid the letter on the table. "We need to let Father know. He boards the train in a little over a week, and he wants Anton to come with him." He gave a sharp nod. "I say, hire him."

"Me too." Hjelmer and Daniel spoke at once.

Toby shrugged. "You know I'm not really on the school board."

"The only one missing is John Solberg, and he feels this is God's design for us."

"Anton also loves music and plays the violin, which he's very good at." Jonathan looked to Thorliff. "Perhaps we can have a music program like Elizabeth dreamed of."

Thorliff shut his eyes and inhaled loudly. "Garth, send our provisional acceptance to David Gould. Jonathan, will they both live at your house then, at least for now?"

"Yes."

"Remember, I offered my house," Toby put in. *My house is too empty.*

"Perhaps we should let Anton make that decision," Jonathan suggested. "Either way is fine by Grace and me."

"All right, back to construction." Thorliff looked over to Toby. "Anything else we have to discuss?"

Toby shook his head. "Just the same old tune we've been piping for months: If we are to meet the fall deadline, we have to have more men."

"Put David Gould and the new school-teacher to work," Hjelmer muttered. He paused. "Have you asked at the hospital in Chicago? Who knows, they might have a handle on the working men there."

"I've run ads in the Grand Forks paper and the Grafton paper. One problem is where will they live?"

"Another tent town?"

Thorliff shuddered. "Look what happened to our people. That fire could have killed or at least burned . . ." He looked to Hjelmer. "Help me on this."

Hjelmer just nodded.

"Anything else, Toby?"

"Not at the moment."

"Thank you, gentlemen." Thorliff stood and pulled his watch out of his pocket. "We've got to cut these meetings shorter."

"We don't usually have to hire a teacher first." Hjelmer started for the door, but as the others were exiting, he stopped and turned back. Toby paused too, frankly, to eavesdrop.

"What are you going to do about the news-paper? I suggest you order a new press and at the same time ask if they know someone who is trained and wants to move west to run it. That way you could write and edit, what you do best, and Lemuel can help this man put the paper out. Before you kill yourself." Without waiting for an answer, Hjelmer headed for the bank.

Toby could only see Thorliff's profile, but there was that furious glare again. Then Thorliff turned away and started gathering papers up from the table. His shoulders sagged. Had Hjelmer's suggestion made an impression at all? John seemed to think Thorliff would come around. Toby was not so sure.

Toby headed for the railroad station.

The train had come and gone. The station-master and two other fellows had already loaded one wagon from the flatcar parked on the siding. The team was tied by the station door, swishing flies and looking bored.

Toby untied them and crawled up into the wagon box. He waved at the two men loading the next wagon. "I'll take this one." *At least I don't have to fight mud this time.*

He clucked the team forward and turned them onto the road past Ingeborg's and ending at the Knutsons' and the deaf school. He tried to keep out of the ruts, but since that was becoming impossible, he kept the team pulling at a jog when they could. That had its own disadvantage; the wagon box bucked and bounced in four different directions. Constantly.

Driving a wagon gave him too much thinking time. He knew he should have left a note or something for Deborah, but he never thought of it until he wasn't home. As if he were ever home longer than to drop like the dead into bed. It was thoughtful, really, leaving food for him. It sure made life a whole lot easier. On the other hand, now he was beholden to her. He didn't like being beholden to anyone, but especially her.

Why *especially her?* That thought struck him. This whole business was getting too complex.

At the construction site, Ilse's husband, George, and two of the boys from the deaf school who'd stayed to work through the summer started unloading immediately. Toby signed *thank you* and strode over to the cook wagon that was now serving as his office and storage. He had nailed diagrams of the basement and forms to the wall. He dropped his papers on the table and motioned for Trygve and Joshua to meet him.

"There's more material at the train. Johnny Solberg is driving the next wagon and will take this one back. How is it going here?"

"It's going okay. Are there nails in one of these loads?" Trygve asked. "We'll be out by the end of the day."

"Also saws to take to Mr. Sam to sharpen."

"Johnny can pick up the saws. I don't know if there are nails." *Lord, we need more helpers.*

"Remember, haying starts tomorrow. Pa is turning hay today, and he says the windrows are drying out fast," Trygve reminded him.

"We're going to lose Heinz Geddick, and Este too."

"I know. You think Emmy and Inga could drive a hay wagon?"

"They're too small."

"I'm going to ask Ingeborg." Toby thought about all the children in this town. Those who were not too young were already working, at least during the summer.

"You be careful. They'll be up on that hay wagon and having the time of their life," Trygve said, waving his arms like children. "I think they would love field work."

"Thorliff and Andrew would kill me."

Trygve grinned. "Doubt it."

Down in the hole that would one day be a deaf school, Toby grabbed a hammer and filled his leather apron pockets with nails. He and Trygve settled into the teamwork born of many hours working together before. Within minutes, he had sweat rivering down his chest and soon his face, in spite of his hat. He pulled his big red kerchief from his back pocket and tied it around his head. When the church bells in the distance finally announced noon, he headed for the water buckets.

"Did you bring dinner?" Trygve asked him.

Mentally calling himself a couple of uncomplimentary names, Toby shook his head. The others were already sitting in the shade, still down in the hole, with their dinner buckets open. Trygve put two fingers in his mouth and whistled.

Emmy popped her head over the hedge.

"Bring more sandwiches, please, and we need more water." He turned to wide-eyed Toby. "Here, we'll start with mine."

"When did that start?"

"Both Ingeborg and Kaaren are sending food out." Trygve handed one of his sandwiches to Toby and motioned toward the shade. "It's a shame we don't get a breeze down here, but at least we can sit in the shade."

"Who's bringing supper out tonight?"

"You missed Deborah here last night." Trygve cocked on eyebrow. "She was looking for you."

Toby snorted and took a huge bite so he needn't answer.

"Oh, and to answer your question, I have no idea who exactly, but someone will. You can always trust the women of Blessing to make sure everyone is fed."

Emmy charged down the ramp they used to haul the dirt out and handed Toby a packet of sandwiches and some cookies. She waved, and back up she went again.

Laughing, Toby almost choked on the last bit he was chewing. He unwrapped a sandwich and this time could eat more slowly. Leave it to Ingeborg. He chuckled both inside and out.

"True. Now if we just had enough hands to get this thing up and ready for winter."

Trygve turned his head and stared at him. "You know what John would say?"

Toby shrugged.

"He'd say we asked for this to happen and now we have to trust that God will make it happen. We just keep doing the best job we can and trust." He leaned a bit closer so he could lower his voice. "And Haakan would say, 'Let the day's own troubles be sufficient for the day.' So, my friend, don't borrow on tomorrow's or next month's trouble." He nudged Toby with his elbow.

"Thanks, I'll try not to."

Both men pushed themselves upright.

"Let's get back at it!" Trygve called. Within minutes, the pounding and sawing commenced.

A wagon arrived with more materials. Johnny yelled down, "Where do you want these nails?"

"Bring two boxes down here and stack the others by the cook wagon."

Toby set to work. "We're going to need a shack of some sort for office and storage before they need that cook wagon for harvest."

"They're going to build one for us at the school woodshop. Lars already told me that. I think they are doing it at night, the way they are all working here." Trygve hollered, "Hey, Johnny, we got saws down here for you to take to Mr. Sam. Tell him we need 'em back tomorrow."

"Will do."

At least in the afternoon one long side of the hole was in the shade. Slowly the forms were framed and then covered with boards. They'd pour the nine-foot walls first and then extend them for the next pour.

That night when Toby staggered into his house, he found a pitcher with cold lemonade in the icebox, a jug of milk, several slices of bread, and some cheese. The note said, "Might help with breakfast too. We are praying for safety on your job."

This time he dug a pencil out of his shirt pocket, turned the note over, and wrote, "Thank you, for the drink, the food—and especially the prayers."

He weighted it down with a spoon, and this time remembering to shuck boots and clothes, collapsed on his bed.

They're praying for me—who? The whole family? Could well be. What Deborah was doing was a Christian service, for sure. Well, it figured. Her father was Reverend Solberg, after all.

Someone's rooster crowing jerked him awake. While it was getting lighter outside, the sun was not up.

He had not even one clean shirt. When could he ever do the wash? Who could he ask? He'd never in his life worked this hard for this long, and before, his mor did the wash. He'd ask Gerald. He knew more about the people of Blessing than anyone.

Dressed again and very aware of needing a bath, he tramped downstairs, poured a glass of milk, and clapped the cheese inside the slices of bread. Why did Deborah keep doing this? As her part in Blessing's huge construction race against time? Or for, well, more personal reasons? He took a big bite of his cheese sandwich. Mmm. This was the good cheese. He headed out the door.

What did he owe Deborah? Something, surely. But then, she didn't have to do any of this, so perhaps he owed her nothing; he'd not asked for anything. *Toby, look what you're doing. Looking a gift horse in the mouth, that's what you're doing. A really good-looking girl is providing you with food you don't have to cook or even buy, and you're trying to think it to death. Accept it, for pity's sake. And make sure she knows you're grateful.*

He had to shake off thoughts of Deborah and get to work. He'd check with Mr. Belin later. Well, sometime. *Thank God we don't have any other jobs to keep going. Lord, I'm not swearing. I do thank you.* He broke into a jog. Trotting to the site was a new habit for him. Walking was just too slow.

The sun burst over the horizon and leapt into the sky like a strong man running a race. Toby paused to suck in a breath and blow it out. It promised to be another hot one. And today they would have fewer workmen. At least today he'd had breakfast.

He joined the crew in the hole, and they set to erecting and nailing.

Some time later, a shout from above made him look up. Johnny was delivering the first load, with a helper. "Benny!"

"I can drive good, Mr. Valders. I'm getting better at climbing up too." His grin made the sun look lazy. "All right?"

All the men in the hole grinned up at him.

Toby blinked. What if the kid got hurt? What if . . . "Who's gonna help your ma make sodas and ice cream?"

"Joy's helping her. Miriam's little sis. So I can drive?"

"You can drive, and thank you."

Trygve clapped him on the shoulder. "Good for you, boss."

"Just pray he doesn't get hurt." *How would I live with myself if he does?*

Johnny yelled back, "Then can I come help down there?"

"You got another driver for me?"

"Working on it."

Yes, Toby realized, he was working on it. Everyone was working on it. Toby was working too many hours, but so was everyone else.

"Get busy, I said, you worthless slug!"

Toby recognized the voice. It was that Josef Tannemeyer, one of the workmen who'd arrived recently.

Toby forgot where the man had come from, but he knew Tannemeyer was a hothead, often picking a fight. *Not here, not now!* Toby ran across to the far corner of the hole.

Tannemeyer was punching Chet Classen's arm. "I said get back to work!"

"Leave me alone!" The fellow sounded weary, not angry. He was leaning a shoulder against the wall.

"So you need convincing, eh?" Tannemeyer drew a fist back to strike the man again.

Toby seized Tannemeyer's arm, twisted it, and shoved him back three feet. Tannemeyer lost his balance and fell on his bottom. He gawked at Toby for a moment and fury flushed his face. He scrambled to his feet and waved a pointing arm at his adversary. "He's loafing, just leaning there! Not pulling his weight! I want him fired!"

Toby raised one finger. "If you so much as threaten another workman, let alone punch him, you're fired. Instantly. Understand?"

"If you're not gonna make him work, I'm not working either! I'm not bustin' my buns while the rest of the crew sloughs off!"

Toby pointed to Chet. "Go up to the office, that wagon."

The man said nothing. He lurched erect from leaning against the wall and slogged toward the ramp.

Toby turned back to Tannemeyer. "Get back to work if you want to have a job yet when dinner arrives. I don't have time to argue with you." He turned his back on the sullen man and climbed the ramp.

He almost got to the wagon ahead of the fellow. It was hot and stuffy in the office, but out here, a welcome breeze made life bearable.

"What was going on down there, Mr. Classen?"

The man leaned heavily against the wagon. "Tannemeyer, he yells at everyone. No big thing."

"I asked what was going on down there."

"I feel tired, outta breath. Don't know why. Rested a minute . . . caught my breath. Just a minute. He yelled."

Toby studied Mr. Classen. He was pallid and listless. His lower lip trembled slightly. "Wait here." Toby climbed into his office, got a piece of paper, and wrote a note to Astrid or whoever was on duty at the hospital. He folded the paper and took it back outside. "Mr. Classen, are you strong enough to walk to town, to the hospital?"

"Hospital? I'm not sick, sir . . . just tired. Outta breath. Not sick."

"Can you?"

"I guess so."

Toby handed the note to him. "Hand this to the person who will greet you near the door. Do whatever the hospital staff tells you."

"I'm not sick. Just—"

"That's an order. You do follow orders, don't you?"

Mr. Classen looked at him for a moment and then chuckled. "Spent half my life . . . following orders, aye, sir. Was a bosun in the Navy . . . for over twenty years." He lurched erect. "Aye, sir, thank you, sir. . . . On my way." He ambled off.

Toby watched him go. An amble was all the fellow could muster; it was obviously his fastest gait. Heat prostration? Heaven knew the day was hot enough. But there seemed to be something more.

Tannemeyer came up over the lip of the ramp. He looked at his former adversary's back. "So you axed him. Good. Good." He turned to Toby, fire still in his eyes. "But you don't never cross me or lay a hand on me again, understand? Not like you did just then, or I'll beat you to a bloody pulp. I don't take that kinda thing!"

Toby stared at him for a long moment and the man met his gaze. "Do you know what a loose cannon is?"

"No."

"It's a fellow who is unpredictable; you can't trust him or trust what he'll do next. I cannot abide loose cannons, Mr. Tannemeyer. They're too dangerous."

"You mean that fellow?" Tannemeyer dipped his head toward the slogging Mr. Classen.

"No, Mr. Tannemeyer, you. You're fired."

CHAPTER 20

Manny shook his head. "I wish you wouldn't do this."

"I'll be fine. You hitch up the other team and we'll get out there." Ingeborg eyed the height of the wagon. She used to do this all the time. *Lord, help me.* She grabbed hold of the hay frame at the front of the wagon and tried pulling herself up. "Go get that wooden box, Manny. You know, the one Haakan used."

He scurried off, and Inga handed Ingeborg her wide-brimmed straw hat.

"Takk. Now you and Emmy take Jack over to Lars' barn to lift the hay in the mow."

"We did it last year, remember?"

"That's right, so now you are old hands at this."

Manny set the box down and stood next to it. "Grab my shoulder. That might help."

She did and swung up on the wagon, tucking her skirts in to stand. *I should have worn my britches.* Even the thought made her smile. She'd hung them out in the woodshed, but they were probably rotten by now. She could've cut down a pair of Haakan's if she hadn't given them all away.

Within minutes they were driving down the lane and out to the field. Ingeborg pulled her leather gloves a bit tighter and lifted her face to the sun, high enough in the heavens to have dried the dew on the windrowed hay. The morning breeze hadn't quite died yet. Yes, Thorliff and Andrew were going to be upset, which she knew was putting it lightly. But all the men were needed with pitchforks in the hay fields or hammers in the hole. She knew she wouldn't last long with either of those tools, but driving horses she could do.

"O Lord, this is so wonderful. Thank you, and please make sure I can last the morning." A chuckle slipped out.

Off in the field, she saw the men gathering around the new hay loader. If it worked the way Lars showed her, loading would go faster and not need as many men on the ends of the hay forks.

When the two wagons stopped, the look on Andrew's face clearly said what he thought of this. He and Lars, who was shaking his head but fighting a grin, stomped over and stopped beside the hayrack.

"You can't mean to drive the wagon, Mor."

"I do mean to. I used to do all of this, and I know I am older now but I *can* drive a team. I've known how since before you were born, so I suggest you hook up the hay loader and let's get rolling." She leveled her mor-has-spoken look at him. "You need hands, and I have two good ones." She held up her gloved hands. One of the horses stamped a foot, setting the harness chains to singing.

"But . . . but . . ." Andrew glared at his mother. "If you start to feel one tiny bit faint, you quit!"

"It'll be all right, Andrew. I will be careful."

"Pull up ahead of the loader."

Within minutes, the loader was clanking along behind her hayrack, and as soon as she guided the team to straddle a windrow, she clucked the horses, and the hay started up the track and dumped onto the empty wagon. She glanced over her shoulder. What an amazing invention! One man on the wagon spreading the hay around and one walking behind to make sure anything left was all picked up, and they moved steadily down the field. The horses' heads bobbed, hayseed flew, and the sweet aroma of fresh hay filled the world around her. Ingeborg felt like dancing.

Near the end of the row, Andrew trotted up to remind her to turn wide so the loader wouldn't bind up. She saluted him, did as he said, and they started down another windrow. She looked at the strip they had finished. Nothing left on it. They'd even managed to pick up the hay flattened by the rainstorm. Round by round, she kept on driving. The men spread the hay out evenly to make it easier to lift off back at the barn and not waste any time or space. When her load was full enough, they hooked the loader up to the other wagon, Lars and Samuel climbed up with Ingeborg, and she drove to Lars' barn, stopping right under the pulley.

"Please get off here while we do the lifting," Lars murmured.

"Oh, I was planning to. I see Ilse has water and something to eat there. Do you want me to bring some to you men? Oh, and do you mind if I slide off?" At the look on his face, she swung her leg over the front and climbed down the frame.

Having her feet on the ground felt mighty good. She pulled off her gloves, grabbed a glass of water, and headed for the outhouse. First things first. It sure was a shame they hadn't bought two of those new loaders. Their ancient one had been repaired so many times that the wood was rotting.

"How are you doing?" Ilse asked when Ingeborg returned for more water.

"It's getting hot out there, but I'm fine. Hoeing the garden is harder work than this."

"Ja, but the hoe won't spook and run off either."

"Our teams are well trained. I think they could do the whole thing without a driver." She watched the load lift from the flatbed wagon, held by the steel forks, and swing up in the air to swish into the open barn door. Ropes and pulleys were another invention that made farming like they were doing now possible. She remembered too well the early years, when even the pitchforks were two prongs of carved wood. Most of the hay was stored in stacks now rather than haymows, which made it weather a whole lot better. She joined Ilse at the table in the shade.

Inga slid her hand into Ingeborg's. "Are you all right, Grandma?"

"Ja, I am good." She tapped Inga on the nose. "How are you two doing?"

"Jack doesn't need us. He knows more than we do."

"I know, the team is like that too."

"Emmy is helping Tante Kaaren." Inga refilled Ingeborg's glass and brought them cookies. "I gotta go." Stuffing her cookie into her mouth, she ran for the back of the barn.

Ingeborg was on her way back with another load when they heard the church bells peal the song of noon. It was probably a good thing she'd not planned to keep on through the afternoon, but she wasn't going to tell Andrew that. Sometimes it was hard to remember that she was getting up in years.

They unhitched the horses and tied them in the shade. Dinner was set out under the cottonwood tree that Kaaren had planted even before they built the house, like Ingeborg had done. On days like this, the shade was so welcome.

Manny filled his plate and sat down beside her. "Grandma, what do you think of Emmy driving the wagon?"

"I think that would be a very good idea. Have you mentioned it to Lars or Andrew?" Her stomach grumbled, so she fed it.

"I will. But I gotta eat first. How come driving a team makes me so hungry?"

"Good question. When you figure out the answer, let me know."

He grinned back at her and leaned close. "You did good, Grandma."

"Takk."

Kaaren refilled her glass and held out the plate of gingerbread. "You were having the time of your life out there, weren't you?"

"I was. Driving a hay wagon is not hard if you don't have to help load or unload it. Manny and I think Emmy should drive this afternoon. I should have taken her on this last load so she'd know what to do."

"We have a shortage of men, that's for sure.

One good thing about haying . . . rather two: You can't start until the dew comes off in the morning, and you have to quit at dusk before the dew starts to fall."

"True. See you tomorrow." Ingeborg stood when the crew did and followed them down to the barn. Since her load was yet to be lifted into the haymow, she led the team back to hitch up again. "Lars, how about having Emmy drive this one this afternoon? She's good with horses and has driven many times."

"I was thinking the same thing. Inga can take care of Jack by herself, even though it gets boring."

"I saw she had a book along." She motioned toward the team. "I'll take them home, then. Freda will help me unharness them."

His eyes twinkled. "You going to ride?"

"Of course." Riding one and leading three was easier than walking, not that she had that far to go. She tipped her hat back on the ribbon and leaned forward to pat her horse's neck. "You are a good old girl."

The mare's ears twitched back and forth. Some things never changed.

That evening, Thorliff was talking with the crew in the hole when Emmy called them all for supper. Ladle in hand, Ingeborg stood at the end of the table, greeting the men when they picked up their plates. She ladled out the rabbit stew, Clara dished up squares of corn bread, Emmy added butter and jam, and Inga handed out glasses of either milk or swizzle, depending on which they asked for.

"We'll bring around the chocolate cake before you finish and coffee if you want," Ingeborg said.

"Mrs. Bjorklund, you sure know how to feed a group of hungry men," one of the workers said. While his accent was heavy, his smile conveyed his feelings.

"Thank you. I hope you like rabbit stew."

Thorliff waited at the end of the line, Toby right in front of him. Ingeborg glanced his way, but the two were talking. Perhaps she would not hear a repeat of Andrew this morning.

"Where's Benny?" she asked the men.

"Ah, they hauled the last load out and unloaded, then returned to town. He said to tell you he'd see you tomorrow."

"He did all right, then?"

One of the men nodded. "But we've got to fix that boy a better way to get up on a wagon."

"It's hard to believe he don't have no legs below the knees. Why, if someone din't tell me, I'd never have guessed," one of the other men said. "That boy don't let nothin' stop him."

"He makes the best sodas too."

Ingeborg enjoyed the conversation. Wait until she told Astrid.

A man with a well-bandaged hand held out his plate. "Thank you."

"You are most welcome. How is your hand doing?"

"Doc wrapped it and said not to get it wet. Or dirty." He shrugged. "Good so far."

When the others returned to the hole, Thorliff refilled his glass and came to sit beside her. "I hear you were driving the hay wagon this morning."

"I was, and I'll be back there tomorrow." She cut a chunk of rabbit into smaller bites. Why should she feel she was being called to account? Thorliff was her son, not her overseer.

"You, uh . . ." Thorliff heaved a sigh that must have started in his toes. "You didn't have to take that chance, you know."

She could tell he was fighting to be tactful. She turned to him. "Thorliff, all of you are working so terribly hard to get the deaf school weathered in. I know what a job that is. I know how valuable every man is. Driving the hay wagon today was a delight for me. I just drove in the morning, and I felt like I was making a contribution."

She raised her hand when he started to say something. "I know feeding hungry men is very important, crucial; with this, I get to do both. Just for a few days, let me have my fun without chiding me. I have promised Andrew that if I feel at all weak or . . . or anything, I will quit immediately. Today I got to see the new hay loader in action, I got to see Benny driving a wagon, and Johnny turning into a man before our eyes. I rode Bess home and let the teams out to pasture." She almost said, *And I remember being young and working nearly to death so we could have this land. Thank God I don't have to do that anymore.*

He raised a hand, slowly shaking his head. "I . . . We won't say any more." He pushed himself to his feet. "Where's Inga?"

"Down at the barn feeding calves. She and Emmy took over that job so Manny could do more important things."

"She could come home and help Thelma with Rolly."

"I know and she knows but . . ." *But she can't bear to see your sad eyes all the time.* "Why don't you bring Rolly out here more often so he doesn't feel left out? Between all of us, we could do it."

"I'll talk to Thelma." He reached for his hat, which he'd laid on the table. "I'll stop and see Inga on my way home. Her story about Manny and the catfish will be in the next edition." He paused. "Wouldn't it be something if she wants to be a newspaper person too?"

She smiled. "Any news about a new press?"

"I've ordered it; they have a man willing to come set it all up, and if he likes it here . . ."

"Really? Then we have to make sure he

likes it here." She tilted her head. "Married? Family?"

"No idea."

"What a relief for you."

"Thanks to Hjelmer. He'd probably have ordered it had I not agreed to do so." He paused to study her in the light of the lowing westerly sun. "How do you do it, Mor?"

"What?" She stood and hugged him with her eyes.

He chewed the inside of his cheek. "Keep on going? All you've been through, and you still want to drive the hay wagon. Feed half the county."

"Thorliff, I have great help here or I couldn't go drive the hay wagon. Our Father brings the healing and the joys of every day." She hesitated, mostly for the effect of the pause. "And He's waiting for you to ask."

Thorliff settled his hat on his head and strode off toward the barn, still carrying all his cares and unable to see the light that hovered around him, waiting for him to even hint at asking.

"Please, Lord, how do we help him let go?" She sniffed back the burning tears as she folded the tablecloth to be used again. *Something has to be a turning point for him.*

&

One week later, Ingeborg gathered with a few of the others on the train station platform.

It seemed like only yesterday they had gathered to send Thomas Devlin and his newly acquired family on their way to a new life in Michigan. Now they were waiting to welcome Jonathan's father, David Jonathan Gould, back to Blessing, along with the new high school teacher, Anton Gendarme. Jonathan had brought the construction project's wagon and team; he stood off to the side with his horses, watching and waiting.

"You seem a bit pensive today." Kaaren wrapped her arm in Ingeborg's. "Is driving the hay wagon wearing you out?"

"Not at all, just thinking on all the changes here in Blessing. Good-bye to one teacher, hello to another. Another friend who has lost his wife, coming here for healing. The hole beginning to look like a real building. Can you believe it all?"

"That's a lot to think about. Let's go have a soda after we greet both an old friend and hopefully a new one. If Jonathan has his way, he'll have his father and his cousin down in the hole even today with a hammer or cranking the cement mixer."

Here came the train, and Ingeborg briefly wondered about train schedules. How the engineer could cover hundreds of miles in all kinds of weather and pull into a station in the middle of the prairie almost on the minute. Every time. Amazing. The black iron monster huffed its way past the platform and sighed to a stop, its wheels buried briefly in spent steam. The doors of the two passenger cars opened, but only two people stepped out.

Jonathan moved forward as the two men stepped out onto the platform and jogged over to embrace his father.

Ingeborg hurried with the others toward the man she knew. "David Gould, we are so grateful you're here! Welcome to Blessing."

He wrapped his big, warm hands around hers. "It is so good to be here."

Ingeborg stepped back to let Kaaren, Ellie, and the others greet him.

David raised his voice. "Thank you all. I am pleased to present Mr. Anton Gendarme, who hopes to teach here in Blessing."

Sophie murmured in Ingeborg's ear, "Every young woman in town is going to want to be in school. What a handsome devil!"

Ingeborg smiled. The young man certainly was mighty attractive physically, but he seemed just as winsome socially. In a smooth, rich baritone, he repeated the name of each person he was being presented to, smiling, nodding.

The train whistle blew, startling just about everyone. Huffing and chugging, the engine strained into motion. With lots of rattles and clangs, the cars one by one started to move as well. They were off to another town.

Jonathan pointed to a pile of baggage. "Is that all yours?"

"I believe so," David replied.

"I'll load it in the wagon, Father." Jonathan headed off to lead the team to the bags.

"Let me help." Mr. Gendarme jogged over to the baggage. Together the two young men began stowing bags and trunks aboard the wagon.

Ingeborg watched the men work. "He seems as strong as he is handsome."

Sophie nodded in agreement. "He doesn't even seem to be wearied by the long ride."

A young man in front of them turned to grin at her and shake his head. "Mr. Valders says let them rest today, but they better have brought work clothes."

CHAPTER 21

D eborah, have you seen the new school-teacher?"

"No, why?" She glanced up from her paper work. "Sophie, this was important enough to bring you out of the boardinghouse?"

"Oh my, yes." Sophie leaned closer. "Perhaps this is the answer to your prayers. You know, in case Toby really isn't *the* one."

"Excuse me?"

"You certainly remember when we all got together and prayed for each other at church. And we prayed that if Toby wasn't the one God intended for you, you'd find the right one."

"Well yes, but . . ." Deborah frowned. She was beginning to regret going to that prayer session. "I suppose you've found him for me, right? And it's our new teacher?"

"Maybe."

"Well, I've not seen him yet. Sophie, thank you for the information and now, if you don't mind, I need to get back to work."

"When are you going to Chicago?"

Deborah could feel her mouth drop open. "It was going to be August, but that's not definite yet. We have to have enough staff here to cover."

"Astrid wants you to go. This hospital desperately needs an administrator, we have more nursing students coming, and . . ." Sophie paused, looking off at the ceiling and barely nodding her head. "Why don't you ask Vera Deming if she would like more work? I mean, running the dental office is—"

"And chasing after her baby, Phillip, who is going to start walking any day now . . . you think Vera is not busy enough? Besides, Astrid asked her some time ago, and she declined. She pitches in occasionally when we get in a real pinch."

"Oh well, see, it was a good idea. Vera needs to become part of the social life here in Blessing."

"Social life?"

"I think I'll ask her to help with the fundraisers. That would be good for us and for her."

Deborah closed her eyes. *O Lord, save Vera from Sophie.*

"I'll be having a meet-the-new-teacher soiree on Saturday at the boardinghouse. Spread the word. I'm going to ask Gerald to pass it on too."

"No grass grows under your feet. He could meet people at church on Sunday."

"I know, but this way we'll all have more chances to meet and visit with him. What shift do you work on Saturday?"

"Days and I have Sunday off, so . . ." She made shooing motions with one hand. "I'm sorry, Sophie, but I really do have work to do."

"Well, keep the new man in mind, and I'll try to get you two introduced before Saturday. Deborah, I really think this might be the one. He is perfect for you." Sophie stepped back. "Talk to you later." And she sailed out the door.

Could this possibly be an answer to prayer? *Deborah, keep your mind on work!* Sometimes that voice could be very stern, and right now she needed that.

"Deborah, could you come here please?" Astrid called from examining room one.

Deborah left the paper work and hurried down the hall.

"We need you to help hold this little one. She's stronger than she looks." Astrid smiled at the mother across the table, where a six-month-old baby girl was squirming. "You hold her head."

"She's sure getting big, isn't she, Mrs. Oblund," Deborah said. "And such a beauty."

The mother nodded. "But she cry and rub her ears."

"And now she's running a temp. I'm trying to check her ears and throat." Astrid stroked the baby's hair. "Babies often have ear trouble, but most outgrow it. Hold on."

The mother held the baby, Deborah held her head still, and Astrid was able to finish the exam. "Thank you both. You can pick her up now." Astrid motioned to the squalling baby. "She has a great pair of lungs, that's for sure." She turned to Deborah. "Please warm some sweet oil, and we'll send some home too, along with a soothing syrup for her throat." Astrid made a note in the chart. "Cool cloths will bring down her temperature. If she is not well in three days, you bring her back, all right?"

The mother nodded. "I understand."

Deborah hurried to the stock room to fix the medication and brought it back, along with the bottle of sweet oil in a bowl of hot water. "Anything else?"

"That's all, thank you."

"Nurse, could you please help me?" Sweet Mabel Ohnstetter waved at Deborah from her chair by the window, then whispered when she arrived, "I need to go to the necessary."

Deborah looked around. "Of course." Where was Mercy? She was working full-time as an aide during the summer and would work again part time after school started.

Deborah was just settling Mrs. Ohnstetter into her chair again when Mercy returned in a rush.

"Sorry, Mrs. Geddick needed a hand in the kitchen."

"And where was Elmer?"

"He is walking our heart patient, Mr. Classen, outside like you asked him to."

"Sorry, I forgot." *We need more help here, that's for sure.* One aide and one orderly with only one nurse per shift was simply not sufficient. It would help when the new people arrived, but they needed three or four more, at least.

The front door opened, and Elmer came in with Chet Classen. Deborah smiled at them as they approached.

"He did just fine," Elmer announced. "Walking steady, and we didn't have to stop and rest but once."

Deborah nodded. "You look so much better, Mr. Classen. Your skin color is good, and you don't look so drawn."

"Thank you. Mr. Valders came by to see me this morning, and he talked to the doctor. Dr. Bjorklund says I shouldn't swing a hammer anymore; my heart might not take it. So Mr. Valders is putting me on finish work. Not as strenuous, he says." Mr. Classen's smile faded and he wagged his head. "That Toby Valders saved my life. You know that, don't you, Nurse

MacCallister? I thought I was just tired, is all. Dr. Bjorklund says if I hadn't come in when he sent me, I probably would have died. So he saved me. He's a good man, Mr. Valders."

Deborah licked her lips. "Uh, yes, yes he is. Toby Valders is a good man."

Elmer smirked.

She sharpened her voice. "Thank you, Elmer. Please take him to his bed. I have the rounds to make. Good afternoon, Mr. Classen."

"Ma'am."

She had fibbed; she did not have rounds just yet. But she had to end the conversation quickly because she could feel her cheeks catching fire.

Everyone pitched in to help serve dinner and settle the six patients afterward.

As Deborah assisted Mrs. Ohnstetter into bed for her afternoon nap, the sweet lady reached up and patted her cheek. "You are all so good to me here. Thank you."

"We love having you here, and besides, we always know someone is praying for everything going on here. We have our own in-house pray-er."

"That's a fact. Say, do you know if Ingeborg is coming today?"

Deborah shrugged. "I know they are awfully busy right now. Is there something you need?"

"I am nearly out of yarn again. She keeps me supplied, you know." Mrs. Ohnstetter tapped back a yawn. "Goodness me, you'd think I'd been out weeding the garden again. I did remind Arthur that the flowers needed weeding."

Deborah kissed her cheek. Mrs. Ohnstetter's son Arthur had died several years ago. She watched as the little woman drifted off to sleep. Sadly, her mind seemed to be wandering more and more.

That afternoon when her shift ended, Deborah thought of going by Ingeborg's to mention the yarn. *You just want to go out there in the hopes you will see Toby.* That voice again. She said aloud, "I'll just telephone, so there!"

"Talking to yourself, I see," Amelia Jeffers called from weeding her front flower beds.

"You caught me." Deborah paused at the fence and Amelia came over. "Your yard is so lovely. The hollyhocks. What are the tall blue ones and pink ones?"

"Delphiniums and foxglove. I need to get another bouquet of roses over to the hospital, don't I?"

"Yes, those we have are about to expire." Deborah inhaled. "Is it just the roses or something else that smells so sweet?"

"See the low-growing white and purple alyssum? I use that as edging so often. It just keeps on blooming. The zinnias are about to start. Along with the cosmos. That's those tall feathery ones over there. Come have a glass of something cold with me. Or are you in a hurry?"

"I better get home and help Ma, but thank you. Do you know who's serving supper at the hole tonight?"

"Ellie, I think—no, several of the new ladies are working together." Amelia leaned closer. "I forget some of their names. So disgusting of me. By the way, wait until you meet Mr. Gendarme. He is so charming. Nice looking too."

Deborah threw back her head. "Is everyone in this town matchmaking for me?"

Amelia patted her hand. "Very subtly, my dear. Very subtly. We women know your wants and dreams, and we want them for you." She snipped several flowers and handed them to Deborah. "Tell Mary Martha hello from me, and yes, I am saving her some seeds."

If Deborah were a whistler, she would have done so on her way home. She waved at Gerald Valders in the phone office, stopped to pick up the mail, and back on the boardwalk, looked up from sorting when she heard her name called.

"Deborah!" Rebecca waved from the front of the Soda Shoppe. "Come try a new flavor of ice cream. Tell me what you think."

So Deborah detoured by the shop, approved the new mint flavor, and hurried on home, making sure she did not look at Toby's house on the way past.

"Amelia sent you flowers," she told her

mother, "and if you make one reference to the new teacher in town, I shall scream."

Mary Martha sniffed the proffered flowers. "How lovely. I think I know where the vase is."

"I'll get it." Deborah reached for the third shelf, but it took standing on her tiptoes to bring the vase down. "One of the canning jars would have worked."

"Ah, so . . . ?"

Deborah pumped some water into the sink. Arranging the flowers took all her concentration, but she could feel her ma laughing behind her.

"Sophie asked if you would bring those delicious new crackers to the"—Mary Martha's eyebrows lifted—"soiree." Her inflection on the last word told her opinion of Sophie going all fancy on them.

Deborah rolled her eyes. "Why not? I . . . we have nothing else to do." She eyed the jars of canned beans on the counter. "I can see you have all been busy. Do the raspberries need picking again?"

"They do, and John asked for raspberry shortcake tonight when he gets back from the hole. I was thinking, do you suppose Toby has someone to wash his clothes? He sure hasn't had any time. When you take the makings of shortcake over for him, how about looking into that?"

"You want me to go upstairs to his bedroom and fetch his dirty clothes?"

"No, you're right. I know, Emily and I will go strip his bed and get his clothes real early tomorrow so they can be dry and back home before he returns. That will work."

Good, at least I work at the hospital tomorrow. When Deborah took the makings for raspberries and shortcake over to Toby's after supper, her note said, *Cream is in the icebox along with the berries. Enjoy.* Making sure she did not look for dirty clothes, she beat it out the back door. Dusk was falling quickly.

At seven on Saturday evening, half of Blessing seemed to be converging on the boarding-house. Deborah brought her large basket of crackers. Others brought their specialties, and soon the tables were groaning. Maisie Landsverk was serving punch, and Helga Larson was pouring coffee. Whether Deborah met the new man of her dreams tonight or not, the food was certainly going to be good.

And then Jonathan and the guests of honor arrived. This Anton Gendarme fellow was considerably taller than Mr. Gould—probably taller than Toby, even—and remarkably handsome. Sophie had a good eye for marriage prospects, that was for sure. Without really thinking about it, Deborah moved in close as Sophie greeted them at the door.

Sophie took Mr. Gould's hands in hers.

"Mr. Gould, welcome and please accept our deepest sympathies on the passing of your wife. Her memory will live on here in Blessing. In fact, we've been discussing naming the new building after her, if you wouldn't mind."

David Gould, looking distinguished with his silver hair, held her hands, nodding all the while. "Thank you, Mrs. Wiste. My wife saw what this deaf school was already accomplishing and foresaw what it could become."

"As we in Blessing are fully aware, your wife wasn't—isn't—the only one. Welcome home."

He bowed over her hand. "Thank you. Allow me to introduce my nephew, Anton Gendarme."

Sophie turned and took the teacher's hands. "We are delighted, Mr. Gendarme, and grateful to you for wanting to teach here."

He smiled and nodded, the perfect gentleman.

"Would you be willing to say a few words when I introduce you? People here are curious to know more about you, and this is a perfect setting for that."

"Of course."

"Just keep it brief," Mr. Gould admonished with a wink.

Anton's right eyebrow lifted and his smile bespoke his understanding. "I will take his advice, Mrs. Wiste. You have put together quite a welcoming. And on such short notice. This is amazing."

"One can do things in small towns that aren't possible in cities."

Deborah almost giggled out loud. And in small towns, busybodies wanting to make matches could get around much more quickly. Sophie should add that.

"Jonathan, would you like to introduce your family?" Sophie led the way to the food tables. Deborah followed. Was she hovering too close?

"Of course." Jonathan leaned closer to Sophie. "And then can I retire to the piano? I learned some new music that I think you will really like."

"You certainly may, and you've piqued my interest." Clapping her hands, Sophie raised her voice. "May I please have your attention?" Conversations continued undiminished. She clapped again and turned to Jonathan. "They all seem to be having a good time."

"They do." He put two fingers in his mouth and blasted out a whistle that made some laugh and everyone fall silent.

"Thank you, Jonathan. Ladies and gentlemen, it is my privilege to introduce our guests for tonight." She stepped back and stood at Deborah's side. Some folks applauded lightly.

"Tonight I want to reintroduce my father," Jonathan started. "I know many of you have met him when he has visited through the years, but this time, I think he will stay longer." More applause.

David Gould greeted them and then motioned to Anton. "Mrs. Wiste gave me the honor of introducing my nephew and your new high school teacher, Anton Gendarme."

Sophie nudged Deborah and whispered, "See, I told you. I have a feeling . . ."

"No predicting the future, Mrs. Wiste."

Hjelmer nearly bumped into Mr. Gendarme, he moved so close. He extended his hand, introduced himself, and started talking about the bank. Deborah admired the way Mr. Gendarme remained cool and collected with so many people milling around him. But then, he was a city person and would naturally be accustomed to lots of people milling around. And being high society like Mr. Gould and Jonathan, he would surely be used to parties of all kinds.

Sophie muttered, "As soon as he finishes talking, I will introduce you."

"By saying what? 'This is our resident spinster, so you should pay attention to her'?"

Mouth dropping open, Sophie stared at her. "Why, Deborah." She put a hand to her bosom. "How could you ever think such a thing?" She tsked for added impact.

Deborah rolled her eyes. "I know you, Sophie Wiste. And I don't trust you any farther than I can throw"—she fought for the right word—"this boardinghouse."

Daniel pushed in ahead of them and posed

a question Deborah was curious about as well. "Some of us were worried that you'd, well, get bored in a small town like this."

"No worries there," Mr. Gendarme said. "I look forward to a more relaxed way of living, believe me. Paul to the Philippians."

Daniel looked puzzled. At Mr. Gendarme's left, John Solberg laughed out loud. "Beautiful!" He told Daniel, "Paraphrased, Paul told the Philippians, 'I have learned whatever state I'm in to be content.'"

Sophie gripped Deborah's arm and nearly pulled her off balance, thrusting her directly in front of Mr. Gendarme. But then Sophie reached back and pulled Astrid forward also. Deborah breathed a sigh of relief. Now perhaps this would not feel so . . . so outrageously staged.

Astrid stepped forward and held out her hand. "I am Dr. Astrid Bjorklund, the head of our Blessing Hospital. You were just speaking to my husband, Daniel. I must tell you how delighted we are that you have come."

"Thank you, I've heard a lot about you." Mr. Gendarme glanced at Mr. Gould. "All good; he holds all of you in the highest esteem." His smile drifted over to Deborah.

"And this is my head nurse, Miss Deborah MacCallister. She is the one who really runs the hospital. I thank God for her every day."

Deborah could feel the flush sweeping up

her face. "We have a small staff here, but it's growing. Like our school. Thank you for choosing to come to Blessing."

He took her hand. "I've heard about you also." He glanced at Mr. Gould, who warmed Deborah with his smile.

Mr. Gould chuckled. "I think Anton was beginning to believe my tales of Blessing were overdone."

"But not anymore?" Deborah smiled at the new teacher, wishing she had a fan. *What a dumb thing to say, Deborah!*

Mr. Gendarme shook his head slowly, never taking his eyes from her face. "No, 'not anymore' is an understatement," he said, touching her arm. He was not just tall and very good-looking, he had a sort of presence—an aura. You could feel him.

The heat burned brighter. If this was what instant attraction meant, she had just wandered into a whole new world. No words came, so she just nodded. *Good grief, what a ninny.*

CHAPTER 22

"You have got to be kidding." Toby stared openmouthed at Thorliff on Monday morning.

"No, I'm not." Thorliff held up his hands, palms out. "This is not my idea. I was being sarcastic when I said we'd do this, but Mr. Gendarme brought a leather apron, leather gloves, and a hammer with him. He is adamant."

"In the hole?"

"Ja, in the hole. He asked if he could start on Wednesday. He wants to go over to the school, meet with John, and get an idea what teaching here will be like, what supplies they need, things like that."

"That's good. Let him do that. Working construction is not like anything he's ever known. Come on, Thorliff, he's a citified dandy.

From the look of him, he's never done a day's hard labor in his life."

"Be that as it may . . ." Thorliff huffed a deep breath. "Look, find him something safe to do, but hard enough that he'll want to quit. Now, Gould is another matter. Remember Gould money is building that school, and if he wants to learn hard labor, he will get a chance. Besides, Mor said he might be trying to work off his grief this way." He stared at the table in front of him, slowly shaking his head.

"It doesn't work, does it?" Toby spoke softly, knowing but not truly understanding what Thorliff was trying to do. What he really knew was how often he ached for Thorliff and his loss. The man had been run through his own printing press in the last couple of years and came out damaged. He figured to work it off.

Thorliff shook his head. "Just put them to work, all right?"

"I will, but I don't have to like it. What if they get hurt on the job? How do I—" He stopped. "I'll set the schoolteacher to hauling wood from the wagons down into the hole. I sure hope he gets so involved in the school that he goes after that. Let him whitewash walls or something."

Thorliff studied Toby. "Remember, you offered him a room at your house."

"I know, and the offer still stands, but I understand he's decided to stay with Jonathan and Grace—for now, anyway. At least maybe I can keep him busy otherwise."

"And safer." Thorliff motioned toward the door. "Whose crew will you put Mr. Gould on?"

"Neither."

"Toby . . ."

"Yeah, boss, I got it. He wants to pound a hammer, I'll give him to Trygve."

A little later that morning, Mr. Gould appeared, ready to go to work. Even in work clothes, he stood out. He was too clean and the clothes too new.

"Thank you, Toby, for letting me be here."

"You're welcome. I figured you'd rather be out haying with Jonathan and the others."

"I've always had a hankering to build something. I do know how to drive nails and measure and rip lumber. I promise to be careful." His half smile and half-raised eyebrows said he had a pretty good idea what Toby was thinking.

Toby nodded. "If you're sure you'd rather not be out haying . . ." When Gould shook his head, Toby waved his arm toward Trygve. "You've met Trygve Knutson on your past trips. He's the foreman on the first of the forms crew, then Joshua's men insert and tie off the steel bars, and Trygve's finish the forms. As you can see, they are all working simultaneously."

"And they have room for another hammer, albeit a slow one?"

"There is plenty to do. Everyone does whatever needs doing here." Toby took Gould over to Trygve, and without a blink, Trygve nodded.

"Glad to have you, sir."

"Please, no *sir*."

"Yes, sir—I mean, fine. Sorry. I'll try to stop."

With Gould set to holding boards and nailing them in place, Toby watched the men at work and then checked the two at the sawhorses. "You need another man or a big kid to fetch and carry."

"That we do. It would speed this up."

"I should have someone for you tomorrow."

"I sure miss that Manny. I'll be glad when the haying is done. At least harvest won't take as many away."

Toby looked up to see John Solberg pulling on leather gloves as he strode down the ramp. "Are you ever a sight for sore eyes, Pastor. Right here. These guys need you."

"It's always good to be needed." He held up his hands. "They're getting well callused, in spite of the gloves."

Toby strode up the ramp to see Benny's team pulling in. One of the two deaf boys grinned at him and they hoisted six one-by-sixes on their shoulders and trooped down the ramp.

"Sure could use two more like those guys."

Benny grinned at Toby. "You want to help me carry a load?"

"Benny, if I see you hauling down that ramp, you'll be off that wagon so fast you won't know what hit you."

"Figured. I do know my limits."

"No you don't. You just figure a way around so you can do it. I bet your ma misses you at the soda fountain."

Benny sighed. "She does, but she agrees this is more important right now."

Toby clapped him on the shoulder. "Keep up the good hauling." *I should go out to Deming's.* Instead, he grabbed his nailing apron out of the shack, rammed the hammer handle into the loop, and headed down into the hole.

When the triangle rang for the morning break, the men climbed out of the hole, mopping their faces and grabbing water first thing. Clara and Freda made sure everyone got a sandwich, cookies, and coffee or swizzle.

"There's plenty for seconds," Freda announced.

John turned to Toby. "I need to meet Anton at the school after dinner, but I'll be back later."

"Every board up counts. Thank you." He turned to Gould and lowered his voice. "How are you holding up?"

"You have strong men here. How about I stop at noon?"

"Wise move. Say, I had a thought. Are you

interested in learning finish work? I know Mr.
Belin, who is running the finish work on the
Deming house, is willing to train someone."

"Really? I like that idea. I worked out in
Lars' shop one time I was here and really
enjoyed it. Haakan did such fine work too."
He took another drink. "Thank you, Toby."

"You are welcome. We'll need a lot of finish carpenters once this building is up." Toby
finished off his sandwich. "Freda, we really
need water jugs down in the hole in the morning too now."

"Ja, I will take care of it."

After dinner, Toby took Gould over to the
Deming house and introduced him to Andrei
Belin.

"You got me hired here," Mr. Belin said
to Gould.

"I thought you looked familiar. I told you
Blessing would be a great place for you."

"Da. My wife and I very busy here. Mrs.
Amelia teaches us English." He paused. "Now
you want to learn to work wood from *me*?"

"I do."

"But . . ." Mr. Belin looked to Toby, who
half shrugged and nodded.

"We need every man we can find. He wants
to work."

"What . . . um, what can you do? Here, I
mean." Mr. Belin gestured to the parlor.

"I worked with Lars in his workshop a few

times when I was in Blessing before, so I am acquainted with the tools and the importance of accurate measuring. I did well sanding for a fine finish. I am hoping you will teach me plenty more."

Mr. Belin glanced once more to Toby, then motioned Gould to follow him. He stopped and turned to Toby. "List of supplies we need is on counter in kitchen."

"Thank you, Mr. Belin." *It's back to work we go. I wonder what Deborah is doing.*

The day dragged worse than most days, and the sun took forever to set. Finally he put his nails and hammer aside and slogged home. At first he had resented that Deborah was leaving him food all the time because he couldn't help but suspect she had some ulterior motive. Not anymore. He was so tired now that he welcomed any food at all that he did not have to prepare.

He stopped at his front door. A package lay there. He picked it up and took it inside. The return address said Pittsburgh. It must be for Mr. Gould. But why would someone in New York mail it to him instead?

He lit the lantern on his table and smiled at today's note from Deborah before tearing open the package.

And sat down with a thud in the chair. Two pages, one of them a formal letter on letterhead and the other in Ma's writing. And in the box were things a woman would own—thirty-seven cents, a few cosmetics, a dainty brooch with roses on it. Ma's brooch.

He read the letter, stuffed everything back into the box, and hurried to Gerald's house. His mind was whirling. He needed something solid. Gerald was solid; Rebecca was solid.

He burst in the door without knocking. "Gerald!"

Gerald was sitting at the table with Mark on his lap, reading aloud. His mouth dropped open. He set Mark on the floor. "We'll read later, son. This looks important."

Toby dumped the box on the table and flopped down in a chair.

Frowning, Gerald stirred a finger through the little pile of belongings and picked up the letters. His lip trembled as he read them.

Rebecca sat down. "Gerald? Toby? What is it?"

Gerald's voice purred soft, slow, and sorrowful, just like Toby felt. "This parcel is from the Pittsburgh Home for Indigents. The matron found our address among Ma's effects and mailed it to us."

"Her effects?" Rebecca pressed her hands to her mouth. "She's dead?"

Gerald nodded.

Toby felt hot tears in his eyes as he pointed to the other page. "The matron found this partly written letter to us; Ma died before she finished it."

"Oh no! No!" Rebecca looked from brother to brother. "What about Anner?"

"She says Pa took a job at a stock brokerage but he wasn't that good an investor, as we found out here in Blessing. He caused a severe loss to his brokerage. They fired him and ruined him. He disappeared. Ma was going to come back here and live with us, but she got pneumonia and died. They buried her in a pauper's grave."

Rebecca covered her face and sobbed. Toby wished she hadn't done that. He was going to start sobbing any second.

Gerald stared at the pitiful little pile. "As I knew Pa, he would have taken care of Ma and not let her be sent to a poor folks home."

"You're right," Toby said. "For all the mistakes he made, he has a strong sense of responsibility. He'd take care of her if he could."

Gerald rubbed his face with both hands. His eyes were red. He sat up straight and sighed deeply. "We'll go get her body and bring her back, rebury her here, where she should be. Probably next spring, when the ground thaws and we can dig the grave." He smiled a very sad non-smile. "I guess she isn't going anywhere until then."

Toby nodded. At least the wondering was over. Now they knew.

Wait, no they didn't. Where was Pa? Dead? Off somewhere seeking a fortune? That would be like him.

Toby stood up and muttered something that was supposed to be "good-bye." Numb, he slogged out into the darkness.

Ma dead. Pa still gone. A mystery solved, but only by half. Would they ever learn anything about Pa?

And then the sobbing came.

CHAPTER 23

Ingeborg closed her eyes and let the sweet aroma of haying season surround her. How she loved the scent. From her porch she could see the fields, the cattle, and the deaf school. The sound of hammers came very faintly from the new construction.

Beside her, David Gould gestured toward the construction site. "I feel guilty sitting here when some of the men are still working down in the hole."

"We all thought it wise when Toby came up with the idea to make Sunday work a choice. Many of the men go to church first, but others want the money, so the crews are smaller. But the forms keep going up."

"And Dr. Deming and his wife really like the day off from workers in their home. He told me so." Gould leaned back against the cushions on the porch chair. "I hate to admit it, but this body is not used to this kind of work."

"I know. You should have heard Andrew and Thorliff when I insisted on driving the hay wagon. By the end of the first morning, no less, I did not dare say a word when I climbed down. The second day was better."

"Ah, but you do physical labor around here all the time." He studied her sitting in the rocking chair across the table from him. "Here I feel like an old man, and you never age a bit."

"Dear friend, is your eyesight going?"

Gould laughed. A real laugh, not a polite chuckle.

"Ah, good." Ingeborg rocked and smiled. "You are leaving New York manners behind."

"Manners are one thing, society etiquette is quite something else." He tipped his head back and stared up into the cottonwood tree, all atwitter with house finches and chickadees. A wren had built its nest in the box set in the eaves of the porch.

"Look, up in the box." He pointed and turned with questions all over his face. "What kind of bird is that?"

"A wren. She's been coming for the last couple of years. Inga brings her hard beef fat or lard crumbles sometimes. Apparently wrens don't eat bread crumbs."

"Where is Inga?"

"She and Emmy put Rolly in the wagon and are taking him home."

"Kaaren served a fine dinner. Thank you all for including Anton and me."

Ingeborg stared at him in mock horror. "But you are family. Once your son married our Grace, you joined this family, whether you planned on that or not." She raised her eyebrows and tipped her head, just slightly. "Besides, we try to make all strangers feel welcome."

He laughed again. A silence but for the birds and the hammering and sawing from the hole settled upon them.

Ingeborg rocked slowly. *Lord, thank you for this marvelous day and now time to catch up with my old friend.* Eyes closed, she asked, "Do you remember when we met?"

"I almost knocked you off the sidewalk on a street in New York City, so I had to grab you to keep from falling into the gutter. And you were lost, and your hat was askew, and you looked so shocked when I answered your Norwegian." He shook his head. "No, guess I don't remember much."

"Oh ja. And you took me down to pay the grocer the penny for the apple. Poor Thorliff, he thought the boys gave it to him, and he was so thrilled to be eating a real apple."

"I've always wondered, did you let him finish it?"

"I have no idea." Her head resting against

the pillowed chair, she slowly shook her head. "And you showed me New York City from a brougham. And the schools. Right then I decided that if my children wanted to go to college, they would be able to. After we got our *free* land, of course."

"Isn't it amazing how God works in lives?"

"You have certainly made a difference in the lives of the people of Blessing."

"But only with money. You and Reverend Solberg and Haakan, Kaaren—all of you here, you take care of the people. You love them and pray for them and feed them and teach them. You serve."

"You build the schools and hospitals and businesses that we serve in."

He nodded. "Geraldine did too, but she never saw the people."

"You miss her terribly."

"Of course. As we both know, grief takes time before it is forced to release its grip on your heart."

"Thorliff is still trapped by it. He can't seem to let go but just drives himself until he falls asleep anywhere."

"Seems to me I remember Kaaren telling me about a woman who did that years ago. So he learned from watching his mother?"

"God saved me from the pit."

"The pit, as you call it, is a dangerous place. There are whole hospitals and institutions filled with folks whose minds and bodies were destroyed by not only disease but the horrible pit."

"Only God. Only our Father can not only draw us back but rebuild our lives."

"I hope He can." David looked dubious.

"He will, if you let Him."

"Perhaps you need to sit down with me and Anton and Thorliff and—" His voice broke and fell to a whisper. "And teach us what you learned."

"Any time. And we will invite Pastor Solberg too."

The silence crept back in. She heard Emmy and Inga giggling over the creaky wagon. The men calling good-night as they walked out of the hole. Manny and Toby laughing at something.

"Can I get you anything?" Freda asked from behind the screen door.

"No, thank you. I think not. I am sated." Gould started to rise but then sat down again. "You know, Ingeborg, I have not mentioned this to Jonathan yet, let alone discussed it with him. I shall, of course. But I will not be returning to the city. Even as the train was whizzing us across the prairie, I could not see going back to the noise and clutter and hubbub. Peace. I am so ready for peace."

"Then you will stay and build here?"

"Yes. I've made the decision."

She smiled. "The way you've always made your decisions. Once you decide, the matter is done. I am so happy, David. You will add much to our town, and with God's help, we'll add much to your life."

He studied her. "Thank you." He pushed himself to his feet. "I'd better get over to Jonathan's house so I can sleep to be ready for Monday morning, early, at the Deming house. Apparently I will be sanding." He picked up his hat. "Thank you."

"You are welcome—always."

"Grandma, we saw a fox! A gorgeous red fox." Inga bounded up the stairs. "Hello, Mr. Gould."

"Hello, yourself." He tipped his hat and waved to Ingeborg.

Emmy and Inga watched him go out the gate. "He sure is a nice man. Did you see his thumb? He said he hit it with a hammer—twice."

"That happens when you are learning to work with tools."

"Grandpa never had smashed thumbs."

"He'd been using his tools for many, many years. They became friends of his, and he took very good care of them."

Manny joined them. "He told me that if you take care of your tools, your tools will take care of you." He breathed a huge sigh. "Grandpa Haakan was a mighty good man." He looked toward the barn. "I didn't even milk tonight. Lars told me to go help Toby, so I did."

"Ja, that is like Lars. We share the work around here, that's for sure. What's Freda doing?"

Inga peeked in the door. "She's mixing something. Clara is changing Martin and . . . and, Grandma, I'm hungry."

"Me too." Manny swatted a mosquito.

"You are always hungry," Emmy said in her mother voice.

"Can't help it, I'm a growing boy." He held out his leg. "See how short my pants are?"

"The pants I can't help with tonight, but I am sure we'll find food in the icebox and cupboards." Ingeborg rose from her chair. "Hey, Patches, are you hungry too?"

Patches thumped his tail on the floorboards and watched them all troop into the kitchen.

They finished haying the Knutson fields and moved over to the Bjorklund place, leaving a full haymow and six stacks and making sure the hay tops were done just right so the rain would run off, rather than soak in.

Once the dew started forming, all the haying crew headed home in relief. The milkers went to the barn, where the cows were lamenting the lack of attention, and the girls wandered to the house. Somehow, though, life did not slow down.

Ingeborg continued driving in the morning, and afternoons and most of her evenings were full of cooking for both construction crews, canning from the garden, making cheese, and falling into bed at night so exhausted she almost forgot to pray. But only almost. Every time Thorliff came to mind, she thanked God for the answers He was working on.

"Uff da, what is that monstrous noise?" Freda looked out the window one evening as Ingeborg was chopping potatoes.

"They're bringing the steam engine to the hole."

Inga ran into the kitchen and grabbed her hand. "Come on, Grandma, let's go watch."

"Come along, Clara," Ingeborg invited.

She shook her head and signed "You go. Freda and I will keep going here."

Freda shook her head. "I have pies in the oven." She made shooing motions to accent her opinion.

With a girl on each hand dragging Ingeborg along, they hurried over to where the steam engine was stopped. Manny threw another chunk of wood into the firebox. Lars and Toby parked the new cement mixer by the belt drive of the steam engine and set to mounting the one on the other. Trygve and one of his crew were figuring how to attach the sluicebox to the mixer.

"It has to be moveable," Toby said.

"I know," Lars said. "Sure wish we could have seen this beast in action."

Lord, give them wisdom beyond what they know. It looks like we need a miracle or two here.

"Grandma, how they gonna—?" As always, Inga had questions, and she was never afraid to ask them.

"I have no idea."

"Look, the cement mixer is turning."

Manny threw his hands in the air and charged back around the steam engine to feed more wood to the fire to keep the steam up.

While the men on the sluice trough had attached it to the feeder from the turning bucket, moving the end to direct the concrete into the form was another story. They clunked and rattled and tried one thing after another.

While that crew was working with the cement mixer, another was building scaffolding along the basement side of the forms for the concrete tampers to work from. All this while the sun had set, and dusk, instead of creeping in, seemed to be galloping.

Toby raised his arms and yelled, "That's it for today, men. You've done a good job. See you in the morning."

Manny walked back with Ingeborg and

the girls. "Wish Papaw back home in Kentucky coulda seen all this. He liked machinery but never had any, other than a plow he drug behind the mule."

"It's hard to believe what is going on," Ingeborg said. "I remember when we got the first hand-cranked cement mixer. We thought that was the greatest ever. Beat mixing with a shovel in the wheelbarrow. And now this beast can do the work of dozens of wheelbarrows, and faster too." So many changes. Wouldn't Haakan have been thrilled to see this? That steam engine that he and Lars brought home. So proud.

Inga slid her hand into Ingeborg's. "You thinkin' of Grandpa Haakan, huh?"

"How do you know that?"

"You got sad eyes."

"But not for long, I promise."

The next day, when the concrete poured from the sluicebox into the forms, everyone started cheering.

That Friday, Ingeborg and her crew were just loading supper into the wagons when she paused. "What's that noise?"

"Sounds like a fight. O Lord, help us." Freda grabbed the wagon handle and headed for the tables by the hole. "Bring your black bag!" she shouted over her shoulder.

Clara dashed back into the house, grabbed

the bag always kept by the door, and ran to catch up with Ingeborg, who was running to the construction site.

"Go back and get ice."

Clara dashed back to the house.

All the men were slugging it out on the floor of the hole, and one was lying flat on the ground.

"Stop it! Enough!" Toby grabbed one man by the arms, but another hit him again, knocking him back against the wall. Joshua grabbed another guy and hauled him back while Trygve grabbed the water jugs and threw the water at the fighters.

John Solberg bellowed, "Stop! Now stop this!"

But they weren't listening. They were shouting at each other in three or four different languages, swinging at each other.

"Please, Lord, stop this insanity!" Ingeborg set her bag on the table. There was plenty of blood flowing, but they would have to come to her. She did not dare go down there. Clara stared up at her, eyes round. Ingeborg shook her head. "It's not surprising tempers flared. They've been working too hard and long."

"Go back at this and you will all be fired!" Toby yelled as things were slowing down.

Two men were down, and those still standing were shouting at each other. But then a miracle: The men seemed to relax; the shouting slowed. Most just stood there or helped the fallen ones up.

Toby waved an arm. "Get up that ramp and let Mrs. Bjorklund see who she can treat and who needs to go to the hospital. Everyone go home after you eat. I don't want to see your faces until morning."

All in all, six men were injured. Ingeborg sent one to the hospital for stitches after wrapping his head. She treated the others, several of whom would not even look her in the eye. Freda and Clara served the meal while Toby and his foremen went back in the hole to put away the tools. Washing the cement mixer took the longest, sluicing it with water from the water wagon that had arrived with it on the train.

All the crew had left by the time the foremen and John Solberg got to the tables.

"It's a good thing we were at the end of a pour," Joshua Landsverk said as he took a full plate and sat down.

"Takk, Tante Ingeborg, for both doctoring and the food," Trygve said. "I guess we should be grateful something like this hasn't happened before."

"Right." Toby took his plate. "Anyone know what or who started it?"

"Someone dropped a hammer on his partner, and he shoved back, and it exploded from there." Joshua shoveled in a mouthful. "Stupid."

Ingeborg put what was left of her supplies

back in the worn leather bag. "I should have sent one of the others to the hospital too. Let's see, Deborah is on duty tonight. She won't call Astrid unless she absolutely has to. No sense getting more people involved."

"There will be some unhappy wives when these guys get home. You'd have thought they'd been drinking." Solberg sat down and Ingeborg set his plate in front of him. "Toby, I know you are under terrible pressure to get this building weathered in, but you can't keep driving the men like this."

"We'll start doing shift work when haying is done or we get more workers."

"Haying should be done by when?" John Solberg looked to Ingeborg.

"Another week should do it."

"Good. You know, Toby, there have been remarkably few accidents on this project. You three men are doing a good job. It's easy to forget to say thank you."

"Right." Toby wrote himself a note.

Ingeborg could read it from across the table. She nodded. "That's a good idea. I'm sure Thorliff and the others will go along with it."

"They better."

The next morning back on the job, Reverend Solberg declared the following Sunday a no-work day. Everyone cheered.

"And later in the afternoon, there will be a baseball game in the Bjorklund pasture."

Another cheer. He leaned over to Trygve. "They've not let the cows out on that field recently, have they?"

"Ja, that's a good pasture, and the cows keep it grazed down. Shame if we had to mow it to play ball." Trygve grinned at him. "Cow pies just add another bit of sport, that's all."

CHAPTER 24

*T*hank you for doing my laundry and all the meals you have provided. *Toby.* Deborah read the note again and felt a smile clear down to her toes. She tucked the note into her pocket and then made sure there was ice in his icebox, where she had left the hard-boiled-egg salad. On the table waited a large square of coffee cake, several slices of bread, and a bowl of raspberry jam, the skimmings of foam off the top.

You are welcome. Enjoy, she wrote, and slid the note under the dish of jam.

When she stepped down off his porch, she paused and turned to look at the house. How long had she dreamed of being the mistress here? With a sigh, she continued home.

Mary Martha was in the kitchen, scrubbing

out the lard bucket. They would be making soap before long.

"Another note from Toby." Deborah showed it to her.

Mary Martha grinned. "I knew he appreciated what we've done; you just have to wait patiently for answers at times."

Deborah nodded, sure her mother meant more than the thank-you note. "Are you going to make a box for the social also?"

Mary Martha gave her daughter one of those *you have to be kidding* looks. "Don't you think I'm a bit old for that? And married? With a family?"

Deborah turned from searching for a suitable container to decorate. "It's all for a good cause."

"I'll bake a cake and two pies for the bake sale."

Deborah smiled. "That was wise of you women to have both events at the same time. So women who aren't auctioning off boxes can take part anyway." Knowing the people of Blessing, the promised dance was going to be the real draw.

"By the way, I saw Mr. Gendarme at Penny's. He was ordering supplies for his classes, I believe."

"I thought he was on the haying crew." Mr. Gendarme had intended to help build the deaf school, but Jonathan had asked for him.

"John says they are about finished with haying, and then Mr. Gendarme can go back to swinging a hammer." Mary Martha smiled at her. "He asked about you."

Deborah could feel her mouth drop. She stared at her mother, at the same time ignoring the heat climbing up her neck. "What did he say?"

"Oh, he was wondering if you might be interested in going for a soda."

Deborah waited. "All right, Ma, and you said . . ."

Mary Martha's innocence looked a wee bit out of place, as if deliberately chosen. Which it had been, Deborah knew well. She should just ignore this and go about her decorating.

"Why, I said of course. What else would I say? You are not beholden to anyone. And he has such lovely manners." She grinned at her daughter. "And you have to admit, he is a fine-looking young man."

"Ma!" She might as well have been out in the direct August sun all afternoon, as hot as her face felt.

"I told him about the box social."

Deborah closed her eyes. "What else did you tell him?"

"That we are grateful he chose to come to Blessing to teach." Mary Martha dried her hands and reached for her sunbonnet. "I'm going out in the garden to pick lettuce for supper. I wish the tomatoes were ripe enough to eat. I want a fresh tomato in the worst way."

"Well, at least you didn't tell him what my box will look like."

"How could I? That would be improper, and besides, I don't know what you are going to do."

And you can count on my not telling you, Deborah thought. Now to decide what to make to put in her box or basket or whatever she decided to use.

So everyone was shifting gears, from Toby to Mr. Gendarme. Deborah was fairly certain she was not ready to dance to this new tune.

Someone knocked at the front door. Now what? As her mother went out the back door, Deborah walked to the front door. The tall, handsome man standing on the porch nearly took her breath away.

"Why, Mr. Gendarme, what a nice surprise." *When did I last fix my hair? At least I'm not wearing an apron, but this dress . . .* The thoughts rampaged through her mind as she stepped back, motioning him inside.

"I know this is not proper, just coming by like this."

"Rules like that don't apply in Blessing." Her mother's comments drifted in and flustered her even more. "Would you like to sit outside, where it is cooler?" She motioned through the house.

"Actually, I wondered if you might have time to join me for a soda. I've heard such high praise that I would like to try one and . . ." He shook his head. "This is very difficult, this informality. I'm sorry to bother you if you are busy. I shall return later."

He started to turn away. Deborah raised a hand. "Please, Mr. Gendarme, we do not stand on ceremony here, and frankly, you are doing quite well for your first venture into casual society. I would be pleased to join you. Let me tell my mother where I'm going." *Of course, she already knows. Is everyone in Blessing a matchmaker?* "Would you like to meet my family?"

"Certainly." He followed her through the kitchen and out the door.

"I know you have met my mother." *She put you up to this.*

Mary Martha's smile widened. "How nice to see you. Welcome to our home. Can I get you something to drink, eat?"

"Mr. Gendarme has invited me to have a soda."

She started to introduce the children but didn't get the words out before Mark looked up from snapping beans and interrupted. "Oh, that sounds so good."

The youngest, Emily, came running. "Are we going for sodas, Ma?" She was almost dancing for joy.

Deborah sent her ma a pleading look.

"Would you mind, Mrs. Solberg, if they all came along? You included, of course," Mr. Gendarme said. He certainly looked sincere, but still Deborah wished she could crawl under the porch.

"Please, Ma, please," the little imps chorused.

"Well, if you are sure . . ." Mary Martha said.

Anton smiled at Deborah. "I have two younger brothers and two younger sisters, and I haven't seen them in far too long. I am delighted to meet yours." He paused and lowered his voice. "Please let me do this."

What could she say? Several ideas flitted through her mind, but practicality took over. "All right." She turned to the eager mob. "You have to wash your hands and faces, and Emily, bring a brush so you don't look like a wild woman."

She and Mary Martha both pinned their hats in place, and out the door they went.

Rebecca greeted them from behind the counter. "Welcome to all of you. Deborah, I was beginning to think you were mad at me or something."

"Whatever for?"

"I haven't seen you in weeks."

"I know. You have met Mr. Gendarme, I hope."

"I did, at the soiree. And I've seen you at

church. I hear they put you to work on the haying crew."

"They did. I will always appreciate how much it takes to ensure that the animals are well fed."

"Now, that's a nice way of saying that. I used to help with haying too, but now I'd rather make and serve ice cream and sodas." Rebecca pointed to the sign on the wall that listed the flavors.

"Why don't you serve the others first while I make up my mind?" Mr. Gendarme stepped back.

"That'll be two chocolate and one vanilla?" Rebecca looked to the children, who nodded and grinned. "And what about you, Mrs. Solberg?"

"The raspberry, of course." Within minutes, the sodas appeared on the counter, and Deborah handed them out.

"Did you decide, Mr. Gendarme?" Rebecca asked.

He nodded to Deborah. "Her first."

"Oh, she wants raspberry. Deborah's helped me choose what to serve, and we both favor the fresh berry ones."

He glanced at Deborah, who nodded. Rebecca handed her the frosted glass with a dab of raspberry syrup on the outside.

"You can have tastes if you can't decide," Deborah said before sucking on her straw.

"No, thanks. That one looks too good to pass up."

Sodas in hand, they joined the others at the tables outside in the shade.

The chatter and questions came thick and fast.

"Are you going to teach at the grade school too, Mr. Gendarme?" Emily asked.

"Funny you should ask. Mister—er, Reverend Solberg and I were talking about that. I might teach a music class there."

"Really?"

"That would be wonderful," Mary Martha said with a smiling nod. "This last year without Elizabeth, our music program, if you could call it that, pretty much died."

"She taught Linnea how to play the piano. Now Linnea sometimes plays with our band and at Sunday school," Emily said.

"I've heard wonderful things about Elizabeth. I can see why she is so missed."

"I heard you play the violin," Deborah said.

"I do and play at some other instruments. Jonathan and I used to play together for our church and some other places. Then we grew up and moved away. In his case, far away."

They all finished their sodas and meandered toward home.

"Thank you for such a marvelous treat." Deborah smiled at him.

"You are welcome." He smiled back at her. "I like your family. They remind me of home."

"You lived in the city, correct?"

"True, but during the summer we move to our beach house on Long Island."

"On the ocean?" Emily's eyes rounded.

"Yes."

"Someday I want to see an ocean." She grinned up at him. "Thank you for the soda."

He turned to Mary Martha. "Thank you for letting me intrude on your afternoon."

"Intrusion? I think not. You are welcome any time. Would you like to stay for supper?"

"No, thank you. I told Grace I would be there, and I have more things to prepare for my classes."

"You will be attending the box social?"

"Of course. It wouldn't look too good if the schoolteacher wasn't there to help in a party to raise money for the new school, now would it?" He glanced at Deborah. "I hear that the creators behind the boxes is a tightly guarded secret."

"We try really hard to keep it that way, but . . ."

"But secrets sometimes have a habit of leaking out?"

"That they do. Thank you again."

He bowed slightly over her hand. "My pleasure."

She watched him jog down the two steps, settle his hat back on his head, and start toward the Gould house.

Now, that was certainly not what she had planned for the afternoon.

Saturday night the people of Blessing flocked to the schoolhouse, where gaily wrapped boxes graced a table and the platform stood in place for the auctioneer and later the band. Tables and benches surrounded the well-packed area used for dancing. The table for baked goods expanded to two as more women brought their gifts.

"Deborah, just look at this! I can't believe we have all that!" Sophie stared at the laden tables. "I mean . . ."

"I would say this is the way some families feel they can help with the fundraiser." Deborah moved a tall cake to the back so that it would not hide a dainty little pink-frosted cake.

"How do we price these?" Mary Martha brought out the box with the change for the cashiers.

Sophie studied the table. "What if everything is the same price? Then we don't have that problem. Make it a nickel or a dime." She turned to Ingeborg, who set three loaves of bread on the table. "What do you think, price-wise? Easier if everything is the same?"

"Sounds like a good idea to me. Did I hear nickel or dime for one serving? Then twenty-five for a whole pie, cake, or loaf of bread." She put a finger to her chin. "And we could be open for dickering, especially as we near the end and someone wants to purchase a lot."

"I would think so."

Freda set down a plate of her famous cinnamon rolls. "Are we open for business?"

"We are." Sophie strode to the platform and picked up the megaphone. "May I have your attention, please?" A whistle from the back did the trick. "Remember, all the money we earn tonight will go into the fund to build and supply our new high school. All of it. And with that, the bake tables are open for business!"

Reverend Solberg took the megaphone. "We'll start the bidding for our box social in half an hour. Please, no eating until all the boxes are sold to the highest bidder. And after that, the dancing will begin."

Astrid and Amelia had agreed to arrange the box social table. Deborah made sure hers was as inconspicuous as possible.

"Do you give hints?" one of the single men asked.

Amelia smiled at him. "No, you take your chances. I can guarantee you will have good food and a charming partner. I'm warning you, the bidding will go fast."

He pointed to a basket with a blue bow. "That one."

"No, Heinrich, you must bid on it when it comes up; you tell the auctioneer what you are willing to pay, then someone else will make an offer. You'll see how it goes."

Deborah crossed the dance floor to help out at the bake sale. When the rush at the bake tables slowed down, she finally had a chance to look around. There was Toby, right over there. Was Mr. Gendarme . . . yes, back there talking to Mr. Belin. He was supposed to have a gift for languages. Were they conversing in English or in Russian? And why was she mooning about him when Toby was right over there?

Her pa picked up the megaphone again. "Come on, folks, we're ready to start the bidding. Garth Wiste will be our auctioneer tonight, and you have fifteen boxes to bid on. Fifteen chances to enjoy a meal with one of our charming young ladies."

Garth took the megaphone, tried talking through it and, shaking his head, put it down. "Raise your hand, please, to bid. We'll start with box one." He took the box Amelia handed him and held it up. "Looks good to me. Who'll bid a nickel?"

Hands shot up.

"Ten cents?" When he upped it to twenty-five cents, three hands were left. "Thirty-five cents?" Two were left. "Forty!" One fellow stood alone.

Garth rapped his gavel. "Do I hear forty-five? Going once at forty, twice at forty . . . sold! To that lucky fellow for forty cents.

And who is the lucky lady who brought this box?"

Rachel Anderson, Goodie Wold's niece, stepped forward with a shy smile.

The boxes quickly sold until only five remained. Deborah made sure she kept a straight face.

Mercy Hastings stood next to her. "Did you tell him?"

"Tell him? No, I did not!" She frowned. "Tell whom?"

"Mr. Gendarme. Or Toby. Whoever."

"No!" Then she added, "But . . . I hope."

Some of the men had been bidding on boxes just to get the bids up, Deborah knew, but they were running out of boxes, and Toby, Anton, Samuel, and a couple of the newer men were still without supper.

Down to three boxes. The highest price so far was one dollar for Maxine Heinrick's.

Garth held up a red and white box, smaller than most of them, with no ribbon, no adornment. Just a box. "Now fellas, this looks very plain and"—he sniffed the box—"smells mighty good. Who'll give me thirty cents?"

No hands.

Garth looked around. "This is a fundraiser, folks, get it? *Fund*raiser, and some of you are hungry. I'm gonna start over. Who'll bid *forty* cents?"

Many hands went up.

"That's more like it! And it really does smell good; fresh bread for sure. Fifty cents. Sixty! Sixty-five? Going once, going twice . . . sold, for sixty cents! Samuel, you got yourself a supper partner."

Mercy breathed a sigh of relief and grinned at Samuel as he took the box. She followed him to a table in the corner.

Deborah and Sophie exchanged glances. *I don't want to be last*. Deborah stared at the auctioneer, refusing to look at the men.

He held her basket up next. Who would she eat with? *You know you hope Toby will get this*. There was that voice again. The bidding climbed quickly to seventy-five cents. She could feel the heat in her neck. *This is all for the school, all for the school*.

"One dollar!" Toby's bid.

"A dollar ten," called another.

"Two dollars."

The crowd murmured.

She refused to look around. Did she want to have supper with Mr. Gendarme?

"Three!" Toby.

Three dollars? *This is absolute craziness*. That was too much money to spend like this. *It's all for the school*.

"Three fifty" came from the back of the room.

Silence. Then, Toby: "Four."

Garth looked at his bidders. "Four going once, four going twice—"

"Ten!" from the back.

People gasped.

"A fortune! Anyone wanna bid two fortunes?" Silence. "Going, going . . . gone to our new schoolteacher, Mr. Anton Gendarme." Garth brought his gavel down.

Was it disappointment she felt? Or out and out embarrassment? She smiled at Mr. Gendarme and handed him the basket. "Shall I go get my family to chaperone again?" she asked.

He chuckled and offered her his arm.

Deborah was happy to see the bidding heat up again on the final box. Now she was not the only one. The price reached three seventy-five and stayed there. Toby would have supper with Naomi Lindquist.

The other single men headed for the bake sale table to purchase their supper. Families brought out their picnic baskets, some offering to share with the men who'd not gotten a basket.

"Where would you like to sit?" Mr. Gendarme asked her.

"Wherever you wish." Ten dollars! The sum still stunned her.

"I was thinking there." He pointed to a spot near Mercy and Samuel.

They sat down, and she flipped out a

tablecloth and set out the food. "First of all, my crackers and some of the Blessing soft cheese."

"Your crackers?"

She nodded. "I came up with the recipe. Freda makes the cheese. Then deviled eggs, sliced beef with horseradish, chicken and lettuce salad, and pickles. And I hope you like potato-bread rolls."

"This looks delicious." He smiled at her. "I figured it would."

"Why?"

"Because from what I've heard, anything you do, you do well."

She studied him. He'd asked other people about her? Was that what he meant? "But you bid on the boxes earlier . . ."

"To help get the bidding going and going up." He took several crackers and smeared the soft cheese on one. "This is really good."

"And you stopped?"

"I was hoping for your basket."

"How did you know which was mine?"

"I gambled." He reached for one of the deviled eggs. "Our cook used to make these. I haven't had any for a long time. Aren't you going to eat?"

"I am." She helped herself.

"And I watched the faces. Teaching school has taught me a lot about watching people to understand them."

"I was careful."

355

"You were, but Mrs. Wiste was watching you. Dead giveaway."

She glanced over to another table when she heard Toby laugh. He seemed to be having a fine time. She opened the salad. "I hope you like this. It's Ingeborg's recipe."

He spread some of the soft cheese on a roll. "Uncle David told me there were great cooks in Blessing. He wasn't exaggerating."

"Tell me about your family."

"Well, let's see. I'm the oldest of five."

As he continued, she watched his face. He ate delicately, like a cultured person, and he seemed so totally at ease. A short distance away, Toby and Naomi were giggling and mock fighting over what was probably the last cookie. It broke, and they laughed with a lot more humor and enthusiasm than the situation seemed to call for.

Deborah forced her attention back to her supper companion. He was talking about his uncle and Jonathan. And his friends. And a beloved old rat terrier named Fred. When he started talking about the chickens they raised during the Spanish-American War, she realized she really wasn't interested in this at all.

Toby laughed again. She didn't have to ask him to tell her about his family. She knew his family.

She was having dinner with a handsome young man who was obviously interested in her, and all she could think about was Toby.

CHAPTER 25

Ah. Rebecca, I don't know how you can cook such a fine supper and make sodas and ice cream all day too." Toby leaned back in his chair. "Thank you."

"It's been too long since you've not been working till dark."

"I should be over there now too."

"That's what you have foremen for." Gerald passed the dishes of ice cream around the table.

"Do I get to keep driving wagons?" Benny asked, grinning up at his mor. "Or do I come back to the Soda Shoppe?"

"Keep in mind you are going to start school in a couple weeks."

"I know." Benny handed Agnes back her spoon. "Now, eat with that. You can't eat ice cream with your fingers."

Nessie shook her head, picked up her bowl, and drank the rest of it.

"Agnes Mary Valders!"

Benny tried to keep a straight face, but a giggle sneaked out.

"Benny, don't encourage her." Rebecca handed him a washcloth. "Here, you mop her up."

Toby smiled at his brother. "Thank you for supper. I s'pose I better head on home."

"It's early yet. Come on outside and we'll see if we can fend off the mosquitoes." Gerald looked toward the kitchen.

"Your pipe is on the stove, where it's supposed to be," Rebecca said.

Gerald flinched. "Oh. Where did I leave it this time?"

"Out on the porch."

Toby looked around the table. Did he want this too? Four children and, looking at Rebecca, it seemed that another might be on the way. Marriage sounded good—being with a good woman, sharing their lives—but kids . . . kids were something else. Was he ready for all that?

"Thanks again, Rebecca," he said as everyone scattered from the table.

Her smile always made him feel welcome. "You've been working too hard, like all the others. I'm glad you agreed to come for supper. I figure you must get lonely in that big house by yourself."

He snorted. "I'm never there but to fall into bed and leave again before sunrise. The garden is thanks to you and Benny, so I do hope you're harvesting all you need."

"Mrs. Sam has been coming with me to harvest, and she did some of the weeding too. She has been drying the string beans, and now we'll let the rest of them mature so we can have plenty of dried beans. I've been saving seed for you too. Or rather, Gerald has. He goes out to the gardens nearly every evening. I think he gets tired of being cooped up inside the telephone office all the time."

Toby lifted Agnes down from her high chair. "There you go, Nessie." He glanced around. "Where did Benny go?"

"He's probably already outside with Gerald."

"And Mark? Out there too?"

"He's probably nagging Benny to push him on the swing. You go sit with your brother. He's concerned about you."

Concerned? Other than the standard brotherly love they shared, why concerned? Toby wandered out to the porch.

"It's so nice to be harvesting tomatoes now," Gerald said, coming back from the garden with a ripe tomato in each hand.

"You've become quite the gardener."

"Thanks to Benny. He needed help digging and raking a couple of years ago, and we've been doing this together ever since. Rebecca was grateful to give it up."

"Push me, Onkel Toby," Mark cried from the swing.

"No, you need to go inside now. Come on." Gerald scooped up his son, put him inside the door, and sank down on one of the chairs on the porch. "Come on, Toby, have a seat. Knowing that wife of mine, she'll be bringing drinks out as soon as she has the children in bed."

"I thought you helped with that."

"I do, but in the summer, Benny and I garden." Gerald picked up his pipe and scraped out the old tobacco, knocking it into the flower pot. "How come you never took up a pipe?"

"No desire to."

"I've heard good things about what a fine job you're doing."

Toby shook his head. "If we get that building weathered in, it'll be a miracle for sure."

"You got outbid for Deborah's box at the social."

"Money talks."

"Are you still going to invite Mr. Gendarme to share your house?"

"Sure. For now he seems content to stay with Jonathan and Grace. But I offered before, and I'll offer again. Why not?" Toby definitely smelled a rat. Which rat, he wasn't sure.

"Oh, I don't know. I guess I thought you were sweet on Deborah."

Oh. Of course. That rat. Toby didn't answer, studying his hands instead. He swatted a mosquito.

Benny clumped up the three steps, half pulling himself on the handrail, his crutches under one arm. "Onkel Toby, you want me to water your garden? Pa and I did ours. Pretty dry now."

"Which is good for harvest and not so good for gardens. Water if you want, but you're still driving the wagon. So when do you have time?"

Benny sank down on one of the chairs and rubbed his legs. "I need new padding for my stumps." He removed one prosthesis and studied the cup, then rubbed the end of his leg.

"Are you getting a sore spot?" Gerald leaned forward. "Unwrap and let me see."

"No, I think it's okay for now. I prob'ly should go back to using my wagon for a while. Give my legs a rest."

When Benny went into the house, Toby said, "He seems so much older and wiser than his age."

"He always has. When I start to get impatient, I think of him, and right away I settle down."

Toby broke the silence beginning to stretch. "You ever wonder what happened to Pa and Ma? I mean, receiving Ma's things in the mail like that—so strange. Even after that, I think sometimes he'll step off that train. . . ."

"He'll never come back. He left under too big a cloud."

"Poor Ma. Why didn't she come home? You think he left her?" Toby shook his head. "So very strange."

"All I know is he sure changed the last couple of years. He wasn't the same man who raised us, that's for sure." Gerald nodded slowly. "But they took us in and gave us a good home. For that, I will ever be thankful."

Rebecca brought them each a glass of swizzle. "Mosquitoes aren't so bad tonight?"

"They don't like us; we're not sweet enough."

"Right. If I brought out a lamp . . ."

"Don't. No thanks."

She sat down in her rocker, but only on the edge of it. Obviously she was not intending to stay. "So, Toby, I was thinking maybe you'd settle down."

Toby grimaced. Here it was again. "You mean with Deborah?"

"Well . . . ja."

"Maybe I'm not the settling-down type."

"Are you afraid of getting married?"

The silence stretched like a new rubber band.

Gerald banged his pipe on the porch rail. "Strange, isn't it? You were always the lady's man, but I'm the one who got married and settled in."

Toby stood. "I better be getting on home. Thanks for the pleasant evening."

Gerald stood as well. "We need to do this more often."

"Winter will come soon enough with long evenings and short days." Toby crammed his hat onto his head.

Rebecca stood up too. "I hope we don't wait until then."

"We won't be working Sundays anymore, now that we're ready to start framing. Both Thorliff and Reverend Solberg made that decision."

"Wise." Gerald walked Toby to the gate. "'Night now."

Toby mounted the three steps to his back porch. Why did he have a feeling his brother had wanted to ask something else but didn't?

The last time he'd had supper at their house, they had invited Deborah too. What a fine evening that had been. The Fourth of July celebration stepped into his mind. The walk home with her had been both memorable and comfortable. Like they had swept back in time to their younger years. When he used to tease her unmercifully but drew the line at anyone else teasing her.

And now? She was changed. He was changed. Now what?

His house was too quiet. Having someone else living here might help with that.

Even if that someone else was Anton Gendarme, who shared Deborah's box supper, outbidding him? With a show of wealth. Whoever heard of spending that much money for a box supper, even if it was for a good cause? What a show-off.

He could always say he changed his mind. Assuming the guy ever actually wanted to move from Jonathan's place.

But that would seem rather strange, since he'd been the one to offer. It's not like anyone asked him. But that was before that ten-dollar bid. Toby didn't even have ten dollars at the moment.

He headed for bed, even though it was early. It would be a busy week, as usual. Instead of falling asleep almost before his head hit the pillow, as he often did, he found himself on his back, staring up at the ceiling, hands locked behind his head.

One would think that as much as he enjoyed Deborah's company and appreciated all the food she had left for him, and the clean clothes and bedding, that he would be smart enough to pursue the relationship. Something told him she was willing. So why did the thought of marriage make him want to jump on the train and head west or east or anywhere else?

Look at Gerald and Rebecca, how happy they are, how they love their children.

Had Mor and Far Valders loved the two

boys they adopted off the train? It was hard to tell, but they had taken good care of them. Toby had forgotten much of their former life on the streets of New York City. What he remembered was screaming and beatings and being hungry and running. Ah, the running. And hiding. The names the man they had called Pa had called them. Even now his heart picked up speed. His hands clenched of their own accord.

Enough! He wrestled the door to those memories shut again. He inhaled a deep breath and held it before exhaling slowly. Perhaps he should talk with Gerald about what he remembered. Gerald was older. If it hadn't been for him getting them on that train . . . and how they stayed hidden until hunger drove them to sneak off the train and into the Blessing Mercantile, trying to find something to eat before the train pulled out.

He rolled over and punched his pillow into a fluffy mound. Probably the reason he couldn't fall asleep was because it was still too light out. Yes, that must be it. Or he was still mourning his mother.

He heard a dog bark somewhere. The breeze flirting with the curtains, a night bird calling, the house creaking into evening rest. No, he would not take back his offer to Mr. Gendarme. This house needed more people.

What it really needs is a woman's touch. He remembered the huge work crew that had come in to clean the house before Anji and her kids moved in, a little more than a year ago. It had felt like a home when they lived here, but now it just felt . . . hollow.

He flipped to the other side and reworked his pillow. What would it hurt if he spent more time with Deborah? And there was always Miss Lindquist or someone else. Lots of prospects. He'd had a nice time with Naomi at the box social. But he hadn't offered to walk her home. Why not? Because as it turned out, some other fellow did, that was why. He had danced quite a few dances with her, though.

You didn't dance even once with Deborah. She didn't seem to have time for him, not that he'd been in a hurry to ask her. But she had plenty of time to dance with Anton Gendarme.

He glanced out the window; the sun was just now sinking out of sight. Maybe he should just give up and go downstairs to read or something.

Toby Valders, is there even the tiniest bit of a chance that you are jealous?

Could consciences snicker?

Deborah stood on the riverbank as the sun began its final descent. Toby, Toby, Toby. In spite of the distraction of the handsome math teacher, her heart kept going back to Toby.

And that was funny in a way. Anton had

lots of money. Toby had almost none. Anton's family spent the summer relaxing in a house on an ocean beach. Toby didn't have much in the way of family, and he himself spent the summer supervising construction crews.

But Toby was . . . well, he was Toby, and she loved him.

However, was this practical? Anton could give her and her children a secure future with enough resources to live well. Anton was smart and witty. Would she be wiser to marry him and put thoughts of Toby away with the other memories of her youth?

The river flowed past her in its casual way. The river did not care one bit about anything. Last year elephants had ripped up the stream-side willows and eaten them. A few months ago on this riverbank, wild dogs had threatened children who were out fishing. Every now and then the river flooded, causing so much damage and loss. And it did not care; it simply rolled on. Perhaps Deborah cared too much. Was that possible? Should she quit trying to make all these impossible decisions and just let life, like the river, carry her along?

She had hoped that taking a walk along the river at the close of day would clear her mind and help her make decisions. Ha. Her thoughts were as muddled as ever.

She paused, frowning. Was that a human voice? Couldn't be. She remembered hearing once that mountain lions sounded like a woman screaming. Surely not! But . . . there it was again, and it came from downstream.

She was right! It was a human voice calling for help. She gathered up her skirts and broke into a run toward the sound.

"No!" The voice ahead was cracked and dry, like an old woman's voice. "Help me!"

There! Beyond those reeds! It was no old woman at all; it was Clara, and she was screaming!

Clara was clutching her baby in its sling against her chest while she kicked at a dog, shoving her booted foot at it. A huge, snarling gray dog. It feinted and lunged. It was trying to grab the baby! *Oh, dear God, no!*

Deborah picked up the first big stick she saw, a torn limb, and ran toward the dog. *This is crazy, Deborah, don't! You can't stop a huge dog!*

The dog grabbed Clara's boot in its mouth and pulled backward. She lost her balance and fell on her side. Instantly she wrapped herself around her baby, protecting it beneath her. She was screaming and sobbing.

Deborah knew she couldn't just swing her stick at the dog like a baseball bat. She tucked it against her side and thrust it straight forward like a spear, jabbing at the dog.

A stroke of luck: the dog turned on her and tried to grab the stick in its mouth, but it rammed partway down the dog's throat.

Deborah shoved with all her strength. The dog's hind legs collapsed and it fell straight backward. She kept pushing and fell on top of it, her body weight and the stick pinning it to the ground. The dog squirmed mightily and its front legs clawed against her, but they ripped her skirt and petticoats without reaching her skin.

She heard more human voices shouting from farther downstream. Clara screamed louder, but her voice was cracking. Deborah shrieked too. She heard people coming, but she couldn't see who it was. It sounded like children.

Manny! Manny was there! He dropped to his knees beside them, hooked his fingers in the dog's nostrils, and dragged that ugly head back. His knife plunged down into the dog's neck and sliced across it. Hot blood spurted onto the ground.

The dog's struggles became weak, and then they stopped.

Manny was panting heavily. He drew in a huge breath. "We're safe now." He released his grip on the dog's head and sat back.

Deborah sat up. "The baby."

Inga was helping Clara sit up.

Deborah crawled to them. "Let me see."

Still sobbing, Clara pulled Martin out of his sling. They were surrounded by children now; it seemed like dozens from the shrill little voices asking questions, but it was only three or four.

Panting and wheezing, Ingeborg came staggering up. "Is the baby hurt?"

Deborah started at the top as the baby squalled lustily, checking his head for injury, then examining his arms and legs. "I think he's fine." She handed the baby to Ingeborg and turned to Clara. "Are you injured?"

And Clara's newfound voice croaked, "No."

It was an hour later and totally dark now, but Deborah's nerves had not stopped chattering. Her fingers still vibrated, and even her lip still trembled a little.

They were sitting around the big slab table in the hospital kitchen. All of them. Ingeborg and the children were drinking juice, and they were giving Clara honey-and-lemon tea for her poor sore throat. Deborah's stomach was still too upset to drink anything, let alone think about eating.

Manny swallowed another bite of his sausage sandwich. "I looked that dog over good. He had healed bullet scars in his shoulder and back, but he was crippled up, and one front leg was useless. So he couldn't chase fast game like rabbits or ground squirrels anymore. His ribs and backbone were all sticking out, so he was starving. Prob'ly why he tried to get the baby."

"So when the men went after the dog pack, one of the dogs survived." Ingeborg looked older than usual.

"I'd guess so."

Deborah asked Clara, "Why were you and Martin down at the river?"

Clara rocked back and forth, holding her son, who was sound asleep. "Cutting wild herbs for Ingeborg. Then she would show me how to dry them."

"I'm thrilled you found your voice; we've been praying that this would happen. But what a horrible way to have to find it." Ingeborg was smiling at Clara as if she were a long lost daughter come home. And in many ways she was, Deborah decided.

Clara's eyes got wet. "I didn't want to lose another one. I couldn't lose another one."

"Another one?" Deborah asked.

Clara's voice was a hoarse, dry whisper, and Deborah had to listen closely. "That man who left me here. He has a cabin in the hills out east, way out in the forest, no roads around. Just him and me, and he said he would kill me if I tried to leave. I had a baby, a tiny little girl, so beautiful. But she had a, uh . . . her foot was like this." She twisted Martin's tiny foot. "But more."

Martin's little hand opened and closed, but he slept on.

"It's called a club foot," Ingeborg explained. "It happens occasionally."

Manny cackled and burst into song. "'Ole Satan wears a clubfoot shoe, way in de middle of de air; and if you don't watch he gonna slip it on you, way in de middle of de air.' We sung that back in Kentucky when I was a kid." He grinned and finished off his sandwich.

When I was a kid? Deborah smiled. Well, he had performed a man's heroic deed tonight; maybe he wasn't a child anymore.

Clara let out a shuddering sigh. "Cal said the baby was deformed and no good. He said, 'I'll take care of it.' He ripped my baby out of my arms and went out the door, I don't know where. I heard her crying and wailing and then they were gone. He was gone all day. He came back after dark without her and never mentioned her again."

Ingeborg stared, aghast. "Surely he didn't kill her. He must have given her to someone or left her on some doorstep."

"I don't know. I don't know. When he yanked her out of my arms and left, that's when my voice left. I tried to cry and shout and I couldn't. Until now. When I was afraid I'd lose Martin too."

Deborah was crying. Just the thought that someone could do that, that Clara had to suffer . . . "Oh, Clara!"

"I named her Lily." Clara smiled slightly. "Every day when I get up, I think, *Someday I will find Lily*. And you know? Someday I will."

Several days later, after a day of canning, when Martin insisted on attention, Ingeborg and Clara adjourned to the porch with cups of tea.

Ingeborg set her rocker in motion while she watched Clara settling Martin in his sling after the final nursing of the day. Since he had started to eat soft foods, he wasn't as hungry as earlier, and he often patted Clara's cheek with his fat little fingers.

"He sure is a good baby."

"Ja, I am grateful." Clara picked up her tea and sipped. "I bee thinking. . . ."

"As always." Ingeborg brushed away a mosquito.

"You never ask me about my life before Blessing."

"I figured you would tell me when you wanted to."

"Why did you name me Clara?"

Ingeborg rested her head against the rocker back. "I had a dear aunt named Clara, and I have always liked the name."

"I was named Sjorn."

"Would you like us to call you that?"

Clara shook her head. "No. That life was not good. I don't want to be reminded of it. Just thought you might want to know. I mean, after all, you gave me a new life, and I don't never want to go back to any part of that."

Freda pushed open the screen door and joined them on the porch, fanning herself with her apron. "Nice out here." She batted at a whining tormentor. "Uff da. Can I get you anything?"

"No, you just sit here and put your feet up for a while."

To Ingeborg's surprise, Freda did just that. Would wonders never cease?

CHAPTER 26

W elcome back, Dr. Johnson." Astrid greeted him as he stepped down from the train, Ingeborg at her side.

He inhaled deeply and looked up and around. "Thank you. Blue sky, sunshine, ah, you are so right. It is good to be home." He moved aside. "And, Dr. Astrid, I brought help with me."

Three, not two, women stepped off the train.

Astrid gasped, stunned; her mouth dropped open. "Mrs. Korsheski! I can't believe you are here! How wonderful!" Astrid threw her arms around the slender woman, knocking her hat askew. She stepped back quickly. "Oh, forgive me, I'm sorry."

"Oh no, dear, now I know for sure I am

welcome, since I came without your knowledge or invitation."

Astrid turned to Ingeborg. "Mor, remember, Mrs. Korsheski is head of nursing at Morganstein Hospital."

The stationmaster interrupted. "Eh, Dr. Johnson, we need to get the train moving. You all have your baggage?"

"Other than what is in the baggage car, thank you," Dr. Johnson called.

"Of course I remember!" Ingeborg smiled as she grasped Mrs. Korsheski's hand. "It's so good to see you again after all these years. What is your secret, that you haven't aged a bit?" Years earlier, Ingeborg had gone to the Chicago hospital for surgery.

Mrs. Korsheski just laughed. "I'm surprised you remember me."

Astrid asked, "How long can you stay?"

"I thought perhaps two weeks. To help get your new nurses settled." She gestured to the two just behind her. "And to see your operation firsthand. Everyone who has come out here sings its praises."

"Ladies, can we move away from the train before the conductor has an apoplectic seizure?" Arms wide, Dr. Johnson herded them toward the station.

"All aboard!" The train was moving before the conductor swung aboard.

Dr. Johnson led a bright-eyed young

woman forward. "Let me introduce our student nurses for the year. Dr. Astrid Bjorklund, Mrs. Bjorklund, I am pleased to introduce Laura Lee Reineke, who has been pleading to be chosen to come here for the last year."

Astrid picked up on his *our*. Apparently Dr. Johnson did indeed consider Blessing home. What a fine way to start his new life.

"I am so thrilled to finally be in Blessing," Nurse Reineke gushed. "You have no idea how we all talk about it in Chicago."

"And Nurse Jane Wisokay, from Cleveland. She is a city girl who is hoping she will like it here."

"I felt exactly that way about Chicago—the reverse, of course, but you can count on being busy here," Ingeborg told her.

"Are we registered at the boardinghouse?" Dr. Johnson asked.

"Yes, your trunks will be delivered there. Now you have a choice: to see the hospital or go to your rooms, if you would rather." Astrid paused.

"Please, the hospital for me," Mrs. Korsheski said with a smile. Dr. Johnson nodded too.

Ingeborg watched the nurses' faces. "If you would rather go to the boardinghouse, I can take you there while the others go to the hospital."

"Nurse Reineke has not been feeling well on the train. Perhaps a rest in a non-moving bed might help," Mrs. Korsheski said.

"Thank you." The girl smiled wanly.

"Do you mind if I go to the hospital?" Nurse Wisokay asked her friend.

"Not at all."

Ingeborg took Nurse Reineke's arm. "Come with me. Hopefully we'll have you up and feeling good again by morning."

"Takk, Mor," Astrid whispered, and they headed off toward Mor's wagon. She waved at the stationmaster. "Could you please have someone take their bags to their rooms at the boardinghouse? Thank you." *Mrs. Korsheski!* Astrid still felt stunned. "I'll introduce you to Blessing as we head east to the hospital, which is that white building you can see next to the machine plant."

On Main Street, she pointed to the left. "Our stores are down there, that is the boardinghouse, and this way, you'll see my house. My mother-in-law is famous for her roses and flowers. Across the street is the Bjorklund house, where Dr. Elizabeth lived. Her husband Thorliff, my brother, owns the newspaper, and he and a group of others own the construction company that is helping Blessing grow."

"New buildings since I left." Dr. Johnson waved at Amelia, who as always had a basket of flowers over her arm. "That woman is a gem."

"That's for sure. Up to the right you see the grain elevator and beyond that is the Blessing Flour Mill."

"They got the grain elevator back up and running mighty fast."

"Desperation is a good incentive. That big building there not only sells machinery, but produces seeders and other parts. And there is our hospital." Astrid motioned to the white building with the portico. "We serve patients from a ten-mile-or-more radius. Some even come on the train."

"And bring their diseases along," Mrs. Korsheski added wryly.

"That too." Everyone here knew about the diphtheria that had come last summer on the circus train.

"Look at the roses here too," Nurse Wisokay exclaimed. "Right at the hospital." She inhaled. "Oh, they smell so good."

"Not like Chicago, eh?" Mrs. Korsheski teased. She inhaled too. "Dr. Johnson, you were so right. Blessing does indeed smell far different than Chicago."

Astrid pulled open the door, and Dr. Johnson took her place, holding the door, motioning the others inside.

Miriam came out of Mrs. Ohnstetter's room, froze, and nearly dropped her tray of dishes. "Mrs. Korsheski!" She set the tray on the floor beside the door and ran forward. "Mrs. Korsheski!" Miriam's smile just got wider. "What a wonderful surprise!"

"I couldn't resist coming." Mrs. Korsheski looked to Astrid. "I won't be intruding?"

Astrid laughed. "Which shift do you want first?"

Miriam, Deborah, and the rest of the on-duty staff lined up in the hall, including Mrs. Geddick and her daughter, Adelaide, who hustled to the end of the line. Astrid introduced her people, then the new people, saying each name at least twice. Mrs. Korsheski smiled at each as they were introduced.

"Dinner in half an hour," Mrs. Geddick announced, and she and her daughter returned to the kitchen.

"That is fresh bread we smell, correct?" Dr. Johnson returned his attention to the group and grinned at the student nurse. "You will really come to appreciate her. This hospital food is like no other. She even has a garden out back." He looked to Astrid, who nodded.

Astrid added, "And when you are not on the floor working, you are always welcome to sit at the big slab table in the kitchen to rest for a moment. Never hesitate to ask Mrs. Geddick for a cup of tea or coffee or a snack to tide you over."

Mrs. Korsheski nodded, smiling. "Good, good."

"It won't take long to show you around." Astrid loved showing off her hospital. She showed them the examination rooms and the room where she performed operations, and even the supply closet.

"That seems rather small," Mrs. Korsheski commented. "You make do with so little."

"We do what we have to do," she replied.

They breezed quickly through the patients' rooms and came to a stop beside Mrs. Ohnstetter, who had wheeled herself into the hall.

After she was introduced, Mrs. Korsheski bent to take Mrs. Ohnstetter's hand. "Thank you for the scarf you knit and sent me. It kept me warm last winter."

"I'm glad." Mrs. Ohnstetter pointed to her basket. "Ingeborg brings me wool that she dyed herself, from her sheep. She doesn't want me to run out of things to do here."

"Let's go on to the last place on your tour, the kitchen and dining area." As soon as they entered the kitchen, Astrid explained, "Mrs. Ohnstetter has lived here for the last year. We found her another home, but she asked if she could live here and be part of us. Besides knitting, she is like my mother, who prays for everything going on here. She is one of our treasures."

"So besides being a hospital, you are now becoming an old folks' home?" Dr. Johnson asked softly.

"Only for her. She has no more family and her heart is not the best. She's very frail."

Astrid turned at the sound of the front door

slamming open. "Uh-oh. Emergency." She headed for the stretcher being carried in by four men, including Toby Valders.

"He fell off the scaffolding. I'm afraid it might be bad," Toby said.

"In here," Miriam beckoned.

Astrid whipped off her hat and grabbed an apron. "Deborah, scrub."

"I will too." Dr. Johnson joined her at the sink.

"If you need me," Mrs. Korsheski volunteered.

Arms dripping, Astrid headed for the examining room, where Miriam was directing the men how to lift the patient onto the table.

"Can you tell us what happened?" Astrid asked.

"He musta stepped wrong and off he went," one of the men said. He looked at Toby.

"I wasn't there, but they called me immediately," Toby said. "We had the stretcher in the office just in case. He hit his head."

While he was talking, Astrid examined their patient. "Did he regain consciousness at all?"

"No."

She looked in his eyes and ears; one had blood trickling from it, as did his mouth.

Dr. Johnson had his stethoscope on the patient's chest. "Heart steady." He started checking arms and legs for broken bones while Astrid felt the man's head and neck.

"Get the ice."

Deborah brought in a pan of ice and some clean cloths.

Astrid stood erect. "Concussion, possible skull fracture. Does he have feeling in his hands and feet?"

Dr. Johnson pinched the appendages and got a flinch on each. "Yes."

"Is he married?"

Toby shook his head. "No, single, living at the apartment house."

"Deborah, please get as much information from Mr. Valders as is available. Especially someone we can notify."

"All I know is that his name is Stanislaw Fredro. I'll ask around among his friends," Toby said, "but I think he is an immigrant from Poland."

"Poland?" Nurse Wisokay came forward and said something in a foreign language.

The patient almost opened his eyes. The lids fluttered and he turned his head slightly.

Nurse Wisokay looked at Astrid. "I asked him in Polish if he had relatives."

"Beautiful. Thank you, Miss Wisokay."

Miriam stepped forward with a donut-shaped pillow. Deborah lifted the patient's head and they slipped the pillow under it, relieving any pressure on the back of his head.

"Unless he has spinal problems, the head wound seems to be it," Astrid said.

Dr. Johnson asked softly, "No broken skin on the back of his head?"

"No blood back there at all, and that's surprising. But the swelling makes it impossible to be certain of broken bones." Astrid adjusted the ice pack as Miriam set cloths soaking in cold water. "Dr. Johnson, if you and our orderly, Elmer, would undress him, please, and clean him up, we'll move him into a room. Miriam, you'll stay with him there. Watch for any changes." She looked to Mrs. Korsheski. "Any suggestions?"

"Not right now. I'm impressed."

"Thank you. I'll notify Mor, and she'll get the prayers going." Astrid glanced at the clock on the wall. "I'm sure Mrs. Geddick has dinner ready, and I know she set up a table especially for all of you. Let's get cleaned up. Come with me, please."

In the kitchen, Mrs. Geddick said, "Elmer is off on an errand. He'll be back in a minute."

Moments later, Elmer returned from his errand.

"You're needed in room one," Astrid told him, and he hurried out to assist.

Dinner was subdued because of the accident as they discussed treatments and prognosis. Dr. Johnson joined the group after they had just begun eating and caught back a yawn. "There's never a dull moment here."

After they finished eating, Astrid explained,

"We did not plan anything for this evening because I thought you might want to have a quiet supper and retire early. I know how wearying that trip can be. Starting tomorrow, one student nurse will be on days and one on nights, basically shadowing Deborah or Miriam. Dr. Johnson, perhaps you would like to—" She paused and looked at him when he raised his hand.

"May I be on call tonight? I will take the overnight shift for our patient. If that is all right with you."

"Are you sure?"

"Oh yes. This is why I came here."

She bobbed her head. "We will introduce you to the town in church on Sunday. Many will, of course, remember you and be glad you have returned. As for office hours, we no longer use the Bjorklund house; patients come directly here. You will take the drop-ins, and I'll see those with appointments. I know the men will be pleased there is a male doctor on staff."

"I thought to talk to Thorliff about housing. I'd rather not stay at the boardinghouse, if we can help it."

"Housing is at a premium here, Doctor. Your best possibility is that we tell the townsfolk you are looking for a place to stay—or rather, live. And put a notice in the paper."

He nodded.

Nurse Wisokay yawned as well. "Would it

be possible for me to take the day shift tomorrow? Hopefully Laura will feel better by evening."

"I have no trouble with that. Miriam is the one in charge of scheduling. Speak with her."

When they all stood, Astrid bid them goodbye and headed for room one.

"Dr. Astrid, is it all right if I just follow you around?" Mrs. Korsheski asked.

"Of course. Since you are such a surprise to me, I . . . I don't know—"

"What to do with me? Let's check on this patient, and then perhaps we can sit down and talk."

"As long as nothing else happens. I know I don't have any appointments scheduled for me today."

As soon as Astrid picked up her patient's hand, all thoughts of Mrs. Korsheski left. His pulse was all right. She lifted his eyelids with her thumb, one at a time. One pupil closed down as light hit it. The other did not. She asked Miriam, "Has he shown any sign of consciousness?"

"No, ma'am. What can we do but change the ice?"

"For now, that's what we can do." *Is there swelling on the brain or a blood clot?* If only there were a way to tell. "Keep checking his reflexes and let me know immediately if there is any change. Dr. Johnson is planning to return to watch him tonight, so you needn't put anyone else on duty to cover this."

"Good. Deborah's on nights, but she's been here half the day."

"Ja, I know."

Miriam raised her voice. "And no, you will not fill in. We now have another doctor to help take the pressure off you."

Astrid patted her arm. "You will not take on more either."

Miriam smirked. "We'll see."

Astrid and Mrs. Korsheski returned to Astrid's office.

"Now can we talk?" Mrs. Korsheski asked.

"I have a better idea. We'll go to my house. I can get back here quickly if there is need. We can sit on the porch, let Amelia fuss over us, and talk all we want."

"Ah, my dear Astrid, that sounds sublime."

They took their hats off the pegs where someone had hung them and, after telling Miriam of the change in plans, left the building.

Seated a few minutes later in the padded chairs on the back porch, with a westerly breeze kicking up, the fragrances of blooming flowers, and raspberry lemonade, along with Amelia's sugar cookies with a touch of lemon . . . perfection. Astrid unpinned her hat and sailed it to a chair. "This is infinitely better than my office or even the dining room."

"A bit of heaven is what I say."

Amelia came with a question. "Now I am of the opinion that you will be staying for supper rather than going to the boardinghouse, unless you would rather adjourn to your room?"

Astrid looked over at Mrs. Korsheski. "It is up to you, but I guarantee that no matter how good the meals are at the boardinghouse—and I know they are good—you can be more comfortable here." A thought struck her; why had it not come to her immediately? Because she was tending to an unfortunate Polish workman. "In fact, Amelia, might we move her here? The bed for sure is more comfortable."

"Astrid, I will not put you out like this. I mean, perhaps I should have told you I was coming."

"I definitely agree." Amelia turned all her charm onto the woman in the chair. "Had we known you were coming, madam, these are the arrangements that would have been made. Please humor me. I so loved it when the student nurses stayed here."

Astrid giggled. "Amelia, for some strange reason, suddenly had new daughters."

"I heard. They came back raving." Mrs. Korsheski dropped her hands in her lap. "All right, certainly, and thank you more than I can say."

"Good. I'll telephone Miss Maisie. She'll be disappointed, I'm sure; she is very protective of her guests. Your things will be right over.

The bedroom on the left at the top of the stairs will be yours for as long as you are in Blessing. Now. What was—"

"Astrid," Mrs. Korsheski interrupted, "I think since I am a guest in your house and we are not on hospital protocol, you should know my given name is Avis. I would appreciate it if you called me that."

"Thank you, but I will probably have difficulty at first." Astrid chuckled. "Now, Avis, can we talk about why you are here?"

"We at the hospital tried to decide how we could best help you. I have an invitation for Deborah to come to Morganstein Hospital from September through October for training in hospital management. I know that is not nearly enough time, but she is such a bright and dedicated student that I think she can absorb a lot in that amount of time. But if I can shadow, shall we say, you and the others for these two weeks, observe how you are doing things, perhaps I will have suggestions for change immediately, but we can also tailor Deborah's time to be even more helpful. Does that make sense?"

Astrid nodded slowly, running her tongue over her lower lip. "I think this is an amazingly wonderful idea." More nodding. "Yes. I can begin to see the possibilities. I mean, we follow the procedures you have already taught us, but seeing in person is always the most effective."

"From this first taste of your level of care, I

can honestly say I'm immensely impressed. The nurses knew exactly what was needed, and the patient was attended promptly and thoroughly. And on our little tour through the building I saw nothing, absolutely nothing, out of place or in want of cleaning. This is extraordinary."

"Thank you, but you'll notice this is a slow time. We only have a few patients. I'm sure when we're full, as we were last summer during the diphtheria outbreak, you would not have been so impressed."

"Probably I would have been even more impressed. Word gets back to us, you know. We were amazed at how well you managed that crisis." She sipped at her lemonade a few moments and Astrid gave her the time. Then Mrs. Korsheski said, "To hear that Dr. Elizabeth had gone on to her eternal reward shocked us all. A tragic loss. Immediately, Kenneth came forward and said, 'They need two doctors there, minimum. I want to go.' I know he will help make your life so much easier."

"You know our financial status better than anyone."

"We will pay his wages for this first year at least. That should give him time to set up a practice and hopefully become financially independent. And if needed, we will help him get there."

"That is exceedingly generous."

Mrs. Korsheski—Avis—shrugged. "After

all, you fed and housed both him and the nurses when they came without requesting compensation. That did not escape our accountant's attention."

"The least we could do."

"Do you have any questions?" Avis drained her lemonade.

"Give me time to think." Astrid trapped a yawn. "Sorry."

"You know what? I'm thinking I would like a bit of a lie-down before supper. That train trip is indeed tiring. And I suggest you do the same. After all, you are expecting, I hear."

Astrid smiled at her. "All I need to do is sit down and put my feet up, and I can be asleep instantly. All the good advice I give to my waiting mothers has come home to haunt me."

"Good." Avis stood and held out her hand. "Come."

"You sound like my mor."

"Now, that is someone else I want to spend some time with while I am here."

Astrid heaved herself to her feet. *Lord, please be taking care of Mr. Fredro. And give me wisdom to know what to do.*

CHAPTER 27

How many town meetings had Ingeborg sat through? Many, many. Some were exciting and most were boring. All were necessary to keep the town together.

As town meetings went, this one wasn't too bad. Sophie reported how much the box social night had accumulated for the new school fund. It was an amazing sum, thanks in part to Mr. Gendarme's generous bid.

Toby stood up to describe the construction progress. "Barring any unplanned complications, we are nearly on-track again, which means we'll have the new building weathered in so we can work on the interior during the winter. The eye beam is now in place, so we can finish the rafters and begin the roofing process. The siding is in process, and now that the windows are here, we'll begin installing those this week. There are a lot of windows in that building. Come on out and see our progress." He paused and looked around the room. "If you think it looks big from town, up close it is huge, especially when you are climbing a ladder with a load on your shoulder. Plenty of room for our deaf school to keep growing." He sat down to a smattering of applause.

Hjelmer reported on the state of the Blessing Bank, another thing that was boring but crucial. People were getting restless; it was a little stuffy in the room.

Mary Martha announced that the quilters would begin meeting the third Thursday of September with a soup luncheon to start it. She added, "Please, for those of you whose wives did not come tonight, tell them about our meeting. Being a fine seamstress is not a requirement. We have lots of sorting and cutting to do too. Also, I have a letter here from Anji Devlin."

"Oh, read it!" Sophie exclaimed.

Mary Martha stood and opened the paper. She raised her voice.

"Dear friends,
"I am writing one letter, hoping you will all share it, as I do not have time to write each one individually.

"Thomas and I are doing fine. Thank you again for the livestock, especially the pig. It has grown into an amazing hog. We were going to butcher it, but Thomas got another idea that he asked his vestry about. The vestry is to our little church what the town council is to Blessing, a governing body, if you wish. They love his idea. So we are going to give the hog to the town as a thanks offering to God for this wonderful parish. A burnt offering, for we will roast it the way Blessing does on the Fourth of July, and everyone can come to the celebration.

"I am busy not just as a housewife and mother, but I help at the church as well, on the altar guild, dressing the altar for the various seasons. There is so much to learn about how it's done. It is kind of like our Blessing church but different in many ways.

"The children are all doing well. Poor Gilbert had a difficult time at first, for he missed his friends so much. He kept begging for us to send him back to Blessing. Then he threatened to run away. You know how calm and easygoing Thomas is. Suddenly he showed a part of himself I had never seen. His voice changed from

that happy Irish lilt to strong and authoritative. He sat Gilbert down in a chair in front of him and addressed him nose to nose, in no uncertain terms. 'You can never run away from problems. I know because I tried that. It doesn't work. You make new problems, and the old problems come along with you. You are a child of God and that will not change. You are a member of this family and that cannot change either. We love you as God loves you and we want the very best for you. Please stay with us and let us help you become the man you want to be.' Those are not his exact words, but very close. And I am happy to say that Gilbert seems to be accepting life here and settling in. And playing with Benny (the puppy, not the boy!) and Frank. He wants to train Benny as a hunting dog. There is good hunting around here.

"All the children and Thomas and I wish every blessing for each of you.

> *"With warmest love,*
> *"Anji*
> *"P.S. No, I am not pregnant."*

Mary Martha sat down. Everyone laughed heartily.

"Thank you, Mary Martha." Daniel checked his list. "Oh, Jonathan wanted me to ask if there are any others here who either do now or used to play an instrument. Between him and Joshua Landsverk, our band is improving all the time. If you are at all interested, please see me after the meeting here. Or stop by the house. John, do you want to give us the closing benediction?"

Solberg raised his hands. "And now, may the Lord bless and keep us. May He shine his face upon us and give us His peace. In the name of the Father, Son, and Holy Spirit, amen. See you in church on Sunday."

Ingeborg looped her arm through Thorliff's. "Walk me home?"

"I can get the buggy."

"It's too nice out." She could tell this wasn't what he had planned on, but sometimes a mother needed to take the first step, always praying it would not be the last one. As they left the schoolhouse, she pointed to the east. "Oh, look, a harvest moon."

Others around them stopped too, and she heard murmurs of *so big* and *beautiful*. Someone else said something in German, then added, "*Sehr gut.*"

"Such a beautiful gift," Ingeborg said.

"Ja." They walked a bit before Thorliff said, "You know, Inga needs to come home."

"She does. I shall miss having both of the

girls together, but we knew fall was coming. She's been helping Emmy tan that deer hide."

"Life is never dull at your house."

"So Dr. Johnson is going to room at your house?"

"For a time. He and I were becoming friends when he was here on his internship."

"Astrid is sure happy to have more help at the hospital."

He didn't answer.

Ingeborg breathed a prayer, then, "Isn't it time to heal the breach between you?"

"Mor, that really is none of your business."

So that's the way it is to be. Ingeborg toughened her spine. "Ah, yes it is," she said firmly. "You are my son, Astrid is my daughter, and family members forgive one another when they need to."

"She stepped over the line, Mor. Way over."

She could hear the anger in his voice. *Lord, help us.* "Thorliff, do you remember after Roald died?"

"Of course. Why?"

"I did what you are doing now, working myself to the point of—"

"So you couldn't think? For missing my far?"

"Ja, that was it. And all the work that needed to be done. I was so terrified that we would lose the land and you would not have your far's legacy. He lived to earn the land."

"What changed for you?" He kicked a clump of rock-hard black dirt.

"Kaaren."

"Tante Kaaren?"

"She sat me down and spoke to me the way that Astrid spoke to you. She said, 'What will Thorliff do if you die trying to save the land?' I was so angry at her. . . ." Ingeborg could feel the surge of it again. "I . . . I wanted to hit her with something. But instead I ran out in the field until I fell on my knees, the agony ripping me apart."

"You've never told me this before."

"I know. I am not proud of the way I acted. But God reached me through my sister-in-law. And together, God and Kaaren pulled me out of the pit and put my feet on solid ground again. We owe her everything." She stopped and turned him to look at her. "Thorliff Bjorklund, I—*we* love you. Our Father loves you. And it is time to let your heart heal. To forgive Elizabeth for leaving you, forgive God for taking her, and forgive yourself, for no matter what you think, you did all you could."

"I don't know anymore. I feel this . . . this rage, and the only way is to work it off."

"No, the better way is to talk it off. You are not alone. You have a daughter who idolizes you, and all she sees are your sad eyes and it breaks her heart. Your little son needs you to be the pa you have been for Inga. It's time."

He stared at her from eyes black with pain and shadows. "I will think on this. But what do I do when the anger attacks me again?"

"You come and talk with me, or Kaaren, or John. Or all of us together. And you talk to Astrid." She reached out and gathered him close. "Ah, my son. We will be praying for you, as I always have. Just ask our Father and He will pour out His love and wisdom upon you—and bring you healing."

"He hasn't been listening."

"Oh, yes He has. You have not heard His answer. That rage creates a wall to make sure of that." While she waited, she pummeled the gates of heaven with her pleas.

Finally, Thorliff murmured, "Thank you." He tucked her arm back in his. "I'm thinking perhaps . . ."

"Ja. Perhaps." She rested her head against his shoulder. "Can Inga stay until Sunday and go home with you after dinner?"

"The dinner is at your house?"

"Ja."

He left her on her porch and headed back down the lane. Was that his whistle she heard? "Thank you, Lord God. Your timing is always right."

The last week before school started was always filled with activity as people tried to cram more into those days than could possibly fit. Emmy and Inga scraped the hide stretched between two posts in the shade of the cotton-wood tree.

"How will we ever get it soft?" Inga asked.

"Indian women used to chew the tanned leather."

"Eww! Ick."

"I didn't learn to do that. But we'll roll it up and beat it, keep working it, a good thing for winter nights, when my people sit around the fires in the lodges and tell stories of long ago and big hunts and—"

"Do you miss that?"

"Sometimes, but Grandma reads to us and we do schoolwork. Manny will do his carving, and I will make gloves or a vest or something from the leather."

Ingeborg joined them with a bucket of corn to be shucked. "Metiz used to make mittens from rabbit hides with the fur inside," she told the girls. "We still have some of them, and the moccasins she made. I wear mine in the winter, as you know. She and Agnes Baard were my good friends. Metiz taught us how to forage like the Indians do and how to live off the land. I know that saved our lives more than once."

"Do you think Manda and Baptiste will ever come back?" Emmy asked.

"I don't know." Ingeborg handed each of the girls a broken piece of corn cob, and they grinned at the first sweet bite. "I finished your skirt and jumper, Inga, for you to take home when you go."

"Thank you." The look on Inga's face wrenched her grandmother's heart.

Ingeborg reached out and drew Inga to her. "We knew this was coming, but I don't think it is going to be as hard as you are dreading. Your pa and I had a long talk. We'll keep praying for him, but I see glimmers of my old Thorliff coming back." She rocked the little girl as she cried. "This has been a wonderful summer. Let's keep enjoying every minute."

Sunday, after dinner and the ball game, Thorliff squatted down in front of Inga. "I know you would rather stay here at Grandma's, but Rolly and I really miss you at home. Scooter too. And Thelma has sewn you some new clothes too. She said you outgrew everything."

"Grandma made me some too. Can Emmy come visit?"

"Of course."

Ingeborg warned her mouth to keep from smiling. He did sound like he used to. *Lord, thank you.*

"But not on school nights."

Inga sighed. "No more staying at Grandma's, no more Emmy, no more kittens and calves and . . ." She hung her head. "Maybe you should move out here so Rolly can be Grandma's boy like I am her girl."

Ingeborg caught Thorliff's eye and shook her head, letting the grin show since Inga was concentrating on her pa. Leave it to Inga.

"And he could learn to go fishing too," Inga continued.

"I think Rolly's a little bit too small for fishing yet. But when he gets bigger, we'll make sure he gets to go fishing." Thorliff creaked to a stand. "You get your things. Maybe we should have brought the buggy to carry it all."

"We could use the wagon, but I don't have a lot." Inga and Emmy turned and headed for the house.

Ingeborg and Thorliff continued at a slow stroll. It certainly was a lovely time of day.

Thorliff licked his lips. "I have a favor to ask."

"Of course."

"Could you invite Astrid out here, and I will come and we will talk?"

"John Solberg too?"

"As you wish."

"I'll find out what night is best for them."

The girls came out with the wagon loaded. Thorliff took the wagon tongue, and together he and his daughter walked away. Ingeborg and Emmy watched the two walk down the lane. Ingeborg felt Emmy's hand slide into hers. Together they picked up the last of the table things and headed for the house.

∾

The next morning, Manny ran in from milking and scrubbed his hands at the kitchen sink. "I have to change clothes, huh?"

"Yes, quick." Emmy dished his oatmeal up at the stove and set it on the table. She finished hers and buttered biscuits for them both. "Grandma, thanks for fixing our dinner buckets. I was going to."

"I know. I'm going to miss you two around here. Just think! You're in the fifth grade this year."

"I know. Inga is in fourth grade. Perhaps we can still sit together." Patches' barking announced the students from the deaf school. "Hurry up, Manny. I have your dinner pail." Emmy hugged Ingeborg and kissed baby Martin's cheek on her way out the door.

Manny drank the remainder of his oatmeal, grabbed his biscuits, and shoved them in his mouth before waving his way out the door.

"I think we should all sit down with a cup of coffee—now." Ingeborg pulled her chair back out. "Why do I feel like a tornado just went through here?"

"A tornado named Manny." Clara smiled. Her voice was still very raspy.

Freda sat down and reached for Martin. "You eat, I'll hold him."

With the deaf school back in session, Kaaren had suggested the construction men bring dinner pails, and Ingeborg would provide coffee for both the morning break and the noon meal. The kitchen staff at the deaf school would bake something once school was in full swing.

Since the harvest crew had gone west and north on their annual trek to harvest for other farmers two days before, and the wagon drivers were now in school, the building force had diminished. Toby had moved all the tools and blueprints and paper work into the new hastily-slammed-together building shack, which was also on wheels for easy moving. But he spent most of his time working right along with his men. David Gould had stayed back from harvesting and continued learning from the finish carpenters.

Everywhere people were cleaning out their gardens, canning the last of the vegetables, and starting to move the fall crop down into cellars. Freda had a cheese shipment ready to go, and Clara took over the coffee pots.

Ingeborg studied the calendar hanging on the kitchen wall. She had asked John Solberg to join them after school today as she, Astrid, and Thorliff would meet at the church—neutral ground, so to speak, where there should be no interruptions. With Freda out in the cheese house and Clara picking dried beans in the garden, Ingeborg put the gingerbread with applesauce to spoon over it in her basket, all the time praying for this meeting to bless them all. When she'd asked Astrid to come, she'd sensed the unwillingness.

"Please, we must," she had urged her daughter.

"Mor, I don't want to go through another time like that with him."

"I understand, but please. One step at a time. This has gone on too long."

"Forgiveness has to go both ways."

John had asked Ingeborg to pray a few days ago, as he was meeting with Thorliff, and she had. But neither had said what happened. Not that John had had time for much with school starting. And helping Amelia get ready to teach.

When Ingeborg heard the school bell releasing the students, she took her basket and walked to the church.

Astrid met her halfway. "Here, let me take that." She sneaked a peek into the basket. "Oh, gingerbread. I've not had that for a long time."

"How are things going to go with Amelia teaching school?"

"I told her I would help with the cooking. Especially now that Mrs. Korsheski has left us. Mor, she is such an amazing woman."

"I know. All these years and she finally came to Blessing. We are so privileged."

Ingeborg waved at the schoolchildren. "When does Deborah leave? I thought it was going to be August."

"It was going to be September. But after Mrs. Korsheski watched us working here, she said Deborah's skills are advanced beyond the course she would have taken. Instead, she's now enrolled in a special course that starts the first of October. While I want her to have the training, her absence will leave a mighty big hole."

As they neared the church, Astrid started dragging her feet. "I don't know why I feel so hesitant."

"You don't want to be hurt again."

"I'm trusting you, Mor, that that won't be the case."

"For that, I am trusting God. I thought perhaps we could just sit up by the altar and pray until the other two get here."

Ingeborg paused when they entered the sanctuary. Sun slanted through the south-facing stained-glass window, the blues and reds glowing on the floor too. The white altar beckoned them forward, the hush embracing them as they dragged four chairs together and set them in a circle. They took their seats and Ingeborg closed her eyes, the better to listen. The voices of children, laughing and calling, floated in the open window along with the song of a meadowlark lilting on the air.

Lord, help us to hear your voice. Holy Spirit, bring peace and harmony—and healing.

She heard John greet Thorliff before they reached the steps to the front door.

"I sure hope this works, Mor," Astrid whispered.

"Me too." Ingeborg stood to greet the men. "Welcome to the most peaceful place in Blessing."

John smiled. "That it seems. After our first day back at school, I can use some peace."

"How did it go?"

"Well, actually. Anton Gendarme mesmerized his students, and those that weren't in his classes were actually jealous."

Thorliff very obviously was avoiding looking at Astrid. "I sent out the ads for another teacher. Talked with the editor of the Grand Forks paper, and he agreed to run a short article. Did you by any chance contact the district superintendent's office to put in a plea?" he asked as he sat down in the far chair.

"I did and he said he'd keep his eyes open. Obviously there were no candidates in the file." John scrubbed his thinning hair back. "We really need someone to do some office work at the school too. Teaching and principaling are getting too complicated." He smiled at them all. "Enough about school problems. It's nothing we can't handle."

He took his chair and relaxed against the

back. "Ingeborg, I think you are right about the peace here. How about we all just sit quietly for a while and then I'll open with prayer?"

Ingeborg nodded and closed her eyes, the better to think and pray. She could feel Astrid relax beside her. Across the small circle, Thorliff settled in. *Lord Jesus, thank you for being here. So there are five of us and you know our hearts and our needs far better than we do.*

One of the men blew out a breath and inhaled gently. A breeze from the open door felt cool, as if an unseen hand were waving a fan. She could feel herself melting into the chair.

"Holy Father, thank you for the peace we are finding here. Speak, please, to our hearts that we might know your wisdom. You bring healing wherever you go. Thank you and amen."

The ensuing silence continued the peace.

Thorliff cleared his throat. "Lord, as Mor said, I have been blaming you for taking Elizabeth when I . . . we needed her so. So unfair, and in my mind, cruel, especially to me and my children. I know I've been like a wounded dog, lashing out at my family, my friends, whoever got in my way. I see that I am bitter and angry and I—"

Ingeborg wiped her eyes. *Lord, help my son.* She heard Astrid sniff beside her.

"Elizabeth must be so ashamed of me." He paused. "John, what do I do?"

"You seem to be doing just fine to me."

"I am so tired." Thorliff's voice broke. "So tired."

Astrid dug in her reticule for a handkerchief and blew her nose. She eased her hand into her mother's. And clung.

"According to God's Word, it is necessary to ask for forgiveness from those we have wounded," John said.

"That's probably half of Blessing." Thorliff pulled a handkerchief from his back pocket and wiped his face. "I lost my father and then my wife. I wanted to go talk to Pa so badly. Two of the most important people in my life. But then I look at Mor. She has moved on." He propped his elbows on his knees. "Other people have moved through the grief. As Astrid said, it is time for me to do the same."

"Ja, you are on the right track."

Thorliff reached across the space for Astrid's hand. "Please forgive me. You were right. I just hope it isn't too late."

Astrid squeezed his hand. "Too late for what?"

"To be your big brother again. To be the pa my two children need."

"You never quit being my big brother. Yes, I forgive you, but you have to do the same for me. I should not have exploded at you like that."

"I think you needed to. I was being extremely hard of hearing." He nodded. "Like John says at communion, you are forgiven."

They rested in the silence.

"I asked for Christ's forgiveness Sunday at communion, and this time it wasn't just saying the words," Thorliff said. "And the verse 'and while we were yet sinners,' that meant me. I have sinned against Him by thought, word, and deed. No longer just words to say on Sunday."

"Sometimes our lives need to nearly be destroyed before we realize He died for us. Each of us," Pastor Solberg said.

"Mor, thank you for all your prayers. I knew you would never quit loving me."

"Good. Then more of my prayers were answered." Ingeborg's handkerchief was soaked. "Inga has prayed for you every night too, as has Emmy."

Solberg nodded. "And I don't know how many others as well. And Thorliff, we'll keep praying for you. Grief will try to strangle you again. It hits you out of the blue at times. You won't forget Elizabeth, but the pain will go away, bit by bit, now that you are willing to let it go."

Ingeborg had a little trouble speaking. "And the good memories will return. Talk to your children about their mother, especially Inga. She is so bright. Poor little Rolly will only remember what you—what we all tell him about his mother."

Thorliff looked utterly broken. "Thelma is another one who has borne the brunt of my actions. I will take care of that too."

Another pause that was no longer uncomfortable.

"Thorliff, my son," Ingeborg said, "be gentle with yourself. I learned that the hard way, and I pray you have, and will too. Someone once said, 'Two steps forward, one step back.' Talk to us, your family, when you need to. I regret I did not share more about Roald with you. Hard work helps one deal with grief, but it is not the healer. Love is."

"I think we can close with prayer, unless someone has something else needing to be said?" When they all shook their heads, John blew out a breath and waited for the peace to settle again. "Thank you, Lord God. You are here with us, around us and in us with your healing love and touch." He laid his hand on Thorliff's shoulder. "Thank you for this son of yours, for bringing healing and newness of life, for the forgiveness we all count on. Draw him and all of us ever closer to you. In Jesus' precious name we pray, amen."

They all stood, and Thorliff shook John's hand. "Thank you. You have no idea how much I was dreading this."

"Oh, I have a pretty good idea. But again, I have had the privilege of watching our God in action through these years. Ingeborg and I say this so often: We pray and ask, and then the best thing is to step back and let God do His work."

"Thank you, Mor." Thorliff hugged her and turned to Astrid. "Thank you for braving the lions' den and being treated so badly."

Astrid wrapped her arms around his rib cage and hugged him. "I don't ever want something like this to happen again. If we can't get along, how can we expect others to?"

"How about we drop you off at your house and I'll walk Mor home?"

"How about we both walk her home and then you can walk me home? I need to walk more, not just around the hospital. That's what I tell my expectant mothers, and this doctor better take her own advice."

"Or her mother will be sure to remind her."

"Remember, Thorliff, I am always here to listen." Pastor Solberg shut the church door behind them. He settled his hat on his head and, with a smile, started for home.

"Do you suppose Rebecca's is still open? A soda sounds awfully good right now." Thorliff looked from his mother to his sister. "That is, if you have time."

"We can take time." Ingeborg locked her arms through her children's. "I haven't had a soda since . . . since I don't know when. The way I feel right now, we should throw a party for all of Blessing."

CHAPTER 28

"May I walk you home?" Anton asked Deborah after church.

She returned his smile. "It's not very far, you know."

"We could make it farther."

She turned as Samuel stopped beside them. "Hi, Deborah. Anton, we're playing ball at the field after dinner. Tante Ingeborg has an open invitation to dinner there, if you'd like to come."

"Thank you. I'll see about dinner."

"Deborah, you can come too, you know."

"We'll see." She watched Samuel wave and stride off, stopping to talk with Thorliff.

"Shall we start?" Anton asked.

Why doesn't Toby ever do this? She ignored the fleeting thought. Most of the people were still visiting in front of the church, including her ma, who nodded when she caught her eye. Deborah and Anton headed north but turned at the new street, as everyone called it, and headed toward the river.

"So how is school going?" she asked.

"My uncle David said I would find the students here excited to learn. He was so right. I have a feeling I can change my plans about what to offer and proceed faster than I had thought. That's exciting for a schoolteacher."

"And you are teaching algebra to the older grades, along with a science, geometry, and ancient history?"

"Yes. The only problem is that it's hard to get used to having someone sign for me. I asked Grace if she would teach me, so we started doing that in the evening. I've never taught where there are deaf students."

"Interesting. We all take that for granted since we've been signing since we could talk. Well, not me, since I wasn't born here, but my sister, Manda, and I learned right away."

"Really? I thought you'd lived here all your life."

"No, Ma's brother, Zeb MacCallister, found us in a dugout near the Missouri River. Our mother had died and our father left one day and never came back. We were both very nearly starving, and I was very sick, so he brought us here to Blessing."

He stared at her. "I have a feeling there are a lot of interesting stories in Blessing."

"There are indeed." The breeze lifted the brim of her straw hat and blew the end of the ribbon around her neck. "What was your life like?"

"Boring in comparison with yours. As I mentioned at the box social, I have two sisters and two brothers, I went to boarding school for high school, and then to college. My brothers are now at that school."

"Your sisters?" They stopped at the junction. "Which way?"

"Would you like to go to Mrs. Bjorklund's for dinner?"

"I think not today. Ma said I should invite you to our house, if you had no other invitations." She shook her head. "I mean—I said that wrong."

"I think I'd like that. I enjoy your family."

They strolled past the newspaper office and Astrid's house, where Amelia waved from the porch.

"Come sit a while," she invited.

Deborah waved back. "Thank you, but not today."

"You all take this so . . . so nonchalantly. This would never happen at the Gendarme home."

"Really? What?"

"Oh, people inviting you to come to dinner

after church, or just stopping to visit, or . . ." He shook his head. "So very different."

"Different is good—I guess." Deborah waved at Rebecca as they passed the Soda Shoppe and then the Blessing Mercantile before turning toward the MacCallister ranch.

"So this is your ranch?"

"No, my pa's. Zeb adopted Manda and me, then after his wife, Katy, died, they all headed to Montana to raise horses, and he asked the Solbergs if they would live here and keep me, as I was too young to go with them."

"That must have been difficult for you."

"At least I didn't get sent off to boarding school."

"I got a good education, and we spent the summers as a family at the beach house." He paused. "That's just what people around us did."

Deborah remembered some of Grace's comments about life in New York City, where Jonathan grew up. "Do the Goulds have a beach house too?"

"Yes, right next to ours. Our houses in the city are near each other too. That's why Jonathan and I became such good friends."

"Sounds like things I've read about in books. I guess I'll get my taste of city living when I go to Chicago."

"I heard you were leaving in September but that got changed."

"Yes. The course of study I will be taking will begin October first." She paused. They had reached the house. "You are staying for dinner?"

Emily burst out the door and stopped in front of her, whining. "Deborah, can you please retie my bow? Thomas pulled on it, and it untied."

Giggling, Deborah retied the bow, and Emily ran back inside. Deborah turned to Anton, ushering him in the door. "Welcome to family life, Blessing style. Come, we'll probably be eating out on the back porch, where it is cooler. Fall seems to be taking its own sweet time coming."

John looked up from the catcher's mitt he was relacing for Mark. "Welcome. You do plan to play ball, don't you? They've asked me to umpire, since Lars is off harvesting."

"Uh, I suppose so. Athletics were not my best pursuit," Anton admitted.

"Then you'll fit right in here. Most of us, the athletics pursue us."

Mary Martha smiled at Anton. "Welcome! What would you like to drink? We have ice water, pink lemonade, or plain water. Deborah, if you would bring out the scalloped corn from the oven. Thomas, bring the salad. Emily, you forgot to put all the silverware on the table."

"You could probably have iced coffee if you

want." John motioned Anton to come to the table.

"Thank you, but pink lemonade sounds delightful." He leaned over to whisper to little Gudrun, who was visiting. "What makes it pink?"

"Thtrawberrieth." She had recently lost her two front teeth.

"Oh good." Anton took the chair John pointed him to.

With the food on the table, they all sat down so Mark could say grace. "Thank you for our good food and that Pa fixed my mitt. Amen."

Deborah watched the emotions play across Anton's face. Did they not say grace in his house, or were the children not permitted at the table or not allowed to talk unless spoken to first? Some things were unfathomable.

After dinner, Deborah helped put things away and do the dishes, while the two men sat in the shade, discussing the school.

Mary Martha nodded toward the men. "John is so pleased with Mr. Gendarme as a teacher. What a gift we have been given."

"It's a shame Mr. Gould doesn't have some-one else to bring here. Ma, as I talk with him, I see that life can be so different in other places."

"True, and coming from an extremely wealthy background, I am surprised that he fits in here like he does. I have to admit, I had my doubts."

"Mr. Gould fits in, but I remember when his wife was here. She wanted no part of us."

"And yet she bequeathed our deaf school all that money, and I have a feeling that Mr. Gendarme will make sure his family funnels money into our public school system too."

"For the new building, you mean."

"He paid for all the textbooks and supplies for his classes. Please don't tell anyone that." Mary Martha stared out the window. "We are blessed in so many ways by so many people. Like Thomas Devlin, who just strolled into town, and look what a difference he made here."

"Pa really misses him, doesn't he?"

"They were kindred souls. We don't meet many friends like that in our lives, so we treasure those given us."

Deborah dried a glass and put it up in the cupboard. What about Toby? Was he a kindred spirit? Was Anton? Was neither of them? Perhaps Toby would never be in love with her like she was in love with him, or maybe his love would be different. Or perhaps Anton . . . maybe God was answering her prayer in a different way. Like Pa had said one time or many, *"Don't pray, telling God what you expect Him to do and how you want Him to do it, but put your requests in His hands and watch to see what He is doing."*

"I see you are miles away." Mary Martha commented while hanging the dish towels on the rack behind the stove.

Deborah nodded. "I've got a lot to think about."

Mary Martha leaned close and dropped her voice. "You had the Toby look again."

"Really, Ma, am I that obvious?"

"Only to one who knows and loves you so dearly, like I do."

"I really enjoy being with Mr. Gendarme. I think we can become friends." She turned to her mother. "But we sure grew up in different worlds."

"Is everyone going to the ball game?" John called from the back porch.

"Looks like it," Mary Martha called back.

"Then we better get over there." He pointed to the hamper on the table. "Is that basket going?"

"Yes."

"I'll take it then," Mr. Gendarme said, picking it up with a smile.

"Do I hafta put my shoes back on?" Mark pleaded.

"Not if you don't want to, but remember, cows live in that pasture the other six days of the week."

"Feet wash easier than shoes."

"It's up to you."

Deborah caught the look of shock on Anton's face. Far different, that was for sure.

At the game, Anton made a place for himself in Blessing when he whacked the baseball over everyone's heads and almost to the river-bank.

Samuel held the ball up. "Good thing it didn't go farther; we might never have found it again."

"Patches would have found it," Manny yelled back from his place as catcher on the opposing team. He caught the ball Samuel threw on the first bounce, but Anton had already run across home plate, pushing one runner ahead of him.

"Score three to two," Solberg called. "Batter up."

Today, Toby was captain of one team and Joshua Landsverk the other. "You can play on my team anytime, Anton," Toby said, slapping him on the back.

"Thank you. What a great way to spend Sunday afternoon."

Halfway through the game, baskets were opened, drinks and food passed out, and the spectators visited. Small children played games started by several of the upper-grade girls, and Inga and Emmy were leading others around on Joker's back.

Deborah sat on a blanket with Astrid and Grace. The thought of leaving, even for a month, sat like a ghoul on her shoulders.

"So have you started packing?" Astrid asked.

"Yes and no. Other than my wool coat, hat, scarf, and mittens or gloves, I'm only taking one dress, skirts and waists to wear at the hospital under aprons, and—"

"Take your woolies too," Astrid instructed. "That wind can be so cold off the lake. You must go walking along the lakeshore, whether it's cold or not. That horizon line seems to stretch forever."

"Is the hospital near the lake?"

"No, but you can take the trolley there."

Dr. Johnson sat down beside her. "Ask Mrs. Korsheski; she'll find someone to go with you. Just riding the trolleys around Chicago is an education in itself. I highly recommend it."

"I've never been away from Blessing since we came here when I was little."

"I was so homesick when I first went to Chicago." Astrid wagged her head. "At least you know you'll only be there a month. And you'll be so busy, I hope you won't have time to be homesick."

I can bear anything for a month. Deborah had been telling herself that repeatedly. She almost believed it now.

"You'll have lots of stories to tell when you get back. I almost wish I could go with you." Astrid trapped a yawn. "Goodness, how can I be ready for a nap again?"

As soon as rounds were over on Monday morning, Deborah went in to check on the schedule Miriam had posted. Who would take her shifts when she left?

Astrid stopped beside her. "All right, what are you worrying about now?"

"We don't really have another charge nurse."

"I know. Miriam and I talked about it. Our two student nurses will take turns on the night shift, and Dr. Johnson has agreed to be on call. If there is an emergency, well, we'll do what we always do."

"Whatever is necessary."

"That's right. And Vera has agreed to fill in at least two shifts a week."

The days passed as a whirlwind. Autumn slipped in, dabbing color on the trees and chilling the night, scenting the air with fall. The first frost touched down with a heavy hand, finishing off the gardens. The harvest crew clanked back into town, and the construction crews started erecting the rafters for the deaf school roof. While the majority worked on top, David Gould worked with the other finish carpenters on the siding.

After her shift one day, on her way home, Deborah walked out to the site to see how the building was growing. It was a good thing she'd worn a shawl, since the wind had the bite of fall to it. She automatically looked for Toby and found him with the crew on top.

"Welcome, Miss MacCallister," Mr. Gould

called. "Watch where you walk; nails seem to be everywhere, especially bent nails."

"You should know," said one of the other men on the ground.

She stared upward. "It's huge, the building. I didn't realize how big it would be."

"It will look even bigger when the roof is on."

"And so many windows."

Mr. Gould looked down the length of it with her. "If we think we have trouble getting teachers for the Blessing school now, this will bring another influx of people who need more housing."

More people. Bigger hospital. Oh my. Deborah said, "I heard that you've decided to stay. Are you are going to build a house?"

"It would take him forever to get it up," another man on the ground teased.

Mr. Gould chuckled. "He's right, actually. No, I'm going to have it built. But thanks to these men, I will have a hand in the building and the finishing."

"By the time you finish the inside of this one, you will be a master carpenter." Deborah smiled at him. "Did you ever dream you'd be in Blessing, working on the buildings?" *Not only helping to finance them?* She decided not to mention the money.

"No, I never did. Jonathan's brothers keep expecting me to move back to New York, but I'm more like Jonathan than I ever realized."

"Or he is more like you?"

Gould nodded. "Like Ingeborg says, you never know what God is going to do next."

She turned to see a wagon of lumber pulling in, Benny on the driver's seat. He waved and climbed down, grabbed his crutches, and stumped over to the empty wagon waiting for a driver.

"You want a ride back to town?" he called.

"No, thanks." She saw Toby walking down the ladder as if it were simply a rather steep staircase. "How can he do that?"

Mr. Gould turned to see where she was looking. "He says it goes with the territory, but I can't do it either." He smiled at her. "And they go up with a load on their shoulders. You see that I am working with both feet firmly on the ground. Well, back to work."

They wished each other good day as Toby walked up to her. "Something to see, isn't it?" he said.

"Up close like this is different than even from the ball field."

Toby pointed to the topmost beam of the roof skeleton. "Getting that ridge beam up, now that was tricky." He pulled off his leather gloves and hooked them over the waist of his leather carpenter's apron. "I need to go talk with Thorliff. Can I walk you home?"

"I . . . I guess so." *Thorliff's house is not really on the way, though . . .*

"Shut 'er down at six," he hollered to his foremen. "So what do you think?" he asked her as they walked back toward town.

"It's huge."

"The biggest building in Blessing. From what I've been hearing, when we do the new high school, that will be two stories too." She could hear the pride in his voice. "Are you really going to be gone a month?"

The question caught her by surprise. "Why?"

"Just seems like a long time to be away." He had slowed his steps to match hers.

What difference does it make?

He smiled. "You know, I don't say thank you often enough, but had it not been for you and your ma, I'd probably never have had breakfast all summer. Or clean clothes and bedding."

"You're welcome. I heard Anton moved in with you. How do you like having someone sharing your house?"

"It's good, especially now that it's getting dark so early. We take turns—well, Anton fixes more meals than I do, but he's good at it. Sometimes I bring supper home from the boardinghouse. And Rebecca either sends over food or invites us for supper." As they neared her gate, he slowed down. "If I don't see you before you leave . . ."

She waited for more. *What, Toby?*

"Well, I hope you have a good trip, learn

a lot, and don't decide to stay in Chicago." He grinned down at her. "I, uh . . . the hospital would be lost without you." He touched the brim of his hat and headed for Thorliff's.

Deborah pushed open the gate. Now, what was that all about?

Time passed way too quickly. Suddenly it was the end of September, and Deborah's bag was all packed. She had said good-bye to her family that morning. Now she picked up the clipboard one last time before leaving her last shift before her departure. The clipboard was instantly snatched from her hand.

"Enough!" Miriam was laughing, which spoiled the stern tone of her voice. "Go. We'll take good care of your hospital until your return."

"*My* hospital!"

Astrid appeared beside her. "Miriam will hold down the fort here. I will escort you to the train."

Miriam hugged her. "Safe travel."

Deborah felt embarrassingly close to tears.

Near the door, Mrs. Ohnstetter called, "Deborah, you are leaving now, ja?"

"Yes." She crossed to the lady and leaned down for a hug. "Be good until I return."

Mrs. Ohnstetter cackled. She reached into the basket beside her and pulled out a thick double-knit wool scarf and hat. "Astrid says you will need this there, even in October."

"Oh, Mrs. Ohnstetter! These are wonderful! Thank you."

Gnarled fingers wrapped around her hand. "You are a blessing, child. Go and learn how to bless us even more."

Now Deborah was really close to tears. She took a deep, shuddering breath and walked outside with Astrid.

The sky was gray today, but the overcast was still too thin to give rain. They walked in silence to the station. The silence continued as they waited for the train.

Deborah pointed. "One thing about flat land, Astrid. You know in plenty of time that a train is coming." The trail of white smoke and steam just barely showed above the trees.

Big and black and ominous, the train rattled toward them, slowing, and puffed to a halt.

"I made it!" Anton ran across the platform and stopped beside them.

"But . . . the school . . ." Deborah almost stammered. "Shouldn't you be in class?"

"John and I agreed that this is a perfect opportunity to give my algebra class a test to see how much they know about quadratic equations. While they're doing that, I am standing here to see you off and asking God's blessing on your endeavors."

"Th-thank you."

Astrid hugged her. "Safe travel, Deborah. Say hello to my friends, please."

"I shall."

"All aboard!"

Deborah turned away from Astrid, from Anton, and from Blessing, picked up her valise, and stepped aboard the train.

There were not many passengers in the car. Deborah tossed her bag into the overhead bin and pressed against a window for one last look. She waved, her hand brushing the glass. Out on the platform, Astrid waved and dabbed her eyes with a handkerchief. Anton waved, grinning brightly.

Toby had not come.

CHAPTER 29

I cannot believe this!"

Gerald looked up from the boot he was trying to patch. "Toby, you have to be more clear. Believe what?"

"Deborah has been gone scarcely a week and I finally figured out what's bothering me."

"That's good. So—what did you learn? Uff da!" He popped his finger into his mouth.

"I miss her. This makes no sense. But all these past months that we've been working so hard, I realized I knew where she was and that if I wanted to see her, I could do that."

"So did you go see her?"

"Well, no. In case you forgot, I was working from dawn to dark, seven days a week. I'd stagger home, and there was always food and a note, and they even started doing my laundry. I had clean clothes and a clean bed and somehow I have to pay them back or do something nice for Mrs. Solberg. I mean, I know . . ."

"You know what?"

Toby heaved a sigh. "Many of those days Deborah was either at the hospital or sleeping. Twelve hours on duty and many times more." Toby leaned over in his chair and brushed the dust off his own boots. While he'd gone home and changed, he'd looked forward to supper with his brother and family. After their last discussion, he'd tried to remember more about their life before coming to Blessing. "Did our father beat you?"

Gerald started to say something but then stopped. "Yes, and our mother, until she disappeared one day. I never knew if he'd killed her in one of his rages or she'd just run away."

"I don't remember him or anyone hitting me."

"That's because when it seemed he might start on you, I took you and hid you in a special place I'd found. But when I couldn't find enough food and I heard he was looking for us, I got us on that train, heading west."

"You never told me this before."

"You never asked. And I've tried to forget."

"And here the Valders adopted us. Knowing Hildegunn and Anner, I—Why do you suppose they took us in?"

"Because they felt it their Christian duty

to feed the hungry and care for the homeless. Two boys needed a home, they had a house with rooms to spare, and so we became Toby and Gerald Valders, no longer White." Gerald had a slight smile with a far-off look.

"What?"

"I remember the first time we sat at their table," Gerald said. "There was meat and canned beans and biscuits, and we even had dessert. An apple spice cake. I'll never forget that meal. Pa filled up our plates and we wolfed that food down. He asked if we wanted more, and I said yes. We both got sick that night. I was mortified."

"I don't remember any of that."

"We both stuck food in our pockets to eat later. We did that until Ma took our clothes to wash and found bread in our pockets. You know how stern she could be. She sat us down and ordered us to never do that again. I was so sure she was going to kick us out. That was a fear of mine for a long time. And then you, you got more spankings because you just couldn't seem to behave. But you'd never been made to behave." Gerald shook his head. "I think we were almost like animals."

"I remember chopping a lot of wood. Andrew and I. At school. Whenever we got in a fight, Reverend Solberg would send us out to chop wood. Hard to stay angry that way."

"Would you two like another cup of coffee?"

Rebecca paused in the doorway. "You need to go up to say good-night."

"Thank you, I will."

Toby knew Gerald read to their children during the long winter evenings and always helped put them to bed. Where did he learn to be a father like that?

When Gerald came back down the stairs, Toby watched him. His brother used to be more frail. Rebecca brought in coffee and leftover pieces of the cake she'd served at supper.

"Can I get you anything else?" she asked.

"No, thanks," Toby answered. "I didn't expect this."

"Why don't you join us?" Gerald asked his wife.

Toby had realized long ago that these two had the same kind of bond he had seen with Ingeborg and Haakan. How did that happen? Something over a long time?

"I have a really personal question," he said.

"You're my brother. Ask away."

"How did you learn to be a pa, like you are?" *And husband*, but he didn't ask that—yet.

"Rebecca taught me. Like she has taught me to be a good husband too. Or rather, continues to teach me." Gerald looked at Toby over the rim of his cup. "I am so blessed. Who knew back when I fell in love with her what life would be like."

"Deborah could be that kind of wife, but I don't think I can be that kind of man."

"Why not?"

Toby stared at him. "I . . . I . . ."

"You're afraid."

"No! I'm not afraid. Afraid of what?" Toby felt like leaping to his feet and charging out that door.

"You've never thought you were afraid, but I have known you all your life, and you were so terrified when you were little. Of everything." Gerald sighed. "And then you got tough. On the outside, at least. All those fights? A boy who couldn't let anyone see he was afraid."

"How do you know all this?" *Wipe that glare off your face; this is not a place to fight.*

"John Solberg. Ingeborg Bjorklund. Reading that Bible." Gerald pointed to the book on the small table by his chair. "There is great wisdom therein. And it says if you want wisdom, to ask for it and God will give it liberally. I know that's a bit of a paraphrase, but where do you think they get their wisdom?"

Toby stared at him. "I guess I never thought about it. I mean, I know we all depend on them praying."

"And look at all the ways God has taken care of us, many times in spite of us. What if— and I'm not saying this is so—you are afraid of commitment? You spend time with Deborah, and then you run the other way."

"No I don't. I've been working so many hours, there's just no time."

Gerald just looked at him. Toby caught himself squirming in his chair.

And then Gerald asked the question Toby absolutely hated. "Do you love—not just as a friend you like spending time with—but are you in love with Deborah MacCallister?"

Toby rested his elbows on his knees and let his hands droop between them. *Do I love Deborah?* He finally looked up. "I don't know." He studied his hands. "Is missing her love?"

"Part of it, perhaps."

"I don't like it when I see her with someone else."

"But you don't want to have to pay her any attention and perhaps you like being able to see someone else?"

"Doesn't sound very good, does it?" Was he really like that? In a burst of honesty, he had to admit that was what he'd done, probably often.

"Maybe now, with her gone, is a good time for you to figure this out."

Rebecca came to stand behind Gerald. "I'm going up to bed. Blow out the lamps when you come."

Toby rose to his feet. "Thanks for supper, Rebecca." He nodded to Gerald. "Thank you—I guess."

"You have a lot to think about."

Toby nodded. "And I'm not a good thinker like you. Building a school is far easier."

Gerald walked him to the door. "I'm always here. Pastor Solberg is too, and he can answer some questions better than I can."

"Good night."

When Toby walked in the door of his house, a lighted kerosene lamp sat in the middle of the kitchen table. How often had he come home to a dark house? Such a simple thing—a lighted lamp. Did he think to do those kinds of things for other people?

Thinking. He hated having to think, and now he must. He fell asleep that night trying to think, but not doing it well.

The next morning he came downstairs still avoiding thinking. "I'll go by the boarding-house and bring home supper tonight," he told Anton, who was just sitting down to eat break-fast when Toby was ready to walk out the door.

"Good. Thank you. I have a lot of papers to correct. Say, who can I hire to do my laundry?"

"There's a washing machine on the back porch."

Toby left, chuckling at the look on Anton's face. *He's probably never seen a washing machine. At least I've helped do the wash. Years ago now, but Ma had me crank the wringer when she had an injured arm.* He had hung clothes on the line too. Just like he had helped in the kitchen, and he and Gerald had to do the dishes, even though as they grew older they realized that was women's work.

But Gerald helps Rebecca with the dishes. Maybe he should ask Rebecca to remind him how to use the washing machine. When he would have time, he had no idea. Unless he didn't work on Saturdays. That would not happen.

At the construction site, he stopped to look up at the bare rafters that now stretched from one end of the building to the other. Today he'd set a crew nailing down the cross timbers and another to start laying shingles on the corner of the roof that was ready for shingling. The siding was now above the windows on the north side and even with the tops of the first-floor windows on the west. When might they be ready for the glass? He wrote a note to check with Thorliff on a delivery date. Always the nagging question: Where could he get more carpenters? Since the grain elevator was in full operation due to the harvest, he'd lost two men to that.

But the other men were back from harvesting, so Samuel and two of the Hegdahl boys were now on the roof, and Laban had taken over driving the wagons back and forth from the siding. As the sun broke the horizon, the men arrived and took over from where they had finished the day before.

Mr. Heinrich stopped by Toby. "My brother coming on train to work."

"Good, thanks. When?"

"Today, I think."

"Does he have tools?" At the headshake, Toby asked, "Has he built buildings before?'

"Houses."

"Good. Bring him to talk with me this afternoon."

"He not speak English much."

"I see. Then he will work with you."

"He not been on such a tall building."

"He will be." One more worker. Every bit helped.

That night Toby stopped to talk with Thorliff regarding the windows and other supplies, then strode over to the boardinghouse and asked Mrs. Landsverk if he could have two suppers to take home. While she sent someone else to get the food, he asked her, "Do you know of some women who would take in wash?"

"Hmm, let me think," Maisie said. "Not right off hand, but I could ask around. The ones who might know would be Mrs. Solberg or Ingeborg. They know most of the wives." She looked up into the distance. "This is for you and Mr. Gendarme, correct?"

He nodded. "Who does the washing and cleaning, and maybe even cooking, for the men in the apartments?"

"One of the wives there. She pretty much runs the place, which is a good thing. Some of them eat here at times."

All we need is a Thelma, only a couple of days a week.

A girl came out of the kitchen with a basket, which she handed to Maisie. She in turn handed it to Toby.

"I'll bring it back."

"I know you will, or you won't get it filled again. That sure is an imposing structure you're building."

"It is that."

That night he sat down at the rolltop oak desk in what used to be his father's office. He found some stationery in one slot and started what was probably the first letter he had written in his life. Other than in school, when they'd learned to write letters in English class.

The inkwell was crusted black in the bottom. So now what? Put water in it? What was ink made of?

Anton was sitting at the table in the dining room, papers spread around him.

"Do you have any ink?" Toby asked him.

"At school." Anton eyed the inkwell that Toby held up. "I could get you some tomorrow."

"Thanks. I'll use a pencil." Pencil was easier anyway. He found two pencils, one with broken lead, the other down to the wood. Taking out his pocket knife, he sharpened both of them and turned back to the paper. No wonder he never wrote letters.

Dear Deborah,

I hope all is going well for you in Chi-cago. I am sure you are learning a lot and I hope you are seeing some of the city too. Although I hear Chicago is a dirty, smelly place.

Now what? He tapped the pencil on his chin.

We are laying the timbers on the rafters and have started shingling the corner we have done. Mr. Gould continues to nail up siding from the ground; he does not like ladders. He said he hopes we can start a house for him come spring.

Fall is here. We've had frost twice now, but we keep praying the rains hold off until we at least have the roof on.

I hear the harvest celebration is in another week. I told the men we would stop work early that day. Sophie has fig-ured a way to make this a fundraiser for the school, as only Sophie can come up with ideas like that.

If you could find the time to answer my letter, I would be honored.

> *Your longtime friend,*
> *Toby White Valders*

He folded the letter and found an envelope for it. An address. He had no idea where to send this. He'd have to stop by the hospital after work tomorrow night. Or he could ask Mrs. Solberg. How could such a simple thing as a letter cause so many difficulties?

Commitment. Gerald had said he was afraid of that. Would a letter be a start on overcoming that fear, if that was what it was? Maybe it was time to talk with Gerald again, or Reverend Solberg.

Y ou have a letter from Blessing," Mrs. Korsheski announced.

"Oh, wonderful!" Deborah turned from the files she was sorting. Mrs. Korsheski claimed that the best way to learn was to do. "Thank you." She looked at the envelope. This was not her mother's or father's writing, nor Astrid's. After slitting the envelope open, she pulled out a sheet of paper. "Toby?"

"I thought that was male handwriting. If you are pleased, I am pleased for you."

Late one evening, Deborah had told Mrs. Korsheski the story of what she saw as an on-again, off-again relationship that always left her disappointed. Deborah had decided it was time to get over any dreams of a life with Toby

Valders. Friends, yes, of sorts, but he did not appear to desire to be husband material.

"Sometimes reason does not triumph over feelings," Mrs. Korsheski had said.

Deborah had frowned. "What do you mean?"

"I mean we think we can reason things out, and that would work if feelings did not get in the way. You have loved him for a long time; choosing to no longer love will take time also. You cannot turn real love off like a faucet."

"But if he chooses not to love me, then what are my choices? To leave? To pretend I never cared? To search out God's will for me?"

"The last one is of course the best." Mrs. Korsheski smiled. "Or you could ask someone to drop a board on his head to wake him up."

They had laughed together over that, but until right now, Deborah had put Toby and Blessing out of her mind as much as possible to be able to concentrate on learning all she could.

She tucked the letter into her apron pocket to read later. Not that it would take long, but it was a letter.

"Our next section is devoted to budgeting and estimating expenses. Many administrators come to work at a hospital not because they are medically trained but rather trained in business and accounting, fields like that. You will spend the next week with our administrators, seeing what all they do."

After class, Deborah asked the instructor, "It seems to me that while I need to understand these broad concepts, at our hospital I would be more like a nursing supervisor than a hospital administrator."

"I think you are right, so we will spend the most time on that, after you better understand the big picture."

Two days later, Mrs. Korsheski handed Deborah another letter. "I see you are rather popular in Blessing."

This one had a return address. "Mr. Gendarme. What a surprise." She again tucked it away for later, but it did get her wondering how everything was going back home. "I wonder what is happening at the hospital."

"Nothing out of the ordinary, or we would have heard. We always hear."

The next day, Deborah felt like screaming, *I am not cut out for this job!* Budgeting! Expense estimates! Assets as opposed to debits! What a nightmare. Life in Blessing, in their hospital, even at the busiest, was not like here.

Yes, but you are here, so make the best of it, she ordered herself. But all she wanted to do was get on the westbound train and get off again in Blessing. Might she dream that Toby would be at the station when she arrived?

Finally, finally, they set her to learning other tasks. Hands-on tasks that she loved to do. At lunch one day she mentioned to Mrs.

Korsheski, "Dr. Johnson told me that I needed to ride the trolley around Chicago and walk on the shore of Lake Michigan."

"He was so right. I'll show you around town; we'll do just that on Saturday. You need at least one day off. Wear warm clothes."

Accordingly, on Saturday Deborah donned her wool petticoat and wore her winter coat, her wool scarf around her neck ready to tie over her hat if need be.

When they stepped down from the trolley car, she crossed the sidewalk to the beach, clapping her hand on her head to keep her hat from ripping off. "This is as bad as a North Dakota wind, but . . . but I've never seen water like this. Oh my." Waves broke on the rocks and the sand. In spite of the sun peeking out from the clouds, her eyes watered from the wind. "There are ships out there."

Mrs. Korsheski nodded. "Boats of all sizes. Cargo is brought clear in here from all around the world."

Deborah knelt down and picked up a handful of sand. "It's so different from our dirt." She looked up. "Would anyone mind if I took some home with me?"

"Not in the least."

Deborah filled her handkerchief with sand and tied the four ends together, carefully setting it in the bottom of her reticule. "Can we walk a bit?"

Walking in the sand was different than walking in North Dakota mud. She glanced down. When she pushed the sand with her boot, it just slid away. It was wet, but not muddy. She shaded her eyes with her hand and stared out as far as she could see. All water. No other shore.

They took the next path up to the sidewalk and caught the trolley at the corner. When they returned to the hospital, Deborah's eyes were gritty from the dirty air and her ears ached from the cacophony of a busy city. It amazed her that the same city that contained the ornate estates of the wealthy also had slums where people were crammed in like penned animals, much like the stockyards where cattle bellowed and hogs poured out of railway cars and into more pens. There were buildings so tall they blocked the sun and others that went on for blocks, housing industries of every kind. They had eaten from a cart that served strange sandwiches, and as dusk fell, electric lights lit signs and windows, as if there were no night at all.

Deborah bathed in the shower down the hall from her room before collapsing in bed. No wonder those who came from here were so amazed at life in Blessing.

A letter from her ma and pa arrived the next day. The third paragraph from the bottom made her jaw drop.

Toby came for supper last night and he asked for a meeting with us, but your father especially. He requested our permission to court you when you arrive home. We said he had our permission but it would depend on if that is what you want. So, dear Deborah, life might be very different when you return home. We love you and miss you. Counting the days, which are nine, until you come home.

Within the letter were notes from her brothers and sisters too.

Deborah dropped her hands into her lap and stared out the window. Even though night had fallen, the sounds of the street still beat against the grimy window. Nothing stayed clean here on the outside of the buildings, which made keeping the inside clean a constant battle. Even in the operating rooms.

Toby—on-again, off-again Toby—had asked if he could court her. What in the world had been going on in Blessing to bring him to that point?

"What in the world is going on in this town?" Toby dropped his muddy boots by the door, shook off his slicker, and threw it on a chair. "It's not supposed to be raining like this in October."

Anton looked up from the kitchen table. "Everyone keeps telling me, 'Oh, it's not usually like this at this time of year.' I'm beginning to suspect you never get normal weather." He was grading math papers. Toby no longer envied Anton his short workday. It wasn't. He worked as long as Toby did, just not physical labor.

"Oh good. You got the mail." Toby flopped down in the chair across from Anton's and picked up the envelopes. Here was another sale flyer from that company that distributed windows. He and Thorliff were both getting sales brochures ever since they'd ordered the school's windows. Did the company think that since they'd bought thirty windows, they'd want to buy lots more? Two letters for Anton that had been opened, and here was one from Deborah! He knew because she had put her return address on it. He had forgotten to do that when he sent her his letter.

He ripped it open. She had beautiful writing—delicate, neat, easy to read. Well, it figured; she wrote all those records and reports at the hospital, and the lines on their paper were close together. She missed Blessing. Lake Michigan was absolutely amazing, and wait until he saw their sand. How was he going to see Lake Michigan sand? The people there were wonderful and she couldn't wait to get home. And she signed it, "Affectionately, Deborah."

She did not mention anything about

receiving his letter, but then, all he'd written about was the school project. That had to be pretty boring for a young lady like her. The more he thought about it, his hotshot letter was not nearly as great as he had first imagined it to be. And he had not even given it a return address.

Then he noticed the return address on one of Anton's two letters. He scowled at his housemate. "You wrote to Deborah too?"

"Of course. Being away from home and familiar places gets very heavy. I know. So I wrote to her a few times."

So I wrote to her a few times. Anton made it sound like no big thing. Writing that letter had been the hardest work Toby had ever done, not counting working dawn to dusk on construction. "All you do is teach math and stuff all day. What'd you find to say?"

Anton shrugged. "I don't remember, really. Small talk. Weather, of course, the new ice cream flavor at the sweet shop, things like that. Ingeborg noticed some wood rot on the north side of her house, so Thorliff, John, and I spent an hour replacing some boards. Nothing big. Like you say, I study four walls all day, one of them a blackboard." He went back to his grading.

Toby smoldered. If Deborah decided to rank him and Anton by the letters they wrote, Toby was done for. Anton had seen her off at the train station; Daniel had said so. Toby had been stuck at the construction site by an unexpected problem that needed solving immediately and couldn't get free until noon, when she was long gone. If she ranked them by that measure, Toby was doomed again.

He had never felt more like pasting Anton Gendarme clear across the room.

Deborah sat in the first row of assembly, and she should have been horribly nervous, but she wasn't. All she could think about was Toby. What did he mean by courting? Had he read the courting chapter in some fancy etiquette book and was going to do whatever it suggested? Was he going to fall back on their school days and tease her and dip her pigtail in the inkwell? Courting how?

Quit thinking about Toby!

She would leave for home in four days. She would not be sad to leave here, other than the people who had been so kind to her and taught her so much. No wonder both Astrid and Elizabeth were grateful to have gone to school here.

In a few minutes she would be speaking to a general assembly of the nursing and medical students. She'd been asked to talk about their small hospital back home and some of the difficulties they encountered.

When she told Mrs. Korsheski that she'd

never spoken before a large group of people before, Mrs. Korsheski simply smiled and said, "Just tell them some of the stories of what has gone on there. Those who have returned from Blessing have shared plenty as well." She patted Deborah's hand. "I'd start with the grain elevator exploding. That will get everyone's attention."

And so Deborah had made a list of five things that had happened that might be interesting. She had no idea if she would make a fool of herself, but there was a high likelihood.

And now Mrs. Korsheski was introducing her. Deborah tried to swallow the butterflies rampaging around in her stomach. When she got on the stage, she was grateful to have the lectern to hang on to. She consulted her list.

She told them about the elevator exploding and setting half of Blessing ablaze. The whole audience was paying attention! This was not quite the disaster she'd been afraid it might be.

She told stories she'd heard of how Elizabeth, Astrid, and Ingeborg worked to save lives before the hospital was built, and how afterward they appreciated the help sent from Chicago to get their hospital on its feet. Some of those stories amazed even her.

She told about the circus train, starting with the elephants, and described the diphtheria that raged through the circus people. She explained about the quarantine tent and how it was easier in some ways to isolate people in a rural place like Blessing.

But how to end her talk? She had some notes for that too. "I've noticed some things that you have here that I am sure we will have one day. You are our future; you have it here first. You have electricity to run not only the lights but that amazing machine, the X-ray. I realize it is a mere oddity yet, a sideshow curiosity, but oh how we could have used it! We had a man who fell from scaffolding. The wound on his head swelled up so fast we couldn't feel if any bones were broken. Curiosity or not, that X-ray could have told us if the skull was fractured. He spent a week in a coma and now is regaining use of his hands and legs. We have hardheaded people in Blessing."

The audience laughed and clapped.

"But we couldn't save them all. One life that was not saved was Dr. Elizabeth's. She died of the diphtheria that was brought in on that circus train. But thanks to her and Dr. Astrid Bjorklund and all the advice and supplies you send to us, we are saving lives, having healthier babies, teaching hygiene, and helping Indians to the north of us and Dr. Red Hawk's tribal clinic to the south. We now have our first male doctor on staff, which you can guess has made some of the male patients more willing to come to the hospital."

Another ripple of laughter. "When you

send us nurses to train, we do our best to give them as many different experiences as possible. Life in Blessing is a different world than life in Chicago. I have learned far more than I dreamed I needed to learn in my month here. I am looking forward to the quiet of Blessing, and we have two young women who want to come back here to school. We'll give them all the training we can first. Thank you for keeping the hospital in Blessing as part of your training program."

She turned to leave but people started clapping, then they stood up and kept on clapping. Deborah looked to Mrs. Korsheski, who joined her at the lectern.

"We are indeed proud and honored to be able to use that small hospital as part of our training program. Thank you, Nurse Mac-Callister. If any of you have questions, we'll adjourn to the dining room, where I'm sure you can ask them all as we enjoy celebrating our special guest." She turned to catch Deborah's nod. "You are all dismissed."

It was all over. Deborah did not have to speak to the crowd again. It was almost time to go home.

❧

"It's all over. Just when I saw what I wanted in my life, it's gone." Toby slouched down in his chair, totally despondent. Across the table from him, Rebecca took another bite of her stew and simply watched him.

Gerald returned from scooping himself a second helping of stew and plopped down in his chair. "So what burr is under your saddle now?"

"Did you see Anton's house plans?"

Gerald nodded, his mouth full.

"He's not building a house, he's building a colony. It's going to be monstrous and out on the edge of town with a nice view of the river."

"So?"

Rebecca snorted. "I get it. You were complaining about Anton writing such great letters and you didn't, and Anton seeing Deborah off when you couldn't, and now Anton is building the Taj Mahal and you live in an old house that needs painting this next summer. And you've convinced yourself that Deborah is going to add all that up on her scoreboard and marry Anton because he's so much better."

Toby stared at her, openmouthed. "H-how do you women do that? Read minds?"

She smirked. "It's easy if the print's large enough. Yours sure is."

Gerald swallowed. "We're at a disadvantage, little brother. Women can read our minds, but when we try to read theirs, they've already changed it, so we can't."

"Why, you . . ." Rebecca glared at him.

Toby sighed. "She's right."

Rebecca barked, "Wrong!" She leaned forward and wagged a fork at him. "I cannot think of a single woman in this town who would sum up a marriage prospect that way. I certainly did not marry Gerald because he's a Valders and the Valders family was well off. I didn't even think about not marrying him because his mother is Hildegunn Valders. None of that. We marry the men we love. And we do *not* keep score!" She sat back and tackled her stew again.

Toby was still staring at her openmouthed, but now it was in amazement. He looked at Gerald. Gerald just smiled and shrugged and continued eating. "All right, so you're saying that Deborah isn't paying attention to all that? She's a smart woman, the smartest I've ever known, so of course she's going to weigh all that."

Gerald asked, "And you're sure you want to court and marry her."

Toby drew in a bushel of air. "Now that it's too late, yes. I'm sure."

Gerald reached over and clapped him on the shoulder. "Good man!" And Rebecca was grinning at him, a wide, happy, almost-in-tears grin.

Toby was never going to understand women.

⁂

Deborah watched the prairie glide by outside the window. The train was slowing, nearing the town she knew best. Home. Soon. The countryside through which the train roared looked increasingly familiar. The only thing not familiar was the confused state of her heart.

Of course Toby wouldn't be there. He'd never leave work in the middle of the day like this. Would Anton? How many tests were his students going to have to take so that he could free himself up to come?

Did she want him to?

Oh, there was the question! Anton . . . Toby . . .

She was very tired. Those last few days at Morganstein Hospital were so hectic and busy even without the assembly and her speech. And she could not sleep the first night on the train. She never could. She sat back, closed her eyes, and let her mind float free. Not thinking, not calling up memories, not anything.

Toby.

What a strange thing. He didn't come to mind. She didn't think of him. He was suddenly just there, as if he were part of her. Her eyes popped open. Was this how God was telling her?

But now the outskirts of Blessing were rolling by and the train was slowing almost to a halt; a cloud of white steam blasted up past the window.

Her pa would be at the school, but she knew her ma, Ingeborg, and possibly Astrid would be there to meet her. The train screeched to a shivery stop at the Blessing station at 11:03 a.m. As the conductor assisted her down the steps, she saw Mary Martha and Ingeborg, as she'd expected. But Sophie, Astrid, Rebecca, Grace, and Kaaren were there too, laughing and waving.

"What is this, a girl party?" Deborah hugged and laughed and hugged some more.

"We're all having dinner at the boarding-house so we can catch up." Sophie took her arm. "Do you have more luggage?"

"In the baggage car."

Mary Martha leaned close and whispered in her ear. "Toby said to tell you to please not make any plans for tonight."

"And?"

"That's what he said. Come, let's go eat."

They started toward the boardinghouse, but Deborah called a halt. "Stop. I have to breathe in some clean air first." She sucked in and blew out a deep breath. Then another. "Real air. Listen. What do you hear?"

"Faint hammering from the deaf school."

"A wagon creaking."

"Male voices over by the train siding." They all had different things to say.

"A crow scolding someone or something."

"Scooter is barking."

"Isn't it wonderful?" Deborah answered.

Astrid and Ingeborg both chuckled. "I felt

the same way when I came back," Astrid said. "I stood in the window at night and listened for the silence after all that ear-breaking noise in Chicago, and then the train clacking and screeching and whistling. When you come home, this is heaven on earth for the ears and the nose."

"And eyes. No more grit."

At the boardinghouse, Maisie Landsverk showed them into the separate room for special parties. "We'll be bringing your dinner right out, so make yourselves comfortable. Lily Mae is bringing cold drinks first."

They sat at the round table and started to catch Deborah up on all that had happened in Blessing.

"And you know the harvest celebration we had? I didn't think Toby was going to come, but he did. He danced with all of us and the older women and none of the younger. I couldn't believe it."

Deborah tried to shake her head, but Rebecca insisted. "You wait; I think Toby Valders has finally grown up. He and Gerald have been doing a lot of talking."

"He really missed you." Ingeborg smiled at Deborah. "Don't look so surprised. It was bound to happen one of these days. Well, at least, that's what we all prayed for."

"He wrote to me." Deborah held up one finger. "I was surprised. So did Anton. I answered each of them. By the way, thank you so much for your letters. I was so busy I didn't have time to answer any others, but I sure thought about you all a lot." She turned and thanked Lily Mae, who was setting the iced glasses around the table.

"So did you like Chicago?" Sophie asked.

"No, not much, but Lake Michigan—oh my word." Where was the sand? In her valise. "I know, Sophie, you saw the Pacific Ocean, and Ingeborg, you crossed the Atlantic, but that lake . . . you couldn't see the far shores at all. And the waves, I closed my eyes and listened to the waves. Like they had their own song."

Once the dinner was served, quiet settled over the group after Mary Martha said the grace.

Deborah looked around at her friends and family. "Thank you all. This is just perfect."

They raised their glasses and said together, "Welcome home."

On the way home after dinner, Mary Martha said, "Toby said he would see you at four, and don't ask me any questions, because I don't know anything else."

"Isn't this rather strange?"

"Yes, but this whole relationship has been rather strange."

Isn't that the truth! "I don't know what to wear."

"I'd say your green skirt with the ivory-white

waist. You look lovely in that. But then, you look lovely no matter what you wear. You could just wrap up in a horse blanket."

"Ma!"

"Well, fall is here and it gets real nippy after the sun goes down."

At four o'clock, Deborah heard a buggy drive up. A buggy? She tossed her shawl around her shoulders, took one last look in the mirror, and stopped when she heard his voice at the door.

"She'll be right here," Mary Martha assured him.

It was only Toby. Why was Deborah's heart pounding like this?

She stepped into the foyer. Surely he was even more handsome than she'd remembered. Of course, she didn't usually see him in a suit, not even at church.

"Welcome home," he said.

"Thank you. I'm glad to be home."

"I thought we could drive west of town and watch the sun go down. Astrid tells me you didn't see a sunset the whole time you were there."

"Did the sun set there? Too many buildings to see it either rise or set." She slid her hand through the bend in his arm, since he offered.

"You look lovely." He helped her up into the buggy and swung up into the driver's side. The smile he gave her set her heart to pounding again. This was crazy. They'd been friends for years. *But he's never taken you—just you—for a buggy ride before.* She tried to ignore the voice in her head.

"Mrs. Sam and Maisie said they would make us something special for supper, but I have something to ask you first." He pulled the buggy over to the side of the road where they had a clear view to the west. The brilliant copper gold disc was on its final descent for the day. The stringy clouds above were already turning to various colors.

"We have been friends or possibly friendly enemies for all these years. I had no idea that when you left, I would miss you. Not just a pang or question once in a while, but—and I know this makes no sense—but I realized I took it for granted that when I wanted to see you, all I had to do was show up at your house, or at church, or at the hospital. And even though I've not taken advantage of that fact very often, I also realized that being busy on the job was always going to be a part of life." He turned to watch the sun.

"But I want more," he continued. "I want a family and someone to love like Gerald loves Rebecca, and your ma and pa, and Ingeborg with Haakan. I finally figured out that I was missing out and, Deborah, it was a shock. Gerald and I talked a lot, and he helped me see that I was afraid of getting married, that I might end up like my real pa." He shook his head slowly. "I know this isn't making much sense, but as I said, I've had to do a lot of thinking."

They both watched the last tiny rim of the sun slip below the horizon, setting the sky and clouds blazing with color.

Deborah wanted to slide her hand into his, like an ache in her middle. Instead she clasped them together on her lap. "So wonderfully beautiful. Thank you for this."

"It's getting chilly. Are you warm enough?"

She nodded.

He turned, his knees brushing hers. When he took her hands in his, she nearly jumped from the charge that went up her arms. "I thought perhaps a courtship would be a good thing so we could learn . . ." He drew a deep breath. "We could find out if we really do have that kind of love for each other. I don't want second best." He squeezed her hands gently. "So I am asking if you will allow me to court you until we both know for absolutely sure that this is God's plan for us."

"Toby Valders, I have been in love with you since I don't know when. So yes, if this is what God is saying for us to do—yes! I have no idea what this really means, but I guess we'll both learn. And I have to learn to trust that you will not back off and ignore me until you get around to it again."

He nodded. "I understand that. I have a lot

to make up for. So for our first step in courtship, shall we go have supper at the boardinghouse? I promise to talk with you, not tease
you."

"Yes. But I have a favor to ask."

"What? Anything."

"Please don't quit making me laugh. We
have such fun when we laugh together."

He coughed on a chuckle. "Deborah, I don't
have any idea how I could stop making you
laugh."

He picked up the reins. She tucked her arm
in his and laid her other hand over the top. Was
that a chuckle she heard on the evening breeze?
He turned the buggy around and they headed
back into town.

Supper and a courtship. What a lot to come
home to.

EPILOGUE

Being courted was rather a pleasant experience.

"You're wearing that dreamy Toby face." Mary Martha smiled at her daughter.

"I'm not surprised." Deborah matched her ma smile for smile. "I never dreamed being courted could be so . . . so delightful." She eyed the huge vase full of fall leaves that seemed to shimmer in the sun coming in the western window. "He said the leaves would have to do until the flowers bloomed again in the spring." She turned to her ma. "Is this what love feels like?"

"Other than dreamy, to what are you referring?"

"My heart seems to leap right out of my chest every time I see him. The sound of his voice melts a puddle in my middle. I'd rather be with him than anyone else. Sometimes he makes me laugh until I get a stitch in my side." Deborah felt the heat flame from her neck up. She and Toby had spent the evening with Rebecca and Gerald, first playing with the children, then drinking coffee and remembering their early years. When he walked her home, he held her hand, and at the door, kissed her on the forehead. When he said good-night, his voice caught. The lamp left burning in the window threw his face into shadows. Her forehead burned for hours. *He kissed me. Toby Valders.*

Surely all these years of waiting were worth it.

"Well, at least he no longer has to keep that backbreaking work schedule of dawn to dark. Not that he's not still doing that, but dark lasts a lot longer."

"I know, and he chooses to spend more of that time with me."

"I think we should have had a celebration when the last window was set into the deaf school, declaring the building weatherproof."

"He said they're installing the furnace this week so it is not too cold in there to work."

"Hmm, that means we could have the celebration there, once the furnace is working." Mary Martha nodded. "I think this is a fine idea." She moved to the calendar hanging on the kitchen wall. "It's two and a half weeks until Thanksgiving. Surely we can get a celebration organized in that amount of time." She picked up the telephone earpiece and spun the crank, asking Gerald to connect her to Sophie. They needed a meeting immediately.

Within two days the celebration was planned. Thorliff moved articles around on the front page to insert a town-wide invitation. The bottom line read, *Raffle tickets available to support the new school building.* Sophie had struck again. The women set to finishing a quilt to raffle off, and Lars' woodworking class began making a trunk, also for the raffle.

One night Deborah answered the door to find Toby smiling at her. She stepped back. "Come in, come in." Her heart picked up the faster beat the sight of him always evoked.

Mangling the hat in his hands, Toby shut the door. "I've come to see your father."

"Oh, well, he's in his office. I'll get him." Something was sure bothering him. What could it be?

"No, that's okay, I'll talk with him there."

Deborah led Toby down the hall and tapped on the closed door.

"Come in," John called.

She opened the door and stepped back. "I'll go put the coffee pot on, unless you're in a hurry."

"Thank you, my dear. We'll join you all in a little bit."

Deborah closed the door behind her and nibbled on her bottom lip all the way to the kitchen.

"Was that Toby I heard?" Mary Martha looked up from where she was helping Emily with her arithmetic at the big oak table in the kitchen.

"He wanted to talk with Pa."

"Oh. Well, we have apple cake left over and cream to pour over it. Why don't you make a fresh pot of coffee?" She returned to her tutoring and supervising of homework.

When the two men entered the kitchen, nothing was said about the talk, much to Deborah's consternation. Curiosity was a wicked taskmaster. They all enjoyed their second dessert, Toby teased Thomas, making them all laugh, and when Deborah walked him to the door, he bid her good-night and went whistling down the path. Whatever had been concerning him seemed to be settled.

Everyone brought food and chairs to the Thanksgiving festival. They served the mountains of food from boards set on sawhorses, and after everyone was filled to groaning, the last call to buy raffle tickets created an air of expectation that shimmered as the big bowl of tickets was set on a table in front of the gathered band.

Hjelmer lifted the bowl high. "Anyone else want to buy a ticket? Remember, six for a quarter. Going, going, gone." He set the bowl back down and stirred the tickets with his hand. "Hmm, I wonder who should have the honor of drawing the winning ticket?"

"Come on, Hjelmer, draw the ticket," a voice called from the crowd.

"We have a lot of tickets here. What if we sweeten the pot?" He pulled out his wallet and tossed five one-dollar bills down on the table. "There, now more people can win something." He stared over the crowd. "I need seven little people to come draw. Let's see, Inga, Emmy, Benny, that's three. How about Carl, Emily, Goodie, and Truth? Come on up here, and let's begin the drawing. You draw the ticket, hand it to me, and I will announce the winner."

The dollar bills went quickly, making five people grin. Mr. Belin tossed his dollar bill back in the bowl. "School need this more than me."

Applause swelled the room.

"Now, Benny," Hjelmer said, "you draw the ticket for the trunk, and Emmy, you will draw for the lovely, warm quilt."

With a grin as wide as his face, Benny pulled up a ticket.

"Looks like Mercy has won the trunk. Perhaps this will make a fine hope chest for a lovely young woman. Come on up here and claim your prize." Hjelmer beamed at her. With Mercy beside him, he opened the trunk. "Why, look at that, this amazing trunk has a few extra gifts in it."

Mercy stared down. "Why . . . why thank you, whoever added sheets, pillowcases, some dish towels, and a doily."

"You can thank the quilters for those," Sophie called. "They thought every trunk needs to hold something."

Trygve and Toby came forward and carried the trunk nearer the door, Mercy dancing beside them.

"And now, the final drawing." He grinned at Emmy. "Stir them up good."

She did and held up one ticket.

"And the winner is . . . Mr. Sten Swedenborg. Something to help keep you comfortable through the long winter."

The broad-shouldered carpenter strode forward and claimed his prize. "Reminds me of home and the quilts there. Tusen takk." He bowed toward some of the ladies.

"And now, let the dancing commence!"

Toby turned to Deborah. "Shall we?" He held out his hand.

With a shiver, she placed her hand in his. "Yes."

The music swelled into a two-step, and partners of all ages whirled around the room, from Ingeborg dancing with David Gould, to grade schoolers, to Thorliff with Inga standing on his feet.

Deborah looked up to see Toby studying her intently. "What?"

"You are the most beautiful of all the lovely young women in this room."

She caught her breath, a smile trembling

on her mouth. "Why, thank you." She nearly choked on the words, or was it the way he was staring at her? "Toby, what is it?"

The final chords sounded, but he held on to her hand. "Come with me."

She pulled back a little. "You could say please."

"Please," he threw over his shoulder and kept on walking until they were both out in the hall and standing in front of a window.

"Toby Valders, what in the world?"

"I just can't wait any longer. I was trying to think of some special way or place, and all I could think was, What if she says no?"

She stared at him, shaking her head. "You are not making any sense."

"I know." He looked down at her, holding both her hands as if to keep her from running away. "Deborah MacCallister, will you marry me?"

Her heart skipped into double time. "Are you sure?"

"I'm sure. I asked your father if I could ask you, and he said it was fine with him and all up to you."

Her heart wanted to scream yes, a thousand times yes, but her mind held back. "I can only marry a man who is sure he loves me as I love him."

"Why would I ask you to marry me if I didn't love you?"

She swallowed. "You've never told me you love me."

"Are you sure?"

"I am."

"You said 'as I love him.'"

She nodded, her hands squeezing his as if to hurry him up.

Toby heaved a sigh from the soles of his boots. "Deborah MacCallister, I love you with all I am and I—"

"Yes."

"Yes?"

"Yes, I'll marry you."

He picked her up and swung her around. "She said yes!"

"Shh, they'll hear you over the music."

"I don't care. I want everyone to know. Deborah MacCallister said she will marry me." He cupped his hands along her jawline and tipped her face up to meet his. The kiss was all she had ever dreamed of. He raised his head, shaking it gently at the same time. "I can't believe this is real."

She stood up on tiptoe to kiss him again.

"I was afraid you might be falling for Anton."

"He has become a good friend, and I hope he finds someone to love again." She tucked her arm in Toby's and leaned against his shoulder. "When were you finally sure you loved me?"

"When you left for Chicago. I realized I was so afraid you would not come back, but after talking with your father, I knew that if I needed to go to Chicago and bring you home, I would."

"Shall we go back and dance?"

"Do you mind if I make an announcement?"

"Really?"

"I want everyone to know at the same time that no more matchmaking is needed."

She giggled. "You know the next question is going to be when."

"When is the wedding?"

"Yes."

"How about before Christmas?"

She laughed. "Let's just say that is not decided yet."

"All right."

The Texas Star square dance was just finishing when they returned to what would become the dining and general purpose room of the new deaf school. Keeping Deborah right beside him, Toby strode up to the platform.

"Jonathan, before you begin the next dance, I have an announcement to make."

"All right, and I sure hope it's what I think it is." He raised his voice to be heard across the room full of laughing and chatting people. "Can I have your attention, please?"

Manny's whistle blasted the walls and silence fell, all eyes on Jonathan.

"Toby Valders has asked if he can make

an announcement." Jonathan grinned at the two of them.

Toby kept Deborah tucked into his side. He choked on his words, cleared his throat, and sucked in a deep breath. "I . . . uh . . ."

"Just say it! We're all laying bets on this anyway," one of the men shouted from the back of the room, bringing out laughter and giggles.

Toby sucked in another breath. "I asked Deborah MacCallister to marry me and she said yes!"

The walls rocked with the clapping and cheering. Both Toby and Deborah wore an instant sunburn.

"When?" came from several places around the room.

"I suggested before Christmas."

"Good idea, since it's taken you so long to get to this point." Surely that was Trygve.

"But she said the date is not certain yet," Toby added.

"You better not wait too long, Deborah. He might run again." *Could that be Thorliff?*

Deborah looked up at Toby, who leaned over to say in her ear, "I will wait as long as you want. Turnabout is fair play."

She looked toward her ma and pa, who both nodded and shrugged. Was her dream of the church filled with lilacs a good enough reason to wait?

The musicians started a slow waltz. "You

two just go on out there and dance. You do not want to make any decisions under pressure." Jonathan gave them a gentle shove.

They stepped down from the raised platform, and Deborah melted into Toby's arms, her gaze never leaving his. As if they had danced together every day of their lives, they swayed with the beat and floated around the open floor.

"Now everyone join in as we celebrate this grand news," Jonathan called.

When the music ended, applause swelled and continued.

"I think they are happy for us." Toby had yet to step back.

"I think so."

The musicians picked up the beat, and the dancing continued. John Solberg was the first to cut in, exchanging his wife for his daughter.

"And now you know what he wanted to talk with me about that day," he said, smiling.

"And you gave him your blessing."

"I did. Something I am very pleased and proud to have the privilege of doing. Your ma and I were talking. If you wait a few months, perhaps your pa and Manda would come for the wedding."

"That is something to think about. But you know, in reality, you are my real father. You are the one who raised me to be who I am today. I want you to walk me down that aisle."

"Ah, Deborah, you have given me the greatest

compliment possible." John hugged her close and swung her gently into the next waltz.

When Toby claimed the next dance, Deborah smiled up at him. "We will have a December wedding. Let's just pray against a blizzard, or it will be a very small wedding."

Toby let out a deep breath, as if he'd been holding it. "Thank you. I'm grateful I needn't wait until the lilacs bloom again."

Pine branches and tall candles waited on the windowsills and decorated the altar. Small candles were clamped on the branches of the pine tree to the side of the altar, with white bows and silver drip cups. Buckets of sand and water waited at the wall, but Manny and Benny had promised to guard against any candle burning too low. Jonathan took his place at the piano, and Anton held his violin at the ready.

The congregation quickly filled the pews and every chair available. Jonathan and Anton nodded and softly began to play a collection of Christmas carols.

In the back room, Deborah smoothed her hands down the pale blue ankle-length gown. "Something borrowed, something blue. Both in one, thanks to you."

Mary Martha pinned a blue circlet with a veil in place on her daughter's head, nestling it into the soft waves. "Something old." She handed Deborah a small white leather Bible. "Something new. Your father and I want you to have a Bible of your own."

"You look so lovely," Astrid said.

Deborah smiled. "Thank you. So do you. And Clara, you look lovely too."

Clara's cheeks turned pink. By rights, Deborah would have asked Astrid to be her matron of honor, but Astrid was going to bear a child any moment now, and she was afraid it would happen on or before the wedding. Clara had agreed to stand up with Deborah in her place. A knock on the door, and Mary Martha opened it.

"Are you ready?" John asked. "They are lighting the candles now."

"Is Toby here?"

"Oh yes, and talk about impatient. Gerald is trying to keep him calm."

"I—we're ready."

"Good, as soon as they finish lighting the tree, Jonathan will change the music. Just like we practiced." He smiled at his daughters, one of the faith and the other by adoption.

The music changed. Mary Martha walked down the aisle and sat in the front row.

He's up there waiting, Deborah's heart whispered.

"You go now." John motioned for Clara to move. He held out his arm for Deborah, and they stepped through the doorway.

"Here she comes!" a very young voice announced, much to the delight of the gathered congregation.

All Deborah could see was Toby standing with Gerald but seeing only her.

While her smile trembled, she felt she was floating. Pa handed her to Toby and then assumed his place as pastor. He smiled at the two of them and then raised his eyes to include all those gathered.

"Dearly beloved, we are gathered here in the sight of God as one family to celebrate the marriage of Toby White Valders to Deborah Norton MacCallister. Let us pray."

When the time came, Deborah gazed into Toby's eyes and repeated her vows with a firm voice but a fluttering heart. His voice never wavered, but she was almost undone when she saw tears glimmering in his eyes.

"To have and to hold, in sickness and in health, from this day forward till death do us part." What powerful words, and she meant every one of them.

"I now declare you husband and wife. Toby, you may kiss your bride."

Gentle, as if acknowledging a treasure, Toby kissed her and smiled into her heart.

"Please welcome Mr. and Mrs. Toby Valders! And join us all in the basement to celebrate."

While the congregation applauded, the music burst forth, and the new couple hugged their attendants first, then John and Mary Martha, before proceeding toward the back of the room, greeting and shaking hands with those gathered. Manny and Benny pinched out the candles on the tree, and everyone trooped downstairs, where a cake baked by Rebecca glowed a pure white.

Toby and Deborah stood near the cake to greet everyone and invite them to have cake and some of the Christmas specialties that many of the women had brought.

"So now are you Mrs. Valders, no longer Nurse MacCallister?" Benny asked.

"Well, actually, now I am Nurse Valders *and* Mrs. Valders."

"But now you are Tante Deborah too, right?"

"For you, I am."

He looked to Toby. "Ma and Pa were beginning to think you were hopeless."

"Benny!" Gerald tried to hide his grin but failed when Benny shrugged. Were it not for the dancing light in the boy's eyes, one would have thought him as innocent as the toddler in Gerald's arms.

"Oh, Ingeborg, thank you for all your prayers and advice." Deborah hugged her close.

"You are most welcome, and you know that will never cease." Ingeborg hugged Toby too and patted his arm. "Just think, you didn't have to wait until lilac time."

"For which I am eternally grateful. As Deborah said, thank you. I know you pray for each of us and for the school and all that goes on around Blessing. What would we do without you?"

"Well, I hope to be around for a good long time yet. I love the line 'from this day forward' in the ceremony. That fits for every day. God gives us new blessings every day. You two are husband and wife from this day forward. To grow together in grace. And yes, I will keep praying for you and all of Blessing."

Ingeborg turned slightly to look around the room at all the ages and families. "Just look at all those whom God has brought here." She looked down to see Carl with his little sister, Goodie, tugging at her skirt. "Yes, little one. I see you." She started to squat down beside her grandchildren, but they each grabbed a hand and led her away toward the food table.

Deborah tucked her arm through Toby's. One day perhaps a child of their own would tug at Mary Martha's skirt or Ingeborg's, asking to be picked up.

Yes, from this day forward. God had been picking her up when she stumbled, and that would never end. What a legacy to pass on.

Lauraine Snelling is the award-winning author of over 70 books, fiction and nonfiction, for adults and young adults. Her books have sold over 3 million copies. Besides writing books and articles, she teaches at writers' conferences across the country. She and her husband make their home in Tehachapi, California.

Sign up for Lauraine's newsletter!

Keep up to date with news on Lauraine's upcoming book releases, signings, and other events by signing up for her email list at laurainesnelling.com/html/contact.html

More From Lauraine Snelling

Ingeborg Strand dreams more of becoming a midwife than of finding a husband—until she meets university student Nils Aarvidson. Could Nils be the man God intends her to marry, or is He leading her toward an entirely different path?

An Untamed Heart

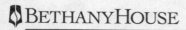